D1651844

#BookTok is raving about *It's Not Her*!

"Expect to find yourself open-mouthed in shock at Kubica's final plot twist."

—Stephanie, @literaryhypewoman

"With red herrings, suspects galore, and ever-increasing tension, I was on the edge of my seat the entire time, my dark thriller heart pounding."

—Suzi Makowski, @lil.bit_reads

"If Mary Kubica isn't on your auto-buy list by now, this book will solidify her spot on your list of must-read thriller authors."

—Jessica, @thrillerschillersandkillers

"Wow! This book reeled me in from the first sentence and kept me guessing until the last page was turned."

—Leisa, @backporchpages

"Warning: do not start this book if you have obligations, because it is UN-PUT-DOWN-ABLE!!"

—Christina, @books_by_the_bottle

"Every page will hold you hostage to the nail-biting events that culminate to a blood-curdling finale!"

—Sav, @gymgirlreads

"This gripping story kept me guessing until the very last page."

—Michelle, @meshellreads

"I recommend this white-knuckle ride with every fiber of my being."

—Linzie, @suspenseisthrillingme

"Without a doubt, 5 stars. Best book of Mary's I've read yet."

—Amie, @the_boozybookworm

ALSO BY MARY KUBICA

The Good Girl
Pretty Baby
Don't You Cry
Every Last Lie
When the Lights Go Out
The Other Mrs.
Local Woman Missing
Just the Nicest Couple
She's Not Sorry

IT'S NOT HER

MARY KUBICA

PARK
ROW
BOOKS

PARK ROW BOOKS™

Recycling programs for this product may not exist in your area.

ISBN-13: 978-0-7783-8799-2
ISBN-13: 978-0-7783-0678-8 (Signed Edition)

It's Not Her

Park Row Books
22 Adelaide St. West, 41st Floor
Toronto, Ontario M5H 4E3, Canada
ParkRowBooks.com

HarperCollins Publishers
Macken House, 39/40 Mayor Street Upper,
Dublin 1, D01 C9W8, Ireland
www.HarperCollins.com

Printed in Lithuania

To anyone who's ever felt alone

IT'S
NOT
HER

COURTNEY

I'm standing at the kitchen sink, washing dishes, when I hear her scream.

My knees lock and I go suddenly upright, drawing in a sharp breath. I glance swiftly up from the hot, soapy water in the sink, losing my grip on a plate that slips from my wet hands and into the basin. Water splashes.

I stand there, rooted to the earth, listening in vain for the anguished sound to come again, or for there to be something else, something that explains it, like tires skidding, the squeal of car brakes, the resident German shepherd (the one that Cass and Mae are both afraid of) barking, or Emily's voice calling out to see if Mae is okay. But there's nothing, only silence, which worries me as much as the scream.

Just moments ago, my niece Mae was here, at our little rental cottage. She and Cass had a sleepover last night, sleeping on the double bed under the slanted eaves of the loft, staying up too late watching Disney movies on DVD and gabbing about whatever ten-year-olds gab about. I fell asleep before they did, waking around three in the morning to check on them and finding them both asleep with the TV still on.

Before Mae left to go back to her own cottage, they stood at the front door, giggling and saying goodbye with their sticky, syrupy faces and hands. I stood in the adjoining kitchen, staring out at them, admiring their friendship. Cass and Mae are much more than cousins; they're best friends, like sisters even. After Mae was gone, I got busy cleaning the small kitchen, asking Cass to go straighten up from their sleepover, and she had, disappearing to the upstairs loft, where the sound of Mae's scream doesn't reach.

I'm the only one in the cottage to hear it, and I thank God, because the sound is tortured, carrying across the property, coming in through the open windows, leaving me feeling shaken and eviscerated though I don't know why, except I've never heard Mae scream like that before.

I reach for the faucet handle and turn the water off, drying my hands on a towel as I hurry toward the front door. I see Mae through the open window first, and my heart catches because she's dashing down the hill and through the trees, back toward us, faster than her small legs can go. Her arms windmill, her hair in her eyes because the wind is pushing from behind. Halfway to me, she trips over something, her feet lifting up from the ground, sending her momentarily airborne before she falls, crashing hard onto the earth. It's not a soft fall. The ground isn't grass, but a bed of pine needles and dirt. It looks painful, though Mae doesn't lie there crying as I would expect her to do, as Cass might do. Instead, she gets back up just as quickly as she went down, glancing over a shoulder in the direction of her own cottage before turning again and running to me.

I step outside, letting the screen door fall closed. Mae comes crashing into me, her arms locking around my waist. "What is it, Mae? What's wrong?" I ask as she buries her face into my abdomen, sobbing, her hands around my back, holding tight as if wanting to disappear inside of me. My eyes sweep the property, searching for signs of something off—a car (a child predator?) pulling away or the mean German shepherd running loose again—but there's nothing that I can see. The cottage where we're vacationing is in the Northwoods of Wisconsin, over five hours north of home. It's on a lake and is one of eight little cottages situated in hundreds of acres of woods. The lake is peaceful this morning; the only people awake besides the girls and me are fishermen in canoes, like Elliott, my husband, who woke up early this morning and left before any of us were awake, hoping to catch something to put on the grill for dinner.

I hear the slow rasp of the screen door behind me. "What happened?" Cass asks, and I turn to see her coming hesitantly out, standing unsure on the deck behind me as I hold Mae in my arms.

"I don't know," I say. "What happened, Mae?" I coax, bending my knees to lower myself to her height, but Mae says nothing, clinging to me, her sticky hands clasped around my neck now, tugging without meaning to on my hair, and it's only when I peel them off with effort and hold her at an arm's length that I see her hands have blood on them.

"What's this? Did this happen when you fell?" I ask, thinking of the way she went down just moments ago. She must have fallen on a rock or a tree root. I take her hands into mine, briefly examining them for an open wound before moving a strand of hair out of her eyes. But Mae only shakes her head, wiping her runny nose on a pajama sleeve before looking back at her cottage for a second time and then lowering herself to the ground, hugging her knees into her chest, rocking.

I lift my gaze. I let my eyes go to Emily and Nolan's cottage next door, which is hard to see through the thick trees. When we arrived at the lake a few days ago, I envied their cottage. Not only had Emily rented the largest one on the property—which came as no surprise, considering she has three kids, two of whom are teenagers and would rather die before sharing a bed with a sibling—but hers was more private than the rest. Once the resort's main house, it's set off at a distance so she can sit on her deck with her coffee and stare out at the placid lake without having a stranger in another cottage at an arm's reach, watching her, listening in on her conversations.

"Is your mom there, Mae? In the cottage?" I ask about my sister-in-law, Emily, and this time, she nods. "Come sit with Mae," I say to Cass, glancing back over my shoulder at her. "Stay here until I come back. I want to make sure everything is okay."

Cass nods as she takes my spot sitting beside her cousin, her hand on Mae's back in a very grown-up way that belies her ten years.

As I start making my way through the trees and toward Emily and Nolan's cottage, quickening my pace by instinct, I feel a wave of unease come over me, though I hold it back, telling myself nothing is seriously wrong, that Mae probably just walked in on them arguing again and got scared or upset. She overreacted. Things haven't been the best between Emily and Nolan of late. Nolan's been out of work for almost six months, and it's taken a toll—on him, their finances and their marriage. He's in the tech industry, where it's almost impossible to find a job these days; companies are laying off in record numbers. Nolan has compared it to something out of *The Hunger Games*. Recently, Emily and Nolan have had conversations about if they need to sell their house (their dream home, the one they planned to retire in) and downsize, which they can't agree on because they can't agree on anything anymore. They fight all the time, but had hoped a couple weeks in the woods with family and away from all the pressures of everyday life would remedy that, though I heard them going at it just yesterday afternoon, and from the way it sounded, things were far from fixed.

As I make my way through the pine trees, the cottage comes into view, looking perfectly peaceful at the top of a small hill—giving it the best view of the lake, another thing for me to envy—with their beach towels draped over the deck rail, drying, though the front door is open, which it never is because Emily is fastidious about not letting the mosquitoes inside.

This far north into Wisconsin, the temperatures drop into the low fifties at night, only ever reaching the mid-seventies during the day. At this time of day, it's barely fifty-five or sixty degrees. I climb the small hill in my robe, which blows open in the cool morning breeze, before I reach for the belt to tie it. Beneath the robe, I have on a pair of thin cotton pajama pants and a camisole. I haven't been awake long enough to shower, put on a bra or run a brush through my hair, but just long enough to rise reluctantly from bed when Cass appeared at the foot of it about an hour ago, asking if I could make pancakes. At the time, I spied Mae, hovering just outside the bedroom door, her hopeful face partially visible from around the edge of the door-frame, and I knew I couldn't say no.

It's unlike Emily to leave the front door open. Even if she and Nolan were arguing, she would have closed the door, and she would have gone after Mae if she knew that Mae was upset. I pick up my pace again, wondering now if something even worse than that has happened, if someone in the cottage is hurt or sick.

I think of Reese, their oldest, who is seventeen. She's been moody and reserved the whole trip. Emily got a hold of Reese's phone the other day because she was worried about her. She read her texts when Reese wasn't looking. **I wanna KMS**, Reese said in a text to a friend. I didn't know what it meant, but Emily told me as we stood on the deck outside, her face grave, her fear acute, and my heart practically stopped, thinking of ten-year-old Cass and how I wasn't prepared to deal with all the anxiety and uncertainty of the teenage years. *Kill myself.*

Do you think she means it or is she just saying it for attention? I'd asked, trying to soothe Emily, to make light of it for Emily's sake, but now I regret that I was dismissive. What I should have done instead was suggest Reese talk to someone when they get back home, like a therapist. I should have seen if my own therapist was available for a telehealth session that same day, not that it necessarily would have worked up here with the internet connection as capricious as it is.

I climb the deck steps and let myself inside the cottage, calling for Emily, who doesn't answer. I leave the front door open behind me, entering the great room, which is a combination of the family room, dining room and kitchen. Like our cottage, theirs is rustic and dated, with limp plaid furniture and knotty pine paneling all over the walls. Theirs, however, is twice as large with a screened-in porch and a second floor instead of a small loft like we have, accessible only by a ladder—which is great for Cass but not very practical for Elliott or me, who can't step foot in the loft without hitting our heads on the low, sloped ceiling.

"Emily?" I say again, as I start to make my way further inside. I listen for them. The first floor is empty, the TV off. There is a strange odor in the air, which I try to place but can't. It's quiet at first, but then, from upstairs, I just barely make out the sound of something faint and indistinct, like the sagging of a mattress from someone rolling over in bed. I stop, feeling uncomfortable all of a sudden, imagining my brother Nolan getting out of bed, coming downstairs half asleep in his boxer shorts and finding me standing in the great room. I think of Mae and how scared she was when she came running back to our place, but whatever scared her might have happened before she ever got to the cottage.

The wildlife around here is abundant. There have been reports of bear sightings in the woods not far from here. The other day, when we were out walking, we noticed what we thought were coyote prints in the dirt. If Mae saw something like a coyote on her way home, it would have scared her—and that means Emily, Nolan and the other kids could still be asleep.

I sink a hand into the pocket of my robe for my phone to try calling Emily, which I should have done first before letting myself into their cottage. I glance at the phone; the cell signal around here is weak though, miraculously, I have two bars. I find Emily's name in my contacts while the signal lasts and click on it, pressing the phone to my ear.

It doesn't take long, split seconds before I hear it: the sound of a phone coming to me from the adjoining screened-in porch, the door of which, I see now, is ajar.

Emily's phone, if not Emily, is out there.

I lower my own phone from my ear. Slowly, I cross the room for the porch, reaching for the handle and pulling the door all the way open.

It's as I step through the doorway and onto the porch that I see it. I reel back, though it takes a second for my mind to make sense of what I'm seeing and for me to realize what it is. The blood is so dark that it blends into the wood paneling and I have to look twice to realize that what I'm looking at is not knotholes in the wood, but blood. It's on the bed that it becomes most evident, where blood streaks the white quilt like paint flicked onto a canvas from the end of an artist's brush.

My breath leaves me. Shock holds me in place, some part of me still trying to reconcile what I'm seeing—to make myself believe that someone has cut themselves with a corkscrew or knife and that they've gone to the hospital, leaving quickly, which explains the open front door—despite the amount of blood on the walls and bed.

The nearest hospital has to be ten or twenty miles away. I wonder if Nolan and Emily would have left for the hospital without telling us. I wonder if they planned to call on the way, but then Emily forgot her phone and Nolan couldn't get a signal.

But then I see it through the porch screens, one flapping loose in the wind: Emily and Nolan's dusty black Volkswagen parked just outside on the drive. The car is still here, which means they haven't gone anywhere.

They're still in the cottage.

My throat tightens. It's hard to breathe as my eyes move around the room. At first glance, the porch is empty, but then I just barely make out bare feet stretched on the floor, overhanging the end of the bed, and I realize the porch is not empty like I thought.

My heart starts to beat faster. A hand rises to my mouth as I feel myself shift closer rather than away by instinct, seeing that the skin on the feet is discolored, the pigment far different than healthy feet. It's purpling, the skin tone now nearly the same as the mauve toenail polish, which I know, before I ever see her face, is Emily's because we went for pedicures together before we left on the trip and I helped her pick out the polish, which matches mine.

I come slowly around the edge of the bed, thinking unrealistically that I can help her, that I can still save her. "Emily?" I ask, the word slipping out of me, weightless and insubstantial until I see her and my knees give, and I have to hold on to the bed frame to keep myself upright.

Emily is dead. The blood beneath her is telling. No one could lose that amount of blood and survive. She's completely motionless, lying on the floor of the screened-in porch on the far side of the bed as if caught trying to escape or to hide. There is no rise and fall of her chest to say that she's breathing, that she's still alive. Her face is turned slightly to the side—her neck not at all angled right—so that I bear witness to the grayness of her face and a cloudy, half-opened eye. One of her arms is bent at an impossible angle too, the shoulder jutting out of place, and her mouth gapes open from a last breath or a final scream. Her phone lies just out of reach, a missed call from me on the screen.

I'm frozen in shock, in fear. Though my every instinct tells me to run, to go back to our cottage, lock the door and call the police, I can't get myself to move.

I hesitate for only seconds. But even that is too much. It's too late.

Before I can get myself to go, there's the sudden, very cerebral sensation of not being alone anymore. A movement in my peripheral vision maybe, or the soft, slow creak of a floorboard.

REESE

Seven Days Earlier

We're in the middle of nowhere. It's been hours since we got off the expressway, since I saw something normal like a Mc-Donald's. At first, we were on some two-lane road surrounded by farms for a while—listening to Emily's playlist, also known as the same five songs on repeat, over and over again until I wanted to die—and now we're on some two-lane road surrounded by trees. We're in the actual forest. Everywhere I look there are trees, so deep and packed so close together you don't know who or what is living in them, though every so often we pass a gravel drive that vanishes into air with tire tracks and signs at the end that say things like *Private Property* and *No Trespassing*, and that's how you know someone lives in the trees. When buildings do crop up, they're dodgy as fuck, like those single-story metal storage units (you just know there's a dead body in at least one of them) or little roadside diners advertising Friday fish frys, whose dusty parking lots are filled with nothing but motorcycles and two-tone cars straight out of the '80s.

This is the kind of place you see on the news, where people disappear and are never seen again.

The parental units are in the front seat, fighting again because Nolan is lost. Nolan always gets lost, because he spaces out and doesn't pay attention to where he's going. At this point, he's missed like three turns, and the GPS is glitchy as fuck because cell service around here sucks, so no one knows where we are anymore. We're just on some road, mostly alone, surrounded by trees. Every once in a while, someone will pass by, going in the opposite direction, but they're all old Ford Broncos and jacked up trucks. They're not like us. A little while ago, there was one truck that flew up from behind with a windshield so tinted I couldn't see the driver's face. He rode our tail for a while, swerving and revving his engine, making everyone nervous. "Just go faster, Dad," I said, while Emily told him to pull over and let the man pass. Nolan did neither, undeterred, saying that if the other driver wanted to, he could pass, which eventually he did, laying on the horn and giving us the bird. When he got in front of us, cutting intentionally close, I saw that on the back glass was one of those bumper stickers of Calvin, peeing with his pants around his knees and his ass crack hanging out, and another of a silhouette of a woman with massive breasts that said *My other ride is your mom*, if that's any indication of the kind of place where we are.

Mae asked what it meant. *My other ride is your mom.*

Emily is mad at Nolan for getting us lost. She thinks he's incompetent. She can't let it go. It's not just that she's mad we're lost, but her anxiety has kicked in and she thinks something bad might happen to us, that we might die out here or something, and if we did, it would be all his fault.

"If you would have just been paying more attention, this wouldn't have happened," she says.

"Do you think I wanted to get us lost? That I tried to get us lost? God, Emily, you just don't know when to shut up sometimes."

Emily goes stiff. She checks her phone then to see if Aunt Courtney texted, but it's pointless because there is no cell signal, which is also somehow Nolan's fault (maybe if we were on the right road, there would be cell service). Emily could just let it go, but she doesn't. She says something instead then about how Grandpa, RIP, used to use an actual map when they went on family vacations so they never got lost because they didn't need Siri telling them where to go, they didn't rely on modern technology, he could just figure it out with his brain. And then, to really drive the point home, she dredges up the one time we were driving in the city—that *Nolan* was driving us in the city—and Siri took us on a tour of some of the sketchiest parts of Chicago, because it was the fastest route, as if Google Maps comes with a feature to avoid areas with high crime. I thought it was funny at the time, but Emily thought we were going to get killed. She kept screaming at us to close our windows and lock our doors.

"You wanna drive?" Nolan asks now. "Here, you can drive," he says, jerking the car onto the side of the road so hard that I crash-land into Mae in the back seat. We skid on gravel, stopping abruptly. I'm not wearing my seat belt and so, when Nolan slams on the brakes and thrusts the gearshift into Park, I fall forward into the back of Emily's seat. "You can drive then, since you're so much better at it than me."

Except he doesn't take off his seat belt or get out of the car, which is how I know—how we all know—he's bluffing. Nolan knows that if Emily drives, we'll go ten under the speed limit the rest of the way—her hands in the ten and two position—and no one wants that to happen because, if we have to stay in this car any longer than is absolutely necessary, someone might die.

"Could you two stop?" I ask, feeling my temper start to flare. "Could you just, like, I don't know, act like fucking grown-ups for a change?"

Emily says nothing, but she gazes over a shoulder at me, looking disappointed, which is no different than the way she always looks at me. Because I said *fuck* in front of Mae. Because I said fuck *at all*. Because I didn't side with her, but chose to stay neutral like Switzerland. If I had just told Nolan to act like a fucking grown-up instead, things might have been different. I might have gotten away with it. Emily is pretty when she smiles—her blond hair a wavy bob with bangs that most people could never get away with, her soft blue eyes making her look kind—but mostly all I ever see is her angry or her resting bitch face and deepening frown lines that she no doubt blames on Nolan or me.

She used to be happy. I remember that. Sort of.

I look away, texting my friend Skylar. **I wanna KMS**, I say and hit Send. It's the summer before our senior year. For months my best friend, Skylar, and I planned to spend it doing things like going to the Indiana Dunes or taking the train into the city to go to Oak Street Beach. Instead, I'm here with these losers. Mae is okay, but the rest of them I can't stand. My brother, Wyatt, sits in the back seat alone, where he hasn't taken his eyes off his phone the whole entire trip, and I know he's probably looking at pictures of naked girls, though every time Emily asks what he's doing, he says *nothing*. It's not nothing. He's lying to her. Because that's what he always does—lies—though, because he's made high honor roll every semester since he started kindergarten and will probably go to college on a full ride baseball scholarship, they think he's like *the perfect child*. He can get away with anything.

As Nolan slips the gearshift back into Drive and pulls back onto the road, Emily starts muttering things under her breath like, "They're going to be there before us," and, "I told Courtney we'd be there by three," as if that matters, as if anyone cares.

"What do you think, they're gonna leave if we're not there by three?" I ask, and she gives me another dirty look over her shoulder. This time, Emily holds my gaze before letting her eyes run down my neck to my clothes. She doesn't like what I'm wearing, which she told me before we left, how people will think I'm a slut if I dress like one. *Is that what you want people to think? That you're a slut?* We were standing in the kitchen when she asked. I didn't know what to say and so I said nothing. I thought maybe she would take it back, that she would realize, because of my silence or the look of astonishment on my face, that her words cut deep and say sorry or something, but she didn't. To be fair, she didn't lead with the slut comment. She started by saying, "You are not wearing that. Please go find something else to wear," and when I said no, she changed her approach.

"Put your seat belt on," she says now, and I want to ask why and what she's going to do if I don't, but instead I put my seat belt on, jamming the buckle in with gusto, the strap shackling me to the seat like a hostage, which is exactly what I am. A hostage.

In less than a year, I'll be eighteen, and then I'm getting away from here. If I survive that long.

Delete that, I type to Skylar, going back to my phone as Emily turns around in her seat, staring out at the forest of trees before us. **I wanna kill someone else.**

The text starts to send, the little blue line moving across the top of the screen until it gets to like 80 percent and then stops, because I lose the cell signal again just then. Just my luck. The message doesn't send.

I hold down on the last message until the option comes to delete it.

COURTNEY

I wheel around, blenching in fear, in anticipation of pain, bringing a hand to my face to cover it. My ears ring, the sound of my own heartbeat pounding in my ears.

Cass and Mae stand in the great room, just inside the front door, the scant light coming in from the plastic miniblinds leaving bands across their faces and arms. My knees sag in relief because it's Cass and Mae, and not the same person who did this to Emily.

I hurry from the screened-in porch and to them, seeing drops of blood on the great room floor when I come at it from this angle, which I hadn't noticed before. "What the hell are you doing here?" I ask, breathless, in a forced whisper. I step in front of them, forcing them to stay far enough back that they can't see the body or blood, lashing out at them because I'm scared, because Emily didn't cut herself with a knife by accident. Someone killed her and from the sprays of blood on the wall and bed, it was violent and unrestrained. "I told you girls to stay and wait for me. You shouldn't be here," I snap brusquely, the hysteria in my voice coming out as anger, looking down only to realize that I'm gripping my phone so hard in my hand that my knuckles have turned white.

Mae's face is ashen. Her body trembles, her eyes looking past me though my body blocks the view. Cass stands behind her, wrapped in guilt and shame. "I'm sorry," she says, her lower lip trembling, because it's not like me to get mad or to yell and swear at her in front of someone else, if at all. Her eyes meet mine, widening and filling with tears. "I tried to stop her. I told her we weren't supposed to leave, that we were supposed to—"

I don't let her get the rest out. I shake my head and she goes quiet. All I can think about is getting these girls out of the cottage, of not letting them see what I've just seen, of getting them somewhere safe. If they see Emily's body or the blood on the walls, floor and quilt, they'll be traumatized. They'll have nightmares. They'll never forget it. The image of Emily's discolored, misshapen body on the floor, surrounded by blood, will be embedded into their minds and will stay with them their whole lives. A defining moment.

But Mae, I realize as I look at her, standing ghost white in the great room, has already seen it.

Is your mom in the cottage, Mae? I asked earlier and she nodded. Yes. Emily was there. Mae saw Emily dead. It's the reason for her anguished scream, it's what sent her running back to us in the first place, and I think of what it would have been like for her, skipping innocently, obliviously in through the front door with her pillow tucked under an arm, smelling of pancakes and syrup with her hair mussed up and sleep in her eyes, eager to tell Emily about the sleepover—only to find her mother like this. Mae would have gone to her. She would have touched her, maybe shaken her and tried to wake her up. It wasn't her own blood on Mae's hands. It was Emily's blood.

"Your mom is hurt, Mae," I say, going to them, wrapping my arms loosely around their shoulders in an effort to steer them out of the house. My voice is quiet because I don't know who is in the cottage with us. I don't know if we're safe. I don't know if we're alone. I don't know if whoever killed Emily is still here, watching and listening. I don't know if the others are alive or if they're dead. My voice trembles as I whisper, "We need to go back to our place and call someone to come help her."

"But you have your phone. Can't you just call?" Cass asks, motioning to it, trying to be helpful, but she's not.

"There is no signal," I lie, dropping my phone back into the pocket of my robe, and Cass believes it.

"Hurt how?"

"I don't know, honey. We're going to call an ambulance so someone can come help her. Let's go."

"Where is she?"

"On the screened-in porch. Come on, let's go. We need to go call for help."

With effort, I turn Mae's body around so she faces the door. I put a hand on her back, pressing her forward, and she goes, following Cass, who moves backward, walking in reverse so that it's Cass, still facing into the cottage, who sees him first. From where I stand, I see the reaction on Cass's face as if in slow motion—the way her eyes bulge as she sucks in a sharp breath, the blood leaching from her cheeks, turning them white, her whole body going rigid—before she releases a bloodcurdling scream, the kind you only ever see in horror films.

My legs go weak. My heart thuds in my chest and up my neck, making me feel dizzy and flush.

I shouldn't look. I know in my mind that I shouldn't because there is something horrible behind me. I should push the girls in the opposite direction and run far away from whatever has Cass so scared.

But instead I turn back by instinct and see it for myself, pressing my hands to my mouth to hold in a scream.

REESE

Emily and Nolan aren't on speaking terms by the time we finally arrive. The air in the car is charged, like gasoline vapors flow invisibly around us. Just one spark would make the whole thing explode.

Nolan is angry. He drums his thumbs against the steering wheel in time to the music (when what he'd rather do, I think, is hit someone, maybe her), which is no longer Emily's music but his, something techno and electronic that he no doubt picked just to piss her off, which is almost exactly what they meant in their marriage vows when they promised to love and cherish each other forever.

Or not.

Emily, on the other hand, is sad. She gazes out the window, her reflection visible in the side mirror. In it, her eyes are empty. She hasn't spoken for twenty miles, not a word.

"What's wrong, Mom?" Mae asks.

"Nothing, honey. I'm just tired," Emily says, not looking back.

The last thing Nolan said to her before she went quiet, between his teeth so we wouldn't hear, though still, I did: "This trip would have been a lot more fun if you just stayed home."

I felt sorry for her, but I also didn't. Because Emily's not exactly innocent either. It's a game at which two can play. The silence, however, is torturous. We all suffer because of it. It was better when they were fighting.

Things go from bad to worse as we pull into the resort lot— the term *resort* used loosely, because it implies to me something bougie and this place is most definitely not. I sit in the back seat of the car taking it in, astonished that I have to spend a whole two weeks here. Two weeks. That's an eternity. I don't know how or if I'll survive it. The trees are thick, shutting us in while, at the same time, blocking out the sun, which pretty much demolishes any hope of going home with a tan, which is the only thing I was looking forward to on this trip. A sad swing set sits beside the lake, looking like something straight out of Emily and Nolan's generation; it's metal with two pathetic swings and a dumpy slide, beside a rusted merry-go-round that's no doubt going to give someone tetanus. Just beside the lake is a sandbox with broken-looking plastic toys and a little kid waddling around in his bulky swim diaper while his mom watches on. The lake itself looks pretty, but the beach we were promised doesn't exist, the trees and grass running right up to the shoreline where there is a slanted pier, which dips sideways toward the lake. I see Emily look at it, and in her mind, I know she's already pitching a fit about how she doesn't want Mae going on the pier alone, as if Mae isn't ten, as if Mae can't swim. But because Mae's the baby of the family, she treats her like one, and Mae milks it for all it's worth.

"Look how pretty it is," Emily says then, finding her voice, though it's phony and forced as if trying to convince herself as much as the rest of us that it is actually pretty. Last year we were in Hawaii, surfing, snorkeling with sea turtles and sunbathing on the warm sandy beaches, but this year, money is tight because Nolan got laid off and still hasn't found a job, despite the fact that his severance package ran out weeks ago and we may or may not have health insurance. I shouldn't know that, but I do, because Emily isn't quiet about telling him it's time to get more motivated about finding a job. She was subtle at first (*How is the résumé coming along? You want me to take a look at it?*), but then I heard her tell him the other day that the mall was hiring. Imagine that. From software engineer to minimum wage retail sales at Gap. I saw the look in his eye when she said it, like he wanted to strangle her. Like he didn't have a degree from MIT.

Are you fucking serious right now? he'd asked. They were standing in the kitchen where anyone could see or hear.

What? she'd asked. *I thought they might have good benefits and it would give you something to do until something better comes along.*

They fought about it later, screaming at each other behind the closed bedroom door as if it was somehow soundproof, him about how she emasculated him, her about how he was worthless and how she couldn't support the family on her own.

I took Mae and we went out for ice cream. She didn't need to hear that shit.

Now our car follows a curvy dirt road through the trees and to our cottage, kicking up dust as we go. The cottage, when we get to it, is grayish green and set a little way back from the lake, on a hill, with trees on all sides. It's bigger than the rest, but that's not saying much, because the rest of the cottages are actually tiny. This place was my Uncle Elliott's idea. He suggested we come here, because he's been here before and liked it, which means I have him to blame for this trip. It's his fault. If he wouldn't have suggested it, we wouldn't have come.

Nolan parks the car and we climb out, getting ambushed by swarms of hungry mosquitoes the minute we do. We go around to the back of the car, lugging our stuff from the trunk, everyone complaining.

"I can barely walk. My legs are asleep."

"Can we just go inside first? Do we have to unpack right this minute? I have to pee."

"Grab a couple bags and we can go in."

"That's not mine. It's Wyatt's. Make him carry it."

"Just carry something. It's all going to the same place."

"Get out of my way unless you want me to pee right here."

"Can everyone just relax, *please*? We're on vacation."

We climb the steps onto a small porch, where Nolan unlocks and throws open the door.

One by one we step inside the dark and dingy cottage, everyone eager to get in, which turns out to be a huge mistake because I soon realize that I don't know what's worse: being trapped in the car together for five hours or being here.

COURTNEY

It's Nolan. My big brother, Nolan. He's dead. His limp body lies at the top of the stairs, hard to see at first from the angle and because it's darker at the top of the stairs, blanketed in shadows, the scant sunlight not reaching there. He lies on his side, his eyes vacant and opaque, staring lifelessly through the wooden balusters and toward the first floor. Blood seeps from the corner of his mouth, draining down the side of his face, drying. Redness blooms from his temple.

I stumble backward, tasting vomit in my mouth. Behind me, Cass still screams, but Mae is much quieter, something more like the whimper of a trapped animal being stalked by a predator.

I tear my eyes away from Nolan, looking back to see that Mae's legs are shaking and she's wet herself. She wears fuzzy gray pajama pants with clouds on them that do nothing to hide the pee, which spreads, broadening and turning the gray shades darker.

"Close your eyes. Don't look at that, Mae. Don't look at him," I snap as I go to her, pressing a hand down over Mae's eyes and forcing her through the open door backward, shoving Cass, who stands behind her, out at the same time. Cass stumbles, tripping over the wooden threshold, managing to catch herself before she falls, sputtering, "What . . . what was that?

What was he doing? *What's wrong with him?*" her voice elevating in pitch until it's screechy and thin.

Outside, I release Mae's eyes. I grab both girls by the hands, telling them to hurry, though they're paralyzed at first, fixed in place on the deck, their eyes stuck on Nolan's body through the open door. I practically drag them down the steps, tugging them by the hands, saying, "He's hurt, Cass. We have to get help," as I try to keep my wits about me, though Nolan's and Emily's empty, lifeless eyes are there every time I blink. "We need to call for help. Hurry. Come on."

We run down the hill for our cottage, slipping on pine cones and nuts, me clinging tightly to both girls' clammy hands, pulling on them because their stride is narrower than mine, their pace slower. I throw a glance back over my shoulder, my eyes skimming the windows on the cottage, which are nearly impossible to see through because of the way the sunlight hits them. I imagine someone behind one, watching us go. I let my thoughts drift to Reese and Wyatt, Mae's older sister and brother, racked with guilt. I think of the sound I heard standing in the foyer, like a mattress yielding to a person's weight. What if they were up there? What if someone, whoever did this to Emily and Nolan, was up there too? I should have checked on them to see if they were safe, to see if there was something I could do to help.

But instead I run, pulling on the girls, saying, "Almost there. Keep running," with a wildness to my voice from exertion and fear, assuaging my guilt at leaving by telling myself I have to save Cass and Mae. I can't save all the kids at once. If I'd have gone to check on Reese and Wyatt, Cass and Mae would have been in danger. Someone might have hurt them, or worse. I pull so hard that Mae falls forward, landing on her hands and knees with a grunt. The slope of the hill is steep and her legs can't keep up with the momentum. I release Cass's hand, telling her to go on without us, to get inside. Our cottage sits at the base of the hill. It's surrounded by a half dozen other cottages that sit close to one another, separated by trees that provide some privacy but not enough that we can't smell each other's food or listen in on each other's conversations.

"Come on, Mae," I say, going back for her, helping her to her feet.

It's as Mae and I run after Cass, our little cottage a safe haven in the distance if only we can get there in time, that I glance back through the trees once more, letting my eyes run from the open front door to the upstairs windows, and this time, I imagine a pale, out-of-focus face looking out through a crack in the curtains on the other side.

REESE

Inside the cottage smells funky. The walls and floors are all wood. It's dark and depressing as fuck, because of a lack of windows and a lack of actual lights. The furniture doesn't match. A red plaid chair sits beside a mangy blue velvet recliner that's seen better days. The sofa is a glorified futon. There are dead flies in the windowsills, an ant trap on the kitchen floor. The curtains are long and pleated, and I'd bet my life there are spiders living in the curtain folds, making spider eggs that will hatch one night while we're asleep, filling the cottage with millions of spider babies.

Emily tries finding a light, which, when she does, turns out to be pointless, because the light the lamp gives off is practically nonexistent. It's sunny outside, but that doesn't matter because the sunlight is not getting past the big trees to reach the inside of the cottage.

Wyatt tries dropping his stuff just inside the front door, but Emily tells him to take it upstairs. "We're not going to make a mess of the cottage the minute we arrive. And someone close the door, please. We don't need those mosquitoes getting inside," she says before going and doing it herself, because none of us is fast enough, because I, for one, am too caught up in grieving last year's ocean views and private lanais to even think about closing the door.

Beside me, Wyatt groans. Nolan says, "Would you relax, Emily? We're on vacation."

"Am I supposed to carry everyone's luggage upstairs for them?" she asks. "Am I not on vacation too?"

I don't know much about parenting, but I do know one thing. You should have a united front. You should at least give the appearance of being in agreement when it comes to things like where the luggage goes. Otherwise the kids will walk all over you.

"No," he says, "of course I don't expect you to carry everyone's things upstairs. Just give people a minute to get settled. It was a long drive."

Wyatt walks away from his backpack. I set my own bags on the floor because if he can, then I can too.

"What's that smell?" Wyatt asks and I'm glad I'm not the only one who notices.

"It's just a little musty," Nolan says, trying to stay upbeat. "We'll open the windows and air things out."

Together, we walk up the wooden stairs, where we find three bedrooms and one bathroom on the second floor. "Wyatt, you can sleep here. And Reese and Mae will sleep in this room," Emily says, and I poke my head into Mae's and mine, seeing just one small bed, which is not happening.

"No," I say, shaking my head. "Absolutely not. I am not sleeping with Mae. She hogs the blankets. She kicks."

"I do not!" Mae argues, crossing her arms against her chest, sulking.

"Yes, you do," I tell her before looking at Emily and saying, "I am *not* sharing a bed with her. No. I refuse. She can sleep with Wyatt. Why should he get his own room? I'm the oldest."

"Because he's a boy," Emily says, as if that's not completely sexist.

"So what?"

"I don't want to sleep with Wyatt," Mae cries, turning on the waterworks because Emily falls for it every single time.

"It's only for a few days, Reese," Emily says, trying to reason with me, but I've already tuned her out because, from the top of the stairs, I make out a porch just off the main room of the cottage, with a bed that I see through the glass panes of the door that connects the porch to the rest of the house.

"Never mind," I say. "Mae can have the room all to herself. I'll sleep down there." I turn and make my way down the stairs, because the idea of being an entire floor away from the rest of them is actually amazing.

Emily sees what I see and decides. "No. You can't sleep on the porch, Reese. It's not safe. What if someone breaks in?"

"Good. They'd put me out of my misery then," I say, bounding down the stairs, not looking back.

"Don't say things like that, Reese. You are not sleeping down there. You're sleeping up here with—"

"Just leave her alone," Nolan says, cutting her off. "Just let her sleep on the porch if she wants to. Who really cares where she sleeps? It's not like anything's going to happen to her."

Emily's attention shifts to him. "You know how much I hate it when you do that," she says, raging as I open the door and slip out onto the porch, into a world of my own, which is basic—just a small bed pushed up against one side of the room with a white quilt and one flat pillow, a tiny nightstand, wooden floorboards with a braided wool rug and slack, flimsy screens that overlook the woods. "You always do that."

"Do what?"

"You always contradict me in front of the kids. You let them do anything they want. They will never respect me because of you. *She* will never respect me because of you. It's your fault she doesn't listen to me. I already told her she can't sleep down there."

"You can't control everything she does. Let her sleep on the porch if she wants to. What do you possibly think is going to happen? She'll be fine," he says, and I hate that they do this. I hate when they talk about me like I'm not here, like I can't hear them. Like I'm deaf. I tug on the porch door so hard that it slams, and then I drop down on the bed, pulling my legs into me, wrapping my arms around them, wishing I was anywhere but here.

I go on my phone to distract myself, to see if Skylar ever texted back. There is no Wi-Fi in the cottages, though there's free Wi-Fi in the lodge. *You've* got *to be kidding me*, I said when the lady at the lodge told us. Emily said I should be glad, that this was my chance to disconnect from technology and enjoy nature, as if that's something I'd actually like.

Nolan, however, appeased me, saying cellular might work, which it does. Sort of. It takes forever to load so that I don't think it's ever going to. But then it does and I wish it hadn't because, while there is no text from Skylar, I go to Instagram and see that she's posted pictures of herself and another girl, Gracie, in Chicago, at Oak Street Beach, doing things she and I were supposed to do together, like lying out, playing beach volleyball and eating hot dogs from the concessions stand. There are stupid little Insta stickers that say shit like *Friendship Vibes* and *BFF Love*, and I wonder if it's for me, if it's for my sake, if she's trying to hurt me because she's still mad at me.

If so, it's working. Because I do feel hurt. Jealous. I can't stand to look at them together and think of all the things I'm missing out on while I'm stuck here. I get even angrier, thinking that I've been replaced—that Gracie is now Skylar's best friend instead of me, and I realize Skylar never responded to my text from before because she's been with Gracie all day. I wonder if she and Gracie saw my text come in together and if, when they did, they laughed, Gracie throwing her pretty blond hair back, rolling her eyes and saying something like *Her again? You should just block her* because it's the kind of thing Gracie would say. Anger floods me until I feel like I could explode. I see them sitting on the beach, laughing, Gracie leaning over Skylar's shoulder to read the text, saying, *Good idea, Reese. Yeah. You probably should kill yourself.* Before I can take a breath or try to stop myself, I reel back, chucking my phone, watching as it arcs across the room, hitting a glass lantern by mistake, which was probably my only source of light out here. The lantern falls. It hits the ground hard, missing the rug by an inch and breaking.

Fuck. Just my luck.

Chunks of glass lie scattered on the floor, but the door to the porch is closed and Emily and Nolan are still fighting anyway; no one notices the sound of breaking glass.

I breathe in. Out. In. Out.

I look out the window where I just barely make out the lake through the trees. There's practically a whole forest between us and the lake. A path cuts through it, some worn, dusty trail that's been beaten down by people's feet. Our cottage is probably the furthest one from the lake, but because of the hill, we see over the trees. Even I can admit it's pretty, though I'd never tell Emily or Nolan that. Never.

I'm feeling sorry for myself—wishing myself dead, imagining myself dead, imagining how sorry everyone would be if I was dead—when all of a sudden I hear movement through the screens.

I look closer. I hold my breath and listen, trying to find the source of the noise. Outside, the trees are still. There is no breeze.

I swing my legs over the side of the bed. I stand up, stepping over the broken glass, drifting closer to the screen. I set my hand on it, feeling the screen give and become looser against the weight of my hand. I wonder if Emily was right, though I'd rather die before admitting it. I wonder if someone could easily break into the porch. There is no door straight to outside, but it wouldn't take much for them to get in anyway, just a little pressure and the screen would give.

I hold my breath as a boy, about my age, steps out from behind the trees, walking alone in the woods with his hands in the pockets of his jeans. The world goes quiet. I forget all about Skylar and Gracie on Instagram, and Emily and Nolan in the next room. Instead, I find myself falling hard, suddenly infatuated with his long, thick brown hair, which is *not* one of those overdone messy cuts that literally every guy in the world has these days (Wyatt included) with the fringe bangs that fall forward into the eyes like a llama's. Instead, his is pushed back so that I can see his face: the thin nose, the sharp edges of his cheekbones and the jawline that looks like it's been carved by a sculptor.

All of a sudden, the door to the porch gets thrown open behind me, ricocheting off the opposite wall.

I spin around. "You ever hear of knocking?"

Emily stands there, delivering my bags, disappointment on her face.

"Sorry to scare you, but I asked you not to leave your bags by the door," she says, setting them down on the floor and then, because she can't limit herself to nagging about just one thing, she says, "You're not going to hide out here for all of vacation. This is a *family* vacation. You're supposed to be with family, not isolating yourself out here."

"Did I not just spend the whole day in the car with all of you?" I ask.

She can't argue with that. And besides, I don't see a single person in the living room besides her anymore. Everyone else has now shut themselves away too, including Nolan, which tells me that Emily is sad and lonely and she's projecting.

"You can at least leave the door open so we know that you're alive."

"Fine. Leave it open when you go."

She starts to. But then she sees the broken glass on the floor and my phone lying just beside it and asks, "What happened? Did you *break* that, Reese?"

A second later, her eyes rise up to the screens. She doesn't wait for me to answer either of her first two questions before she asks, "Is someone out there?" while searching, something outside having caught her attention.

"No," I unhesitatingly say. "I don't think so. I didn't see anyone."

But he is still there. Emily just doesn't see him.

Because, when I look for myself, I catch sight of him hidden further in the trees, listening to our conversation, his dark eyes watching me.

COURTNEY

It wasn't real. The face in the window. I imagined it, I tell my-self as I slam the cottage door closed behind us. I lock it, flick-ing the dead bolt into place, jiggling the handle to be certain it's locked and that no one can get in. I lean into it, resting my forehead against the door, trying to catch my breath, which feels impossible.

When I turn around, Cass and Mae stand behind me in the room, Cass four or five inches taller than Mae, because Mae, like Emily, is petite, and because she hasn't hit puberty yet. She's still waiting for a growth spurt, which happened for Cass a year ago. It gives the impression that Mae is much younger than she is, though she's ten, like Cass, just one year away from middle school. Emily and I were pregnant at the same time. We gave birth just five weeks apart. It comes rushing back to me in that moment: the baby shower we shared, Emily and me pos-ing for pictures with our baby bumps, her going into labor first and then downplaying it, so I wouldn't be scared. *It really didn't hurt, not as bad as they say.*

And now Emily is dead.

I shudder at the thought, some sort of feral, guttural sound coming out of me. My hand rises to my mouth as I squeeze my eyes shut tight, trying not to, but still picturing her lying on the floor of the screened-in porch, her mangled body bloodied, practically magenta from the way the blood pooled inside of her. I see the expression on her face, fixed forever in place in a wide-eyed, openmouthed scream. I throw up in my mouth thinking about it and swallow it back down, the reflux making my throat burn.

Someone killed her.

Someone killed Nolan.

They're both dead. Murdered. My best friend and my brother. Gone.

I open my eyes. In front of me, Cass is wide-eyed, wild, her chest heaving, crying. But Mae is in shock, quiet, her skin sallow, though I see her heartbeat through her thin cotton shirt. She breathes through an open mouth, her nostrils flaring. The knee of Mae's pajama pants is torn from when she fell. There is still blood on her hands. It's on her knee too, staining the edges of the tear red. Her hair, like Cass's, is in her eyes. It's practically the same color hair, a light caramel brown—like Nolan's, like mine—so that when you see them lying side by side sometimes you don't know where Cass ends and Mae begins.

I drop to the arm of a chair. I pull them into me, wrapping my arms around their small waists, holding them as they press into me. I look back over my shoulder to double-check that the front door is closed and locked, which it is, though that doesn't mean someone couldn't just kick it in or break a window to get in. I picture Emily and Nolan's cottage. Did someone let the killer inside, or did the killer break down the door? I try to remember if the door was open, or if the weak wooden frame was splintered by force, but I can't recall. Still, I think about pulling a chair in front of our door, but I don't know that it would stop anyone, and someone could just as easily come in through the open windows.

"Are you girls okay?" I ask quietly, the words coming out fast, urgent. It's a stupid question. Of course they're not okay.

None of us will ever be okay again. Still, Cass—always a people pleaser—nods, but Mae says nothing, her body palpitating in my arms. "I need to call for help," I tell them, finding my phone in the pocket of my robe but seeing that the two bars I had next door have disappeared and I have none.

"Shit."

Cass looks at me with fear in her eyes. "What's wrong?"

"The cell signal," I say, wishing more than anything that Elliott was here, that he hadn't gone fishing today of all days, that he would come back home. I don't know what time he left, though early morning is the best chance to catch fish, and so my guess is he was out on the lake just before dawn. I slept through it. I didn't hear him get up, I didn't hear him leave. The sun rises around five or five thirty, which makes me think he slipped from bed sometime before that and was drifting out into the lake in the canoe soon after with a thermos of coffee and his fishing gear, which he brought from home, tucked inside the hull.

"What are you going to do?" Cass asks, her voice trembling.

"I don't know," I say, rising up. "Just give me a minute to think."

I wander around the cottage with my phone in the air, searching for just one crucial bar, which I don't find. I move toward the window, hoping the signal might be better there than behind a solid wall. I peel the curtain back, pressing my phone to the glass. *No service.* "Dammit," I mutter under my breath, looking outside where the day is pristine, the lake and sky bluer than I've seen. The cell signal is better up on the hill, by Emily and Nolan's cottage. Since the day we got here, that's been the case, because the higher elevation is closer to the cell tower, or so Elliott said. That said, I don't know that I can get myself to go back up there to make the call. I don't know what's happening inside the cottage. I don't know who is there. I don't know if when they're finished there, they'll come for us.

I let go of the curtain, watching as it swishes closed.

I can't stay here. I have to get help. I have to *do something*. Reese and Wyatt might still be alive. I have to save them before it's too late. I have to save the girls and me.

"I have to go to the lodge for help," I decide, turning away from the window and looking back at Cass. The lodge is where the rental office is. There is free Wi-Fi there and, even better, a landline where I can call the police. "You girls stay—"

"No," Cass says, shaking her head and cutting me off, though it's not as decisive as it sounds; it's scared, whining before she bursts into tears. "You can't go," she begs, shaking her head.

"It will be fine, Cass," I say, my voice turning buoyant, breezy, trying to convince her, as if suggesting she stay in the car while I run into the convenience store for a gallon of milk. "I'll run. I'll go fast. You girls stay here and lock the door behind me. Don't open it for anyone until I come back. Keep the curtains closed. When I'm back, I'll let myself in with the key."

"No. *No.* You're not going."

"There isn't another option, honey. It will be fine," I say again, drawing the last word out for emphasis. "I need to get to a phone so I can call for help. I have no signal."

"You're not leaving us here." She reaches for my hand, fastening to it like glue, tugging so hard it hurts. Her eyes are pleading, desperate, and I give in. There is no good option. Maybe it's better that we stay together. I could never live with myself if I left them behind and then something happened to them.

We leave out the front door, trying to be silent and invisible. I pull the door closed quickly behind us, to prevent the hinges from squeaking, holding on to the handle until the latch is aligned with the plate and it slides noiselessly into place. I ease the screen door closed.

Cass tries to take off immediately, but I grab her by the hand and we stand on the deck, our backs pressed to the weathered wooden siding, searching the trees with our eyes. In the cottages around us, people still sleep with doors closed and curtains drawn, while overhead a flock of loons soars by, landing gracefully on the lake.

I count down on my fingers—3 . . . 2 . . . I mouth the word, *Go,* before we leave the deck, running. Cass darts ahead, but again, Mae lags behind because her steps are smaller than ours. I tug on her hand, practically dragging her along the path and through the trees. Cass takes the lead, sprinting in the direction of the lodge—she knows the way by heart because of all the times the kids have gone together to play pool or foosball or rent DVDs.

Cass gets there first, but the German shepherd stops her in her tracks. It's tied to a tree, though it rises up, showing its teeth. Cass cowers, and I have to tell her that she's fine, that the dog can't get her because of the rope, and only then does she go on, slipping quickly past, pressing on the lodge door, running inside but stopping so abruptly that Mae and I stumble into her, practically falling.

It's dim inside the lodge. The lights are wanting. The ceilings are low, the wood paneling dark. It takes a minute for me to orient myself, for my eyes to adjust to the lack of light, but when they do, I see that we're not alone. That the lodge is not empty, as it should be at just past seven in the morning.

There is a man sitting at the bar alone. I've seen him around the resort before. In fact, the other day, I saw him stop and say something to Reese by the pool. I don't know what he said, but I noticed her reaction from behind: the clenched hands, the nervous laugh. She walked away, and as she did, she stole a hesitant glance back to see if he was still there, and he was, his smile smarmy.

Now he looks up as we come in, one of the only people awake at the resort besides us. He's on his laptop, presumably working, though he has a beer at 7:00 a.m., which he reaches for, saying nothing as the lodge door clicks closed, taking the sunlight with it.

As it does, Cass backs into me, scared.

A woman comes out from the office, muttering under her breath, "That better be you, Daniel, you little shit. You think you can just waltz into work whenever you want and—"

She stops, pulling back. I stand just inside the door with Mae and Cass beside me, pressed in close, Mae clutching a fistful of my robe in her hand. My heart hammers inside me, and I want to scream at the woman to call the police, but I'm doing everything in my power to stay strong for Cass and Mae, to not fall apart, to not lose control. I hear a noise from behind and I gasp. My eyes dart back, panicked, expecting to see Emily and Nolan's killer coming into the lodge with us, but it's not; the sound is from an arcade game. I look back, my mind all over the place, frantic. I can't stop wondering what happened, who killed them. Was it someone we know or was it random? Did the killer think Emily and Nolan were someone else? Did they go into the wrong cottage and still kill them anyway? I can't stop thinking about Reese and Wyatt in the cottage now. They're dead. Of course they're dead. They have to be. I can't stand the idea of going back, of seeing their bodies like I did Emily's and Nolan's. It would kill me. I wouldn't survive it.

"Oh," the woman says, seeing us, taken aback because we're not who she expected to see, and because of the way we look: pale, tear streaked, breathing hard. She regroups. When she speaks again, her voice is softer, changed. "I'm sorry. Pardon my French. I thought you were someone else." She pulls her eyebrows together, bends down and leans in toward bloodied Mae. "You need something, honey? Are you hurt?" she asks, smiling, and I think she believes something inconsequential has happened, like that Mae's fallen and we've come for a Band-Aid. She has a kind, gentle face, pear shaped with rolls of skin on her neck. Her name tag reads Greta Dahl. I've seen her before. She was here the day we checked in to the resort and got our keys.

I step closer to Ms. Dahl. "There's been a . . . a . . . an accident in cottage number eight. My brother and his wife. They're . . . they're . . ." I glance back, aware that Cass and Mae are listening. I lean in, quiet my voice, my eyes pooling with tears. "They're dead."

But Cass still hears, her voice rising in pitch as she asks, "*What?* They're *dead*?" as if only now realizing, and I nod, watching as she cries harder. Beside her, Mae presses her hands to her ears, blocking out the sound of Cass's sobs.

"What do you mean they're *dead*?" Ms. Dahl asks, her smile vanishing as she takes a step back, a look of shock and disbelief on her face.

"I . . . I went this morning to see if everything was okay," I say, explaining how Mae came to our place, crying and upset. "The front door was open. I went in. It was quiet. I thought at first that they were all asleep. I found my sister-in-law on the screened-in porch. The blood. Oh God," I say, bringing my hand to my own mouth, pressing hard as tears spill out and over my cheeks, seeing it all over again, the color of Emily's skin, the way her contorted body was sprawled on the floor, mouth open, eyes wide and opaque like murky lakes, blood everywhere, and the smell—I remember now—something coppery that I couldn't place at the time. It was the smell of blood.

"My brother is dead too. I saw his body. Someone did this to them," I say, crying, speaking fast. "Someone killed them."

"No," she says, shaking her head, finding it impossible to

believe. Her eyes go to the man at the bar and then back to me, saying, sputtering, "There must be some mistake. That can't be right. Are you sure . . ." But then she stops and asks, "Have you called anyone, honey? The police? Are they on their way?" Her movements are brisk as she steps past me for the door, which she dead-bolts, looking through a window and outside to see if anyone is there, if anyone followed us here. I feel grateful, believing we're safer inside with the door locked, believing it's better that we're not alone, that someone is here with us.

"No," I say, shaking my head. "No. I tried, but I couldn't get a signal. We came here to see about a landline."

She nods, spinning back, away from the door. "Yes. Of course," she says. "I'll call right now." She speaks quickly, her words choppy, punctuated, her movements fast. She brushes past me for the office, where she closes the door and I hear nothing, which I'm grateful for because that means the girls can't hear it either, that they don't have to listen for a second time as someone says that Emily and Nolan are dead.

"Here," I say to them, "let's sit."

I help them to stools at the bar. At the same time, the man says, "Must've been a hell of a thing to see," while reaching for his beer, and I nod. I look away, but when I look back a minute later, he's still watching me.

I drop my eyes to my phone. My fingers shake as I text Elliott. **Come home. Something's happened.** Because of the Wi-Fi in the lodge, the message sends, but I don't know if, out on the lake, Elliott receives it.

When Ms. Dahl comes out, she gets us glasses of water from the tap. She says, "They're on the way. Shouldn't be too long," and I see on her face and in her body language that she wants to ask more, to *know* more, but she doesn't for the girls' sake. "Does anyone need anything?" she asks instead, her eyes tight. We say no, but still, she gets the girls snacks from the vending machine because she's anxious and can't stand still, though no one is hungry. No one wants to eat.

The bags of Fritos sit untouched on the bar. I reach for Cass's and Mae's barstools, pulling them closer to mine. I ask for a garbage can for Mae, who's begun to feel sick. I think of all the pancakes and syrup she ate earlier today and know that eventually, they'll come back up. Ms. Dahl brings us the garbage and a wet rag, which I press to Mae's face, crooning, "Breathe. Just try to breathe." It doesn't work. She begins to vomit into the small plastic can as I lay the rag on the back of her neck to cool her.

"How long did they say?" I ask Ms. Dahl, anxious for the police to come, for them to be here. Bile rises up inside of me at the thought of Reese and Wyatt inside that cottage. Of what might be happening, of what they might be going through. Of me, standing idly by, letting it happen. It crosses my mind to leave Cass and Mae here, to go to the cottage alone, to see if they're safe or if they're hurt, but the idea of going back, of leaving Cass and Mae with strangers, is more than I can bear.

Ms. Dahl paces behind the bar. With each pass, her eyes rise to the door, though from where we sit, it's impossible to see outside. "They didn't say, honey. Just said they'd send someone."

I nod, rubbing circles on Mae's back. Cass, herself, looks green, and I don't know if it's from seeing Mae puke, from the smell of the vomit in the trash can, or from everything else that's happened. I stroke her cheek. "I can't imagine there are too many emergencies around here," I say to no one in particular, desperate for the police to arrive, though I imagine too, that in a town this size, there aren't many police.

The man decides to leave, to go back to his cottage and check on his wife and kids. Ms. Dahl tries to object, saying, "I don't know if that's safe, not until the police get here. I think you should wait." But he goes anyway, Ms. Dahl walking him to the door, where she gazes vigilantly out before unlocking and opening it. Once he's gone, she flings the door closed, flicking the dead bolt. She comes back to the bar, looking for something to do, for some way to keep busy until the police arrive. She puts the man's dirty glass in the sink and then starts wiping down the bar with a rag, glancing at us as she does, sweat starting to appear on her upper lip. "You doing okay, honey? Anything you need?" she asks.

I tell her no. No, I don't need anything. But also no, I'm not okay. My brother and his wife are dead. I don't know where Reese and Wyatt are, if they're alive, if they're dead, and the guilt eats at me. Ms. Dahl moves the bar rag around in aimless circles, and at first I'm lost in thought, staring blindly at her rough, worn and calloused hands and the movement of the rag on the countertop, thinking about the last thing I heard Reese say to Emily last night, until I feel eyes on me and realize that Ms. Dahl is staring at us with a cold, fixed gaze as she wipes down the bar.

Cass notices too, pressing into me, hiding her face against my arm.

Greta Dahl's staring gets under my skin, until the paranoia sets in and I start to wonder if it's taking so long for the police to come because, when she went into the office to make the call alone, closing the door behind herself, she never called them.

REESE

"Where are you going?" Emily asks. It's a few minutes later. She stands in the dumpy kitchen, wiping everything down with Lysol wipes because she won't let our bags of food touch anything that hasn't been cleaned, and for once, I don't disagree. I stare at her for half a second. She's still sad from what happened with Nolan before. Her eyes are dull and she looks tired, which maybe she is, or maybe she's just sad. He's upstairs in the room they're supposed to share, with the door closed, and I think how lonely it must be being Emily.

"For a walk," I say, reaching for the door handle.

"I don't want you going for a walk alone."

"Why not? What do you think's going to happen to me?"

"I don't know, but we just got here. You don't know your way around yet. You might get lost."

"I won't get lost."

"Take Wyatt and Mae with you then."

"Why? So we can all get lost?" I sigh when she says nothing. "Do I have to? I just want to be alone for like five minutes."

"Yes," she says, "you have to."

I throw my hands up in the air, calling for Wyatt and Mae. Mae is upstairs, but Wyatt is outside, taking practice swings at nothing with his four-hundred-dollar baseball bat (if I never have to hear about its light weight or alloy barrel again, I'll be thrilled). They take forever to get ready so that by the time Mae's shoes are on, Wyatt's bat is set safely inside and we're finally ready to leave, there's no use looking for the boy I saw before because he's gone.

"Keep an eye on Mae, Reese. Don't let her wander off," Emily says as we leave.

"Where do you guys want to go?" I ask them.

Mae doesn't care, but Wyatt wants to go back to the lodge, which is the place where we checked in to the resort and got our keys, because there were arcade games there that he wants to play. I say fine, whatever. I don't care, so long as Emily and Nolan aren't there.

It's a short walk to the lodge from our cottage. The path there is no different than the trail that goes from our cottage toward the lake. In fact, it's probably the exact same worn-down path that goes across this whole stupid resort with little wooden arrows saying stuff like *Lodge* and *Pool*, so that, contrary to what Emily thinks, you'd have to be an actual idiot to get lost.

When we get there, there is a man standing outside the lodge entrance, smoking as we approach with his eyes on me; if Skylar were here, she'd tell him to take a picture because it lasts longer. Skylar always knows what to say in situations like these. Me? Not so much. Instead, his staring makes me self-conscious, and I think about what Emily said before. *Is that what you want people to think? That you're a slut?* I adjust my shirt, avoiding eye contact as the man barely steps out of the way to make room for us to pass. He takes a long drag from his cigarette, almost blowing the smoke in my face before letting his eyes drift to Mae, who's fallen behind Wyatt and me. As I watch, he takes in the thin, bare legs that stick out from beneath her denim overalls, one strap too big so that it slips to her upper arm. "Hurry up, slowpoke," I say to her, seeing her spaced out, kicking up rocks and dirt with the toe of her gym shoes.

"You walk too fast," she whines.

"You walk too slow. Hurry up."

I make Mae go inside before me, praying to God this creep doesn't follow us in and that he's not still here when we leave.

Inside the lodge, slot machines and arcade games line a wall, which Wyatt takes immediately off for, leaving Mae and me behind. Mae spots the DVD rentals and asks if we can get one. I have three dollars in my pocket and so I say fine, whatever, if she gets Emily to pay me back, because they cost a dollar each and I'm not a bank.

"Why do you call her that?" Mae asks.

"Call her what?"

"Emily."

"Why not? It's her name, isn't it?"

"Her name is *Mom*."

I roll my eyes. I don't call them Emily and Nolan to their faces. Not anymore, not after Emily told me it was a "sign of disrespect" and that I was "devaluing her authority." Now I just think it and say it behind her back, because that's what Skylar does, she calls her mom *Caroline*, like they're friends.

I watch as Mae wanders away to peruse the infinitesimal selection of DVDs, which look like they were made before I was born, while Wyatt feeds quarters into some arcade game, feeding his own gambling habit. He's gotten into trouble for it before: for online gambling, for stealing Emily and Nolan's credit card for things like buying loot boxes and other in-game purchases, for racking up debt on fantasy football. I don't know how he got around the whole legal-gambling-age thing, but he did. When they caught him, they took away his phone and computer for a month and made him do chores to pay back the money he stole, which was in the thousands. They think it solved the problem. It didn't. Instead, Wyatt started selling his old Pokémon cards and Grandma's antique silverware (she's not dead, not yet, but she's getting ready for it, offloading things she no longer needs) that Emily keeps in a bin in the basement for cash to gamble with, but they haven't noticed and I'm not going to be the one to tell them because if I did, Wyatt would murder me in my sleep.

I wander aimlessly, killing time. The lodge is a dive. Kids walk around barefoot and wet, like they've just come from the pool or beach. There are giant taxidermy fish on the walls beside neon Budweiser signs. There is a sign for some missing girl. I go to the sign and read it, seeing that the girl was four foot ten and ninety pounds when she went missing. She was last seen riding her bike home from a friend's house almost five years ago, which tells me the odds of her still being alive are slim to none. There is a Facebook page to find her, *Help Find Kylie Matthews*. The sign asks for anyone with information to call the police or visit the Facebook page. Mae sees me looking at the sign and comes over to ask, "Who's that?" about the girl, and I say it's no one.

"It doesn't look like no one," she says, and I roll my eyes. "Then who's that?" she asks, pointing to another picture beside the first one, on the same sign.

"Same girl," I say because it's an age-progressed picture.

"No it's not," Mae says, giving me a look like I'm dumb.

"Yes it is. That's her before," I say, motioning at the first picture. "And that's what she'd look like now if—" I start to say, moving my finger to the next picture and wondering what it would be like for her family to see her grow up in pictures but not real life.

"If what?" Mae asks when I cut my words short, not wanting to say to her: *if she's not dead*, because I don't want to scare her, for one, and because she'd probably say something to Emily and then I'd get in trouble for talking about dead girls.

"Did you find a movie yet?" I ask instead.

She hasn't. Mae runs away, and I go to the other side of the room, where there is a coin-operated pool table with torn felt where a couple kids play while their parents sit at the long wooden bar with mugs of beer, getting drunk, having fun. I doubt they get out much if they think this place is fun. It's dim in the lodge. The walls and floor are wood, and the only lights look like they've been here since 1970, which they probably have. They're covered in dust and grease and give off a nearly nonexistent amount of dull, yellow light. I take a picture of the stuffed fish for posterity's sake (hashtag worst vacation ever) and am feeling sorry for myself again—wishing I was anywhere but here—when I see him through the small window on the other side of the lodge, the boy I saw earlier walking in the woods, and from the minute I see him, everything changes.

My heart catches. All of a sudden, my body feels lighter, like I'm floating. I lose track of time, tuning out the rest of the world—the music, the people at the bar, the smell of fried fish, Wyatt, Mae—so that it's only me and him.

I forget all about what Emily said about keeping an eye on Mae.

COURTNEY

Cass screams. Mae draws back, blanching at the sound of someone tugging roughly on the door handle before battering the lodge door, which is locked, as if with the heel of a hand.

I fold my arms around both girls, drawing them into me, pressing their faces against my chest. My heart pounds as I wonder who's at the door and whether it's the police or if it's someone else.

Cass's scream is a reflex, something involuntary, but then, realizing what she's done and knowing she needs to be quiet so that whoever is on the other side of the door doesn't know we're here, she clamps both hands down over her mouth and goes silent, her eyes wide as full moons.

Ms. Dahl looks toward the door. She sets the rag down on the countertop, stepping out from behind the bar as Cass pulls away from me, crying out in a scream whisper, "No! Don't open it."

"She won't, honey," I say in a low voice, stroking her hair. "Not until she sees who it is. Isn't that right?" I ask for Cass's sake as well as mine. We're easy targets. I don't know who I can trust, if I can trust anyone. I regret not taking a knife from the cottage before we left or Elliott's multitool, something like that, something to protect ourselves with. I search the bar with my eyes, seeing a box cutter, though it's out of reach. I could lunge for it if I need to, though the blade on a box cutter is something like an inch or two. I don't know how much damage it would do.

"That's right," Ms. Dahl says. Still, I feel scared as she closes in on the door, my heart pounding in my chest and up my neck.

"No," Cass whines again. "Don't look. Don't open it."

"What if it's Dad?" I ask to comfort Cass, hoping she can't hear the fear in my own voice. "What if he's looking for us?"

It could be Elliott. It really could be. I texted him earlier. If he saw the text, he would have come immediately back from the lake to see what had happened. I wish more than anything that he was here, that he hadn't gone fishing today, because he would know what to do. He would keep the girls safer than I can. He'd keep me safe. Unlike me, Elliott would have gone back to the cottage to check on Wyatt and Reese; he wouldn't have left without them in the first place. I think of Elliott out there in the canoe on the lake, in the dark. He has no idea what's happened. He has no idea that Emily and Nolan are dead.

Last night, Elliott and I were at Emily and Nolan's place until sometime just after eight. It was mostly dark when we left, the sky softly glowing, though the sun had already slipped beneath the horizon. We said goodbye to Emily, who stood alone on the deck, waving until we could no longer see her though the trees. I had no way of knowing that was the last time I'd ever see her alive. Cass and Mae were already in our cottage, waiting for us to come home. They were lying up in the loft, giggling when we came in. *What's so funny up there?* I remember Elliott calling out to the girls, and them, in unison, holding their laughter back.

Nothing.

It doesn't sound like nothing, he teased.

"It's okay," Ms. Dahl says now, gazing out the window. "It's the police." She reaches her hand up to undo the dead bolt. I hold my breath, only releasing it when the door opens and I see them for myself: a few men, standing tall and broad shouldered while, behind them, red-and-blue police lights pulse through the trees.

I close my eyes, pressing a hand to my heart, sagging forward in relief. "The police are here. We're safe now," I whisper to Cass and Mae.

It's only as the police step inside the lodge that I see him: my nephew, Wyatt, standing behind the officers, getting swallowed up by their larger size.

Tears of relief leave my eyes, falling down my face. "Wyatt," I cry out, moving from my stool to go to him, taking him into my arms, and though Wyatt is fourteen and averse to things like affection and hugs, I feel his body give freely to me, slackening in my arms.

"Are you okay? Are you hurt?" I ask, running my hands through his hair, pushing it out of the way so I can see his eyes, which shun mine. Like Mae, Wyatt is languid, his reactions slow, his eyes bemused. Slowly, he shakes his head, leaving me to wonder which question of mine he's answering: if he's okay or if he's hurt, because it's hard to know. There is no blood, no obvious sign of an injury, but he doesn't look okay.

One of the officers, a young, ruddy redhead with freckles on his face and hands, steps forward, asking Wyatt who I am and if he knows me.

Wyatt is slow to nod. "Aunt Courtney," he manages to get out, pulling his body away from mine. His voice is meek, his shoulders rounded forward, which makes him appear smaller than he is, though Wyatt is taller than me.

"I'm Wyatt's aunt," I say to the officer. "Courtney Gray. I'm the one who found them." *Them.* I practically choke on the word, my throat tightening, my mouth all of a sudden watery, what little I've eaten today threatening to come up. I bring a hand to my mouth, trying to swallow away the image of Emily's and Nolan's gnarled bodies on the floor, watching as the officer stands there, taking glances at me out of the corner of his eye as if he doesn't know what to do, as if discomforted by my display of emotion.

"Is there anything you need?"

"Can I speak to whoever's in charge?" I ask, curling my shaking hands into fists. My eyes leave his, moving to the two men who stand behind him, because they're older than he is and closer in age to me.

But the young redhead says, "That would be me, ma'am. I'm Detective Evans," and I look again to see that, unlike the other officers who are in unform, he's dressed in everyday clothes, long sleeves and pants under a black tactical vest, and I wonder what a person has to do to be a detective, how old they have to be or how much experience they need to have and if he has any. "You can speak to me if you want." I nod, forcing my eyes closed, where I see the blood spatter on the wall, though I try not to, though I try to purge it from my mind. I breathe in, holding it before exhaling, over and over again until the nausea subsides.

I open my eyes to find him still watching me. I look away, glancing at Wyatt. "Is he hurt?"

"No."

"Where did you find him?"

"He was asleep in one of the upstairs bedrooms," he says, and I pull a face, wondering how it's even possible that Wyatt was asleep when they found him, until I look again and this time see that there are still pillow lines on Wyatt's face.

Wyatt was asleep? How can that be?

"Can he sit?" I ask, because Wyatt looks pale and he's unsteady, like standing in the ocean and feeling the shifting sand beneath your feet.

"If he wants." I go to Wyatt. I take him by the elbow, helping him to a barstool beside Cass and Mae, and then I turn back.

"Can we talk over there?" I ask, pointing before following the detective to the far side of the room, where I can still see the kids, who are quiet, statue-like, no one speaking. "Did he see them?" The detective turns to face me, his stance wide, his hands on his hips. "My brother and his wife," I say, when he says nothing. "The bodies. Did Wyatt see them?"

"He did. To a limited degree."

"To a limited degree. What does that even mean?"

"It means that we did what we could to get him out of the house without him seeing any more than he needed to see, but unfortunately we can't move the bodies until the medical examiner comes."

I nod, understanding. I imagine the police leading Wyatt out of the house with a tight grip on his arm, of them steering him past Nolan's lifeless body in the upstairs hall. I wonder if Wyatt closed his eyes or if he looked straight ahead, if he avoided looking at Nolan lying on the floor. A knot forms in my throat, thinking how this will stay with him and how he'll deal with the fallout his whole life. How he'll never be the same again.

"Who did this?" I ask.

He shakes his head. "We've just begun—" he starts to say.

I cut him off, asking instead, "How were they killed?"

"We don't know that yet. The medical examiner will have to determine a cause of death, but as soon as she does, we will let you know."

"And Reese?" I ask, clearing my throat, fighting tears. "Where is she?"

"Reese?" he asks, with a slight headshake. "I'm sorry, I—"

"My niece. Is she—" I start to ask, interrupting, but the words get away from me and I can't finish my question. *Dead. Is she dead?* Of course she's dead, because if she wasn't, then she would be here too, with Wyatt. While Wyatt slept, someone came into the cottage and killed the three of them. Miraculously, he's the only one who survived.

But the detective's response is unexpected. "There wasn't anyone else in the cottage. We only found the two deceased and him."

"I . . . I don't understand," I say, feeling a tightness spread through my chest. "She has to be there. Did you check all the rooms, the closets?"

"We searched the entire cottage. There was no one else there."

"That can't be right. She must be there."

My first thought is that they're incompetent, that they've somehow missed Reese in their search. I get angry. But he insists, "No, ma'am. It was only the two deceased and him," lifting his chin to Wyatt.

I feel my body temperature rise. I'm hot all of a sudden, sweating under my arms and near my groin, feeling claustrophobic in my robe, wondering what's worse, if Reese is dead or if whoever killed Emily and Nolan took her, and if so, what unimaginable things they're doing to her. My stomach roils, a sour taste in my mouth.

I think how last night, while we were asleep, someone came into their cottage and killed Emily and Nolan and took Reese. Elliott and I had the bedroom window open last night. There is no air-conditioning in the cottage. Though the temperatures drop into the fifties overnight, Elliott runs warm. The fresh air these last few nights has been a blessing. When we left home, it was something like ninety degrees with air quality alerts and unmerciful humidity. As a result, I've relished the crisp, earthy, pine-infused air slipping into the room with us at night, curling around us like fog. I can't remember ever sleeping as well as I have these last few nights, despite the fact that the resort has aged since Elliott was here five years ago and isn't as charming as he remembered. When we got here, he felt guilty for even recommending it; I told him it was fine and that we weren't expecting the Four Seasons.

Last night, there was a cross breeze coming in through the open windows. I wrapped myself in the patchwork quilt, pressing up close to Elliott to absorb the heat off his body, which he thought was me coming on to him and I had to tell him no— while gently pushing his hands away—not with Cass and Mae awake just twenty feet away. Unhappily he obeyed, wrapping his arms around me instead, and we fell asleep like that. I woke up at three in the morning to check on the girls, finding them asleep with the TV on, though now I wonder if I woke up all on my own or if something woke me.

"How old is your niece?"

"Seventeen. Her name is Reese. Reese Crane."

He asks if I have a picture of her, and I find one on my phone, taken just a day or so ago of her standing on the deck beside Cass, with her hand on Cass's shoulder, her skin natural and makeup-free. She wore an oversize tee that day, which came down to her upper thigh, her legs beneath it bare, her hair air-dried so that it was tousled and wavy. Cass adores her cousin, but Reese blows hot and cold in her affection toward Cass, though when she pays attention to her, I can visibly see Cass's self-worth increase.

He barely gives it a glance. "And the deceased—"

"Please stop calling them that," I say, interrupting, my words so sharp he does a double take.

"Pardon?"

"*The deceased.* They have names, you know? They're Nolan and Emily Crane."

He glances to the other side of the room to see if anyone heard me, which they did, because the other officers look up. Wyatt does too. Detective Evans turns back, his ego hurt. He gives me a hard smile and says, if only to placate me, "I'm sorry, ma'am. You're right. Of course they do. Mr. and Mrs. Crane then, they're Reese's parents?"

"Yes."

"How did they get along?" Detective Evans asks then, in

the same casual manner of someone asking what kind of pizza they like.

"Excuse me?" I ask, his question—and its implication—making it suddenly hard to breathe.

"I asked, how did they get along?" he says, as if I didn't hear him the first time. I don't answer right away because I can't, because it's too horrible for words, thinking of the carnage next door and of Reese somehow being responsible for it, which is what he's suggesting.

"You think Reese did something to hurt them?" I ask, shaking my head and feeling defensive. "No. *No.* That's not possible. That's not what happened. Someone has Reese. Someone *took* Reese," I insist.

But even as I say it, I think of last night, before Elliott and I said goodbye and left to come back home to our own cottage for the night. Reese was upset with Emily, which wasn't unusual, because it seemed like Reese was always upset with Emily. I didn't know why she was mad last night, because it could have been something as simple as the way Emily looked at her or a comment Emily made about Reese's clothes or hair that set her off.

But I remember Reese's vitriolic words as she stomped up the wooden steps, slamming a bedroom door so forcibly the whole cottage shook, an awkward silence sweeping over the rest of us before Elliott patted my knee and suggested we leave.

I hate you. I wish you'd die.

Detective Evans is watching me. He asks, "What makes you say that, ma'am? What makes you think someone *has* her?"

"It's just . . . it's just that I know Reese. And I know she would never hurt her parents," I say, telling myself that she was only angry and that people say things they don't mean when they're angry.

"Do you have a reason to believe someone took her? Was she afraid of someone? Was she being threatened?"

"We're not from around here, Detective. We don't know anyone here."

That said, I think of the man at the bar just now. I think of the men—grown men, married men—leering at Reese sunbathing in her bikini by the pool.

Anyone could have done it. Anyone could have taken her.

"When is the last time you saw Mr. and Mrs. Crane alive?"

I think back to last night, how everything happened. Cass and Mae asked if they could have a sleepover. We were at their cottage at the time and Emily suggested the girls stay there, so that Elliott and I could have a night alone. For a short-lived moment, I felt excited by the idea, because Elliott and I almost never had any time to ourselves anymore. With an only child, practically everything we do involves Cass. Family movie night, family game night. I thought about opening a bottle of wine, about staying up late sitting on the sunken sofa, talking.

But Reese was the one to complain, to put a kibosh on those plans. *They are not sleeping here. No fucking way. I am not listening to them all night.*

I didn't want to make Emily feel bad for the way Reese reacted, and so I said no, that Elliott would probably just go to bed early because he planned to leave early to fish. *We can keep them,* I'd said. *And then another night they can sleep at your cottage.*

Now there would never be another night. A moan rises up inside of me as I think about how close Cass and Mae came to being killed too. I picture them lying on the floor of the screened-in porch beside Emily. I see them dead. I see blood on their small bodies as thoughts fill my mind of Emily and Nolan dead. Murdered. Dead. Murdered. I say it again and again in my mind, until the words lose meaning and I can't make sense of them anymore. I can't process the fact that Emily and Nolan are no longer living. That they're gone. I think about their last moments alive and wonder if they knew they were going to die, if they were scared, if they fought back or if it happened so fast they didn't have time to react.

Someone brings me a glass of water that I don't want. Detective Evans takes it when I don't, holding it before looking around for someplace to set it—settling on a dusty windowsill—and turning back to face me.

I don't know how much time passes before I can answer. "Last night," I say. "Maybe half past eight. My husband and I were at their cottage. Wyatt and Reese were there too. The girls, Cass and Mae, were back at our cottage alone. They're ten," I say, as if feeling the need to defend my decision to let them stay home alone for a few hours, though he's too young to know anything about raising kids. "And we were just next door. We assumed they'd be fine and they were. The four adults played cards, had a few drinks, and then my husband and I said good-night to come back and check on the girls. That was the last time we saw Emily and Nolan alive."

I've said something, sparking the detective's interest. He stands up straighter, looks around, noticing Elliott's absence for the first time.

"Where is your husband?" he asks slowly, cocking a head, his words, however benign, getting under my skin.

REESE

I drift to the window like a leaf caught in a breeze, getting carried away by the wind. I stand there watching as the boy unloads boxes from the bed of a rusty pickup truck, completely hung up on his arms: the suntanned skin, a tattoo partially visible from beneath the short sleeve of a white t-shirt and the way his biceps flex when he lifts the boxes, carrying them across the parking lot and then stacking them beside an open door. I can't look away. I'm hypnotized. Transfixed. I feel warm all over, my heart fluttering as he closes the truck's tailgate, thinking how good he looks in his tight t-shirt and jeans as he turns and walks toward a vending machine on the side of the lodge. He slides money in before reaching down for a Pepsi that he uncaps and throws back, and then I watch him drink it, completely obsessed with his neck as he swallows, on the sweat that tumbles down the sides of his face—envying it because of its closeness to his skin—and on his dark eyes that slowly lower as he finishes drinking, locking with mine.

My heart stops. I freeze like a dummy, telling myself that he can't *see* me in the window, that there must be a shadow or a glare blocking his view.

But then a smile pulls on the edges of his lips, and he lifts his hand and waves.

He can see me after all.

I fall away from the window. I hide myself, feeling my cheeks burn. Embarrassed, I ask Wyatt and Mae, "You guys ready to go?" though it isn't so much of a question.

Only Wyatt answers. "Not yet. Once I get past this level we can go."

I turn around, thinking Mae is behind me. She's not, though she should be back by now. It shouldn't be taking this long to pick out a movie, especially when there were only like ten to choose from. I let my eyes go to the wall of them, irritated that she's being a snail again, though Mae is always a snail. Normal people do everything Mae does in half the time, but she gets a pass because she shouldn't even be alive.

The area by the movies is empty. Mae isn't there; she's gone.

My heart beats hard again, but for a completely different reason than before.

"Where's Mae, Wyatt?" I ask, but he doesn't hear me because he's too caught up in his game. "Wyatt," I say again. "Where is Mae?"

"How should I know? You're supposed to be watching her, remember?"

I don't know how much time has passed since Mae went to look for a DVD. I don't know how long I was staring outside, if it was five minutes or fifteen.

"Help me look for her," I say, my eyes darting around the lodge, but Mae is nowhere. "Mae!" I call out, that creep from before suddenly living rent free in my mind, the way his eyes went from me to Mae when we walked in. I think of every worst thing I can imagine in that moment. Child predators. Human trafficking. "Mae!" I shout out, loud enough that people turn to look.

Before anyone can offer to help, she appears from behind a dark curtain—her eyes wide and her face white—with some guy's hand on her shoulder. A sign on the curtain reads *Adults Only*.

"I think someone's a little lost," he says, chuckling.

"Get over here," I say, snatching Mae by the arm and pulling her away from him. "What were you thinking? Can't you read, idiot? That section's for grown-ups," I say, pointing to the *Adults Only* sign.

"I didn't know," she says, on the verge of tears, so that I almost feel bad for calling her an idiot. Almost. "I'm sorry."

"You should be. You scared the shit out of me. Do you have any idea what could have happened to you?" Mae shakes her head, tears in her eyes, because she doesn't know, because she can't imagine the creeps that live in this world and the things they do to little girls like her, and I'm not going to be the one to tell her.

"Did you find something?" I ask. In her hands is *The Parent Trap*, which she holds out to me. "Give me that," I say, yanking it from her so I can pay and we can leave.

"If you're not careful," I say to Mae on the way out, as we pass by the poster of that missing girl again, "whatever happened to her is going to happen to you."

I watch as Mae stares back over her shoulder at it, scared. Good, I think. She should be. Then maybe she won't wander off like that again.

"Are you going to tell Mom?" she asks later, as we make our way back to the cottage, following the same worn-down path through the woods.

"Definitely not," I say because it wouldn't be Mae's fault. Mae can do no wrong in Emily's and Nolan's minds. It would be mine for not keeping a better eye on her.

"Yeah well, I might," Wyatt says.

"You better not," I tell him.

"If you want me to keep quiet, it's going to cost you."

"You're such a jerk. Besides, I have two actual dollars," I say, reaching a hand into my pocket for the cash, which I try handing to him. "Here. You can have it if you want."

But he doesn't take it. "You have Venmo," he says, but there's no way I'm letting my little fourteen-year-old brother blackmail me again. Wyatt is a shark. The time he caught me breaking curfew cost me twenty bucks. The time he caught me leaving the house with a bottle of Nolan's Tito's in my bag cost more.

"Screw you, Wyatt. I'm not giving you shit."

We get back to the cottage. Aunt Courtney and Uncle Elliott are there now, along with my little cousin Cass. The adults have been drinking, which I know because Emily's voice is high as fuck and her skin is red like it gets when she's lit up. There's an Old Fashioned in her hands too—her favorite and probably not her first. No, definitely not her first. Nolan stands just behind her, his hand on her shoulder like they actually like each other, though I know it's a front for company's sake. Aunt Courtney sits on the sofa with Cass. Uncle Elliott plays bartender, standing in the kitchen with a bottle of bourbon, and I know that if I ask nice later, when no one is looking, he might just give me some.

"There you are!" Emily exclaims, setting her glass down and coming to us. "How did it go? Did you find something?" she asks, leaning down to see what movie Mae picked out.

Wyatt's eyes come to mine, looking down because, despite being three years younger, he has inches on me. "You want to tell her, or should I?" he asks.

"Tell me what?" Emily asks, standing up. I think how it would go if Wyatt told her I lost Mae, that I let her wander into the porn section alone, that I let her wander into the porn section *at all*, and that she saw things that would make any normal person want to bleach their eyes.

"Nothing," I say. "Just that you owe me a dollar for the movie."

As Emily goes for her wallet, I pull up Venmo on my phone and pay Wyatt his hush money, knowing it won't be the last time I pay him to keep my secrets quiet.

COURTNEY

"Fishing," I tell the detective, feeling my throat tighten, knowing that Elliott is still out on the lake, unaware of what's happened. He never replied to my text, which means, as far as I know, he never saw it. "My husband is fishing." I think of what the girls and I have been through this morning and how he's completely clueless. He'll come back, celebrating his catch. It's not his fault. There is no way for him to know what's happened, and yet I feel resentful that he's not here and that I'm going through this alone.

"When did he leave?"

"Early this morning."

"What time?"

"Five o'clock."

"You were awake when he left?" the detective asks.

"No."

"But you heard him leave?"

"No. I didn't. I didn't wake up until the girls woke me."

"And what time was that?"

"Six thirty or seven maybe."

"So your husband may have left before five o'clock?"

I've walked right into it. "He said he was leaving at five. I don't know why he would leave any sooner than that to go fish."

In fact, last night, when we were still at Emily and Nolan's place, Elliott checked the sunrise on his phone. It would rise at 5:18. If he left at five, it would have been mostly dark, the sky illuminated just enough for him to see where he was going as he made his way out through the trees and to the lake, as he put the canoe in the water and boarded it.

"But you don't know for sure what time he left. Is that correct?"

"Yes," I say, thinking carefully through my words, knowing what he's getting at, the assumptions he's making. "That's correct." He raises his eyebrows. "But it wouldn't have been before five. He wanted to be on the lake at dawn because that's the best time to fish," I say, repeating the same thing Elliott said to me last night.

I try to remember waking up at three in the morning to check on the girls. I wonder again if I woke up all on my own or if something woke me. I remember that I came to all of a sudden, sitting up in bed, hearing voices and realizing only after a minute that they were coming from the TV. I tiptoed from the bedroom, seeing the soft, eerie glow of the screen from the upstairs loft. I pulled myself up the ladder, crawling on all fours to the TV to shut it off. The girls were sound asleep in bed with Elliott's iPad tucked under Cass's arm like a security blanket. They must have been playing games on it before bed. I slipped it out from under her arm and headed back downstairs with it, leaving it on the kitchen counter, making a mental note to talk to Cass in the morning to remind her that she's supposed to ask before using Elliott's iPad.

I remember coming into the bedroom. I pulled the door and got back into bed, feeling blinded by the light of the TV. My eyes struggled to adjust to the sudden lack of light now that the TV was off and the cottage had turned pitch-black.

What I can't remember is if, when I spread out on the saggy mattress, pulling the covers over myself and giving in to sleep, Elliott was there, beside me in bed.

It takes effort to get the kids and me back to the cottage from the lodge. The police escort us, keeping us between them, their hands on their sidearms, their eyes sweeping the property as we walk while, in the distance, the sound of sirens rings out, additional units coming in to assist.

Along the way, people step out of their own cottages to see what's happening, examining us from their decks like we're something in a petri dish, leaned over railings, taking in Mae's torn pants, the blood on her knees and hands, the vacant stares on all of our faces.

"Everything okay, Officers?" one man asks as we pass by him, standing on his deck with his coffee.

"Go inside and lock your door," Detective Evans says, and the man straightens, calling for his kids, who play catch on the lawn.

My fear is acute. I look around us as we walk, my eyes skimming the trees, my muscles tense and ready to run. Even with the police right beside us, I feel exposed, like nowhere is safe, like there is nowhere the kids and I could run to or hide.

At the same time, the grief sits heavy on my chest like an elephant, making it hard to breathe, the pain dulled only by disbelief.

Maybe this isn't real. Maybe it's not happening. Maybe it's just a dream.

Elliott is waiting for us at the cottage when we come back. He's outside, pacing the small deck with his phone in hand, worried out of his mind about us. "Oh my God," he says, taking the deck steps two at a time to come to me, wrapping his arms around my shoulders and pulling me into him. I sag against his chest, feeling my legs practically give. I press my face to his shirt, breathing in the ripe, damp smell of him. The relief is overwhelming. He's here now. I'm safe. I don't have to do this alone.

But at the same time, I feel pangs of anger and resentment at the sight of his fishing gear on the deck, the rod and tackle box he bought just for this trip, a cooler with his morning's catch.

Elliott says, pulling away, his hands cradling my face as he looks me deep in the eye, "I was so worried about you. I tried going to Em and Nolan's place, but the police wouldn't let me in. I asked, but no one would tell me what's happening. I saw your text. What's going on, Court? Is everything alright? God," he says then, answering for himself. "Of course not. Of course it's not alright."

Elliott is visibly stunned when I tell him they're dead. His face contorts. He stumbles backward, blinking my words into focus. "Dead?" he asks, shaking his head, running his hands through his hair, grabbing for the back of his neck. "What do you mean, they're dead? That's not possible. We just saw them last night. No," he decides, "there has to be some mistake. They can't be dead."

"They are," I breathe, my voice barely a whisper. "It happened sometime last night after we left, or early this morning, I don't know. They were killed, Elliott. Someone killed them. I found them in their cottage this morning. *Mac*," I say, stepping closer to him, "found them in their cottage this morning. The blood. Oh God," I say, fighting the image in my mind. Elliott reaches for me as I start to cry, pulling me into him by the shoulders, holding me.

"Do they know?" he says into my ear, letting his eyes run over the three of them standing like zombies behind me, quiet, unemotional, their shoulders drooped and their arms hanging limp at their sides.

"They know."

"Where's Reese?"

"She's missing."

He pulls away again, searching my face, my eyes. "What do you mean, she's *missing*?"

"I don't know. I think whoever killed Emily and Nolan took her." I imagine Reese kicking, resisting, getting hoisted off the ground and carried out of the cottage by some faceless man, whose large hand is pressed to her mouth to keep her quiet.

"You *think*, Court? What do you mean you *think*? Why do you think that?" he asks, his words incredulous because he's frustrated that we don't have all the answers, that we don't know where she is. He's not mad at me; he's afraid for Reese. I'm afraid too. "Was there a note or something? Some kind of ransom demand?"

"No," Detective Evans says, standing beside us. Elliott's eyes dart to him, as if only now realizing that while we've been talking, someone else was there. For a long time, Elliott stares until Detective Evans says, "There was no note. No ransom demand."

"Elliott, this is Detective Evans. Detective Evans, my husband, Elliott."

Elliott nods. He brings his gaze back to me, asking, "If there was no note and no ransom demand, then how do you know someone took her?"

"Because if someone didn't take her," I say, "where else could she be?"

Elliott pulls back. He takes in my words, his mind veering in a different direction all of a sudden. He says nothing, but he holds my eye, a silent conversation happening between us, and I know we're both thinking the same thing.

I hate you. I wish you'd die.

Reese didn't kill them.

That's what I tell myself as I sit on the edge of the bathtub with my knees spread apart and my head between my knees, trying not to puke though I already have, the vomit swirling like Bran Flakes in the toilet water, the smell repulsive.

She didn't kill them. I know she didn't. There is a killer out there somewhere, but it's not her. She wouldn't do this. She *couldn't* do this. I think of the slaughter next door, of the bloodshed inside that cottage. She's a victim, just like they are. Someone has her.

"Are you okay? Do you need anything?" Elliott asks through the bathroom door, gently rapping his knuckles on it. I don't know how long I've been in here, but long enough that Elliott has gotten worried and come looking for me.

I sit up and wipe my mouth with the sleeve of my robe. "I'll be right out," I say.

It takes effort to stand. I'm exhausted. All I want to do is climb into bed, pull the covers over my head and sleep. I want to pretend this isn't happening, that this isn't real, but I can't. Detective Evans is in the cottage with us. He's waiting for me to come and sit with Wyatt and Mae so that he can ask them questions. We can't do it later; we have to do it now, though I don't know that I have it in me. Still, I have no choice. I have to do it for Nolan and Emily. If the situation were reversed—if I was the one who was dead and they were alive—they'd do it for me. They'd help the police find my killer, and they'd find my missing child and bring her home.

I flush the toilet, and then I stand at the bathroom sink, staring at my face in the mirror's reflection. I hardly recognize myself. I'm a wreck. My face is blotchy, my eyes and cheeks swollen and red. I haven't brushed my hair today and it's knotty, though I don't bother brushing it because I don't care what I look like, and I don't have the capacity to even drag a brush through my hair right now. Emily and Nolan are dead. What difference does it make what my hair looks like? I still have on the same clothes

I've worn all day—my robe over my pajamas—though there is vomit on the collar and sleeve, and blood on the cuff.

I lean over and take a sip of water directly from the tap, swirl it around in my mouth and spit it out, seeing traces of vomit in the sink.

I open the bathroom door and breeze past Elliott in the doorway, our elbows bumping. "Where are you going?" he asks, reaching for me, though I steal my arm from his grasp, walking away.

"I just need to change my clothes. I'll be out as soon as I can. Can you tell the detective please?" I ask, going into the bedroom and closing the door without giving him a chance to reply. In the bedroom, I sit on the edge of the unmade bed, fighting a headache, hating the detective for putting these small seeds of doubt in my mind, no matter how inadvertent.

So your husband may have left before five o'clock?

I think again to last night. I try to take myself back in time, to remember if Elliott was here at 3:00 a.m. after I climbed up into the loft, turned the girls' TV off and came back to bed. I close my eyes, imagining the feel of the soft mattress sinking beneath me, trying to feel Elliott curl around me from behind, his warm hand slipping onto my hip, the heat from his body or the sound of his shallow breathing as he slept. I can't, but that doesn't mean anything, I tell myself, because I was half asleep and I don't remember the absence of him either, I don't remember coming back to a cold and empty bed alone.

Elliott was here. Of course he was here.

I change into a pair of jeans and a t-shirt. I take a breath, steeling myself for what comes next.

I step out of the bedroom to find Elliott upstairs now and not waiting in the hall for me as I imagined. He's in the loft with Cass, sitting with her so that the detective can speak to Wyatt, Mae and me alone.

In the living room, Wyatt slumps on a saggy chair, staring down at his phone. He might have internet connection or he might not. He might just be playing some game offline because cell service is fickle; it comes and goes as it wants. The pillow lines have disappeared from his face, and I think of what he must have gone through this morning. I picture him sound asleep in his bed, maybe lost in a peaceful dream before waking up to the sound of police clearing rooms. They wouldn't have knocked on his bedroom door when they came to it; they would have let themselves in, and I envision that: the police violently throwing open the door so hard it ricocheted off the opposite wall, finding Wyatt in bed, drawing and aiming their guns at him, screaming for him to freeze as if he's a suspect, as if he's the one who killed them. He must have been confused, scared out of his mind. I wonder what happened next, if the police told him his parents were dead. They must have, because they would have had to prepare him to leave the bedroom and to walk past Nolan's body in the hall. I wonder if Wyatt cried. If he was afraid. If the police comforted him.

Wyatt and Mae haven't had a second to grieve. I wonder if they've begun to process the fact that their parents are dead, or if they're in denial, harboring false hope that this isn't real, that Nolan and Emily might walk through the door any minute. They've had nothing in their life to prepare them for death. They've never had a pet die. Emily's father died, but he had Alzheimer's for years and so they were never close to him before his death. They didn't mourn him, not like they will Emily and Nolan.

I set a hand on Wyatt's shoulder. He looks up, and when he does, I see so much of Nolan in him, it takes my breath away. It isn't so much in the hair or body shape—because Wyatt, though tall, has yet to fill out—but in the facial features like the dark brown eyes, the round face, full cheeks and ears that stick slightly out. Wyatt has a scar just above his right eye. He's had it for years as a result of a baseball injury. I remember when it happened, the night he took a hit to the eye, because Emily called from the emergency room to see if I could come pick up Reese and Mae. The bleeding was profuse, both externally and inside the eye. They were worried he might lose some of his vision, which he didn't, thank God, but still, he had an impressive black eye for weeks and now the scar.

"Do you need anything?" I ask.

Wyatt shakes his head, his mop of dark, coarse hair falling in his eyes, hiding them.

"Okay," I say. "Let me know if you do."

I take a seat on the sofa. Mae shuffles over and sits beside me, pressing a leg close to mine, her face vacant, her eyes red. I wrap an arm around her shoulder, feeling her collapse against me as Detective Evans lowers himself to a chair across from us, and I watch him, taking in his height, his athletic build, his red hair, his freckles. I went to high school with a redhead who was ruthlessly teased because kids can be mean. Detective Evans, on the other hand, seems to embrace his redheadedness. He sits confident on the chair, his legs spread wide, taking up space, and I doubt that he's ever been teased or had an issue with getting girls to like him.

"What are you doing to find my niece?" I ask, worried that the police aren't doing anything and that they don't see Reese as a victim but as a suspect.

"We are looking for her, Mrs. Gray," Detective Evans says. "We've issued an AMBER Alert and have entered her into the NCIC Missing Person File. We've set up roadblocks to try to apprehend her or anyone who may have her. We're doing everything we can." He looks to Wyatt then, who's on his phone. "How about you put that away for a little bit," he says.

But Wyatt doesn't put his phone away. Instead, he hesitates, looking from the detective to me, wondering, I think, if he has to. "What if I don't want to?" he finally asks, testing Detective Evans's patience, looking him right in the face. Detective Evans doesn't balk, though I'm sure he's not used to being told no, least of all not by someone Wyatt's age.

My tone is soft, pleading. I feel afraid, for Wyatt's sake, wondering how Detective Evans will react if he continues to say no. "Put it away, Wyatt. Please. Just for a little bit."

But Wyatt still doesn't, and I'm not sure if he's trying to be defiant or if it's the grief speaking, being rebellious so that he doesn't break down and let us see him cry. Still, I worry about what Detective Evans is going to do, about what he's going to say. He watches Wyatt for a long time (Wyatt's own eyes dropping to his phone), his face deadpan.

"You remind me of myself when I was your age," Detective Evans finally says, his voice controlled, and Wyatt looks up, imagining, as I do, Detective Evans at fourteen.

"Yeah?" Wyatt asks, doubting. "How's that?"

"I didn't like people telling me what to do. I hated authority figures as a result. Teachers, parents, coaches, you name it."

Something he says registers. Wyatt doesn't say as much, but he shifts, slumping further in his seat, still staring at his phone.

"I'm going to ask one more time," Detective Evans says. He nods at the phone. "Do you think you can put that away for a while and answer a few questions of mine so we can find your sister and figure out who hurt your parents? You do want to find her, don't you?" he asks. This time, Wyatt reluctantly puts the phone away, mumbling something under his breath about *the stupid internet not working anyway*, turning it face down on the arm of the chair.

Detective Evans leans back. He asks, "Did you hear anything in your cottage last night?" Wyatt shrugs. "Is that a yes or a no?"

Wyatt says nothing. He sits in his chair, silent, staring down at his hands.

"Wyatt? Did you hear the detective's question?" I ask, and then, when he still doesn't respond: "Wyatt? Did you hear me?"

"I already told you," he says, his eyes darting up.

"You already told us what?" I ask, taken aback by the anger in his eyes.

Wyatt says nothing.

"Listen. Wyatt. I know this is hard," Detective Evans says, the unexpected softness in his voice momentarily endearing him to me. "I want to find the person who did this to your parents and to find your sister. I think you can help me do that. The thing is, the sooner we start looking, the more likely we are to find them. But we can't do that unless you talk to us. You are the last person who saw the three of them, which means you might be the only one who can help. Try to think back to last night, in your cottage. Did you hear anything unusual? Did anything out of the ordinary happen?"

Wyatt shifts in his seat. "I dunno. I don't think so," he says this time.

"You don't think so?"

"No."

"Okay," Detective Evans says. "Take me through last night. Your aunt and uncle came for dinner, is that right?" Wyatt nods, sitting slouched in his chair. "What time did they leave?"

Wyatt looks to me and asks, "What time did you leave?"

"Maybe eight or eight thirty," I say, going through it again in my mind, playing cards and sharing a bottle of wine and a couple beers with Emily and Nolan before that argument between Emily and Reese happened, and we left.

Except that this time, as I play it back in my mind, I remember something I'd forgotten. As Elliott and I were leaving, Emily leaned in to him and said, her words guarded but not so under wraps that I didn't notice, "Do you think I could talk to you tomorrow in private? I have something to ask you," and Elliott hesitated, stiffening as if caught off guard, and then said yes.

After we left, I didn't think to ask Elliott about it. I forgot all about it, because he and I were so laser focused on what happened with Reese that it slipped my mind.

"What happened after your aunt and uncle left your cottage?"

"It was . . . I dunno . . . it was quiet."

"Quiet how?"

Wyatt shrugs. "Like no one was talking."

"Had they gone to sleep?"

"I was in my own room. The door was closed. How would I know?"

"Fair enough." The detective thinks and rephrases his question. "Were you awake for a while after your aunt and uncle left?"

"Yeah. I guess."

"Do you remember what time you went to sleep?"

"Not for a while. I couldn't sleep. I tried to, but I couldn't. My nose was all stuffy, so I went downstairs and told my mom and she gave me medicine."

"What kind of medicine?"

"Allergy medicine I guess."

"Do you know what kind?"

He shrugs. "It was pink."

"Was it Benadryl?"

"Maybe."

Detective Evans looks up. Our eyes meet.

Benadryl. Emily gave him Benadryl, which has a sedative effect. It would have made Wyatt sleepy, which explains things, like how he slept through the night, through everything that happened and why he didn't wake up this morning until the police woke him.

"Okay. Good. That's helpful, Wyatt. Do you know what time it was when you came downstairs for the Benadryl?" Wyatt shakes his head. "That's alright. When you came downstairs, you said your mom was there. Was she alone or was someone with her?"

"She was alone." I picture that: Emily staying up later than the rest, cleaning the cottage from our night, and I regret that Elliott and I went home when we did, that we didn't stay to keep her company or help clean.

"She was sad," Wyatt offers all on his own, his voice flat. He sits on his chair, gazing down at his hands, picking now at a black woven bracelet on his thin wrist.

I have trouble breathing because of his words. Emily was sad. It hits a nerve, though I knew that, didn't I? When Elliott and I left last night, waving to Emily on the deck until we couldn't see her anymore, I knew that she was sad.

Emily was my best friend. I've known Nolan my whole life, but I knew her better. She and I were friends since we were Cass's and Mae's age. We met the first day of fifth grade, when I was new to the school and Emily took notice. She saw me sitting on the playground alone and was the only one in the whole fifth grade who came over and talked to me. From that moment on, we were inseparable. At first, Nolan was just my big brother to her, someone we both thought was annoying and gross. Until, all of a sudden, Emily didn't think he was either of those things anymore. I caught her staring at him in my kitchen once, gazing at him over her Oreos and milk. She liked him.

I pretended to vomit when she confessed to me that she thought he was cute.

Are you mad? she asked.

I didn't see the appeal, but I told her no. Of course not. I don't think there is anything Emily could have ever done to make me mad.

That said, I knew as well as anyone that Nolan could be a

jerk, that, even as a grown adult, it was as if he sometimes had the emotional intelligence of someone who's eighteen. He made her sad, and though I loved him, there were times, in hindsight, that I wish I would have talked her out of marrying him. They weren't compatible. They had almost nothing in common, not when we were kids and not as adults.

I regret that last night I didn't stay and talk to her, that I just left with Elliott.

"How do you know that she was sad?" Detective Evans asks. "Did she tell you?"

"She didn't have to. She was crying." As he says it, my hand goes to my mouth and tears fill my eyes. It breaks my heart, thinking of Emily alone and upset after we left. She'd had that argument with Reese. All week, her and Nolan had been fighting. Of course she was upset. I should have made more of an effort to be there for her, to comfort her. I shouldn't have left when I did. I should have sent Elliott home alone to check on Cass and Mae, and I should have stayed with Emily.

The detective asks, "Did she tell you why she was upset?"

Wyatt says, "She tried to hide it, to pretend she wasn't, you know?"

"To pretend she wasn't crying?"

"Yeah."

"Did you ask her what was wrong?"

"They'd been going through hard times," I offer when Wyatt shakes his head—tightening my hold on Mae, who I don't realize is crying until she wipes her nose with a sleeve—because I don't want the detective to make him feel bad for not asking Emily what was wrong. Emily is strong; she's stoic. It would have killed her for Wyatt to see her upset, and if he had asked, she would have told him that nothing was wrong. "My brother has been out of work. Money is tight and it's caused tension in their marriage."

"Were they fighting?"

"Not around us. Not where we could see. But yes," I say, "they were fighting."

"Did you notice that too?" the detective asks the kids, though Mae just turns away from him, burying her face into my arm.

"You'd have to be deaf not to," Wyatt says.

"What did they fight about?"

"What didn't they fight about?"

"Was it just words?"

"What do you mean?"

"I mean, did they ever get physical?" Detective Evans asks, and I wince, wanting to say no, *never*. But he's not asking me and I don't know what went on behind closed doors.

"You mean like hitting each other?" Wyatt asks.

"Yeah. Like hitting each other." I hold my breath, wondering what Wyatt is going to say, if there was something going on in that house that I didn't know about.

But, to my relief, Wyatt says no.

Detective Evans says, "Okay. What else can you remember about the last few days? Anything unusual? Any strange run-ins, threatening calls or texts? Did someone have an enemy?"

For the first time, Mae speaks, pulling her body away from mine, her eyes gazing up at me, not the detective, as she says, as if divulging a secret, "Reese met a boy," and it sparks a memory.

It was a couple days ago. They were behind the little pool shed: Reese and some boy. I came around the corner to see her standing there in her flimsy red strappy bikini top with a towel tied loosely around her waist, her hair and tanned skin dripping wet as if she'd just come out of the water. She was barefoot, tossing her hair as she laughed a high-pitched laugh, her smile a mile wide. In the moment, there was no denying she was completely smitten with this boy. I stopped and backed quietly away, not wanting to embarrass her in front of her friend.

I nod. "You're right, Mae, she did." I look at the detective. "I saw them at the pool the other day. I don't know if that means anything, if it's relevant."

"At this point, everything is relevant," he says. "Do you know this boy's name? Is he staying in one of the cottages?"

"No. He's an employee, I think," I say, because I saw him from time to time, in his t-shirt and low-slung jeans, doing things like cleaning the pool, yard and maintenance work, going into and out of other people's cottages, carrying a toolbox, fixing things, letting himself in with some master key.

"Can you describe him?"

"Tall," I say. "Brown hair, I think. I'm sorry. I didn't get a good look."

"What about you, Mae? Is there anything that stands out about this boy? Anything you can remember?" Detective Evans asks, and I see Mae blush when he speaks directly to her, calling her by name. I look at her, at the way her hands shake on her lap, dried tears clinging to her cheeks like the blood on her knee. I let my eyes go to the blood, realizing in that moment that poor Mae is still in the same clothes as before, the ones with urine on them too, because she wet herself earlier. I feel a sharp pain in my chest from guilt, because I didn't remember, because I changed my own clothes but didn't think how she needed to change hers, though I don't want to call attention to it now and embarrass her.

"Mae?" I ask, bringing my eyes back to her face, gently nudging her. "Is there anything you can tell Detective Evans about the boy?"

She nods. "He had a snake tattoo on his arm."

"A snake tattoo," Detective Evans repeats, and Mae looks cautiously toward him and nods again. "Did you ever talk to him?" She shakes her head. "Did your sister ever mention anything about him to you? His name maybe?"

Again Mae shakes her head. She says, "But I saw them together. And I heard him one night."

"You heard him? Where?"

Mae glances at me, as if nervous to go on, her tangled hair in her eyes. "It's okay," I say, sweeping her hair off her face. "You can tell him. Don't be scared."

Her lower lip trembles as she says, "I don't want to get Reese in trouble. I don't want her to be mad at me."

"You won't be getting her in trouble, Mae. I promise. Reese isn't in any trouble. We're trying to help her, that's all. We're trying to find her. She won't be mad."

Still, Mae hesitates. Her hair falls back in her face and it takes a minute for her to say, "He was in our cottage."

"How do you know?"

"I got up in the middle of the night to go to the bathroom. I heard him."

Nolan and Emily must not have known. They would have been out of their minds if they knew Reese had a boy over in the middle of the night.

"What did you hear, Mae?" Detective Evans leans in to ask. "Can you tell me?"

Mae doesn't say at first. She's apprehensive. She looks away from the detective, her eyes coming to mine. "It's alright," I assure her, tucking her stubborn hair gently behind an ear so that it stays put this time. "You can say. Help us help Reese."

She nods. "I heard her scream," she says. "And then she was crying."

My heart rate changes. It's been years since I've seen Reese cry. "Your parents didn't hear?" She shakes her head. "Why was Reese crying? Do you know?"

She shakes her head again.

"Did you hear anything else?"

Mae nods.

"What did you hear?"

She says, "Reese said he was hurting her. That he was scaring her."

My chest feels heavy again. There is a pain in the back of my throat, and I want to shake Mae and ask her why she didn't wake Emily and Nolan and tell them about the boy in the cottage and that he was doing something to hurt Reese.

But it's not Mae's fault. She didn't know any better, but I did. I start to shake, regretting that I didn't ask Reese about this boy when I first saw them together, that I didn't ask who he was or how they met or what he was like. I should have expressed interest at least, let her know I saw them together, because maybe she would have opened up to me about him. Maybe she would have told me if he was coming on too strong, if he was making her uncomfortable or if she thought she was in danger. Maybe she would have told me things she couldn't tell Emily because Emily was her mom and, God love her, a bit controlling and inflexible sometimes. Not because she didn't love Reese, but because she did.

"Did you hear anything else that night, Mae?" She shakes her head. "Did he come again, maybe another night?"

"I don't know."

"Anything else you can remember about the last few days? Anything unusual?"

I think back. "One of the cottages was broken into," I say, remembering then, recalling how uneasy it made me feel at the time. Until it happened, Elliott and I had been a little too lax about leaving the front door unlocked when we were home or when we ran to Emily and Nolan's cottage for something. It didn't cross our minds that we had to worry or even think about someone coming in and taking our things.

"How do you know?" Detective Evans asks.

"I overheard some women talking about it one day at the pool."

"When was this?"

"A couple days ago."

"Did they file a police report?"

"I don't know. I just know that one of the women's wedding bands was missing and she thought it had been stolen from the cottage. I heard her say that she took it off to swim, left it on top of a dresser and that, when she came back, it was gone. They reported it to the resort."

The detective nods and then he asks me more about Reese. Any drug or alcohol abuse, history of depression, is she suicidal. He doesn't lower his voice for Wyatt's and Mae's sake. He just asks. I say no, but then I think of the text Emily saw on her phone, the one in which Reese told some friend *I wanna KMS.* Kill myself. Did she mean it? I don't have time to tell Detective Evans about it before he asks for Reese's height and weight— which I can only guess—her hair and eye color, if she has any identifying features like a tattoo or birthmark. I say no, not that I know of.

"What was she wearing last night?" Detective Evans asks and I draw a blank, seeing Reese stomp up the stairs with her chin held high and nostrils flaring. Her face was red and she practically spit her words at Emily, *I hate you, I wish you'd die,* before slamming the bedroom door so roughly it didn't latch and it bounced back, and she slammed it even harder the next time, her anger escalating because of her frustration with the door. Emily froze with shame, paling; after Reese was gone, she had a hard time looking me in the eye.

All that said, what she had on escapes me.

"I . . . I don't know. I can't remember. I'm sorry." He asks Wyatt and Mae, but none of us can.

"That's fine." He asks that I AirDrop the picture of Reese to him and then, once I've done that, he stands up. He thanks Wyatt and Mae for their help before shifting his attention to me. "It's best if you stay here and wait for Reese to come back," he says, and I nod, finding it impossible to believe that Reese will come walking in the door on her own.

"Are we safe?" I ask, knowing we're not, because how could we possibly be safe when there is a killer out there somewhere?

"We're going to have an officer outside, keeping watch, for as long as it takes. You'll be safe here," he assures me.

I don't believe it. He can't guarantee our safety.

I worry more about the kids than about Elliott and me. I'm not leaving without Reese, but they don't need to be here. I tell him, "I'd feel better if the kids could go home. They can stay with their grandparents while Elliott and I help look for Reese."

But Detective Evans shakes his head. "I'd like everyone to stay put while we finish the investigation. You never know," he says. "We might need to speak to Wyatt and Mae again. We might have more questions for them. Now," he says, leaving no room for discussion, letting his eyes rise to the loft to where Elliott and Cass watch TV with the volume so low it could be on mute, "if we could just speak to your husband before we leave."

REESE

My first night on the porch is cold. The dark, crisp air slips in through the screens, surrounding me. I try to wait it out, telling myself I'll get used to it, but it doesn't work. I sit there for a long time, thinking about nothing but how cold and dark it is (my only source of light lying broken on the floor—pieces of glass that I have to avoid because I haven't bothered to sweep them up), until eventually I dig sweats from my bag and pull them on, wrapping myself in blankets, refusing to go inside where it's warm because the last thing I need is for Emily to be right about this. I'd just as soon die of hypothermia than go inside.

The darkness is inescapable. It closes in on me like some tactile thing. There are no streetlights and no house lights. No one bothered to leave a light on inside. I'd be lying if I said it didn't weird me out, not knowing who or what lies just beyond the screens, and for a while, I sit on the edge of the bed, staring out into the darkness and waiting for a face to press against the mesh, thinking of Pennywise, of Jigsaw, of Samara Morgan from *The Ring* in that white dress, her long, dark hair covering her face as she crawls out of the TV. The screens are weak. Other than keeping bugs out, they don't serve any real purpose. If someone wanted to break in in the middle of the night, they could.

I think about the creep at the lodge today, the one who stood there, smoking his cigarette, his eyes feasting on me and then on Mae. I wonder if he's staying at this resort. I wonder if he watched us leave the lodge, if he followed us back to our cottage, if he knows where we're staying and if he's out there in the woods right now, watching me.

Sometime after midnight, it starts to drizzle. The rain is a fine mist that comes in through the screens, threatening to get anything within two feet of them wet. On the side of the bed closest to the screens, it just misses. I hold my hand out, letting it dangle over the edge of the bed, feeling rain.

I lie in bed, cocooned in the quilt, looking at Instagram and Snapchat, trying to distract myself, to not let myself be scared. Cell service is less glitchy at night than before. For whatever reason, it just works better. There was a bonfire tonight, back home, at Marshall's house, because it sits on like six acres of land in the middle of nowhere and his parents go to bed at nine o'clock so that—according to Marshall—they never hear what happens at the far edge of their own property late at night. There are pictures of the party online, including one of Skylar dancing around the fire—Liam Morris grinding behind her—drinking from her bottle of Poland Spring, which everyone knows is not water, but vodka.

I text Skylar my picture of the taxidermy fish. It's two in the morning. I don't expect her to be awake or sober. Still, she sees my text but leaves me on read, and I wonder if there was a sleepover after the bonfire, if she's with Gracie again and if she's having more fun with her than she has when she's with me.

In the morning, there's just one word from Skylar in response to my picture of the fish. **Cool.** Which means it's not. Which means it's lame as fuck. I'm actually embarrassed I sent it.

Did u and Liam Morris hook up? I start to text, but I don't send it because what's even more lame than sending pictures of taxidermy fish at two in the morning is spying on your friends on Instagram, especially when they're mad at you. I told her I was sorry about what happened before, before we left. I said it would never happen again, and she said, *Whatever, forget about it, it's fine.* I don't think it's fine. In fact, I keep replaying it again and again in my mind, wishing it was a bad dream, that it never happened.

Emily wants us up and out of the cottage by nine, so we can stake a claim to chairs at the pool. I get dressed in the one bathroom everyone shares, getting naked before stepping into the bathing suit I bought for this trip, the bikini bottoms high enough to hide my new tattoo that Emily and Nolan know nothing about, because if they did, they'd kill me. It's a butterfly on the side of my hip, because butterflies represent freedom and transformation, which seemed fitting and hopeful. The tattoo is sexy too, except for when I have to hide it, like now. I stand before the mirror, making sure the high waist of the bikini bottoms covers it.

When I come out of the bathroom, Mae is standing there, wearing my pink sweatshirt, which she's obsessed with because it's pink and because it's super soft and fleecy, which means that when I was getting dressed, she went onto the porch and went through my things. "Take it off," I say, more pissed about her snooping than about her wearing my stuff. The sweatshirt is too big on her anyway, though she poses with it slouchy and off the shoulder with her hands on her hips, doing the duck face like those stupid tween influencers she's infatuated with on Instagram and YouTube, which Emily knows nothing about because Emily somehow still believes Mae idolizes Disney princesses. She thinks Mae hasn't discovered social media yet, though she has, because she's ten and doesn't live under a rock. She also knows Santa doesn't exist, but Emily doesn't know that either. Mae doesn't have her own phone (in our house, you have to be in middle school to get one) but she steals mine or even Emily's sometimes and does whatever she wants on it and Emily and Nolan are completely clueless.

"No," Mae pouts, crossing her arms. "I don't want to."

"Take it off now."

"But I'm cold," she whines.

"Find your own sweatshirt. That one's mine."

"No. Please."

"I'm counting to three. If you don't take it off yourself, then I'm ripping it off your head. One . . . two . . ."

By the time I get to three, Mae screams, and Emily comes running, out of breath when she arrives, stepping between Mae and me like she thinks I might hurt her. "What is it? What's wrong? Is everything okay, Mae?" When I tell her, she looks disappointed with me, like this is somehow my fault, and asks, "Can't you just let her wear it, Reese? She already has it on."

"No. Give it to me," I say, dragging it off Mae's head and telling her to leave my shit alone.

When we get there, the pool is small. It's cold, like sixty-eight degrees outside, though Emily swears it's going to get warmer as the day goes on. I watch as some guy skims twigs and leaves from the pool, but it comes back again, falling from the sky like confetti. The only redeeming quality is that there aren't as many trees here, which means the sun gets through somewhat. If I drag my plastic chair with its broken brown straps into the patches of sunlight, moving it throughout the day with the sun, I might stand a chance of going home with a tan. Then, when people ask, I can say I went somewhere cool like Cancun or Cozumel and not Wisconsin.

The day is never-ending. It moves by at a snail's pace. Mae and our cousin Cass are cojoined. Whatever Cass does, Mae does. Synchronized swimming, tea parties at the bottom of the pool, pretending to be mermaids. They want me to play with them, but I say no. I don't know where Wyatt is. All I know is that he's not here, which doesn't seem fair, because he can do whatever he wants, while I can't even go to the bathroom without being interrogated.

"Where are you going?" Emily asks, as I stand up from my chair, adjusting my bathing suit. She glances up from her book, shielding her eyes from the sun.

"To pee. Or is that not okay?" She says that it is. I ask for the key to the cottage.

"There is a bathroom in the pool house," she says, but I went in there once and I don't ever want to have to do it again. The words *pool house* are deceptive. It's a dingy little building like a shed with a grungy concrete floor that pools with water from people going in barefoot and sopping wet.

"Can I not just go back to the cottage to pee?"

"What's wrong with the pool house?"

"Have you seen it? It's disgusting. And there are bugs in there."

"Fine," she reluctantly says. "But come right back when you're done."

In the chair between us, Uncle Elliott drinks beer from a can in a koozie. He has a cooler of beer beside his chair, which he and Nolan share, stacking their empties on the concrete deck, seeing who can stack theirs higher before it falls, as if it's Jenga, as if this isn't the most redneck vacation ever.

Earlier I looked over to find Uncle Elliott staring at me, and I didn't know if he looked when I looked or if he was already looking, but he smiled and there was something a little cocky but also guilty-looking about it, like he got caught red-handed, leering at his teenage niece in her bikini. It's gross, though every family has that one slightly pervy uncle and Elliott is mine, which isn't the worst thing in the world, because he's also hot.

He says now, "Hey. Can you bring me back something to eat?"

But Emily tells him, "We're going to have lunch soon," as if she planned the whole day's agenda and no one's allowed to deviate from it.

"What do you want?" I ask, ignoring her.

He smiles, crinkles forming around his brown eyes. Aunt Courtney sits on the edge of the pool, her legs dangling in the icy water, though she doesn't go in because Aunt Courtney can't swim. Imagine being like forty years old and not being able to swim.

Instead, she tosses some pool toy for Mae and Cass to race to, as if they're dogs playing fetch. She glances back over her shoulder, catches Elliott's eye and smiles. Aunt Courtney and Uncle Elliott are an *it couple*. They're both cool and hot, so that I find it impossible to believe that she and Nolan share the same genes. She teaches preschool, he's an attorney, which feels so dead-on for them, like they couldn't have picked more fitting careers if they tried. They live in a big house. They're relationship goals, like Blake Lively and Ryan Reynolds or Emily Blunt and John Krasinski. They've been married exactly eleven years, which I know because I was their flower girl when I was six, the summer before kindergarten. There are pictures of it, of me in my little white dress scattering red rose petals down the aisle of some big, fancy church, which feels perfect and fairy tale–like in my memories, except that Uncle Elliott was married before. He had a wife when he met Aunt Courtney, which is another one of those things I shouldn't know, but that I do.

"I don't know. Why don't you surprise me," Uncle Elliott says, and I glance down to find him still looking up at me from his pool chair, shirtless, smiling though his sunglasses now cover his eyes. His abs are ripped. I try not to look at them as I walk away.

Some guy in another chair who I don't know says to me as I pass, "Hey. Can you bring me something to eat too?" his voice low and throaty. He's grinning when I look, like he's pleased with himself, like he thinks he's funny. Except he's not looking at my face, he's looking somewhere lower than that. My throat tightens. I can't think of anything to say and so I stay quiet, smiling awkwardly and praying he doesn't follow me when I leave.

I push my way out of the squeaky pool gate. There are trees between the cottage and me, dozens if not hundreds of them blocking out the sun, darkening the world around me. I take the path through the woods, the temperature dropping so that I'm instantly cold, goose bumps cropping up on my arms, making me wish for a towel, which I left on the pool chair so that I'm just in my bikini and slides.

I haven't gone far when my brother Wyatt's voice comes to me, disembodied from somewhere in the woods. I inch closer, crouching down when I see him. I pull back on a tree branch to get a better view, peering through the leaves.

On the other side of the trees, Wyatt stands less than twenty feet away, talking to some guy I've never seen before, their voices dulled down as they speak. The guy, who looks like he's forty, shoots nervous glances into the woods, over his shoulder and then back again at Wyatt, making sure they're alone. That no one can see them. Wyatt looks like my brother, but he doesn't sound like him, he sounds like someone else, like someone older than he is and less of a bot. He slips the guy something. The guy gives him something back. The guy shoots another glance over his shoulder before taking off, and then Wyatt stands there, counting his cash. I shake my head in disbelief. He's an entrepreneur. Always figuring out ways to make money, though never in the normal sense, like getting an actual job. Instead, blackmail and now this: being someone's plug. Wyatt doesn't use drugs. His body is a temple and all that. But just because he doesn't use them doesn't mean he can't sell them. Weed is easy enough to get back home. It's legal. You just need someone old enough to walk into a dispensary and get it for you. Wyatt also has a prescription for Adderall because, supposedly, he has ADHD, because he probably faked his way through some test for a doctor to say that. Last I checked, he doesn't take the pills. He stockpiles them and sells them for fifteen or twenty bucks each. Kids get especially desperate around final exams.

I wonder how he even does it, what the initial setup looks like and how he goes about finding random people to sell drugs to.

I think I underestimate him sometimes.

Wyatt slips the cash in a pocket. I turn around to go back. But as I do, I realize there's more than one path through the woods. I pick one, figuring either will take me out of the woods and to the cottages. I walk faster now, looking back over my shoulder, for Wyatt. I don't want him to find me here, because I don't know what he'd do to me if he did. I'm cold. The mosquitoes are thicker in the trees. There are clouds of them that I have to walk through, that buzz close to my ear. I shoo them away, feeling the sharp bite of one on my thigh and I slap at it, coming up with a dead, bloody mosquito on my hand. I lean down to wipe my hand on the dirt because I have nothing else to wipe it on, and it's then, when I'm bent down low, that I hear footsteps approaching quickly, moving in on me faster than I can react.

I turn, jerking upright, my eyes searching the woods for Wyatt's ugly face. I hear people laughing in the distance, the sound of them carrying from the pool.

I wonder if I screamed, would anyone hear?

My heart beats fast. I see his shadow on the ground first.

"It's okay," he drones, becoming visible in the trees. "I didn't mean to scare you. You don't have to be scared. I'm not going to hurt you."

COURTNEY

I stand at a distance, watching out the window as Detective Evans speaks to Elliott. Elliott's back is to me so I can't see his face, but the detective leans against the deck railing, an inch or two taller than my husband and broader, with his arms crossed. He nods, says something, then nods again, and I wonder what he's asking and what Elliott is telling him. My jaw is clenched, though I don't know I'm doing it until I feel the pain radiate up the side of my face and into my temple.

"What did he say?" I ask when Elliott returns, turning his back to me to close and lock the door.

He turns back, lets his gaze run over the kids before meeting my eyes. Everyone is quiet. Mae has barely moved since Detective Evans was in here speaking to us, her body wilting over the arm of the sofa, her eyes empty.

"That we should shelter in place in the cottage while they decide if it's safe to be outside," Elliott says.

I nod, but that's not what I meant. That's not what I was asking. I take a breath. "But what did he ask you?"

Elliott shrugs. "What time I left to go fishing, if I saw or heard anything unusual outside, if I caught anything, what my relationship with Nolan and Emily was like." He pretends not to care. He pretends that line of questioning doesn't bother him, but I can see in the tautness of his face that it does.

"Did you?"

"Did I what?" he asks, defensive as if I've just asked him if he killed Emily and Nolan.

"Catch anything," I say.

He shrugs, nonchalant. "Couple bass."

"I suppose they have to ask questions like that," I say, meaning questions in general to rule him out as a suspect. If they didn't, they wouldn't be doing their jobs.

"I suppose. What did they ask you?"

I tell Elliott what we talked about. The arguing, the Benadryl, how Wyatt said he saw Emily in the kitchen crying last night. "Mae remembered too, that Reese had been hanging out with some boy around the resort. She heard him in their cottage. She said Reese was scared of him. What if he did this, Elliott?" I ask, thinking of this boy creeping into the cottage late at night. I picture his face, his eyes, and the way he looked that day by the pool at Reese, his gaze smoldering and intense. *Young love*, I thought at the time, envying Reese for it, wanting to be seventeen all over again and have some boy look at me like that. But what if I misread the situation? What if something different was going on?

Elliott shrugs. "I don't know."

"I remembered something too."

"What?"

"Last night as we were leaving the cottage, Emily said she wanted to talk to you today. She had something to ask you."

But Elliott's face goes blank. He pulls his eyebrows together and shakes his head, asking, "She did?"

"Yes. You don't remember?"

"No, but I'd been drinking," he reminds me, and I nod, wondering just exactly how much Elliott had to drink. I only had a glass or two of wine and sobered up quickly when Reese and Emily started arguing. But maybe he had more to drink than I think.

"You don't know what she wanted to talk to you about?"

"No. I have no idea, Court. If I did, I'd tell you."

I feel numb. Physically and emotionally drained. I replay the day's events in my mind. It's just after eleven in the morning now. All that's transpired has taken place in less than four hours. Waking up. Making pancakes. Finding Emily. Finding Nolan. The girls and me running for our lives to the lodge, waiting for the police to come, being questioned by them. It feels like it's been four days, even four years. I step away from Elliott, lowering myself to a chair, my legs weary, thinking how it's not possible that this is the same day Cass woke me up to make pancakes for her and Mae, and that it's not possible Emily and Nolan are dead.

"Courtney?" Elliott asks.

"I just need a minute."

Elliott watches me for a while, and then he goes back to the window, looking out at the police, who continue their investigation, going from door to door, speaking to people in neighboring cottages, and I wonder what they're asking and if they're asking things about us.

What are they like?

Did everyone get along?

Did you ever hear them fight?

I look away. I let my eyes go back to the kids. Wyatt sits in the chair with his posture slumped, staring at his phone. Mae's body still lies flaccid over the arm of the sofa while, at the other end of it, Cass sits there, picking absentmindedly at her skin. They're all quiet, but Mae in particular has barely spoken since we found Emily and Nolan next door. I go and sit beside her, between both girls, putting my arm around her shoulder, my hand on Cass's knee. I don't know what to say to the kids, and so I say nothing of value, only things like, *Can I get anyone anything to eat?* and *Does anyone need something?* I put a movie on the

TV to try to distract them—as if some slapstick comedy might be enough to shift their attention away from what's happened—though we're all grateful for the noise because the silence in the cottage is more than any of us can stand.

The day crawls by. All day I try to be strong, to be stoic, to not let myself fall apart, though that's exactly what I want to do: to cry, to throw and break things, to scream, to hide. Instead, I spend the next few hours in a delirious daze of disbelief, taking care of the kids, trying to get everyone but myself to eat because I can't eat. I try, but it comes back up and I find myself in the bathroom again, on my knees, vomiting into the toilet until my stomach is empty and there's nothing left to throw up.

I have phone calls to make: to Emily's mom and to Nolan and my parents, but for the longest time, I can't bring myself to call them. It hangs over me all day like a dark cloud that I keep putting off because I don't physically think that I can do it.

"Do you want me to call?" Elliott asks, his tone solicitous, and I know he's trying to help, but I say no.

"They need to hear it from me."

By the time I'm ready to make the calls, there is no cell reception in the cottage. I step out on the deck with my phone, knowing that I'll have to climb the hill to get a signal that lasts long enough to make the calls—either that or go to the lodge for the Wi-Fi, which I don't want to do either. Detective Evans told us to stay inside, but I can't keep postponing this.

Cautiously, I move down the wooden stairs. I leave the alleged safety of the deck. I look around as I step onto the thin, patchy grass, feeling only slightly less vulnerable because of the police on the property, still collecting evidence in cottage number eight.

Would the killer be so bold as to come back when the police are here?

What if the killer is still here?

What if the killer never left?

I cross the yard. I slip past other cottages for the hill, climbing it. A cool breeze blows, and I watch the leaves in the trees tremble like I do. I hold my phone in my hand, staring down at it, waiting for a bar to appear. As I reach the top, it does.

I call Reese first. I don't expect her to answer and she doesn't. Her voicemail has not been set up, so the voice that greets me isn't Reese herself; it's something automated, soulless. *The number you are trying to reach . . .* I click end and try again. *The number you are trying to reach . . .*

I pull up Instagram instead. I search for Reese's profile to see if she posted anything since she's been gone, like a cry for help, a hint of her whereabouts, something, anything. She hasn't. Instead, her posts have been completely wiped clean. There are none. In their place are the words: *No posts yet*, though I know for certain Reese *has* posted to Instagram before. I can picture her posts, most of them of her and that one good friend of hers, posing, taking selfies, and the comments from her friends that always made Elliott and me laugh, nonsense things like *You ate*, which, as far as we could tell, had nothing to do with food.

Reese has deleted every single one of them from her page.

When I call, Emily's mother sobs, gasping, choking sobs so that she can't speak, but my own parents are silent for a long time at first. When they finally do speak, they say that they want to come, to be with me and to look for Reese, but I say no, that they can't. My father is on dialysis for end-stage kidney disease. He goes three days a week and my mother drives him; she sits with him, holding his hand until it's through. Not going to dialysis isn't an option, because without it he could die.

"No," I say decisively. "I will let you know when we find her."

After I end the call, I clutch my stomach, folding an arm around it and bending at the waist. I press a hand against a tree, leaning into it. I cry, a moaning, no-holds-barred cry, because I'm alone; no one can hear me from here. But it only lasts for a moment before the sound of slow and deliberate footsteps coming from the woods startles me, and I stand sharply up, gasping, holding my breath.

I stare out at the landscape, more acutely aware of my own mortality than I've ever been.

A police officer appears in the depths of the trees. He's tucked back, his head sloped, watching me from a distance. "Everything okay, miss?" he calls out, and I nod. "You shouldn't be outside. You should go inside, where it's safe."

Safe. Is anywhere safe?

Did Emily and Nolan think they were safe inside their cottage?

I nod again, hurrying down the hill and back to the cottage, and then I go inside, close the door and lock the dead bolt.

"Did you get a hold of them?" Elliott asks, and I say yes. I walk past him for the bedroom, feeling his warm hand graze my arm as I do.

We're better off during the day, but as darkness falls, the five of us grow more alert, jumping out of our skin with every noise, from the sound of the wind whispering through the trees, to footsteps passing by the cottage or a police car pulling slowly down the gravel drive, the crunch of it like walking on snow. I stand at the window, staring outside, searching for Reese, thinking of her out there somewhere, alone in the darkness.

The police car comes to a stop just outside our cottage. I wait for the officer to get out, but he doesn't. Instead, he lowers the window, kills the engine and turns the headlights off. He rests his elbow in the open window and I realize that he'll be there all night, that he's been sent to keep us safe, as Detective Evans said.

All of a sudden, the officer turns. He sees me staring and he stares back, his eyes beady black pools. I wonder why I should feel any safer with a complete stranger just outside, watching over us. The police continue their work at Emily and Nolan's, even after dark. They will be there most of the night, Detective Evans said, and I should feel safer knowing that too, but I don't.

Elliott makes dinner, a box of macaroni and cheese that the five of us sit around the small table and share, still not finishing it. I sit there watching Wyatt, across from me, line the tines of his fork with the elbow noodles, never eating them. "You need to try to eat, Wyatt," I say gently, watching as he gazes slowly up from his plate, his cold, hard stare holding mine so long that eventually I look away and start gathering dirty dishes for the sink.

We get ready for bed early in the hopes of a break from reality and to surrender ourselves to sleep. Wyatt and Mae don't have any pajamas of their own and so they borrow from Elliott and Cass, but still they don't fit. It seems strange seeing Wyatt in Elliott's shorts, which he has to tug on the elastic waistband of, tying it so they don't slip off. I start to turn away as he takes his own shirt off, until a big black bruise on his chest catches my eye and I look back.

"Do you mind?" he asks, glaring.

"Sorry," I say, turning fully away, not asking where it came from because I'm embarrassed I got caught staring at his chest.

Cass and Mae ask to sleep in the bedroom with me, and I say yes, of course. Neither of them is doing well. Cass's sadness seems to come and go in waves—one minute, she's seemingly fine as if she's forgotten, and in the next, the memory of what happened slams into her like a wall and she starts to cry—while Mae is lost in a mental fog, tired, barely speaking, her body heavy as she shambles into bed.

Wyatt sleeps on the sofa bed, which Elliott pulls out as I

search the cottage for extra sheets and a blanket, finding a thread-bare set in a musty dresser drawer. Elliott takes the loft, which isn't made for a man his size, but he manages to shinny himself up there and fit.

"I miss my mom," Mae confesses, which are maybe the first words she's spoken since Detective Evans left hours ago, so that they take me by surprise. I can't see her face in the darkness, but I imagine, from the quivering of her hushed voice, the way her chin and lower lip tremble as she fights tears.

"I know, honey," I say, wrapping an arm around her shoulder and pulling her into me. "I miss your mom too." My throat is tight. I take a breath and ask, my voice lowered, "Do you girls understand what's happening?"

I should have had this conversation before. I shouldn't have let the whole day go by without speaking to them. Cass knows a thing or two about death. She had a classmate die last year from acute myeloid leukemia, but this seems different—worse—because Emily and Nolan didn't die of a disease. They were murdered.

Mae's voice breaks as she says, "Someone hurt them."

"Yeah," I say, struggling to keep my own voice under con-trol, "someone did. Someone really bad. And Detective Evans is going to find out who." I hesitate, steeling myself before I ask, "You know that they're not just hurt though, right, honey? You know that they're dead?" Mae lets out a soft moan. I feel her nod against my arm, Cass, on the other side, crying. "You understand what that means? That they're not coming back?"

Mae's tears, when they come, are overflowing, choking her. "I want my mom," she sobs again, coughing, gasping for breath this time, her body convulsing.

"I know, honey. I know you do."

She cries herself to sleep, keening and then whimpering for

hours for Emily, until her body succumbs to exhaustion. Even when she sleeps, she moves restlessly in bed and I wonder what her dreams are about.

All night, I lie awake. I don't sleep. I don't dream. I stare at the dark, cavernous opening that is the bedroom doorway, waiting for someone to come through it and kill the girls and me.

It's not unsubstantiated. It's justified. It could happen.

If it happened to Emily and Nolan, then why not us?

Every time I close my eyes and try to sleep, I see it happen. I watch it play out. I see someone in the woods just outside our cottage, standing tall, thin, featureless like Slenderman, unnoticeable in the darkness and in the trees. I watch him advance slowly, slipping unseen past the police officer. In my musings, he walks with confidence and poise. He steps out of the trees, quietly climbing the deck steps, picking the lock to the front door. Coming in. Killing every single one of us, one at a time, while the rest of us watch, paralyzed, helpless.

Time moves by in slow motion. I check the time on my phone. Midnight. One o'clock. Sometime just after two, I hear a faint sound coming from somewhere in the house. I slip out from under Cass's leaden arm, which is flung across my chest. I sit up in bed, holding my breath, listening while my mind goes to the worst things it can think of: to someone circling the house, creeping around the periphery of the cottage to find a way in, and I wonder if Elliott remembered to close all the windows like he said he was going to do. I wonder if he remembered to lock them. The windows have sash locks. I know because our first night here, I went around the cottage unlocking and throwing them all open for fresh air.

But what if Elliott missed a window or if he didn't slide the lever all the way into the catch?

I lift the covers. I rise from bed, moving across the wood floors in my bare feet, scared and wishing that Elliott wasn't all the way upstairs. It seems like whenever I need him, he's not here.

I stop before the bedroom door. I set my hand on the doorframe, summoning the courage to step out and see what the noise is.

It's Wyatt. When I come out of the bedroom, I find him sitting up on the sofa bed, the soft glow of his phone lighting up his face, making it ghostly.

"Can't you sleep?" I ask, whispering, relief brimming over as I step out into the room with him.

"Nope."

"Do you need anything?" I stand there, waiting for a reply that doesn't come. "Wyatt," I ask again.

He looks up, his face inscrutable in the dark, and I'm not sure if he's going to tell me to fuck off, to break down and cry, to ask me to stay and keep him company, or something else.

His eyes drop again to his phone.

"What is it, Wyatt?" I ask. "What are you looking at on your phone?"

They rise back up.

He says, "I know where Reese is."

REESE

His eyes are dark, like melted chocolate, like black tea. I dissolve in them. He steps out of the trees, running a hand through his dark hair, moving it, though it falls right back into place. He smells like sweat, bug spray and weed. His t-shirt has the name of the resort on it, which is how I know he isn't like me, that he works here.

"Hey," he says, grinning, his gaze cutting and intense.

I can't help myself. I smile because something about his is contagious.

I say, "Hey," standing there in my bikini and slides in the woods, one foot on top of the other.

"I saw you yesterday, at your cottage. What's your name?"

"Reese."

"Reese?"

"Yeah," I say, "like the candy," wishing I could take it back the second it leaves my mouth. *Like the candy.* I could die. "What's yours?" I ask.

"Daniel." I say it in my mind. I wonder if he ever goes by Dan or Danny, or if it's always Daniel. "Is your mom always like that?" he asks.

"Like what?"

"I don't know." He pauses. "A nag."

The corners of his mouth pull up. I smile too. Because, for maybe the first time in my life, someone gets me. Someone sees the world the way I see it.

"Yeah," I say, grinning. "Pretty much."

"*This is a family vacation. You're supposed to be with family,*" he says, parroting Emily and the conversation he overheard yesterday from the woods, and we laugh at her expense. "Sorry," he says, his smile flattening. "I shouldn't talk shit about your mom."

"No. It's fine. I do."

"Yeah, but she's your mom. You're supposed to talk shit about her," he says, like it's my birthright, like every kid is out there talking shit about their moms. Many are, but then there are the ones like my little cousin Cass, who actually hero-worships her mom, or Skylar, who has spa dates and goes on shopping sprees with hers, where her mom, Caroline, splurges on Lululemon and shit.

I ask, "What's your mom like?"

He shrugs, saying that she's dead, and I recoil. "Oh my God. I'm so sorry." What happens next is totally unexpected. My hand moves as if all on its own, reaching out to touch his before pulling back. In the real world, I'd never do that. I would never touch him. I would just stand there, feeling awkward, hating myself for asking the question as if I should have somehow known that his mom was dead, and maybe it's the fact that I'm on vacation and may never see this guy again that makes me realize I can be anyone I want to be. I can do anything I want to do.

He shrugs again. "Don't be. It's not your fault. You didn't kill her." He looks away. When he looks back, he says, "I actually saw you twice yesterday. At your cottage and again at the lodge. I waved at you." He waits for me to say something, but when I don't, he says, "You didn't wave back."

"I didn't see you."

"No?" he asks, his smile playful this time, and it takes every-thing in me not to smile back and give myself away. "Because it seemed like maybe you did."

Heat fills my cheeks. I think of the way I stood at the win-dow yesterday, watching him unload boxes from the pickup truck. I wonder what he could see from the other side of the window, just the faint outline of my face or the look on it as I stared, imagining what he looked like under his shirt.

"Well, I didn't," I say. "It wasn't me. I wasn't even at the lodge yesterday."

"That's too bad. I was kind of hoping it was you, because whoever I saw was pretty as hell."

My face goes red. I'm about to take it back—to tell him it was me at the lodge after all—when all of a sudden I hear the sound of voices in the distance, carrying through the woods, closing in on us, and my heart sinks because I know they're about to ruin this moment for me because they ruin everything.

When I see them, Emily's arms are crossed. She tries hard to keep up with Nolan, who walks ahead, the gap between them widening with each step because she can't keep pace. I don't know if Nolan is trying to intentionally ditch her or not because he always walks ahead of her, like he can't ever slow down, like he has only one speed. "Why do you always do that?" she asks, her voice out of breath from trying to keep up, and I don't even know what they're talking about, but it doesn't matter. It's the same argument, different day.

"Do what?"

"Why do you always contradict everything I say? Why can't you agree with me for once?"

He stops, wheels around to face her, his voice loud and un-checked. "Why can you never just fucking compromise? Why do you always have to tell everyone what to do?"

"Can you just be quiet? Can you lower your voice, *please*?"

"Why?" Nolan asks, his voice escalating because it can, just to piss her off, to embarrass her. "Why do I have to be *fucking* quiet? When are we ever going to see these *fucking* people again?"

I take Daniel by the arm and drag him deeper into the woods.

"Where are we going?" he asks.

I put a finger to my lips and whisper, "Shhh."

Emily says, "You're only acting like this because you're drunk."

This time, when she says it, Nolan steps up close, entering her personal space with such velocity I'm not sure he's not going to hit her. Emily feels it too. She backs away from him as he says, "I am not drunk. I had two beers."

"You had at least three, if not four."

"Are you *counting*? We're on vacation, Emily. You need to relax."

Suddenly, Daniel's hand is on my arm. I turn toward him, losing myself in his eyes. "What are you doing later?" he asks, his voice low.

But Nolan's tone is aggressive, incensed, pulling my attention away again as he says, "You're ruining everyone's trip, Emily. Everyone would be having a far better time if you weren't here." He turns, walking away from her again, and I feel Daniel's hand on my cheek this time, turning my face, making me look into his eyes.

"When?" I ask.

"Tonight," he says. "I want to show you something."

"Show me what?" I ask, but the truth is that I don't care what he wants to show me. Whatever it is, if it means being with him, then I want to see.

He shrugs, the sun hitting his eyes just right so that they actually twinkle like stars in a night sky. "Just something."

I look at Nolan, climbing the hill to the cottage. This time, Emily doesn't follow. She doesn't want to go where he's going, because his last words—*Everyone would be having a far better time if you weren't here*—cut deep. She throws a look back over her shoulder and toward the pool, wondering if she should go back and be with Aunt Courtney and Uncle Elliott. But she doesn't want to do that either, because they're happy and having fun and their energy doesn't match. She doesn't want to bring everyone down. In the end, she turns and climbs the hill for the cottage, following Nolan at a distance, her arms still crossed, her head down and looking at her feet. I almost feel sorry for her. Except that Nolan isn't wrong. Everyone would be having a better time if she weren't here, telling everyone what to do.

"I don't know if they'll let me leave," I say, though I think that if I have to spend the entire night in the cottage with them either fighting or giving each other the silent treatment, I might actually kill myself.

He's grinning out of the side of his mouth. "Do they have to know? Do you tell them everything?"

My stomach flips. Butterflies dance inside of it.

"No. Not everything." I smile back, a gust of wind sweeping in from behind, blowing my hair forward and into my face. I clutch a fistful of it by my neck, waiting for the breeze to pass. I glance again at Emily and Nolan in the distance and say, "Let me see if I can sneak out after they're asleep."

"Okay. If you can, meet me by the beach, on the pier. If you can't—" he starts to say, but I cut him off, my words free from doubt this time.

"I'll be there. Wait for me."

COURTNEY

Wyatt's words bring me to a sudden stop in the living room, which is dark save for the glow from his phone screen, the blue light brightening his face but, at the same time, casting shadows on it that make it impossible to read.

I know where Reese is.

"Where?" I ask, breathless. I step closer to him, wanting to see what he's looking at on his phone. I reach the sofa bed and lower myself to it as Wyatt turns his phone slowly around and shows me. On his screen is a map with a cute little avatar of Reese in a tiny pink tee and cutoff denim shorts that looks almost exactly like her.

"What is this, Wyatt?" I ask, reaching for the phone, bringing it closer so that I can see it better. He has cell reception, one piddling bar that might disappear at any time, though reception tends to be better at night, when fewer people are awake and fighting for it.

"Snapchat," he says, his face dark now that the phone's light isn't shining directly on him.

I don't use Snapchat. I'm not familiar with how it works. "What is this map?" I ask, fixating on the bright smile on the likeness of Reese's face, on the tiny details that are just right, down to the double piercings in her ears and the shape and spacing of her eyes.

"Snap Map."

"How does it work?" I ask, and he explains. It's a location sharing feature. It allows friends to see where friends are in real time, by putting these avatars of them on a map.

My stomach tightens. "You mean, anyone can see where you are all the time?" I ask. The idea of it makes me feel sick. I think of all the ways that could go wrong, how the wrong people could find you, like old boyfriends, people you don't get along with, friends you're in an argument with or boys who like you but you don't like back.

He shrugs. "Yeah. If you want them to."

"What does that mean, Wyatt?" I ask, looking at him.

"You can put it in ghost mode."

"What's ghost mode?"

"Where no one knows where you are."

I nod, understanding. You don't have to let your avatar be on this map. You don't have to let people know where you are. You can opt out of it if you want, but kids don't think like that. They aren't cautious like adults. They don't consider all the bad things that can happen, only how they can find friends at parties and show up at places where their crush is, things like that.

I zoom in on this Snap Map, bringing Reese closer so that not only can I see her exact location, but I can see how long it would take me to get to her.

Five minutes.

Reese is only five minutes away.

I push myself from the sofa bed, taking Wyatt's phone into the bedroom with me, my heart racing as I feel the bedside table for my own phone, relieved to see that I, too, have a single bar before searching for the number I stored in my contacts earlier today.

Detective Evans's voice is woolly when he answers.

"Detective Evans," I say, trying to keep my voice low for the girls, who still sleep. "It's Courtney Gray."

"Is everything okay?" he asks, shaking off the morning voice, and I imagine him sitting up in bed, rubbing the sleep from his eyes. There's a noise in the background, and I picture a woman beside him, a girlfriend maybe, rolling away, drawing a sheet over her head to lessen the sound of his voice.

On the other side of the curtains, the night is black. It's sometime after two, maybe three, in the morning. The sun won't rise for hours.

"We know where Reese is."

"Where?" he asks, his voice suddenly more alert. I tell him, texting him a screenshot of the Snap Map from Wyatt's phone.

On the other end of the line, Detective Evans is quiet at first; he doesn't have the same reaction as me.

"What is it? What's wrong?" I ask, because of his silence.

"How much do you know about Snapchat, Mrs. Gray?"

"Not much. Almost nothing."

"These maps are not always reliable. They're only as good as the last time a person logged in to the site. That means Reese might have been there last night, but it doesn't mean she's still here now. And we have no way of knowing if Reese logged in to the account herself or if someone else logged in to it."

"You're not going to look for her?" I ask, exasperated, hearing him sigh through the phone, and though my heart sinks, it doesn't matter because I've already decided that even if he isn't, I still am.

But he is. He says that he is going to look for her, and I imagine him sweeping the covers from his body, swinging his feet over the side of the bed, standing up.

"I'll meet you there," I tell him, already reaching for a pair of jeans that lie folded on the top of my closed suitcase.

But he says, "No, Mrs. Gray," his voice firm, resolute. "You can't do that. I need you to stay there, at the cottage. It's dark outside. You don't know the area like we do."

"But—" I try to object. He stops me before the words can get out.

"You need to take care of the other kids," he says, as Mae whimpers, crying out for Emily in her sleep.

I know Detective Evans is right. Still, I hate the idea of sitting idly by while the police search for Reese. But this part of Wisconsin that we're in is made up of vast forests with millions of acres of trees and thousands of lakes and swamps. It's the type of place where people can get easily lost or disappear in.

"I can't have anything bad happening to you too," he says, promising to call with news.

I come to early in the morning, woken by a sound. I don't know where I am at first. I only know that this isn't my bed and this isn't my room. Before I ever open my eyes, I can tell that something is off. It feels all wrong to me. There are fewer pillows on the bed than I'm used to, and my downy duvet has been reduced to a quilt that lies like deadweight, leveling me in bed.

And then reality crushes and drives over me and I remember: the little lakeside cottage in the woods.

Emily and Nolan dead.

I inhale a sharp drag of air, the memory of it settling in my stomach like rocks. This can't be real. This can't be happening. For one split second, I can almost tell myself it was a dream, a nightmare, but then, a second later it solidifies, becoming concrete, and I know.

It is real. It happened.

They're dead.

I blink open my eyes, which are all but swollen shut. With effort, I sit up in bed, my phone sliding off my chest because I must have somehow drifted off to sleep, waiting for Detective Evans to call, exhaustion pulling me under against my will.

The sound, I realize, is my phone.

Desperately I grab for it, turning it to face me, Detective Evans's name splayed on the screen.

"What happened?" I ask. "Was she there, Detective? Did you find Reese?"

After a failed attempt to find her themselves overnight, the police arrange a ground search for Reese, asking the community for volunteers to help look in the location where she was last seen on Snapchat. I decide to go while Elliott stays behind with the kids. He wants to go too, but we can't take the kids with us and we can't leave them alone. It's not safe for them.

Before I leave, Elliott follows me to the window, standing behind me. I peel the curtain back to gaze out, beyond the police officer who's still parked in his car on the driveway. Outside, it's bright and calm, a glitch in the matrix. The weather should be stormy, the lake raging, the wind wild and rushing through the trees. Instead, there are more boaters and fishermen on the lake than I'm used to. They sit along our shoreline, enjoying the peaceful view.

"Why don't you just let the police and volunteers look? Why do you need to go?" Elliott asks.

At the same time, I say, "Busy day for fishing," taking in the surplus of boats on the lake, though finding it impossible to believe the world still exists, that life still goes on, that people are able to do ordinary things like go boating and fish.

Elliott steps closer, looking past me and out the window. "They're not fishing, Court."

I look again and this time see it for myself. The boats aren't out there slowing to troll for fish as I first imagined. Instead, they're trying to get a glimpse of Emily and Nolan's cottage from the lake, searching through binoculars or taking pictures of it on their phones and on cameras with telephoto lenses to share online with horrible little hashtags like #crimescene or #murderhouse, reducing our family's nightmare to a social media post.

Rage builds inside of me. "What do you think they can even see from the lake?" I ask, trying to keep my voice calm, level, but as I do I remember how Emily used to relish her undisrupted view of the lake from the cottage's deck. While the rest of her family slept, she spent her mornings there, drinking coffee and taking it in: the reflection of the sky and the shadows of the trees on the still blue-green water.

"I don't know. Probably not much," Elliott says to indulge me. But I know he's wrong. They can see practically everything.

"Why don't the police make them leave?"

"I don't think they can. It's public property and it's not like they can rope off a lake." Elliott turns me around and again he asks, "Why don't you stay here today? Let the police look for Reese. If she's there, they'll find her. They'll bring her home."

I shake my head. "I have to go, Elliott. She's my niece. Emily would do this for me." He nods, pensive, and I can tell he wants to say more. "What?" I ask, feeling frustration build that I even have to explain to him why I would want to go.

"It's just . . ." His eyes stray. He won't look at me as he says, "I keep thinking about what she said to Emily the other night. She was just so angry. I've never seen her like that before."

I hate you. I wish you'd die.

I take a breath. "What are you saying? That she killed them and ran off?" The words are hard to get out. They're harder to imagine. Elliott is quiet; he can't bring himself to say yes, that that's exactly what he thinks. "She didn't do this," I say. "You know her. You know she would never do this." But even as I say it, I wonder: Did either of us know Reese that well? Once upon a time, when she was young, we did. Reese was exuberant then. She had the best smile, the best laugh, and she was always very liberal with her hugs. Before Cass came along, Elliott and I adored being the fun aunt and uncle, without all the duties of parenting. We'd have Reese over to our house from time to time and spend the day watching movies and playing games, sending her home before the drudgery of bedtime. When she was young, Elliott taught her how to play hide-n-seek. Reese was a quick learner. I remember finding her at the back of my closet and not just standing there, but fully dressed in a shirt and skirt of mine and in my shoes. At least twice I looked right past without ever noticing she was there. Hidden in plain sight. Elliott was impressed; he said she was like some child prodigy of hide-n-seek, which she thought was hilarious, though she had no idea what *prodigy* meant.

But this new Reese, this defiant seventeen-year-old Reese, is almost a stranger to me. That girl that we knew as a child isn't her. It's someone else. "She was just mad. She said things she didn't mean. We've all done that."

"No, you're right," he says. "Of course she didn't. Like you said, she was just mad." The change of heart is too quick; I can see in his eyes that he doesn't believe it.

My head throbs. When I looked at my face in the mirror before, it was swollen from crying and there were tiny marks, like broken blood vessels, on my cheeks and around my eyes from vomiting. The kids, all three of them, sit on the unmade sofa bed in their makeshift pajamas like deer in headlights, their eyes glazed over and stunned. Mae's face is puffy from crying half the night. As I watch, she sniffles and then wipes her nose with a sleeve. Beside her, Cass stares down at her own hands before getting up and moving to the loft to be alone.

"You'll take care of the kids?" I ask, worrying about them, feeling conflicted by the need to find Reese but also my desire to stay here and be with Cass and Mae, to comfort them.

"Of course I will." I press the heels of my hands to my eyes.
"Are you sure you can do this?" Elliott asks.

"Yes," I say. "I'll be fine."

"Okay," he says, reaching out for me and pulling me close,
"if you're sure. Just be careful. Stay alert. Stay with people and
don't ever let yourself be alone."

"I won't."

The police officer steps out of his car when I go outside. Up
close, he's maybe fifty years old, tall, lanky and balding. "Everything alright, ma'am?" he asks.

"Yes," I say, moving down the steps, veering away from him
and in the direction of my own car.

"Going somewhere?"

I stop and turn back, feeling my breath quicken, that flight-
or-fight reaction kicking in. "Am I not allowed to leave?" I ask,
defensive.

He waits too long to answer. When he does, he asks, "How
can I keep you safe when I don't know where you are?"

I tell him, "I'm going to help the search party look for my
niece." I don't ask if that's allowed, or if I'm just supposed to
stay in the cottage all day like a prisoner.

As I jog the rest of the way to the car, my neck stiffens with
that sense of being watched.

I open the door and get in. I slam the door closed and lock it.

From the front seat of the car, I search the woods, wondering
if that sense of being watched is just my imagination or if it isn't
my subconscious, picking up on something my eyes cannot see.

REESE

My horoscope this morning said to take risks, to reap the benefits of not playing it safe. I'm not usually a risk-taker. My idea of taking risks is watching horror movies, riding roller coasters and things like that, things that scare the shit out of you but are safe, that can't really hurt you.

This can, I think, as I disappear into the trees, getting swallowed up by them. Outside, the night air is cooler than I thought. I shiver from the cold, trying to forget about things like being cold and about being scared to death of the dark, though the darkness is so close I can feel it, like some concrete thing. It's not just an absence of light. It's not something intangible like love or hope or dreams. It's real. I feel it against my skin as I walk, touching me. I try not to think about how scared I am. I try to think of Daniel instead, of him at the beach, waiting for me on the pier, like he said. I picture his face. I imagine him alone, searching the dark horizon with his eyes. I fantasize about the moment I step out of the darkness and we see each other again. In my illusion, I say something witty and brilliant. He laughs, coming to me.

For a while, thinking about him makes me forget about being scared. But then I hear a sound from behind—the snap of a tree branch and the soft crunch of leaves like from beneath someone's feet—and I freeze, momentarily paralyzed, thinking this is how I die. Out here, alone, late at night.

No one knows where I am.

No one would even know I was missing until the morning, when Emily and Nolan woke up and found my bed empty. By then, I'd definitely be dead.

I picture that: Emily finding my bed empty and being mad first, before she finds out I'm dead.

Everyone was asleep when I left. I waited for Emily to go upstairs last as if she was putting off going to bed with Nolan, who went out of his way all night to ignore her. Even when he did say something, it was mean. He went to bed first, closing the bedroom door. I wasn't sure she was ever going to go. I waited a long time, and then, after she did, I waited even longer for her to fall asleep. I carried my shoes out so no one would hear me go, wrapping my hand around the doorknob, turning it a little at a time so as not to make a sound. When it was open, I grabbed the knob by the other side so that the latch stayed put, not letting go until the door was closed and even when I did, it was slow as fuck, the latch crawling back into place. From downstairs, I could hear Nolan, snoring like he does, which is why Emily wears earplugs when she sleeps. Nolan sleeps like the dead, so much so that he's always sleeping through his alarm.

I left the front door unlocked because I don't have a key, which means that anyone can get in while I'm gone, if they wanted to.

Now I wheel around at the noise. I narrow my eyes, searching the woods, my heart pounding in my chest. I try to see through the darkness, imagining someone coming out of the trees and killing me horror movie style, with a chain saw or an ice pick. I can almost hear the music playing in the background, something super minimalist but creepy as fuck. In horror movies, it's always the dumb, slutty cheerleader who dies first, and I wonder if that's me, if I'm that trope: the stupid blonde, sneaking out late at night to walk through the woods alone to meet up with a complete stranger.

If something were to happen to me, would people say it was my fault? That I had it coming to me? That I deserved to die?

"Hello," I whisper out into the darkness, my voice soft, shrinking. I feel cold and I'm shaky all over. My legs are weak and there's a steady pulse in my neck, a *thump thump, thump thump*. "Is someone there?" I ask.

Thump thump.

No one says. But then the sound comes again, even closer this time, and I retreat slowly from it, too afraid to turn my back to whatever it is, to turn around and run. The face of the man from the pool—the *Hey. Can you bring me something to eat too?*—flashes into my mind, as does the face of the man at the lodge the other day, the one who checked out Mae, his eyes moving from her overalls, down her bony little legs to her shoes.

I should run to our own cottage, where it's safe. I start to, backing further away. But before I can go, a dark shape steps in front of me and I gasp. It's too late for me now. There's no time to run before he smashes a damp, sweaty hand down over my mouth, and my heart goes wild. I try to pull away, to jerk free from under his grip.

"There's no point fighting," he says as the moonlight shines down on him and lights up his face so that, for the first time, I see who it is. I go still. Stiff. My breaths become shallow, my whole body overcome with panic and fear.

He comes even closer. I yank back, slamming into a tree, trapped. His face is straight, his stare piercing and cold as he looks down on me and says, "You should've known better than to trust a guy like me. Did you really not think I might try to hurt you?"

COURTNEY

I take the car, leaving Elliott and the kids carless, not that it matters because they won't go anywhere. The resort is nearly empty now. All day yesterday, I watched out the window as other families packed their bags and left, driving away from this awful place, so that Elliott and the kids have it all—the pool, the beach—to themselves now, not that that matters either, because they won't leave the cottage. It's not like anyone is in the mood for a swim, but even if they were, they couldn't, because it's not safe for them to be outside.

I leave the resort. I pull from the parking lot and onto the main road, which is a two-lane highway through town, though the term *highway* is misleading, because it gives the impression of a main artery, when this is nothing more than a small vein, not much different than any of the other roads around here. I drive through the small village with a population of something like four or five hundred people, though I don't know where they live because houses around here are so infrequent. It feels like it's stepped back in time. There is a Laundromat in a tired storefront with a rusted sign. There is a psychic and a seedy-looking liquor store—with crooked signs that hype *beer, ammo, bait*—and gas stations with convenience marts in place of grocery stores. There are restaurants, but nothing high-end, everything local and modest like the dive lodge at our own resort.

I drive the couple miles it takes to get to the location Snap Map pulled from Reese's phone. The further I go, the more the road narrows. Trees draw nearer the street; their branches over-hang it, the sun coming through in mottled swathes that move on the asphalt with the wind.

As I drive, I can't stop thinking about Reese on these same roads two nights ago. There's an image that plays over and over again in my mind like a song on repeat until I can't get the lyrics out of my head: Reese with a blindfold over her eyes, a sock in her mouth gagging her scream, and zip ties on her ankles and wrists. In my vision, she lies on her side in the hard bed of a pickup truck with her hands bound behind her with her knees pulled into her chest, struggling in vain to get free.

It's been about thirty-six hours since she's been gone.

She could be in California by now. Or she could be here, just like the Snap Map said.

I try not to give in to paranoia and fear. I try not to think that for the last thirty-six hours, someone—whoever took Reese—has been keeping watch on the cottage, that they watched me leave and that they're following me.

No one is following me, I tell myself, as I steal a glance in the rearview mirror to see that the street behind me, which nar-rows until it's almost only one lane, is empty. I'm completely alone, which is the one thing Elliott told me not to do: *Don't ever let yourself be alone.*

If something were to happen to me right now, no one would know. No one would see.

My fear lightens when I see cars parked up ahead. They're pulled to the side of the road, just off a wooded trail not far from a waste disposal site, which is the kind of place where people bring their own recycling and trash. I pull onto the shoulder. I turn the engine off, and then I sit in the front seat of the car, taking in the wide expanse of trees that surrounds me.

People gather at the edge of the trees, including Detective
Evans. As I get out of the car, hearing the low growl of an ATV
in the distance, he starts to make his way toward me, and we
meet in the middle, where the dewy grass reaches my knees,
the moisture coming in through the mesh of my gym shoes and
making my feet wet.

"I didn't know you were coming," he says.

"Why wouldn't I come?"

"I thought you'd want to stay home and be with your family."

"Reese is my family."

He nods. "Of course. Listen," he says, as I let my eyes go to
the people behind him, wearing orange vests, a small group of
civilian volunteers who stand around doing nothing, with no
sense of urgency, and I wonder if it's because they've already
found Reese, if it's because they've found her body or something
else to suggest she's dead.

"What is it?" I ask, starting to panic. "Has something happened? Have you found her?"

"No." He shakes his head. "It's not that. I just wanted to
say, you shouldn't get your hopes up," he says, and it's hard not
to notice how he gazes over my head then, surveying the area
around us.

"What's that supposed to mean?" I ask, feeling my hands start
to tremble. I wouldn't say that my hopes are up, but my emotions are charged and run the gamut of hope, grief and fear to
an overwhelming, paralyzing sense of dread.

Maybe Reese is here. Maybe she's not here.

Or maybe we will find her dead.

I think of what that would look like. I prepare myself for it,
to come across Reese's dead body in the damp and overgrown
grass or deep in the dark woods, shaded beneath the mantle of
trees where the sun can't reach.

He lowers his eyes to mine, though it's fleeting before his

eyes leave mine again to graze the area, his hand moving slowly, intuitively to his hip, where his gun sits, and this time, I'm unnerved by his attentiveness.

He thinks someone is out there in the woods.

He thinks someone is watching us from the depth of the trees.

When he looks back at me, he says, "Reese might be here. We might find her phone. Or we might find nothing." He waits a beat to let his words sink in, and then says, "It's best if you keep your expectations to a minimum. Hope for the best but prepare for the worst."

Detective Evans walks with me to the rest of the volunteers, where we're given directions before splitting into small groups to search. We work under the guidance of the police and trained search and rescue volunteers, moving outward from what the police call Reese's last known position, which is where Snap Map picked up her phone signal the other night. We move slowly, methodically in the area to which we're assigned, though it's not known if Reese is on foot or if she's in a vehicle—that image of her bound and gagged in the bed of a pickup truck comes rushing back—and so there is no way to know just how fast she's traveling or how far away she is from the trail by now, if at all. It's not only Reese we're looking for. It's things too, like her phone, footprints, drag marks, blood, a shoe.

Around me, as we search, people call out her name, so that I'm surrounded by a chorus of *Reese*.

Reese.

Reese.

Reese.

I worry about what we'll find or if we'll find anything. There aren't as many volunteers here as I'd have liked. There are five people in my group and the area is so large that, at this pace, we won't cover much distance. We stay quiet, intensely focused, concentrating on the rocks, the soil, the blades of grass, so that our eyes almost never leave the ground until thirty or forty minutes into our search, when one of the women in the group says to me in passing, "Yours isn't the only pretty girl who's gone missing, you know?"

Her words, and the way she says them, make the small hairs on the back of my neck stand up.

"What do you mean?" I ask, looking sharply up, my heart rate accelerating.

"Joanna over there," she says, and I follow her gaze to another woman who searches nearby, picking her way through the tall trees. "Her and her husband's little girl went missing a couple years back."

"What happened to her?" I ask, keeping my eyes on the woman in the distance, Joanna, whose head is bent, taking in the earth beneath her feet, long dark hair falling down to veil her face.

"Hell if I know. Your guess is as good as mine."

"What do you mean? They didn't find her?"

"No. They looked everywhere for her, but she was just gone."

"Gone," I echo, wondering how it's even possible that a person—a child, anyone—could completely vanish like that, into thin air. "What was the little girl's name?"

"Kylie Matthews."

There is a poster in the resort lodge for a missing girl. It's her, Kylie Matthews. The poster asks *Have you seen me?* in big, bold red letters along the top of the sheet. My eyes have grazed over it more than once, never really processing the words or seeing the face of the missing girl. Instead, I breezed casually past it. I never gave it pause, which I feel guilty for now. I shouldn't have been so blasé. She's a child, someone's daughter. At the time, I chalked it up to just another missing child, thinking that this girl and I had nothing in common, believing this missing child had nothing to do with me.

"Excuse me," I say, turning and making my way deeper into the woods, where the terrain varies from dirt trails to bog bridges when the ground becomes too soft and spongy to cross. Wildflowers and mushrooms grow beneath the trees where the sun doesn't reach. There are houses in the area, though they're intermittent and small, mobile or ranch homes, five hundred to a thousand square feet at best, so spread out and hidden away that my mind fills with horrible possibilities that make me afraid.

What if Reese is in one of the houses?

What if someone is keeping her in there?

I make my way to Joanna.

"Excuse me," I say, my voice bridled, her back to me as I approach. She straightens and turns, and as she does, I'm taken aback by her hollowed-out cheeks and the wasting away of her body. Knobby collarbones bulge at the base of her neck; there are half-moon-shaped shadows beneath her eyes. It takes my breath away and I see another version of myself in a few years from now, one that scares me. "Are you Joanna?" I ask, my words a whisper.

She nods.

"I'm so sorry to bother you. I just . . . I'm Courtney," I say, struggling to get my words out. "Reese—the girl we're looking for—she's my niece."

"I know," she says, explaining how she saw my car pull up before and how she saw me speaking to Detective Evans. "I'm sorry for what you're going through," she says. Then she sighs exasperatedly and adds, "*I'm sorry. I shouldn't have said that. It's such a cliché, if not a completely inadequate thing to say. Sorry.* When my daughter went missing, everyone was *so sorry.*"

I feel her anger, her grief. "I heard about your daughter," I tell her. "Someone in my group mentioned her."

Before I can say more, a man comes up from behind, his face—like hers—sad, with sunken eyes, their slender bodies not only thin, but atrophied, like people who are dying, and they are, I think, not of any physical thing, but of anguish and grief. He sets a gentle hand on her shoulder. She turns and looks back at him, her smile sad and full of regret. "This is Sam, my husband," she says before bringing her gaze back to me. Neither Sam nor Joanna can be much older than me, and yet it's clear that tragedy has aged them, making them appear much older than they are.

"It's nice to meet you, Sam."

"This is Courtney," she says to him. "Hers is the girl who's missing."

"Reese. My niece. Her parents—" I start to say, but I can't get the words out. They get lodged in my throat like gravel, making it hard to speak and even harder to breathe. I see the blood on the walls again, Emily's bent shape and the color of her skin, the same color as the mauve nail polish on her toes, taking me back to us getting pedicures together less than two weeks ago, in another lifetime, back when she was alive, sitting side by side on spa chairs, talking about things that don't matter anymore, like her annoying coworker, some new diet she wanted to try that supposedly reverses signs of aging, and whether we should both get Botox.

"Will you tell me about your daughter?" I ask instead, changing the subject. "Will you tell me what happened to her?"

Sam closes his eyes for a minute. He breathes. When he opens his eyes, he says, "I'm going to go see if they need any help," his stare distant and empty.

Joanna looks up at him and says, "I'll catch up with you later," before watching him go. "He doesn't like to talk about it," she says, once he's far enough away that he can't hear.

"I'm so sorry," I say, the words slipping out, feeling guilty. "I shouldn't have said anything. I shouldn't have asked."

"No. Please. Don't be sorry." Joanna pauses. When she speaks again, she says, "I like talking about her. It keeps her alive in my mind. Kylie was bold, a free spirit," which reminds me of Reese. She stares down at her empty hands. "It was five years ago this August that it happened, that she left us. There are days that the pain is so real and raw it feels like it was just yesterday, and then there are other times when I struggle to remember the sound of her voice or what her face looked like when she laughed, and it feels like it's been an eternity since I last saw or held my child. They never found her." She pauses, gazing up at the horizon, searching as she says, "She could still be out there somewhere. I'd like to believe that." And then she brings her eyes back to mine and says, "Or maybe she's not. Maybe she's dead. They say mothers have some intuition about this, about whether their child is dead or alive, but I don't. I don't have that gift."

"Did they ever have any suspects?"

"Some, but nothing that ever panned out. Without a body, it was hard to say what really happened to her. The police said they couldn't be sure she hadn't just run away, though I knew she hadn't. She wouldn't do that. Kylie was happy."

I nod, wanting her to go on, to say more, and she does. "Kylie was eleven when she disappeared. She would be sixteen now, going on seventeen. Her birthday is next week. Every year, I bake a cake, red velvet because it was her favorite. Sam," she says, turning to look at him in the distance. He's rejoined his group, searching the forest floor for signs of Reese, combing through pine needles and leaves. "He wants nothing to do with it. Every year on her birthday, he leaves the house early and stays at work longer than he needs to because he can't stand to be at home."

She looks back at me. "Sam was the one who suggested we come today, to look for your niece. To be honest, I said no. I wasn't sure I could do it, that I could mentally go back to those days of searching for Kylie. But Sam and I know what it's like to lose a child. We know what you're going through," she says, and I feel grateful for her, to have someone here who knows what I'm experiencing and feeling.

"How do you survive it?"

She's quiet at first. "It gets easier the longer they're gone," she eventually says. "But that's when the guilt and the shame kick in, because it shouldn't ever get easier. The day that Kylie went missing wasn't all that different than this. In fact, it was almost exactly the same, sunny, warm with a gentle breeze. It was the summer that Kylie started her period and got her braces off, that she discovered boys and had her first crush," she says, and I think of Cass at age ten, just a year or two younger than Kylie and not so far away from any of these things. Braces. Her period. Boys.

"Kylie was a wonderful contradiction at that age. She wanted to be independent, to wear makeup and real bras—not sports or training bras, but ones with wires and lace. But at the same time, she needed to sleep with her stuffed animals at night. She would climb into our bed during thunderstorms and lay in the space between Sam and me, her arm around my waist. She had a bin of Barbie dolls that she kept hidden under her bed in case she ever wanted to play with them alone, in private, so as not to let her friends see. She was growing up fast and excited about it, but she didn't want to let go of her childhood either. Not yet."

She hesitates before going on, the nostalgia transforming into something different, something darker.

"The not knowing," she says, holding my stare, "is the hardest part. Even if the answers you get are not the ones you want, they're still answers. Sam and I don't have that. Maybe we never will."

REESE

All of a sudden, he changes. His shoulders slouch, he cracks a smile. The tautness of his face disappears just like that. Like magic.

He laughs.

"I'm just fucking with you. You know that, right? I'm not really gonna hurt you," Daniel says, his voice all of a sudden different too, and I believe him.

The smell of weed carries through the air. Up close, I see in his eyes that he's stoned, not like super, super stoned, but he's definitely been toking a joint.

He says, "If I move my hand, promise you won't scream?"

I nod, not sure how to feel. Humiliated, mad, maybe scared.

But mostly I'm just happy and in disbelief that he's here, that he came. That I'm out in the woods, alone with some hot guy in the middle of the night. Nobody would believe it if I told them. He stands close. Tears of relief well behind my eyes, though I hold them back, tension leaving my body and getting replaced with something else, something I can't name, but that makes my skin flush and my heart beat hard.

"You're a feisty one," he says, grinning as he moves his hand. "I like that."

"I thought you said to meet on the pier," I say, trying to catch my breath.

He shrugs, says all nonchalant, "I changed my mind. I got tired of waiting."

It took me longer than expected to get out of the cottage. I think of Daniel, waiting all that time for me, wondering if I was ever going to show or if I was ghosting him. He would have known where to look because he knows which cottage is ours, because he heard Emily and me the other day on the porch. He would have known where to find me. It doesn't cross my mind to be weirded out by it. Instead, I'm actually flattered and ecstatic. He came looking for me because he wanted to see me. That never happens.

"Sorry it took so long."

"It's alright. I would have stayed out here all night if I had to. Anything to see you."

Anything to see you.

He steps even closer, standing so close now that I feel his shirt against mine, his breath on my skin as he breathes. There is an urgency to this, which makes me think of when Nolan puts lighter fluid on the grill, how it accelerates the fire, makes the flame flare up and makes everything happen faster. Bigger. This is what that feels like. Like someone has doused us with lighter fluid and struck a match. He reaches out, runs the back of a finger down my cheek. There is an actual gleam in his eye, which makes me simultaneously crush hard and wonder if he's done this before, if he's hit on other girls at the resort before and taken them to see whatever it is he wants me to see.

I wonder if it matters.

I wonder if I care.

"How long are you here for?" he asks, and when I tell him, he says, "That's all?"

"That's all."

"Then we have to make the most of it."

Around us, crickets chirp. A breeze blows through the trees, moving the leaves.

He leans in and asks, "Where are you from, Reese like the candy?"

He smiles and I melt in it, dissolving completely.

"Chicago."

"You have a boyfriend back home in Chicago?"

I shake my head. "No."

"Why not?"

"No one thinks of me like that."

He makes a sound under his breath. "I doubt that."

"No, it's true. I haven't had a boyfriend since like fourth grade."

I want to die. I can't believe I just said that. I feel stupid, but before I can take it back—say it's a lie or that I'm kidding or something, tell him I *do* have a boyfriend after all—he says, "Then either those guys are intimidated by you because you're so beautiful, or they're a bunch of idiots."

He touches the ends of my hair and my heart actually stops. No one's ever called me beautiful before, except for maybe Emily saying something like how I *could be* so beautiful, if only I dressed different or wore my hair different or didn't hide myself under so much makeup.

"What did you want to show me?" I ask, because I don't know how to respond to that, because I don't know what I'm supposed to say now that he's said I'm beautiful. *Thanks* seems lame. *No, I'm not* is even more pathetic and self-deprecating than everything I've already told him, and I don't have the nerve to tell him he's beautiful too, though he is, he's fucking hot. Like Timothée Chalamet hot. Guys as hot as him don't ever talk to me unless I'm in their way and they need me to move. Most guys don't like me, not normal guys anyway, only the weird gamer and cosplay ones, because I'm niceish to them when no one else is. Unlike everyone else, I don't tell them to fuck off or to kill themselves.

He lets go of my hair, lowers his hand to his side. "I'm sorry if I'm making you uncomfortable."

"You're not," I say, wishing he would touch me again, wondering if I'm massively screwing this all up, if I'm doing everything wrong, if I'm saying the wrong things.

"I'm not?" he asks. "Your face is red," he says, grinning, and I know it is—I can feel heat fill it, I can feel my whole body flood with warmth—I'm just surprised he can see it in the dark.

I swallow, my saliva thick and difficult to get down. It takes effort, conscious thought. I don't look him in the eye as I admit, "I'm just not used to people saying things like that I'm beautiful."

He puts a finger under my chin, lifts my face so I look at him. "Well, you are," he says. "You are beautiful." He stares hard and then he asks, teasing, the moonlight slipping out from behind a cloud just then, flickering off his eyes and making them glow, "You have kissed a boy, haven't you? Or is that not since fourth grade too?"

"Yeah," I say, breathless. "I have."

"When?" he asks, like he doesn't believe me.

And I could tell him it was exactly three weeks ago yesterday, though the guy was so bombed out of his mind there's no way he remembers and probably wouldn't have kissed me if he was sober, but instead I take a page out of Skylar's playbook and say, "It's not nice to kiss and tell. Besides, it's none of your business," which he likes because he grins.

He says, "Well played, Reese like the candy. Well played. I like you."

All I hear is *I like you*, which I overthink. Does he like me-like me, like actually *like* me, or is he not serious? Is he kidding? Is it just something you say?

He says, "You know, we could just kiss and get it over with," and my knees go weak. My heart almost explodes out of my chest. And I want to say yes. Let's kiss. Because it's all I've been thinking about since the first time I laid eyes on him yesterday afternoon: what he would taste like and what his tongue would feel like in my mouth. I've imagined it again and again in my mind, trying to manifest it, to make it happen, trying not to think about how many other girls like me he's kissed out here in these woods.

"Why do you think I want to kiss you?" I ask, because Skylar always says to play hard to get, because it makes them want you more.

"You don't?" he asks, looking hurt.

"No. I don't," I say. "At least not until you show me what I came to see."

"Are you scared?"

"Of kissing you?"

"Of what I'm going to show you."

"Should I be?"

"No," he says. "I'll protect you."

"Protect me from what?" I ask.

What is he going to protect me from?

Is there something I should be afraid of out there in the woods?

"You'll see."

We turn, following the path through the trees, which narrows with every step. I lose track of time until, eventually, I'm not so sure we're even on a trail anymore. The brush gets taller. It comes to my ankles first and then my knees, making me wonder what lives in there, though I try *not* to think about those things, but to think about something else instead, like the soft stroke of his shirt against my arm as we walk or his deep voice saying, *You know, we could just kiss and get it over with.* I play it back in my mind a thousand times, fantasizing about how it will happen, about if it will happen. If it will be gentle, his soft lips grazing mine, my face cradled in his hands, or if it will be fast, frantic, urgent, our hearts wild, our breathing heavy, hands drifting.

Or if it won't happen at all.

If he'll decide at some point that he doesn't want to kiss me, that he doesn't even like me.

Branches scrape against me as we walk. Twigs pull at my hair. The sound of crickets is rhythmic, throbbing. I feel it in my chest. Daniel reaches for my hand, his warm despite the cool night. He pulls me closer to him, steering me through the trees and over fallen logs and exposed tree roots as if he's got night vision, as if he can somehow see in the dark. I hear him say it again in my mind, *You know, we could just kiss and get it over with.* And this time I fantasize about him stopping us where we are, about him turning and pressing me into a tree, feeling the knobby bark against my back as he leans in and kisses me.

"How do you know where you're going?" I ask.

"I just do," he says, and then he asks, "Do your parents always fight like that?" and though they're the last people in the world I want to talk about, it's easier than talking about things like boyfriends and kissing.

"Yup. Pretty much."

Except it's not true. It wasn't always this way. There was a time they got along, and I don't know if that makes things better or worse. Emily and Nolan were never the PDA type, but they used to like each other, I think—either that or they had the willpower to fight where we couldn't see or hear, which is unfortunate for Mae because they don't give a crap what she sees or hears now. Sucks being the third kid.

"Sometimes I wonder why they don't get a divorce when it's obvious they hate each other. It's not like there's anything wrong with that. People do it all the time," I say. What I don't say is that I wonder sometimes how long it will take for one of them to snap and actually kill the other, and that I wonder—sometimes late at night when I can't sleep—which one of them it would be, hedging my bets on Nolan because Emily's ability to provoke people and push them to the limit is next-level. Sometimes I think I could kill her myself.

"Does it bother you when they fight?"

"Sometimes. But mostly I just try to ignore it, to imagine I'm somewhere else."

"Like where?"

"I don't know. Anywhere they're not."

"How old are you?"

"Seventeen."

He says, "Soon you'll be gone and you won't have to listen to them anymore."

I'm counting down the days.

Except the way he says it—*soon you'll be gone*—is ominous.

He mocks Emily again. "*This is a family vacation. You're supposed to be with family, not isolating yourself out here.*" It lightens the mood. I laugh, but then he gets more serious and asks, "What would she do if she knew where you were right now? If she knew you were with me?"

"Ground me. Literally never take her eyes off me for the rest of the trip. Never let me go anywhere without her. Never let me see you again."

He says, "I wouldn't let that happen," and my whole body warms, because I've never had anyone in my corner like that, except for Skylar, but she's not my friend anymore, I don't think.

Daniel stops walking. He lets go of my hand all of a sudden, turning to face me, and I think that this is where it happens, this is where we kiss.

But we don't. Instead, he asks, "Wanna hit?" while reaching

into a pocket for a joint, which he lights, rotating the tip in the lighter's flame, the flame so close to his face that it illuminates it with an eerie glow, the fire reflected in his eyes.

I hesitate because I've only smoked weed like twice in my life—and only ever with Skylar, alone—watching as he sets the joint between his lips, a smoothness to it that I could never replicate.

"Is that a no?" he asks, pulling the joint from his lips, because of my hesitation. My throat tightens. When I say nothing, he says, "Don't be afraid. It's just you and me, Reese like the candy. No one will know. It will be our little secret." He cocks his head, asks with that same voice from before, "You have smoked weed before, haven't you?"

"Yeah," I say. "Of course."

"Then show me."

I take the joint. I press it between my lips. I breathe in, feeling my lungs instantly ignite. I fight the urge to cough though, inevitably, I do, and he asks, "You good?" grinning, his smile teasing and hot. He moves closer, setting one hand on the crest of my hip, lighting my whole body on fire, saying, "Don't worry about it. Happens to everyone," as if he can feel my embarrassment.

"I'm fine."

"You sure?" he asks, because I'm still coughing. For a minute, the clouds above us part, and in the moonlight, there is an intensity to his eyes, his eyes like black holes. He doesn't blink, not often, so that I have to look away to lessen the intensity of his stare.

"Yeah."

He takes the joint from my hand. "You've got to take smaller hits and slow your inhale, like this," he says, showing me, and this time, I watch. I learn, like he's the mentor and I'm his protégé. "Try again," he says, his voice patient but persuasive, so that

I couldn't say no if I wanted to. He holds out the joint. I reach for it, taking another hit, and this time, I don't cough. This time, a lightness blooms through my body, spreading to my limbs.

He sees it on my face and in my eyes.

"There you go," he says, smiling, pleased. "Good girl." He leans closer so I feel his breath on my cheek. He asks, "Can I kiss you now?" while reaching out a free hand to move my hair out of my eyes.

And I want to say yes. Kiss me. But again, I think of what Skylar said about playing hard to get, about how when you give guys what they want, they don't want you anymore. "Is this what you wanted to show me?" I ask.

He shakes his head, says, "No."

"Then no," I say. "Show me."

He stares too long, his face too close so that I think he's going to kiss me anyway and if he did, I'd let him. I wouldn't say no. I'd let him do more than kiss me. But then he doesn't. He takes the joint back. He takes another hit and then stubs it out, saving it for later.

We keep walking, down a small hill and eventually into a clearing, which I know, not because I see it (it's too dark to see) but because I feel the change in the terrain, the scrub no longer reaching out to touch my knees. The trees widen so that, all of a sudden, there's space. Breathing room. The air around us changes too, becoming heavy, moist, and the temperature drops.

He says, "This is it. We're here," and I stop dead, holding my breath, squinting and trying to see through the darkness.

"What is this place?" I ask.

I shiver, an actual chill moving up my spine, everything all of a sudden more acute. My shoulders jerk, which he notices, asking, "You feel that too? Not everyone does. I thought it was just me."

For the first time, I feel scared.

"Feel what?" I ask, though I do feel it. The sense that we're not alone. That someone, or something, is here with us, just beyond reach, just beyond what we can see.

He says, "The cold."

"Yeah," I say. "I feel it." I wrap my arms around myself, afraid to turn around and see if someone's behind me, because there's a different energy at my back all of a sudden. A felt presence, like someone is there. "What is it?" I ask, about the cold, thinking of the lake effect back home and how we must be close to the lake, and that's what's causing the change in temperature.

Daniel doesn't tell me, not in words. Instead, he shines his phone's flashlight just out in front of him and I make out names and dates on stone tablets before me. Millie Green. 1889–1925. Dorothy Frank. August 19, 1902–June 1, 1919. Janice George. 1912–1968.

A cemetery.

The chill in the air has nothing to do with the lake.

"They say it's haunted," he says, his voice toned down, doomy, so that I start to shake. "They say that sometimes, late at night, you can hear the sound of someone crying. And that some nights there's a girl in white, holding a baby and asking for help." I can feel his eyes on me in the darkness. "Are you scared?" he asks, and I know that's what he wants.

He wants to scare me.

He wants me to be scared.

"No," I say, except I am. "Because there's no such thing as ghosts." But as I say it, a sound like gnashing teeth, like driving on gravel, comes from behind and I flinch, spinning, crying quietly out as we both turn at the same time, staring into the darkness, searching but seeing nothing.

It doesn't matter.

I don't have to see it to know. Someone or something is there.

I picture her with long, flowing hair like cobwebs, a gaping mouth, hollowed-out eyes.

But then no one and nothing emerges from the woods and I start to second-guess myself. Maybe I didn't hear anything. Maybe nothing is there. Maybe it was just my imagination.

Except that he heard it too.

"How do you know?" he asks after a minute.

"Know what?" I ask with my back to him.

"That there's no such thing as ghosts."

"I just do."

Except I don't. Because after Grandpa died, I was pretty sure he came back and that he left coins for me on my dresser. I didn't know him, not really, because he had dementia for most of my life and half the time thought I was Emily and the other half that I was her mom, my grandma. Emily used to say how he collected coins his whole life, how he hunted flea markets for them, how he went to coin shows and auctions, how he kept them in hard plastic storage cases at home. She thought it was a dumb hobby, a waste of time. I thought it was cool. He always wanted to tell me about his coin collection and it was like the only thing he ever talked about that made sense. He couldn't remember my name or who I was—that I was his granddaughter even—but he remembered everything about his coins, like where he got them and what they were worth.

And then one day after he died, I came home from school to find three silver dollars waiting for me on my dresser, including a Morgan silver dollar, which, when I googled, was actually worth something, not anything life-changing, but something.

If he didn't put them there, then who did?

"Then what are you looking for, if there's no such thing as ghosts?" Daniel asks. He doesn't wait for me to say. "Don't be scared," he says then, like he knows I am, even though I said

I'm not. Like he can see through me, even in the darkness. He comes up from behind, standing so close that I feel his breath on my hair, moving it, the sensation making my stomach flip like when you're on a roller coaster, coasting out of control down the first big hill, free-falling, and my heart and stomach are somehow detached from the rest of my body, floating in space. That's how it feels. His arms wrap around me. He leans in, breathes into my ear, "They're not going to hurt you. They're harmless. They're just lonely and looking for someone to vibe with, like me."

He turns me around, putting his hands on either side of my face. He leans down, bringing his face closer to mine, and as he kisses me, it feels like getting caught in a rip current, like it's pulling me in, pulling me under, and all I can think about is don't fuck this up. Don't do something stupid.

Because girls like me don't get second chances.

COURTNEY

We search all day through the woods. I don't know how many miles we cover, but it's not enough. Because we have to be so diligent in our search, we don't cover as much ground as I'd have expected, as I'd have hoped. The forest is dense and covered with things like branches and leaves that we have to sift through to make sure we don't miss anything, that something isn't buried beneath.

As time goes on, what little hope I had of finding Reese wanes, and I resign myself to going back to the cottage with nothing—with no news, good or bad—when I hear a voice carry from fifty or a hundred feet away.

"There's something over there."

My back arches. I stand upright, turning to look, tenting my eyes with my hand to block out the lowering sun. I follow the direction of a man's hand as he points to something in the distance, seeing the wispy strands lift up from the grass in the breeze.

Without thinking, I start to run, a clumsy, desperate run, my feet kicking up dirt. I call out, my heart racing, my vocal cords tightening so that it comes out shaky and strained, "What is it? Is it her? Is it Reese?"

On the way, I step by accident into a shallow pit in the earth, my ankle turning. I fall and land on the ground on a hip, grunting; someone reaches out to take me by the elbow and help me to my feet, and I keep running, past trees and over fallen logs.

A group of volunteers forms a circle around it and from the looks on their faces, I know.

"Is it Reese?" I ask again, already starting to cry.

It's her. It's Reese. She's dead.

I stop just short, stumbling, taking in the vacant, glass-like eyes, the dried blood smeared on the dirt and across what's left of the flesh, though it's been sloughed off and torn away, flaps of skin lying beside the body in the grass.

The head has been detached from the body.

The bushy tail resembles human hair.

Whatever it is has been dead for days, its body hollowed out by maggots.

It's an animal, a fox or a coyote, though it's hard to tell, because parts of its body are missing, carried away by scavengers.

All I know for sure is that it's not human.

It's not Reese.

My legs give and I fall to my knees in relief.

But it's temporary, because we still don't know where she is.

I make my way out of the woods, feeling frustrated and berating myself because we didn't find anything and wondering if there was something *I* missed.

"We wanted to see how you're doing," Joanna says, coming to me. She and Sam hang back as everyone else starts to leave, while, around us, the people in charge, the incident command team, pack up supplies, like first aid kits, water, maps.

I feel demoralized. Beaten down. Any hope I had of finding Reese before the search began has been reduced, and I imagine how, in the next few minutes, I'll have to walk into the cottage and tell Elliott and the kids that Reese is still gone.

"I don't know," I say, shrugging. "Not great."

Sam and Joanna exchange a look. It isn't pity, but more like empathy because they've been where I am; they've been in my shoes. I don't have to tell them how I'm doing because they know. Joanna looks back, the expression on her face mirroring mine. "I can't think of anything worse than what you're going through right now," she says, and I feel thankful that she doesn't try to fill me with empty promises or false hope, but that she instead asks for my phone, plugging her own number into my contacts, in case I need anything, in case I ever want to talk.

"We live on Found Lake Road," Sam, beside her, says, his own voice gentle, subdued, and my eyes leave Joanna's to go to him as he offers a small, sad smile, his own eyes reddening as I imagine, in his mind, that all day as he searched for Reese, he spent reliving the day Kylie disappeared. "It's the only home you can see from the street, with a brown picket fence. Can't miss it. You're welcome anytime."

Tears prick my eyes. "That's kind of you, but I wouldn't want to intrude."

"You wouldn't be," he says, gazing softly at Joanna, who stares back, reaching for his hand, giving him the same sad smile he just gave me. "When we were going through this, we didn't have anyone. Lots of people were sympathetic, but no one really knows how it feels to lose a child until, God forbid, it happens. The least we can do," he says, bringing his eyes back to mine, his moist so that I feel overwhelmed with gratitude for them, but also sad for their own grief, "is lend an ear."

Detective Evans walks me to my car when we're through. I don't know what time it is or how long we've been out here, but long enough that above us, there are signs of darkening, sapphire and eggplant purple overtaking the once-azure sky.

"You were right," I say to him as we walk.

"About what?"

"That we wouldn't find anything."

He says nothing to that. Instead, he says, "We asked around about that boy you mentioned. The one Reese made friends with, with the snake tattoo."

"And?"

He stops walking and turns to face me. "That boy isn't a teenager, Mrs. Gray. He's twenty-four. And he hasn't shown up for work in two days."

My jaw slackens. Twenty-four. He's an adult. A grown man. Reese is seventeen. I don't know what the age of consent is in Wisconsin, and I don't know that they did anything more than flirt, but I do know that that seven-year age gap is almost half of Reese's lifetime. By the time I was twenty-four, Elliott and I were dating, if not engaged. I had gone to college and graduated and started my career.

Reese is in high school still.

"There's something else," he says.

"What?"

"The medical examiner determined a cause of death."

My body grows stiff. I tie my arms into a knot against my chest, bracing myself. I want to know, but I'm afraid to know. "What is it?" I ask. "How did they die?"

"Blunt force trauma," he says. "We found multiple skull fractures and crush wounds on both Mr. and Mrs. Crane's heads. Mrs. Crane had a severed spinal cord, and Mr. Crane's aorta had been lacer—"

"Stop," I say. "Please. Just stop."

I close my eyes. It's too much. Too many details. I don't want to know anymore. I press my hand to my mouth, trying not to picture someone hitting Emily in the back so hard it severed her spinal cord—cutting off contact between her brain and the lower half of her body, meaning that if she had lived, she would have been paralyzed—or Nolan so hard that his aorta, the largest blood vessel in his body, tore.

"I'm sorry," he says. "If it helps, we can assume their deaths were relatively painless. The disruption of brain function means that Mr. and Mrs. Crane didn't feel pain, even if they didn't die right away. They would have lost consciousness quickly."

It doesn't help.

I imagine them dying a slow death.

Of them lying on the cottage floor, paralyzed and bleeding out.

"Did someone break into the cottage that night or were they let in?"

"The door wasn't broken," he says. "It appears that someone either let the killer in or that the killer was already there, in the cottage."

I nod, my throat tightening. "What killed them?" I ask. "The object," I say, when he says nothing. "What is the blunt object that killed them? Do you know?"

He nods, though it takes a second for him to tell me.

"A baseball bat."

I wince as he says it, seeing someone, some shadowy, ambiguous shape standing behind Emily that night on the screened-in porch, the bat hoisted over a shoulder. I see him hitting her so hard with the bat—putting his whole body into it—that Emily's spinal cord severed, that her legs gave completely out, losing function; I see her buckle and collapse onto the floor, and I wonder if the injury to the head came next, after she was already incapacitated and lying on the ground, or if that came first, and if she was already bleeding and losing consciousness when she was hit in the back.

There is a bad alkaline taste on my tongue all of a sudden.

It doesn't matter how it happened. Either way she's dead.

"How do you know it was a bat? How can you be certain?" I ask.

"We found the bat," he tells me. "It was just outside the cottage, a black and teal alloy bat. A Louisville Slugger. It had blood on it still." He's quiet a minute, letting me process that. Then he says, "We compared the blood to Mr. and Mrs. Crane's blood. It was a match. There were prints on it as well. We're running those now."

I nod, despite knowing the bat will have all sorts of prints on it. Wyatt's, Reese's, Elliott's, mine. The police won't be able to glean anything from it, because every single one of us touched the bat that night.

It's dusk by the time I get back to the cottage. Over the last few minutes, the sky went from a medley of colors to a dark, saturated inky blue. As it did, a million glittery stars came out to dot the night sky, which is clear and moonless.

We don't see skies like this back home. Under different circumstances, it would be magical. I'd stand in marvel, taking it all in, never imagining there could be so many stars in one sky.

But tonight the darkness scares me, a creeping-up, closing-in sense of blindness, a blackening out of the world around me. I pull onto the gravel drive and park behind the police officer whose car is on, the engine idling with the window closed. In the side mirror, I just barely make out a reflection. The eyes, when they look back, are different than before. This is someone new, and though I can't see his whole face, I can assume from the width of him and the height of his head in the front seat, just barely skimming the ceiling of the car, that it's a man.

I look away. I gaze past the police cruiser and toward the trees, which are dense, dark silhouettes under the ink-stained sky. The police have finished their investigation next door. There are no more police cars parked at cottage number eight and no more cops raking the area for evidence. Most, if not all, the guests have left the resort. It's just us, as far as I know, though there is a light on in one of the cottages further down, and I wonder if someone is there or if someone forgot to turn the light off before they left.

Maybe we're not alone after all.

Maybe someone else is here.

I kill the car engine. I don't have to look to know that the police officer is still watching me in his mirror. I avoid his gaze, letting my eyes go to the cottage instead, where Elliott left a light on outside for me, a dusty iron sconce that sits to the right of the front door and gives off a dull light that moths and beetles fly circles around. But it's light nonetheless, and I'm grateful not to have to step out of the car and into total darkness.

I open the door and step quietly out, the night air terrifying as it wraps its cool arms around me. Outside, crickets have begun to surface, their high-pitched chirps screaming out into the night, the temperatures dropping with the sun. I close the door and make my way to the deck steps, which I climb, my fear swelling, feeling the officer's eyes on me from behind and not knowing who or what else is out here with me.

I walk faster toward the door. I reach out a hand to unlock it when, all of a sudden, the door swings sharply open and I gasp, dropping the keys, the sound of them hitting the deck brassy and loud.

Elliott stands in the open door, a dish towel in his hands. He looks out, his face softening when he sees me, quivering in the faint glow of the porch light. "Shit. Sorry. I thought I heard something and came to check. I didn't know it was you. I didn't mean to scare you."

Tears sting my eyes, rolling down my cheeks. Elliott pulls his eyebrows together, misreading my reaction, asking, "Did something happen, Court? Did you find her?" meaning Reese.

But I shake my head, wiping my eyes. "No," I say, feeling like a child for crying. "We found nothing. She wasn't there. I just . . . You scared me."

Elliott runs a hand the length of my hair and says, "I'm sorry. I didn't mean to." He pulls me into him, wrapping his arms around me, and I nod against his chest, feeling a slight chill as I imagine the police officer, watching us from the front seat of his car.

Elliott steps back, looking at me. I'm exhausted, my eyes heavy, swollen and red, though I know that even when I lie down, I won't sleep. I can't sleep. I'll lie there thinking again about someone circling the cottage, looking for a way in.

"Come inside," Elliott says, his voice tender as he takes me by the hand and tries pulling me in.

I pull back and say, "I'm coming. Just let me get my keys," as I bend down, lowering myself to retrieve my keys from the deck, where they landed beside Elliott's shoes. He took them off yesterday, leaving them outside because they were wet from fishing. Now the light from the wall sconce shines down on them, and in the pale yellow glow of the exterior light, I see something I hadn't seen before: pinpricks of red dotting the toe and the side of the rubber sole.

Blood.

I blink away, feeling the rhythm of my heart change.

"You coming?" Elliott asks, and I glance up to see he's gone further inside the cottage now, stopping to turn back and look for me. He stands there in a short-sleeved gray Henley and jeans, his hands in his pockets, his shoulders broad, days of stubble turning into a beard.

I try to be nonreactive, but my stomach roils, and I hate Detective Evans all over again for planting this small seed of doubt in my mind. Why would my first thought be that Elliott did something to Emily and Nolan instead of that he pierced himself with a fishhook or slipped and fell yesterday morning in the canoe?

I know my husband. I know he could never hurt someone. Never. He left our bed at five in the morning like he said to go fishing. Besides, Elliott loved Emily and Nolan as much as I did. He has no reason in the world to hurt them. None.

But in the same breath, some voice in the back of my mind asks *what if?*

"Courtney?" he asks again, his head tilted, his eyes tired like mine with dark circles beneath them.

"Yeah," I say. "I'm coming."

I sweep the keys up off the deck and follow him inside, taking one last look over my shoulder at the police officer before closing the door, separating us from the outside world.

The girls scramble down from the loft when they see that I'm back. They stand before me, their eyes wide and hopeful as they look around the room, excitement turning to doubt and then defeat.

"Where's Reese?" Cass asks, her voice crushed as, beside her, Mae lowers her chin to her chest and stares down at her hands when I say we didn't find her, that she wasn't there.

"I thought she was," Cass says. "You said she was."

I did say that. I told Detective Evans on the phone last night that I knew where Reese was, because I had seen her on the Snap Map.

"Well, she was, honey, at some point, we think. But she's not there now. We're not done," I say, my voice elevating with a modicum of hope for their sake. "We're still looking. The police are doing everything they can to find her."

I watch as Mae rubs her eyes before they turn in unison and climb sluggishly back up into the loft, with none of the same enthusiasm as when they came down. They fall asleep up there, watching a movie. Elliott carries his pillow downstairs and back to our bed to sleep with me. I stand at the bedroom door after Wyatt has gotten settled in bed, wondering if I should close it, if I should lock the door. I'm afraid, for many reasons, and know I'd feel marginally better with the door locked, but if the kids need me in the middle of the night, I won't be able to hear them.

Elliott lies on his side in bed, his head propped on the palm of his hand, watching me. "What are you doing?" he asks.

In the end, I leave the door open. I turn off the light, climbing under the covers and pressing into Elliott, letting him wrap his arms around me from behind.

As we lie there in silence, all I can think about is the blood on his shoes just outside the front door.

"What are you thinking about?" he asks after a while, as if he can sense it, as if he somehow knows.

I'm hesitant to tell him, not wanting it to come out as an accusation because I don't know how he'll react.

"There was blood on your shoes," I say softly, under the cover of darkness.

"What do you mean?"

"Outside, when I dropped my keys and leaned over to pick them up, there was blood on your shoes."

Elliott rolls me briskly over onto my back, suspended above me, though I can't see his eyes because of how dark it is in the room. His voice is astonished, louder than it needs to be with the size of the cottage and how close we are to the kids. "What do you think, Court? That *I* killed them?"

"Shhhh. No. Of course not," I say. I don't think that. Really, I don't.

"Then what are you trying to say?"

"I . . . I don't know. I guess I'm just wondering why there was blood on your shoes."

He sighs. "It's probably from the fucking fish, Courtney. Jeez." He drops down onto his back, lying flat beside me, our heads on separate pillows.

We're quiet for a minute. I breathe hard, feeling the rise and fall of my chest, feeling Elliott's indignation beside me like heat from a fire.

After a minute, I say, "I didn't know fish bled." I've never been fishing before and I don't know that I ever want to go. Killing something and watching it die isn't for me.

He's slow to respond, but when he does, I hear in his voice that he's no longer mad, that he's already forgiven me for the accusation. That's the way it is with Elliott. He gets angry and then he gets over it. "You bleed them."

"How?"

"Don't ask. You don't want to know."

"I do want to know. Tell me."

"By cutting the artery that runs through their gills."

"Why?"

"They taste better. And die faster."

I grimace. "I'm sorry I said something," I say.

"It's more humane. Honestly, Courtney. It takes seconds and then they're gone. It's better than suffocating to death."

"That's not what I meant. I meant about the blood on your shoes. I know you didn't kill them. God, of course you didn't," I say, rolling toward him. "My mind is all over the place. I just . . ." My voice cracks and I start to cry, quiet, choked-back tears, so the kids don't hear.

"Hey now," Elliott says, turning his body to mine.

I press into him. "I'm just so fucking scared," I confess, whispering as he strokes my hair.

"I know. Me too," he says, though those words are at odds

with his behavior. Elliott hasn't once seemed scared to me, and I wonder if it's because he's not or if he's trying to hold his emotion back for the kids' and my sake. He hasn't cried. He hasn't broken down like me.

I weep softly into his chest, thinking about Emily and Nolan, thinking about Reese out there all alone for the second night in a row, wondering what's happening to her, where she is and who she's with.

"I can't stay here," I say to Elliott.

"I know. I can't stay here either. Not with what's happened." There is a pause, and then he says, "But we can't go home. The police won't let us."

"We can't go home without Reese," I say plainly, getting hung up on the fact that I have to explain that to him. Elliott should know I'd never leave this place without Reese. Never. Even if the police said we could, I still wouldn't leave without her. I owe it to Emily and Nolan to find her, to bring her home.

"No. You're right. Of course we can't." He rubs my back, says then, his tone more solicitous now, making me wonder if I've been too sensitive, too critical, "In the morning, why don't I see if I can find a hotel nearby, somewhere else we can stay."

I nod, thinking it would help, to get out of this cottage.

"You really don't know why Emily wanted to talk to you the other night? You don't know what she was going to ask?"

He says, "I already told you, Courtney. No. If I did, I'd tell you."

Long after Elliott falls asleep, his breath becoming shallow, I lie awake, thinking through things, belaboring every moment of the past forty-eight hours: wishing I hadn't left Emily and Nolan's place when I did; wondering what a twenty-four-year-old man wants with a seventeen-year-old girl; thinking how fish blood isn't any different than human blood, how it's red like human blood and you wouldn't know the difference just by looking at it.

I can't sleep. I reach for Elliott's iPad on the bedside table to pass the time. I adjust the brightness so it doesn't wake him and then I go to his photos app to browse. Elliott likes to take pictures. Unlike me, who usually forgets, Elliott is the one who chronicles our life together. I scroll through the vacation photos on his Camera Roll, finding images of us around the campfire, a selfie of him and Cass by the lake and a picture of me that I have no memory of, taken when I wasn't looking.

And a picture of Reese.

Or rather, I should say, *pictures* of Reese. A series of them as if taken in quick succession, like the stop motion movies Cass used to like to take on my phone, positioning her LEGO minifigures so that, when played back, they looked like they were moving. The time stamp on these images is from five days ago at 12:03 p.m. The location: here. This resort.

Why does Elliott have pictures of Reese on his iPad?

My heartbeats become shallow.

The first few are clearly candid. She didn't know he was taking her picture, which is almost worse than if she did. In fact, it *is* worse. I think of Elliott sitting there, sneaking pictures of her on his iPad. It makes my stomach hurt.

But the last one takes my breath away. In the picture, Reese sits beside the pool in her little bikini. She's lying on her stomach on a beach towel, the cheap plastic chaise lounge chair slats leaving indents on her arms, propped on her elbows so that it's a straight cleavage shot, that hollow between her breasts chasmic, a beaded gold necklace lying over her collarbones, getting covered by her windswept hair. I can't get a good look at the bikini top, but I can see from this angle that the cups are cut short, the straps wide. The bottoms are higher waisted, but they have a cheeky cut so that you can see her bum, which she makes no attempt to hide, and I envy her, knowing how at my age, my skin has lost its elasticity, making the cellulite more visible despite being relatively thin. I'd never go around showing myself off like this. That said, even at seventeen and with a body like hers, I don't know that I would have had the guts to do it either.

But what gets me the most isn't the bikini. It's her face. The look on it, the angle of her head and the way her lips are parted. I can't quite put my finger on what it is, whether the look is emboldened, playful, flirtatious, angry or something else, something that cuts to the quick.

There's also the fact that she's flicking Elliott off with her finger, which feels so ballsy and inappropriate to me. He's her uncle. He's more than twice her age. I can't imagine ever behaving like that to an adult in my life when I was her age.

I imagine Elliott on the other side of the camera lens.

I imagine the way he looks back at her. The expression on his own face or what he said that would rile her up enough to merit her giving him the finger.

I remember that day—12:03 p.m. would have been about lunchtime. I had gone back to the cottage to make peanut butter and jelly sandwiches for everyone, to bring back to the pool for lunch. Cass and Elliott stayed behind, with everyone else. Cass was in the pool playing Marco Polo with Mae when I left; she didn't want to leave, and so Elliott stayed, sitting on a lounge chair, drinking a beer, keeping an eye on her.

I didn't mind. I don't swim and I was grateful for a minute alone. After days of being with extended family nonstop, I needed the quiet. It was bliss. No one was fighting. No one was talking at all. It only lasted two minutes before I heard the door handle turn and I looked up. The cottage door swung open. Elliott came in, tanned and toned and shirtless, bringing the smell of chlorine into the cottage with him. He kicked the door closed, saying nothing, but the single-minded look in his eye said all he needed to say. He crossed the room in what felt like three steps, and before I could even put the jelly knife down, he was behind me, his mouth on my ear, his hands moving under my gauzy swim coverup, lowering his own damp swim trunks, tugging aside my bathing suit. We didn't speak. What happened next was fast and urgent, so that I never had time to worry about whether the front door was locked, about if someone—Cass—might have followed him to the cottage, and that she might come in and find us like that, bent over the kitchen countertop. Before any temperance or self-restraint could kick in, it was over and I was left breathing hard as Elliott hoisted his swim trunks back onto his hips, grinning like a teenage boy before he kissed me gently on the cheek and said, "I better get back to the pool and check on Cass. Do you need any help with those sandwiches?"

It was so unlike him. Not that I minded.

Spontaneous and bold.

I wondered at the time what had gotten into him. I wondered if it was because we were on vacation, totally at ease, free from worry, spending more time together than usual, or if it had something to do with me and the fact that I'd been working out more, trying to lose the extra five or so pounds around my waist and hips, and he'd noticed. It made me feel good about myself, that my husband still found me so desirable after eleven years and a child together.

But now I think, looking at Reese's teasing, sun-kissed face on the iPad screen, I might know.

And it wasn't me.

REESE

Someone is awake when I come back to the cottage.

The shape is a silhouette, a black, featureless outline on the edge of my bed, which I see from just inside the front door. My hands shake and I start hatching excuses like that I couldn't sleep and decided to take a walk or that I was sleepwalking, that I went to bed and the next thing I knew, I woke up in the woods.

As I step out onto the screened-in porch, I make out Wyatt's smug face. He turns slowly to me in the darkness and I feel my heart beat faster, my temperature rise.

I slur in a whisper, "Get the fuck off my bed, loser."

He says, smirking in the moonlight so that I want to slap the smile off his ugly face, "It's not your bed."

"Yes it is."

"No it's not. It's the lady who owns the resort's bed." It's such a stupid thing to say. Still, he stands up like I asked. He hovers at the side of my bed, asking, "You want me to go?"

"Yes, you idiot. Get out."

"For twenty dollars, I'll go."

"Fuck you. I'm not giving you anything."

He shrugs. "Suit yourself," he says, stepping past me for the open door. He stops just before it and turns to face me. "I'll go, if that's what you want. But I'm sure Mom and Dad will love to hear about this in the morning."

"Hear about what?" I ask. "About you breaking into my room in the middle of the night like a creep?"

"No," he says. "About you sneaking out in the middle of the night to hook up with some rando."

I feel my whole body tense up. Heat fills it so that I could explode. My mouth is dry as I spit my words at him. "I'll tell them you're lying. That you're a fucking liar. That you're making it all up."

"Yeah," he chuckles, his sangfroid triggering as hell so that I clench my jaw, grind my teeth, curl my hands into fists beside me. "I'm sure they'll believe that," he says, and it makes me rage to know he's right, that they would believe him over me, even if it was only his word against mine.

But it's not only his word.

Because he has proof, on his phone. He holds it out so I can see, scrolling through pictures he's taken of Daniel and me together. They're blurry, but that doesn't mean they're not good enough to make out our faces. There are pictures of us standing close, smoking weed and standing in the cemetery together.

"It was you," I say, incredulous, taking in the dark, shadowy headstones in the background. "At the cemetery. You're what we heard."

Wyatt sneers. "*They say it's haunted*," he says, mocking Daniel, and I picture him crouched down in the trees, taking pictures of us. What I imagined as a ghost with long, flowing hair like cobwebs, a gaping mouth and hollowed-out eyes was actually Wyatt.

He followed me out of the cottage.

He followed us through the woods and to the cemetery.

He saw everything. He *heard* everything.

I feel sick. Embarrassed. Mad.

No, more than mad. I feel enraged.

When he plays it, the video is so much worse than any of the pictures.

How do you know? Daniel asks from behind me. We're dark, shadowy, but undeniably there on the phone's screen.

Know what? I ask, staring into the woods, almost directly into Wyatt's camera lens, my voice sounding different than the way I hear it, higher in pitch.

Daniel says, *That there's no such thing as ghosts.*

I tell him, *I just do.*

Then what are you looking for, if there's no such thing as ghosts? Don't be scared, he says after a second, coming up and wrapping his arms around me from behind. I don't want to watch Wyatt's stupid video, knowing what comes next. I try to look away, but he only brings the phone closer, shoving it in my face, saying, "You don't want to miss this, Reese. This is the best part," and I think how much I hate him. How much I fucking hate him.

They're not going to hurt you, Daniel says on screen, his own voice mellow and cool. *They're harmless. They're just lonely and looking for someone to vibe with, like me.* He turns me around. Shame seizes hold of me as I watch Daniel cup my face in his hands, as I watch him kiss me, as—even worse—I see myself kiss back, the wet mouth sounds loud as Wyatt slides the volume higher.

"Can I kiss you now, Reese like the candy?" he mocks, laughing hysterically, and then he makes kissy faces that make me literally want to puke. I feel dirty. Violated. Every special thing about tonight has been destroyed by him.

My mind homes in on only one thing in that moment. I ignore everything else.

I think only about obliterating the smile from his ugly face.

It happens before I know it's happening. I lunge across the room at him, grabbing him by the shirt, thinking how much I want to hurt him. How much I want him dead.

Wyatt loses balance. He stumbles and falls. It's not a fast fall. He tries catching himself, but he can't. When he goes down, I go down too, falling on top of him. Wyatt is bigger than me. He's stronger, an athlete, but I use my rage to my advantage. With him on his back, I climb on my hands and knees onto his chest, my knees digging into him as he squirms, not able to get out from under my body weight.

I see it in his eyes, fueling me at first: the fear.

Wyatt is scared.

Just beside me, on the floor, is the glass from the broken lantern. I reach out for it, snag a long, slender chunk of it in my hand, its edges digging into my own palm, the end of it razor-sharp and pointed, and I think of the relief I will feel as it perforates his skin. As it slips into his organs. As he bleeds.

I don't think about the repercussions.

I think only of what he did to me.

I raise the piece of glass above my head. I watch as he flinches and writhes beneath me, the scar above his eye still visible from last time. When anyone asks, Emily tells people it was from a baseball injury, but that's not true. It's from me. I did that to him.

All of a sudden, Wyatt gets a second wind. He fights back, pushing me off him so hard that I fall away. He jumps to his feet before I can get up, calling me names, saying stuff like, "This is why you have no friends," and, "This is why no one likes you," as he runs his hands through his messed-up hair and fixes his dumb shirt.

I lie there on the ground, gasping for air.

"The price just went up," he says, standing out of breath above me, looking down. "Forty dollars. Forty dollars or I tell, not just about this," he says, reaching down to scoop his phone up from the ground, "but all of it," meaning not just about Daniel, but that I tried to stab him too.

After he leaves, I lie there on the floor, my heart racing, wild thoughts filling my mind.

I wouldn't really have stabbed him with that glass. At least I don't think so.

I'm not capable of that, of *murder*, I don't think, though Emily made me see that therapist for a while because of poor impulse control. Because of *intermittent explosive disorder*, as the therapist called it in my diagnosis. Because of the angry, racing thoughts that would make me rage and slam my bedroom door and break things and say things that hurt.

That was when I was twelve. She said that, with therapy, I'd grow out of it. We talked about other ways to control my anger, like deep breathing and going to my "happy place" aka this hilltop I remember from when I was a little kid, where I picture myself lying on the soft grass at the top of the hill with nothing visible but the endless blue sky.

The therapist said the tantrums and outbursts would lessen over time and in severity.

I don't think they have.

COURTNEY

Somehow I must fall asleep.

When I wake up, it's hot in the bedroom. The windows are closed, and there is no air-conditioning in the cottage, so that it's unventilated and close. I wake up with a slick of sweat running between my legs and breasts, my thin shirt adhering to my wet skin. I push the covers off and rise from bed.

It's dark in the cottage. My eyes struggle to adjust, the blackness unbearable, so that I want desperately to turn on a light, but I don't because I don't want to wake Wyatt.

Alone, I feel my way to the kitchen. I run my hand along the knotty pine walls and then, when the wall ends, I put my hands out in front of me, casting around for the counter, touching it. I hunt for a glass in the cabinet, not bothering to run the water to let it cool before filling my glass and throwing it back.

All of a sudden, the floor behind me creaks, the sound of it like a rusty gate blowing shut on a stormy day. I jump, nearly letting go of the glass and dropping it into the sink.

I whirl around, just barely hanging on to the glass, gasping. Wyatt is there. He's not much more than a dark figure that I know is him by his shape: as tall as Elliott but much more slender with his hair in his face, a dark mass like a mophead.

I throw a hand to my heart, breathing hard.

I didn't hear him get out of bed, not the rustle of sheets nor the keening of the mattress springs as he rolled over and pushed himself to his feet.

"I'm so sorry, Wyatt," I whisper, turning back to set the glass on the countertop. "I didn't mean to wake you. I just needed some water."

Wyatt is quiet. Unresponsive. He stands there, motionless, and I ask, tilting my head, pulling my eyebrows together and searching through the darkness for his face. "Are you okay? Is there something you need?"

He's quiet at first, his breath audible in the stillness of the cottage.

"Come on," he says. "Hurry up or we're gonna be late for school."

School.

He breezes past me, and as I watch, Wyatt goes to the refrigerator, bumping my elbow as he passes. He pulls open the refrigerator door, the light from inside an advantage. "Where's my lunch?" he asks, searching the empty shelves, getting agitated because he can't find it. "Where is it? Where'd you put my lunch?"

When he looks at me, I see in the refrigerator light that, though his eyes are open, they're glassy, looking through me more than at me, and I realize then that he isn't awake. He's sleepwalking. And he's agitated about his missing lunch.

"Can you hear me? Or are you fucking deaf? I asked where's my lunch," he says, though I can't find the words to respond at first. I've never seen Wyatt sleepwalk. I've never seen him angry like this. I've never heard him curse.

My voice is gentle when I finally do speak. "You don't have to go to school, Wyatt. It's summer. We're in Wisconsin, remember?" I ask, trying to explain without saying too much so that it all comes snowballing back to him. Emily. Nolan. Reese. It doesn't matter. Wyatt ignores me; he bends down and looks into the refrigerator again and keeps searching for his lost lunch, shoving a gallon of milk and leftover macaroni and cheese roughly aside, and I let him, thinking maybe he will give up on his lunch when he can't find it and go back to bed.

But then, all of a sudden, he jerks his head to the side. He stands fully upright, staring hard at me. There is a tightness on his face, his eyes cold as ice.

He breathes fire when he speaks.

"I'm going to kill you if I'm late for school. It will be all your fault."

Kill you.

It takes my breath away.

Still, I move toward him. I set a gentle hand on his arm while easing the refrigerator door closed with my opposite hand because he doesn't mean it of course. He's just dreaming.

It's not like he's going to hurt me.

"Wyatt," I say, pulling him away, trying to lure him from the refrigerator, to wake him from his dream. "Your lunch isn't in there. You're not going to be late for school. You don't have to go to school. It's the middle of the night. You're dreaming. Come on, let's get you back to bed."

I grasp his arm more firmly in an attempt to draw him away and walk him back to the sofa bed. But Wyatt reacts. He shakes off my hand, pulling his arm fiercely back. It happens so fast that I can't process what's about to happen, I can't react. I don't even see it coming. Wyatt winds up and then, all of a sudden, there is the loud smack of him hitting me across the side of the face with an open-hand blow. The shock is overwhelming. I almost don't feel the pain of impact. I'm too stunned. My eyes water and, by instinct, my hand goes to my face, while at the same time, Wyatt rears back, positioning himself to hit me again.

"Wyatt!" I scream with everything I have, waking everyone else in the cottage.

From upstairs, Cass cries out, "Mom!"

Elliott, too, calls for me, stumbling from the bedroom in the darkness, tripping over something on the floor. "Courtney? What's wrong?" In the living room, he turns on a lamp, dousing the cottage in light, and for the first time I get a good look at Wyatt: shirtless, in Elliott's gym shorts, his hair a mess, the bones of his rib cage showing, though his arms are toned, his chest still bruised.

The ruckus, the noise, the light must wake him.

He comes to life, blinking repeatedly. "I . . . I . . . ." Wyatt stammers, his face bemused. He looks around the cottage, trying to make out where he is and what happened.

"You were sleepwalking," I say to him, explaining, struggling to catch my breath. "You're safe. You're with Elliott and me, remember? In our cottage." My heart hammers inside of me, my face now throbbing. I feel a bruise start to form on the upper cheekbone, the pain of it radiating all the way to my teeth.

Wyatt looks around. He's breathing hard in confusion and fear, a memory washing over him. "There . . . there was someone here. They were pulling me by the arm. They were trying to take me." His fear is acute. It's on his face and in his eyes, the wide-eyed, feverish look of someone who was, just a minute ago, scared to death for his life.

"It was a dream, Wyatt. You were just dreaming. You're safe." I set a timid hand on his arm, afraid of what he'll do, of how he'll react to my touch this time. "There is no one here. It's just Elliott, the girls and me. No one is going to hurt you, Wyatt."

"Someone was here."

"No," I tell him definitively, shaking my head. "No. It was just a dream."

His nod is hesitant and I can see on his face that he's not sure if he believes me.

Cass finally makes her way down from the loft, with Mae

just a step behind her, their eyes like slits as they adjust to the light. "What happened?" she asks.

"Everything is fine, honey. You girls go back to bed."

"But why did you scream?" Cass asks.

"I . . . I couldn't see where I was going. I ran into the corner of the door. I bumped my face. That's all. I'm so sorry I scared you. Mae," I say, looking at her. "Are you okay, honey?" Mae nods, her hair falling in her eyes as she does, but it's meek and unbelievable.

A knock comes on the front door then. Elliott goes to it and I turn away, knowing who it is but not wanting the officer to see my face. I hear Elliott say to him that everything is fine, that one of the kids just had a bad dream, and the officer, barely glancing inside the cottage to verify that Elliott's story is true, leaves.

Elliott closes the door. He gets the kids back to bed while I excuse myself for the bathroom. Standing before the dark wood vanity with its harvest-gold laminate countertop, I get my first look at the black-and-blue mark starting to form on my cheek. I lean in closer to the mirror. In the glow of the vanity lights, I see the red impression of Wyatt's fingers where they made contact with my skin, more bruised where the heel of his hand hit.

The door opens. "Cass asked to sleep with us. She's scared. Jesus," Elliott says, coming up from behind me in the bathroom, looking up and really seeing my face for the first time.

I turn to him. "I just . . . He was scared. I scared him. It's my fault. I should know better than to wake someone who's sleepwalking."

His expression changes. His head slants and his eyes widen. "Did he hit you?" he asks, astonished.

"It's not his fault," I say, rather than answering Elliott's question directly. "I think he thought that I was an intruder and that I was trying to kidnap him. He was protecting himself. After everything that's happened, you can't blame him."

There are tears in my eyes. In all my life, I've never been hit like that. My cheek smarts and I wonder, if it's already starting to bruise, what it will look like come morning and if by then it will be the full imprint of his hand.

Elliott steps closer to me. He sweeps a gentle thumb across my face and I wince, pulling back. "Does it hurt?" I nod. "Let me see if I can find some ice to help bring the swelling down."

I leave the bathroom for the bedroom, where I climb into bed beside Cass. Elliott goes to the kitchen, returning with a cool washcloth because there isn't any ice in the cottage; he leans over me and lays it gently on my face.

"Do you want me to close the door?" he asks, standing beside the bed before getting into it, lying on the other side of Cass like another defensive wall.

This time I don't hesitate.

"Yes," I say. "And can you lock it too?"

REESE

The thing about intermittent explosive disorder that people don't always get is that it comes out of nowhere and goes from zero to sixty just like that. Like one second I'm fine, and the next I'm throwing shit and screaming at people and it doesn't matter who sees or hears.

The other thing people don't get is that I feel guilty after, like when I wake up the next morning and think about how close I came to stabbing Wyatt with that glass, I feel bad. Embarrassed. Sometimes scared.

Sometimes it's just thoughts. Like when I'm driving through the school parking lot and kids are walking real slow right in front of me, blocking the way, being assholes, and I think about stepping on the gas, about running over them. I wouldn't do it. At least I don't think I would.

But there are times when it's not just thoughts. When I act on it. When that happens, it's like my body is on fire, burning from the inside out, spreading out of control across my chest, up my neck and down my legs and arms like wildfire. Or like when the Hulk transforms from Bruce Banner into the Hulk and goes all scorched-earth on everyone. That's how I feel. Like I'm not myself. Like I'm someone else, someone I have no control of. And then it's over and I shrink back down to Bruce Banner size, left with the guilt and shame of what I've done, knowing you can only say sorry so many times before no one believes it, before no one says, *It's okay, Reese,* anymore. Which is what happened with Skylar. I said sorry one too many times to count and she can't forgive me this time. Because swearing and kicking over a garbage can in the middle of physics on the last day of school with everyone watching—all because your friend made plans with a different friend and not you—is not cool.

It didn't help that someone in class got a video of me kicking over the garbage can on their phone. That they posted it to TikTok. That it was viewed thousands of times by the end of the day, so that even if Skylar wanted to forgive me, she couldn't. She couldn't be friends with me anymore, because by then everyone knew I was a freak.

When people saw me in the hall after that, they called me Robbie Gould, which, under different circumstances, would have been a compliment (greatest Chicago Bears field goal kicker of all time, according to Nolan). But they didn't mean it like that. It wasn't a compliment. They were making fun of me, referring to the way I kicked the garbage can, the way it went airborne, flying across the room, trash going everywhere.

They pointed at me and laughed. *Hey look, there's Robbie Gould!*

Some kids stopped me in the hall and asked for my autograph.

I almost felt sorry for Robbie Gould, that he would be associated with me.

Incandescent with rage. Seeing red. They're real things, not just idioms or metaphors or whatever. They're real. Because when I get mad enough, I feel hot, like I actually glow, a redness creeping into the periphery of my vision until everything I see is bloodred.

When I'm mad, I actually explode. Relief—release—comes first, followed by guilt, regret, humiliation, shame. Thinking everyone would be better off if I was gone. If I was dead.

Which is how I feel when I wake up in the morning and remember what happened with Wyatt last night, knots forming in my stomach as I lie there in bed, think about kneeling on his chest, about holding the chunk of glass above my head, and hoping something like that never, ever happens again.

Everything would be so much better if I was dead.

I leave the cottage before anyone else is awake. I go outside, dragging the door closed behind me, careful not to make any noise. I turn around, looking out at the world, which looks different today, and I think it's because of Daniel. Because I kissed a boy last night.

I smile without meaning to, without really knowing that I am.

Our cottage sits on top of a hill so that it overlooks everything else. Down the hill from us there are other cottages, which are quiet now, everyone still inside for the night. The sun is just coming up. It sits low in the sky, a giant glowing red orb on the horizon, surrounded by wispy gray clouds that I see over the lake, the light pouring sideways like spilled paint, turning the lake red.

The morning air is numbing. I jam my hands into my pockets to keep warm, and then I head into the woods, following the same path I took last night, trying to go back over my steps, to remember which way Daniel and I went to the cemetery, wanting to see what it looks like in daylight.

I thought finding it again would be easy. But the woods are different during the day. Even with the sun coming up, they're disorienting, almost as disorienting as they are at night, but for different reasons. Instead of seeing nothing like last night, all I can see are trees, though there are so many of them and they're packed so closely together that it feels like the trees are moving. There are no markers and no landmarks. There are only trees, which all look the exact same to me, tall and brown, the bark covered in moss, the roots exposed and lying on the ground like a disembodied hand, like Thing from *The Addams Family*, some of which I trip over, swearing as I lurch forward and then catch myself before I can fall.

The path is wide at first. It's easy to navigate. But over time it narrows, closing in on me until it's almost the exact same width of my feet and I wonder if it's a path at all or if it's just what happens when the grass gets worn down by enough people's feet. There are noises in the woods, which makes it feel like the woods are alive, like they have eyes. Rustling leaves. Falling pine cones. Squirrels.

And then there are the sounds of things I can't see.

When I get there, it hits different during the day, when I can actually see what's around me. It's less creepy and more sad. Tombstones surround me. They're matching and mostly old with square tops that sit sunken down into the earth. A broken chain-link fence wraps partway around the cemetery while, inside, some of the tombstones are cracked, the granite severed, and I wonder if it happened all on its own or if vandals broke them. They're smaller than I remembered. Their edges crumble. Moss grows like carpeting on them, staining the gray green. I take a closer look at the dates etched in the stone, most of which are ancient, though there are a few that aren't. Born: 1931. Died: 1972. Twin daughters of Dorothy Frank. January 3, 1926–January 3, 1926. Mother. Father. Beloved son.

Flowers lie on a Jessica Clarke's grave, which has no headstone, but only a flat marker, her name and the dates 1985–2019 etched in it, and I wonder what's so special about it that it has flowers when none of the others do.

I'm staring down at her grave when I hear a noise from behind and I jerk, turning around.

I'm not alone like I thought. Someone else is here.

The woman stands at the far end of the cemetery. I've seen her before. I know who she is. She's the same woman from the resort, the one who was in the lodge that day we checked in, who gave us our keys to the cottage. The sun comes up behind her, its glare making it harder to see. I put a hand to my eyes to block the sun, watching as she bends to lay a handful of pink wildflowers on someone else's grave (the same pink wildflowers as on Jessica Clarke's grave), their delicate petals lifting up in the wind.

I start to back away, but in my retreat, I step by accident on a stick. She hears it, throwing a glance over her shoulder. When she sees me, she turns around. "This is a private cemetery, honey," she says. "Didn't you see the sign?"

"What sign?"

"The one that says no trespassing."

I turn, looking for it.

"No," I say, looking back, shaking my head. "I didn't see it. I guess I got lost."

She watches me, her short, gray-streaked shag blowing in the breeze, neither of us speaking until she says again, "This is private property. You're not supposed to be here."

"I'm sorry," I say. "I didn't know. I'll go."

As she watches, I leave through the broken chain-link fence, though I don't go back to the resort like she thinks. Once I'm out of view, I step off the path, creeping deeper into the woods, and then I squat close to the ground, in the trees, making myself as small as possible and wait for her to leave.

Eventually she goes. I watch her leave and then, when I'm sure she's gone, I get back up and cross the small cemetery for the flowers she left behind.

When I come to them, there is no marker and no headstone, though the earth is somehow different when I look, the ground concave, the grass patchier than the rest of the cemetery, like someone dug a hole in it and the grass didn't grow completely back.

I wouldn't know for sure, except for the flowers, which are undeniable, like a buried treasure, X marks the spot.

If it wasn't for them, you'd never know someone was buried there.

COURTNEY

In the morning, I'm awake before everyone else. I slept for a few hours, but not well. It was a restless sleep. I get out of bed, careful not to wake Elliott or Cass, and go to the kitchen for coffee. I stand in the kitchen while it brews, looking out at Wyatt, sound asleep on his side on the sofa bed with his knees pulled into his chest so that his feet don't overhang the edge of the thin mattress.

Asleep, he looks harmless. His hair goes every which way and he has acne, not much, but some along the jaw and chin. He doesn't have any facial hair yet. His body is trim, athletic, quickly developing into that of a young man. Over the last year, he's grown four or six inches, if possible. His voice has gotten deeper too, to the point that there have been times in the past when I was speaking to Emily on the phone, heard Wyatt in the background and was convinced there was another full-grown man in their house.

No, Emily told me, giggling when I asked. *It's just Wyatt.*

My face hurts. It's tender to the touch. There is a dull pain, made worse by a headache, the kind that slinks up the base of my skull, wrapping around my temples, settling between my eyes.

Growing up, Nolan would sleepwalk from time to time. It's hereditary, though I didn't know it was something Wyatt did too. Emily and Nolan never mentioned it, and I wonder if last night was a one-off triggered by exhaustion and stress, or if it's something that happens often. Either way, sleepwalking is usually the kind of thing a person outgrows by the time they're Wyatt's age. With Nolan, it didn't persist past age nine or ten, I don't think. Our parents would find him wandering the house in the middle of the night and march him back to bed, and it was never a big deal; it wasn't even worth mentioning come morning unless Nolan did something hysterical that we laughed at.

I hear footsteps on the deck. I look up, my heart rhythm changing as someone raps their knuckles on the door. I hold still, thinking that, if I don't make any noise, whoever is there will go away. But no such luck. The knock comes again, more tenacious this time. Wyatt stirs in bed, rolling over, and I realize that I'd rather take my chances with whoever is at the door than have to face him alone before Elliott and the girls are up.

I go to it. I peel the curtain back to find Ms. Dahl from the resort, who I haven't seen in days, not since the girls and I ran for our lives to the lodge and she called the police. I pull the door open. "Good morning," I say, my voice still weary from sleep. Outside, I'm immediately assaulted by the cool morning air, the thin cotton pajama pants and camisole I slept in making me feel cold and exposed.

The lake is green this morning. Algae blooms sprung up as if overnight.

"Good morning. I hope I didn't wake you," she says as I pull the door closed.

"No," I tell her. "I was already up."

"I just wanted to check on you. See if there was anything you need."

"That's sweet. Thank you, but I think we're fine."

She turns her head, gazes up the hill and toward the cottage in the distance. "I also wanted to tell you the police finished their investigation next door. They've released it. You can go in if you want and get your family's things."

I look toward the cottage. This should be good news, but still, my stomach sours at the thought of going back in again. "Have you been inside yet?" I ask, thinking of Emily's, Nolan's and the kids' things inside the cottage and wanting them back, like the kids' own clothes and Emily's favorite go-to cardigan that she pulls on over everything when she's cold, which is almost always. I want it. I want to slip my arms into the shirtsleeves and wrap myself up in it.

"No, not yet. But I thought you might want to." She reaches out, holds out a flat metal key, which I take, curling it in my hand. Everything won't be there. The police will have taken things from the cottage too, for evidence, like their cell phones for example, if they found them.

Ms. Dahl quiets, her eyes examining my face. "Are you sure there isn't anything I can do for you?" she asks, her tone changing.

"I'm sure."

"What'd you do to your face?"

I touch my cheek by instinct. "Last night," I say, glancing away because I can't look her in the eye as I lie. "I went to get water in the middle of the night. It was dark. I couldn't see where I was going. I ran into the doorframe."

She stares too long.

"I didn't know doorframes had fingers."

I don't know what to say. I don't know if I should let her think that Elliott did this to me—which is what she thinks—or if I should tell her it was Wyatt.

"Actually," I say instead, my throat tightening, lowering my arm to my side. "I was going to stop by later this morning to let you know that we won't be staying here much longer."

"No?"

"No. I'm sure you can understand, but we can't stay here, given what's happened. My husband, Elliott, is going to see if there are any other accommodations in town with vacancy for us to stay."

"Let me save him some time. He won't have any luck," she says, her words catching me off guard.

"What do you mean?"

"I mean that most places around here book up months in advance. Some of them have been booked since last summer."

I nod, say, "Well, he's going to try. Maybe there was a cancellation," my voice hopeful. I cross my arms against my chest, feeling the morning breeze blow through me. Ms. Dahl turns to leave, but before she ever reaches the steps, I ask, "Can I ask you a question? About an employee of yours?"

She turns back. "Daniel," she says, before I can ask.

"Excuse me?"

"Daniel Clarke. Snake tattoo, right?"

"How did you know?"

"The police came around asking about him too."

"What did you tell them?"

She shrugs. "That he's a less-than-ideal employee. That if he was anyone else, I would have fired him by now. But I didn't hire him because he was qualified for the job. I did it as a favor to his mom, who I was friends with before she died."

I nod and say, "The police say he hasn't shown up for work in a few days."

"That's nothing new, honey. Daniel comes and goes when he wants to. Doesn't mean he had anything to do with all this. Daniel is mostly harmless."

Mostly.

"Do you know where he is?"

"The police asked that too. Hell if I know. I haven't heard from him. He's like a cat you let outside to roam. It's gone so long, you think it's dead—that a car or a coyote got it—but then one day, he just reappears as if no one was ever looking for him."

"Where does he go when he's gone?"

She shrugs again. "I don't ask and he doesn't say." She stops there. She frowns, clearing her throat, and I can see on her face and in her hesitation that there's something more she wants to say.

"What is it?" I ask, searching her eyes.

She starts to tell me, but then she stops and shakes her head. "No. I shouldn't."

I feel a desperation mounting, a need to know. "You shouldn't what?"

"I shouldn't say it."

"Say what? Please," I beg, reaching out to touch her hand, "if you know something, tell me."

She tilts her head to the side, says, "I'm sorry to be the one to tell you, but your girl's dead."

I gasp, letting go of her hand like it's hot lava, my hand rising to my mouth. "What?" I ask, breathless, shaking my head, pressure building in my chest. "What do you mean? How . . . how do you know?"

"Because this is what happens when girls go missing. They don't come back."

I don't understand at first. It takes a minute for her words to sink in, for me to process what she's saying. Ms. Dahl doesn't actually know that something's happened to Reese. It's hypothetical. An overgeneralization.

"Why . . . why would you say something like that to me, if you don't actually know, if you don't have any proof that Reese is dead? She could be alive. For all you know, she could be *fine*."

"Because it's best if you come to terms with that now, honey, so that you don't end up like that other girl's family, always looking, never done. I tried telling them that too, that their girl was dead. They didn't want to hear it."

I don't know what to say, how to respond to that. Instead, I say nothing, watching as she turns to leave and then, after she's gone, I stand on the deck, composing myself, trying to catch my breath, to convince myself that Ms. Dahl doesn't know anything, that she doesn't know what she's talking about, that Reese might still be fine.

I turn to go back inside. And that's when I see the cooler on the deck beside Elliott's rod and tackle box. It's what Elliott would have carried his fish home in the other morning after being out on the lake. It sits there on the deck beside his shoes.

I eye the cooler from a distance. I glance at the cottage door, listening for voices, for signs of life, and then, slowly, I step closer to the cooler. I hunch down, reaching for and unfastening the cooler's latches, wondering what a two-day-old fish cadaver looks and smells like, wondering if, after he bled the fish, Elliott cut off their heads or if I'll open the cooler to find their glassy, lifeless eyes staring back at me.

I hold my breath. I press a hand to my nose to fight off the smell.

I lift the lid. I peer inside, inhaling a sharp breath of air.

The cooler is empty, the rigid plastic interior spotless.

The door suddenly swings open. "What are you doing out here?" Elliott asks, rising above me. I gasp in surprise.

It takes a second to respond, and I wonder if, in that second, Elliott picks up on the lie. "I . . . I was worried about the fish. I didn't know how long they would stay good in the cooler. I thought about putting them in the fridge."

I stand up. As I do, Elliott takes a look at my face and says, "That looks awful. Does it hurt?" I nod. "I still can't believe he did that to you." He reaches out to move my hair, to get a better look at it. "I got rid of them," he says about the fish.

"I can see that. When?" I ask, my throat tightening, thoughts of Reese's picture on his iPad returning to me just then, of that day in the cottage and the peanut butter and jelly sandwiches. That feels like a lifetime ago.

"Yesterday when you were gone. I didn't think anyone would eat them."

I nod. He's right. These days, we're hardly eating anything at all. "What did you do with them?" Elliott gives me a quizzical look, lowering his hand to his side, and I say, "I only ask because I worry they might smell if you put them in the trash. They might attract bears."

"There's a Dumpster over by the lodge. I threw them in there."

I nod, my eyes rising, searching for it.

Maybe he did and maybe he didn't. How would I know?

REESE

Later that morning I step into the bathroom alone. I close the door, pressing the little push button to lock it, though it doesn't stay locked, because everything about this cottage and this resort (aside from Daniel) is actually defective.

I stand before the mirror, staring at my reflection. I think back to last night, to meeting Daniel in the woods, wondering if it was real, if it happened or if it was just a dream. Guys like him have never had any interest in me, which makes me wonder what he sees in me and if it's something others don't. I try to see myself the way he does. I like my eyes. They're green, which people say is one of the more attractive eye colors in the world, depending on who you ask. My smile is fine, a little gummy if anything, which makes my teeth look small. But I don't hate it.

That said, there are things about my face I definitely don't like, at least not when compared to other people I see online with their flawless skin, their perfect eyes and their perfect little lives. No matter how hard I try, I could never be like them. I've watched TikTok videos on forehead reduction surgery and nose jobs, imagining myself with a less bulbous nose that doesn't flare when I laugh so I have to cover it so no one sees, because of the one time a girl called me *Hoover*. I do, however, like my hair. It's one of the few things about myself I'm legit happy with, because it's low maintenance. I can get out of bed and go.

I step back from the mirror, so I can see more of myself than just my face. I listen, making sure no one's coming, and then I pull my shirt over my head and step out of my jeans. I stare at my body, at the way my sides curve inward and the crest of my hips, imagining Daniel setting his warm hand on one last night, leaning in, *Don't worry about it. Happens to everyone*, as I choked to death on the joint. I'm skinny, which most people think is enviable. But it's not, not always. There are things I don't like about being thin, like how people always assume I'm weak or iron deficient, or that I have an eating disorder, that I must be secretly bingeing and purging, or that every time I turn down food because I'm not hungry—or don't want to waste money on stuff like movie theater popcorn—it's because I'm actually anorexic. I'm not.

My skin is pink from the sun; it turns white when I press on it. There are lines from the bathing suit straps and red, swollen mosquito bites from getting eaten alive in the woods. I let my eyes go to the fine, delicate, tangled lines of the minimalist tattoo I drew myself. Skyler's cousin did the tattoos for us, because we're underage, because you have to be eighteen in Illinois to get a tattoo. But he was working as an apprentice at an actual tattoo shop and wanted to practice, so we said he could practice on us. We said we wouldn't tell if he didn't. It hurt more than I thought it would, but Skylar held my hand the whole time as I lay on her bed, a towel beneath me in case it bled, saying *Promise it will be worth it*, and then when it was done, she said, *It's fucking amazing, Reese. It's fucking hot*, and it was.

I close my eyes now, imagining Daniel's warm hands moving under my shirt, across my stomach to my ribs as they did last night when we kissed. With my eyes shut tight, I put my own hand on my stomach, and though it's not the same—I don't feel the same rush and my whole body doesn't explode in goose bumps—I retrace where his hand went, moving up my side, over my raised ribs, brushing against the side of my breast when, all of a sudden, the bathroom door handle jiggles violently and I throw my body against it to make sure the door stays closed.

Emily calls through the door, "What are you doing in there? Is everything okay? Other people need to get ready too, you know?"

She jiggles the handle again and I press my body harder against the door.

Rage fills me. I scream, "Can I not just have five fucking minutes alone?"

On the other side of the door, Emily goes quiet.

My heart pounds as I pull on the same high-waisted bikini bottoms I've worn for days to cover the tattoo, as I put on my bikini top and pink sweatshirt, as I open the door and slip silently past her, knowing she's still standing there, watching me go.

Aunt Courtney tells me, "Pink is your color, Reese." We're at the pool. We've just gotten here and so far the day is cold, like sixty-five degree cold. The only ones who want to go in the water are Mae and Cass. The rest of us sit on our chairs, killing time, waiting for the day to warm. Uncle Elliott is in the chair beside mine. Aunt Courtney is next to him, and then Emily and Nolan are on the other side of her, not speaking. "It goes well with your skin tone," Courtney says, and when I look, she's smiling over at me like she actually likes it, like she thinks I look pretty in pink. For a minute, it makes me feel good about myself. I smile back and say thanks, feeling my self-worth increase, because I'm not used to people saying nice things about me.

And then I hear Emily lean in and tell her how I went and ruined a perfectly good, fifty-dollar sweatshirt, how I mutilated it with a pair of scissors, cutting the neckline wide, and it ruins everything. Every. Fucking. Thing.

I feel crushed. Aunt Courtney looks again and this time she's not thinking how well the pink goes with the color of my skin. She's taking a closer look at what I've done to the sweatshirt and silently judging me.

I sit on my chair feeling sorry for myself, sulking, hating everyone here. I try not to think about them but to think about Daniel instead, and somehow my mind must manifest him, I must think him into existence, because all of a sudden Daniel's there, and when he appears, coming out from behind the little pool house, everything changes.

He stands on the other side of the pool, skimming the water's surface with a net, scooping dead bugs from the top of it before dumping them over the other side of the fence. As he does, he finds and watches me, his dark eyes so intense that I get chills. No guy has ever looked at me like that before. It makes me feel lightheaded, weightless. My mind starts to wander. I bite down on my lip, imagine a scenario where Daniel and I are the only ones at the pool (though the water is warm and it's not this stupid little pool but somewhere else, somewhere nice with palm trees). I feel my face and my neck get red, my heart beating faster at the thoughts that slide all on their own inside my head, thoughts of Daniel and me floating in the water together, of him wrapping my legs around his waist, leaning in, breathing into my ear, *You have gone all the way with a guy before, haven't you?*

From the other side of the pool, Daniel's eyes consume me. I have to look away and when I look back, he's still watching me. Someone comes and stands in front of me, blocking his view, and Daniel scooches aside. He moves to a different location to see me better, looking around this man, a smile building on his lips, the kind that makes me crush hard. I smile back, closing my eyes, going back to my daydream again, losing myself in it, telling him that *No, I haven't gone all the way with a guy before*, and in my fantasy, he shows me how.

"Reese, did you hear me?" Emily asks, and I throw my eyes open. I come to, my face red, my breath shallow, to find her on the chair beside me now, Uncle Elliott in the water with Mae and Cass, trying to get Aunt Courtney to go in too, but she says no.

I don't know how much time has passed.

"No," I say, embarrassed, swallowing hard. "I didn't hear you. What did you say?"

"That boy," she says, looking across the pool at him, making no attempt to be surreptitious, so that Daniel catches her staring and he looks away, pretends to be doing something else. "He was looking at you just now."

"What boy?" I ask, playing dumb.

"Over there. On the other side of the pool," she says, and I look.

"So?"

"Do you know him?"

"No," I say, shaking my head. "How would I know him?"

"I don't know. It's just the way he was looking at you . . ." she says, her words drifting, getting lost.

"What way?" I ask, though I know what way.

"I don't know," she says. "Like he knew you, I guess."

On the other side of the pool, Daniel moves closer to the pool house. He catches my eye when Emily isn't looking and gives a sign for me to follow.

"Where are you going?" Emily asks, as I swing my legs over the side of the chair, standing up. When I tell her I'm going to the bathroom, she says, "I don't want you going back to the cottage alone. I'll come with you."

She makes an effort to stand, but I say quickly back, "No," my voice firm before it softens and I say, "I mean, I'm not going back to the cottage. I can use the one in the pool house," as if last time I didn't refuse.

She stares too long. She looks to the other side of the pool, where Daniel just was, and then she looks back to me. "I thought you didn't like that one. You said it was disgusting."

"No, I didn't."

"Yes, you did."

"I didn't," I say again, and then I ask, "Are you really not going to let me pee?" walking away without waiting for her to say.

Daniel is waiting for me on the other side of the pool house when I get there.

"What was that all about?" he asks, looking past me, glancing around the edge of the building as if he can see Emily from here.

"What was what all about?"

"Your mom," he says. "Was she giving you shit?"

"It's no big deal. She just wanted to know where I was going."

"What did you tell her?"

"That I was going to the bathroom."

He makes a sound under his breath. "You can't even go ten feet without her wanting to know where you are?" he asks, getting angry, and then he echoes again, *"This is a family vacation. You're supposed to be with family."*

He laughs, but it has an edge.

He beckons for me to come closer then, hooking me in with his finger. When I get close enough for him to reach me, he reels me in by the arms and says, "You're almost eighteen, and then you can do anything you want."

I nod, holding in a smile as he puts his finger under my chin, as he lifts my face to him.

He says, "I can't stop thinking about you. All day, all I've been thinking about is you."

My cheeks glow. He leans down to kiss me then. It's soft, gentle. He reaches up and runs his hands over my hair. "I dreamed about you last night. Is that weird?" he asks, pulling back, and I grin and say no, feeling butterflies in my stomach.

In my whole life, no one's ever dreamed of me before. No one has so much as thought about me before. I wonder what I was doing in his dream, but I don't ask.

"I can't believe you don't have a boyfriend yet," he says, and I smile again. He smiles back, telling me he likes it when I smile before saying something that makes me laugh, and I think of the quizzes Skylar and I used to do, about how to tell if a guy likes you. Do you find him staring at you in a room? Does he find reasons to touch you? Does he try to get you alone and does he tease or compliment you? Does he make you laugh?

Daniel likes me. I just don't know why.

When he steps back, he asks, "Meet me by the beach again tonight, on the pier?"

"I'll try," I say, thinking of Wyatt and wondering how I'll get out of the cottage without him finding out. It's not just Emily and Nolan I have to worry about anymore. It's him too. "If I can."

Daniel draws back. He lowers his head all of a sudden, cocking it to the side, his eyes looking down like he's hurt. "Don't you like me?" he asks, his voice vulnerable, his smile nervous now, like he thinks I might really not like him, and I wonder in what world a girl like me would ever turn down a guy like him.

"Of course I do," I say.

"Then come," he begs. "If you like me, you'll come. Meet me on the pier."

I know I have to do whatever it takes to be there.

COURTNEY

Elliott takes the car, driving around town to see if there is vacancy in another resort, despite Ms. Dahl's telling us there wouldn't be any. I'd be lying if I didn't say I felt marginally relieved for him to leave, feeling unsure about many things, but none more than the picture of Reese on his iPad. I want to ask him about it, to know why he took this picture of our niece, but then I see him last night, rolling me briskly over on my back in bed, asking *What do you think, Court? That I killed them?*

Of course he didn't, I tell myself. Elliott wouldn't do that. There's another reason for it.

Cass wakes up after he's gone, emerging from the bedroom in a daze. When she sees me for the first time today, she pauses, asking again what happened to my face and I have to say the same lie about how I ran into the door in the dark, watching Wyatt out of the corner of my eye to see if he has any reaction to it, but he doesn't.

I pull my robe on over my pajamas. I split the last of the cereal and milk among the three kids. I call them to the table to eat and then I pour myself more coffee and stand in the kitchen with my back to the countertop, watching them peck at their food, swirling the cereal around in the milk like tiny ships on the lake. They're all despondent, and I want to say something comforting or uplifting, but I don't have it in me. The energy isn't there. The words aren't there either, and even if they were, they would lack conviction. The kids would know I was lying.

The kitchen is silent, the only sound the occasional ding of the metal spoons striking the ceramic edges of the bowls. There is a fly in the cottage with us. Occasionally it will buzz, quietly thumping against a closed window to get out, drawn to the glass by the light and warmth. In the corner of the room hangs a ribbon of twirly flypaper with at least a dozen gnat and fly carcasses on it. In a different life, I would catch the fly and let it out of the cottage before it can get stuck to the paper and die. But not now. Now I watch it thrash against the glass, unable to find the energy to steer it into a jar and let it out.

The sense of being watched is sudden but strong. I turn to find Wyatt staring at me.

"Do you need something?" I ask, my voice unsteady, my heart thrashing in my chest like the fly against the glass.

I'm going to kill you if I'm late for school.

He lowers his eyes to his bowl without answering. I watch him for a long time, and then I gaze up and out the window just in time to see Detective Evans pull up to the cottage. I set my coffee on the counter and I leave out the front door, grateful for the reprieve, to be able to get away from Wyatt and the deathly quiet of the kitchen.

Detective Evans and the other officer are talking when I come outside, Detective Evans leaned down and speaking to him through an open car window, their laughter like a thousand knives. "Did you find anything?" I ask, interrupting, not waiting for a reply before I ask, "Like Daniel Clarke? Did you find him?" Detective Evans sobers. He stands up, turning to face me as I stand on the deck, far enough away that he can't see the swollen handprint on the side of my face, using my hair to hide it.

Detective Evans cocks his head and says, "I don't remember

telling you his name." When I say nothing, he says, "But, to answer your question, we went by his house. He wasn't there. We're still looking for him."

I let my gaze go around the property, which is now desolate. "Everyone in the resort has checked out and left. We're the only ones here. Why did you let them leave? How do you know one of them, another guest, didn't do this?"

"We spoke to everyone who was here. No one had motive and everyone had an alibi. We told them they could leave." He crosses his arms. "Forensics has finished their investigation next door. There are a few things I wanted to update you on."

"Such as?"

He looks at Emily and Nolan's cottage, and then he looks back at me, matching my energy. "Such as that they found a knife in the cottage."

"Where?"

"In a nightstand drawer on the porch. There was blood on the blade that didn't belong to either of the victims."

My heart pounds. I picture this knife, though I've never seen it and I don't know what it looks like. Still, I picture a long, honed blade with crimson blood dripping from the tip. "Is it Reese's?" I ask, and then, without giving him a chance to respond, I ask again, clarifying my question, "Does the blood belong to Reese, Detective?"

"We don't know. We're comparing the blood to hair samples we found on a brush in the cottage, to see if the DNA matches. There were two sets of fingerprints on the knife," he tells me. "Again, neither belonged to the victims. There were prints found elsewhere in the cottage, some made with blood," he says, giving me a minute to let that sink in, to process it, to envision bloodied fingerprints all over the cottage walls. "We'll need the five of you to come to the station today, to get your fingerprints taken."

"*Our* fingerprints?" I ask, unable to hide my disbelief. "Why would you need those?"

"So we can eliminate your prints from the ones we found in the cottage," he says, though I wonder if that's the only reason.

Maybe this other police officer hasn't been here all night to keep us safe, but to keep us under surveillance.

"You think one of us did this. Are we suspects, Detective?"

"I didn't say that, Mrs. Gray. I said for elimination prints."

"You haven't made any progress at all then," I decide. "You're no closer to finding my niece or the person who killed my brother and sister-in-law than you were a day ago."

He stands taller, squaring his shoulders and putting his hands on his hips. "We are making progress. We have Mr. and Mrs. Crane's phones now, which we found in the cottage, and we're searching them for information."

"What kind of information?"

"Text messages, emails, call history, browsing history, location data. Cell phones," he says, "can be a wealth of information."

"What about Reese's phone?"

He shakes his head. "No. I'm sorry. Without her phone, it's harder to get information from it. We've tried pinging the phone," he says, explaining to me what that means, how the cell phone carrier sends a signal to the phone, asking it to reply with its location. "But if the phone is off or dead, then it's not useful to us. It's just a dead thing in her pocket."

"But what if the phone isn't off or dead?" I ask, thinking how she appeared the other night on that Snap Map, though that was thirty-six hours ago now, so any charge she had left at that point would be gone by now, if she isn't in a position to charge it.

"The results can still be imprecise. We can track phones to a broad area, and not always an exact location. I promise you,

Mrs. Gray, we're doing everything we can to find her and bring her home."

I nod, my heart sinking.

The world feels suddenly so vast and, in it, Reese so small. I feel scared for her, but then, in the next breath, I think of the girl in that picture on Elliott's iPad, the gritty, unafraid look on her face, flicking Elliott off, and wonder if I should feel scared for her, or if I should feel afraid for everyone else.

I hate you. I wish you'd die.

I see the answer on Elliott's face when he comes back to the cottage an hour or so later. "They all say they've been booked for months," he tells me, looking chastened—as if it's somehow his fault that there isn't vacancy in the other resorts—tossing the car keys onto the kitchen counter with a clang.

"There was nothing?"

"No," he says. "Not quite nothing. There was one place. A motel. It had vacancy, but it looked like a rathole, Court. I don't think you want to stay there. We may just have to make do here."

"How much longer do we have to stay?" Cass asks, hearing him, her voice whiny in a way that gets under my skin. "I want to go home."

Wyatt looks up from his phone with such suddenness that I hold my breath, worrying about what he might say or do to Cass. I speak first, before he can. "We all want to go home, honey. As soon as we find Reese, we can."

"Then why aren't we looking for her?" she whines. Beside her, Mae is quiet, her face puffy from another night of crying herself to sleep.

"The police are, Cass. They're looking for her."

I glance around the room. This cottage is small, musty. Now that the windows are always closed and locked, the air suffocates me until all I can think about is the dank, stale smell, knowing there must be mold in here somewhere. The cottage is seven or eight hundred square feet at best with a single bathroom; it was on the small side when we first checked in, but now there are five people living in it, and nothing about it is homey or inviting anymore. It's our prison.

I reach for my coffee, which has no doubt gone from lukewarm to cold, but is still caffeine. I lift it to my lips, but before I can sip, I see the fly from before, dead and floating in it, its black body bobbing on the surface like a buoy.

My stomach roils. I set the mug down, feeling physically ill at the idea of staying here in this cottage any longer. But we can't leave, and there's nowhere to go, not until we find Reese and the police find Nolan and Emily's killer.

I curl my fist around the car keys lying on the countertop. "I'm going to run out for a few things."

"Where?" Elliott asks, looking sharply up, surprise in his eyes. "For what?"

I hold his eye. "I used up the last of the cereal and milk this morning for the kids. I'm going to run to the store and stock up on a few things."

I don't like lying to him. But if he knew where I was going, he wouldn't want me to go.

REESE

That night after everyone's asleep, I sneak into the cottage from the porch and then out the front door, Venmoing Wyatt twenty bucks in advance to keep quiet.

I move through the woods alone. When I step out of the trees, I find Daniel's dreamy, out-of-focus face hazy against the backdrop of the night sky, which is spotted with a million tiny stars.

Tonight, he stands on the end of the pier, as promised, waiting for me.

"Hey," he says.

"Hey," I say back. I step onto the pier. As I do, it sways and I hesitate, afraid and wondering if it can hold us both.

"You're okay. I won't let you fall," Daniel says, reaching for me. I go to him, feeling anchored and safe in his arms.

Once there, I tell him, "I found the gift you left me."

"What gift?" Daniel asks, smiling, giving himself away.

When we came back from the pool today, there was a flower waiting for me on my bed, which meant only one thing: that when we were gone, Daniel was there, inside the cottage, that he let himself in with his key, that he was still thinking about me. It made me happy. For the rest of the day, I found myself grinning at nothing. Mae asked what I was smiling for. I told her I wasn't, and then, when she wouldn't shut up about it, I asked, *What? Am I not allowed to smile?*

She giggled and said, *I thought you weren't smiling.*

"That wasn't from you? Oh," I say, giving him a gentle shove, knowing I've never done anything like this before, I've never flirted with a guy like him in my life. I feel different, like I'm not me, but someone better, someone new. I grin and say, "Must've been from one of the other guys I've been sneaking out at night to see."

He wraps his hands around my wrists and whispers into my ear, "You better tell all those other guys to get lost, 'cause you're mine," and I feel a rush of adrenaline as he says it, thinking of all the boys from back home that never liked me. If only they could see me now.

Daniel and I lower ourselves to the end of the pier, where we sit with our legs dangling over the edge. The night is clear, though the lake itself is so dark I almost don't know it's there.

"You drink, don't you?" Daniel asks, as he pulls a can from a six-pack's plastic rings and holds it out to me, though I hesitate because it's hard to see what I'm reaching for in the dark.

"Yeah," I say. "Of course."

"You sure?" he asks, because of the way I hesitate.

"Yeah."

I do drink, but I almost never drink beer. I don't like it. I hate the taste of alcohol, and so, when we want to get drunk, we get the cheapest, most disgusting vodka we can find to get drunk fast. Skylar has a thing for the flavored vodkas like Burnett's, which her cousin buys for us, and then we sit in her bedroom taking shots out of the bottle before we go to parties that she was actually invited to (I just tag along, and as long as Skylar's there, no one really cares), though that was before, when we were still friends and people didn't think of me as a freak.

"Then let's see," he says.

Sitting beside me, so close that our legs almost touch, he cracks open his can, waiting for me to copy, which I do. I try not to think about the taste as it goes down, about how much I don't like it. Uncle Elliott was the first person who let me drink beer, when I was about nine. I remember still, him holding out his glass when no one was around, grinning, a mischievous look in his eye. *Wanna try?* he asked, and I did. I didn't like it. I almost spit it back up. He laughed and told me it was an acquired taste, that I'd get used to it one day. *Same with boys*, he said. *You think they're gross now. Just wait.*

He was right.

"I went back to the cemetery today," I tell Daniel as he slides closer to me on the dock so that our legs actually do touch.

"You did?"

"Yeah."

"Why?"

"I wanted to see it in the daytime," I say.

"And?" Daniel asks.

"It's not haunted like I said. And there's an unmarked grave."

He hesitates. "I don't know anything about that," he says, taking a long swig of his beer before setting the empty aside and tugging another from the plastic ring. He offers me one, but I say no. "Don't you like it?"

"No, I do," I say, because I don't want him to think I'm ungrateful or that I don't like his beer. I lift mine to my mouth to show him, to prove it to him, and after a few sips, the beer goes down easier so that my edges start to blur.

"I have something for you," he says.

"You already gave me something," I say, meaning the flower on my pillow.

"This is something else, something better. Close your eyes

and hold out your hand." I do. When he says, "Open your eyes," I look, reaching into my hand and holding it up to the moon to see: a gold chain with beads.

I don't know what to say. No one has ever given me something like this before.

"What's this for?" I ask, as he turns me around, as I lift my hair and he fastens the chain around my neck, the soft stroke of his hands on my neck making my heart race. I look back at him and say, "You didn't have to get me anything."

"I know I didn't have to. But you like it, don't you?"

I touch the necklace. "Yes," I tell him. "It's beautiful."

"It's because I like you. A lot," he says with a smile in his voice. "I'm actually kinda obsessed with you." I hesitate, only because no guy has ever said something like that to me before. In my whole life, I've never had someone so super into me, or even remotely into me. I don't know what to say. I don't know how it feels to be liked by a guy, because it's never happened.

He lowers his head. The look in his eyes is hurt and then he turns away, gazing out over the lake.

He says, his voice quieter now, "If you don't like it, you don't have to keep it."

"No, it's not that," I say, scrambling for words. "I told you I did. I said that it was beautiful."

"What then?" he asks, taking it the wrong way, feeling rejected. His eyes come back to mine and he asks, "You don't like me?"

"No," I say, speaking fast, reaching for him. "I do."

"Do you? Or are you just saying that because you don't want to hurt my feelings?"

"I do. I like you, Daniel," I say. "A lot."

He hesitates, not sure if he believes me at first, and then he softens. He smiles. He squeezes my hand and says, "I like you a lot too." He stares at me. He reaches out to stroke my cheek, angling his body toward mine. He says, "I think I could fall in love with you, Reese like the candy." And I say nothing because I can't breathe. I can't think. "It's too soon, right?" he asks, laughing at himself, something self-deprecating that only makes me like him more. "You probably think I'm crazy. We've only known each other a couple days, if that. It's just that I've never met a girl like you. And when you know, you know, right?"

"Yeah," I say, breathless. When you know, you know. "It's not crazy," I say. "I've never met anyone like you either." When I smile, he leans his face down to mine. We kiss, moving fast, not letting a second go to waste. We stay outside like that, kissing on the end of the pier until color creeps back into the edges of the nighttime sky.

Only then does he walk me home. He waits outside the cottage while I go in, and after he leaves, I lie in bed, wondering if this is real or not, if it's just a dream, and if, when morning comes, I'll wake up to find it never happened.

Because it feels almost too good to be true.

COURTNEY

Found Lake Road is narrow, winding and wooded. As I drive down the street, the brown picket fence gives it away though, like Sam Matthews said, it's the only home you can see from the street, the rest with long, private gravel drives that sit hidden behind dense and overgrown trees.

I park in the driveway and get out of the car, hearing the drum of a woodpecker striking a tree, though the woods are so deep I can't see it. Sam answers the door when I knock, his face broken up by the fiberglass screen.

"Courtney," he says, surprise in his voice that I took him up on his offer and came. I realize then that he wasn't expecting it, which makes me feel guilty for not calling first, but accepting the invitation and wondering now if it wasn't so much an invitation as a polite gesture.

"Hi, Sam. I'm sorry to just stop by like this. Is this a bad time?"

"No. Not at all." His kind smile puts me at ease. "I told you you were welcome anytime. Joanna's just in the basement, doing laundry. Let me get her for you." He turns away, going to the basement door and calling down for Joanna, who comes up, smiling but short of breath from the steps.

"Courtney. Hi. Please, come in. Excuse the mess," she says, coming and pushing the screen door open for me, gasping as she takes in my face. "Oh my God. What happened?" she asks, Sam looking too and seeing it for the first time, his expression changing to concern.

By instinct, my hand goes to the bruise. "It's not what you think. It was an accident. My nephew, Wyatt, was sleepwalking. I tried to wake him. I should have known better. They say not to wake up people who are sleepwalking, that they can become disoriented and lash out by mistake."

"He hit you?" Joanna asks, stunned, her eyes wide.

"It's not like that," I say. "He was having a dream. I don't even know if he knows he did this."

They're both quiet, not sure what to say, processing what I've said. For a moment, they lock eyes, and then Sam suggests, "Why don't I go finish the laundry and let you two talk."

She nods, and then to me she says, "Please, sit," as he leaves, Sam pulling the basement door closed behind himself before I hear his heavy footsteps jog down the stairs. Joanna takes a chair for herself, offering me the sofa, and then she leans forward in her seat so that her elbows are on her knees, asking, "Has he done this before?"

"No," I say. I shake my head. "I don't think so. My brother and sister-in-law never mentioned Wyatt sleepwalking, though my brother was a sleepwalker when he was young, so maybe. I've heard it runs in families."

Joanna is quiet at first. She's circumspect. She visibly hesitates, angling her head the opposite way and then leaning back and crossing her legs before asking, "What I meant was, has he hit you before?"

The question takes me by surprise. I inhale a long drag of air, sitting up straighter on the sofa. "No," I slowly breathe out. "God, no. Never. Wyatt isn't like that. Like I said, he was having a bad dream."

She nods. "Have you heard anything from the police?"

I tell her what I know, which isn't much. "I want more," I say, my sigh heavy, frustrated with the lack of progress. It's been forty-eight hours now since it happened. The first forty-eight hours are the most critical time in finding a missing person. I know the stats; I've looked them up. The more time that goes by, the likelihood of finding Reese dead, if at all, increases.

"I know how you feel," Joanna says. "Waiting is the hardest part. It's excruciating. So many times we thought we were onto something only for it to turn into a dead end. People would call the police station and claim they saw Kylie somewhere—the library, some street corner, on a bus two hundred miles away—but when we went to look, she was gone. Or surveillance footage that turned out to be someone else. Tracing shoe print patterns through the woods, only to find out they belonged to someone with an alibi or that the prints themselves were inconclusive. We'd get our hopes up for nothing, over and over again. It broke our hearts. It made Sam and me crazy. We wound up turning on each other, because we had no one else to take our frustration out on, and we needed someone to blame."

"What do you mean?"

Joanna pauses, throwing a glance over her shoulder to be sure Sam is in the basement still and can't hear. When she speaks, it's thoughtful, slow, thinking carefully through her words, her voice low. "When Kylie disappeared, I wondered if Sam had something to do with it."

"Why would you think that?"

I watch as she gazes down at her hands, turning her wedding band around and around in circles before saying, "He had gotten home late from work that night. When I asked why he was late, he said there was a freight train stopped on the tracks. But I wasn't sure I believed him, because Sam is almost never late. It seemed too coincidental that it would happen on that night of all nights."

"What did you do? Did you tell anyone?"

She lifts her eyes to mine and admits, "Yes. I told the police." Her shame is evident, making me think of the blood on Elliott's shoe, the photo of Reese on his iPad, him rolling me briskly onto my back. *What do you think, Court? That I killed them?* Maybe I'm just looking for someone to blame. "They looked into it. There is no worse feeling in the world than telling the police you think your husband may have had something to do with your daughter's disappearance. It didn't make sense. There was no reason for it. Sam loved Kylie more than anything in the world. He never would have hurt her."

"What did the police say?"

"It just so happened there was a camera at that train crossing. The police looked at the surveillance footage. Sam," she explains, looking so sad my heart breaks, "*was* telling the truth. He was there. The police saw his car and they saw him—his face—through the windshield. His worst transgression was being on his phone while driving, because there was, indeed, a train stopped on the tracks, just like he said."

I ask, "Did he know you went to the police?"

"Yes. The police spoke to him. They asked him questions."

"Was he upset?"

"No. Sam almost never gets upset. He said he understood. He was so forgiving, in fact, that I hated myself for days for even thinking it. If anyone was to blame, it was me. I was the only one home at the time, and Kylie was supposed to be here with me. She'd gone to her friend Abby's house that day. She rode her bike there, and then later she left on her bike to come home. Her friend saw her leave. Abby remembers how they raced down the street, until eventually she stopped and waved, and Kylie kept going, riding away with no hands, so that I've had this image of Kylie for all these years, laughing, tempting fate, her arms held out to the sides, her hair getting carried by the wind."

I picture that, and the image gets cemented in my mind.

"The night that Kylie disappeared, I told her to be home by five o'clock for dinner. She never came and at first I was upset that she didn't listen, that dinner was getting cold on the table and that neither she nor Sam was home to eat it," she says, pausing before going on. "I don't know if I can ever forgive myself for that. For being angry at her instead of knowing that something was wrong, that something terrible was happening to my child in that moment."

"How would you have known?"

She shrugs. "I don't know. Instinct? Sam never blamed me. He was never angry that I sat here all that time, feeling upset, instead of getting in my car and going to look for her or calling over to Abby's house to ask her parents to send Kylie home. I should have known. Kylie was never late. She was always so responsible. It wasn't like her to be late for dinner. I've wondered all these years—if I had gone to look, would I have been able to stop whatever happened from happening?"

"You can't blame yourself, Joanna."

"I can. They found her bike three days after she went missing, in the woods. They never found her."

Tears fill her eyes. I look away to give her space to grieve. My eyes wander, coming to a picture of the three of them on the fireplace mantel. In it, they wear earth tones, Sam in a white shirt and beige pants, Joanna in a camel-color dress, Kylie in dusty pink, a beaded gold chain around her neck. Sam and Kylie make silly faces—Sam cross-eyed with his tongue sticking out, and Kylie with her eyes wide, curling her upper lip under to show her teeth, while Joanna laughs, her smile bright, beaming; it's the face of someone completely different than the one sitting across from me, one who is happy and carefree.

But there's something else, something more, something about the picture that's vaguely familiar. I find myself holding my breath, leaned forward in my seat, searching, my stomach heavy but I don't know why. I can't put my finger on it.

Joanna sees me looking. She says, "That picture was taken the summer that Kylie disappeared. It's one of the last pictures I have of the three of us together. For the longest time, I regretted that we hadn't all smiled for the picture, that it wasn't more formal, more posed. But this," she says, "is so much more authentic. This is us. This house used to be full of laughter. Sam and I, we don't laugh anymore."

She takes me to see Kylie's room. We step in through the open doorway, and the first thing I see is the light filtering through the louvered blinds and into the room. The bedroom, which is the embodiment of a tween girl, seems to be untouched for the last five years, the bed sloppily made, one side of the wooden bifold closet doors open to reveal the clothes inside: ruffled and eyelet dresses that hang beside graphic tees, none of it any different than what Cass would wear. There are shoes on the closet floor, not placed in a neat row but lying in a messy pile on their sides, and I imagine that's the way Kylie left them, practically seeing her kick off the pair of pink-and-white-checkerboard Vans in the days before she went missing.

I stand just inside the open doorway, watching as Joanna floats around the room, her fingers running over things. She turns around, and when she does, there are tears in her eyes, which are infectious. "I'm sorry," she breathes. "You'd think after all this time, I'd get numb to it, that coming in here wouldn't have this effect on me. This," she says, "is how I cope, by keeping her bedroom a shrine that I can visit from time to time. Sam," she says, listening for him, "won't come in. He won't even look. He never opens the door."

"How does he cope?"

"He doesn't. He keeps everything bottled up, though in the early days, he resigned himself to finding her. He made that his mission, his reason for living. It was all he could do, all he could think and talk about until he became obsessed. *Finding her.* He wouldn't give up. He was all over Reddit, trying to find and interact with people who might know something, connecting with parents of other missing kids, finding internet detectives to work with. He kept a shoebox of newspaper articles about her disappearance, as well as evidence that the police dismissed, collected with his own latex gloves and stored in plastic bags. He said if the police couldn't find her, he would. He was dead set on it, to the point that sometimes I wished she was dead, that we would have proof of it so we could move on. So there could be closure. That's awful, right?"

I say, "No, it's not," and then I ask, "Does he still have it? The shoebox?"

"Yes."

"Will you show me?" I ask, and she nods, leading me to a den, where she pulls a shoebox from a built-in bookshelf, lifting the dusty lid while I watch. In the box, newspaper articles sit stacked beside miscellanea like bottle caps and chewing gum wrappers.

She picks up one of the bottle caps, kept safe inside a plastic bag, as promised. "He found these on the street where Kylie was last seen. Never mind that it was windy and these things probably just blew out of someone's trash. I didn't tell him that because this was a defense mechanism of his, a way to cope, to keep his mind off the fact that our little girl wasn't ever coming home. He wanted the police to check for DNA. But there was never a suspect to compare it with, and so they said no, that they couldn't."

Joanna reaches for a newspaper article, which she unfolds, holding it out to me. There on the newsprint is a picture of

Kylie's sweet face, with a headline that reads *The search for Kylie Matthews enters its second week.* The image is one of those over-priced school photos with the stock blue background. Joanna says, "That's the last school picture Kylie would ever take."

There are Polaroid photos in the box too. "Sam took these himself, his own crime scene photos." The Polaroids are pictures of a home, which is inviting, if not small. It has wooden siding and green shutters and is well-kept. Trees surround it, steeping the land, the home, in shade. Some are closeups of the house—of the window boxes that spill over with pink impatiens, the crooked *Welcome* mat on the porch floor—but others are taken from further away so that the whole property is visible and I see how, at the edge of the property, a green shed sits—the shade of green an exact match to the shutters. "This is Kylie's friend Abby's house. It's where she was the day she disappeared. The police searched it. They searched the shed, the woods, everywhere, in case Kylie never left. They questioned the family, her parents, Abby and her older brother, Josh, but it was all the same: Kylie and Abby biked away together that day. But only one of them came back.

"Greta Dahl came by not long after it happened," she says, looking up at me all of a sudden. "Do you know what she said?" She doesn't wait before she says, "She said that Kylie was dead. And that the sooner I started believing that, the better off I'd be." I feel weighed down, an ache in my throat, picturing Ms. Dahl standing on her front porch like she had mine, saying to her, *I'm sorry to be the one to tell you, honey, but your girl's dead.*

"I'm sorry she did that. She had no right."

On the way out, I walk again past the picture of the three of them, Sam, Joanna and Kylie, on the fireplace mantel. My eyes run over it, that vaguely familiar, elusive thing still sitting on the tip of my tongue, though, no matter how hard I try, my mind can't retrieve it.

REESE

"What's that?" Emily asks. It's the next morning. She and I are outside on the deck, her with her coffee. It's cool out. Fog rises up over the lake.

"What's what?" I ask. I'm leaned against the deck railing, looking down at her, her hair wet from a shower, drying. She sits at the table, her hands around a chipped mug. Emily doesn't wear makeup. She's one of the few women in the world who doesn't look naked without makeup, mostly because I've almost never seen her with it on.

My hand follows her eyes. It goes to my neck, coming down on the necklace Daniel gave me last night, fingering the beads.

I forgot all about it. I fell asleep with it on.

"That necklace," she says.

"What does it look like?" I ask.

Emily takes a sip of her coffee. She sets the mug back down. "But what does it mean?"

"What do you mean? It doesn't mean anything. It's just a necklace."

"The beads," she says. "They form a pattern." If they do, I hadn't noticed. "Where did you get it?"

My throat tightens. "Does it matter?"

Emily raises her eyebrows. "It's just that I've never seen it before."

"It's Skylar's, okay? She let me borrow it," I say, getting defensive, and then, turning around to look out over the water instead, I mutter, "I didn't know I had to ask your permission to wear my friend's necklace."

She's onto me, I think.

That afternoon, we're at the pool. I lie face down on my chair, listening to Mae and Cass scream and run around the pool deck, which Emily has told them at least a thousand times not to do because someone might fall and get hurt.

"Mae, please. I said *no running*," Emily says again, for the millionth time, as Mae runs and cannonballs back into the pool like she's invincible or has some death wish.

"Cass!" she screams out when her head surfaces. "Let's play Marco Polo!"

Cass gets back in the water, and then all I hear until Aunt Courtney says she's heading back to the cottage to make peanut butter and jelly sandwiches for lunch is, "Marco! Polo! Marco! Polo!" screamed at the top of their lungs.

I put my headphones on to drown out the sound. I close my eyes and think about Daniel.

A few minutes later, I feel drops of water like from rain.

I look up, lifting my head. Mae stands next to me, her wet hair raining pool water down on me. I look over. Uncle Elliott is gone. I don't know where he went, but beside me, his chair is empty, Mae and Cass trying to squeeze together into it, soaking wet, wrapping themselves in his towel.

"Can you two stop?" I ask.

"Stop what?" Mae asks. "We're not doing anything."

"Stop getting me wet."

I put my head back down. I try to ignore them, but not ten seconds later, they start to laugh, a big belly laugh that's impossible to ignore even over the sound of my headphones. I lift up, propping myself on my elbows just in time to see them tuck something under the towel to hide it from me.

"What's that?" I ask, pulling the headphones off.

"What's what?" Mae asks, looking over at Cass, who presses a hand to her mouth to stop herself from laughing, though they're not fooling anyone.

"That," I say, pointing at the towel. "Whatever you're hiding."

They look at each other and crack up, saying in unison, "We're not hiding anything."

"You two are such liars." I reach out. I tug on the towel. Beneath it, they have Uncle Elliott's iPad, which they're not supposed to use unless they ask. He must have forgotten all about it; he must have left it behind in his chair when he went wherever he did.

"Put that away, you idiots. You're not even supposed to be on that thing."

They don't put it away. Instead, still giggling, Cass lifts the iPad and starts taking pictures of me, which is what they were probably doing before I noticed, so that there must be a dozen of me on that stupid thing.

"Say cheese," Mae says.

I don't say cheese. Instead, I flick her off and say, "Put it away, or I'll tell Uncle Elliott when he comes back."

I don't have to ask for a third time, because they know they'll get in trouble for being on the iPad. They leave it behind on the chair. They throw the towel off and go running across the concrete, ignoring Emily, who tells them not to run again, calling out, "If you're not careful, you might fall!"

I wish they would at this point, to teach them a lesson if nothing else, though thinking thoughts like that is bad karma.

That night, I put Daniel's necklace on. I run my fingers over the beads, thinking about what Emily said, about them forming a pattern, though I don't think she's right, I think they're just beads. I slip back into my jean shorts from my pajamas, pulling a different shirt over my head. There is body spray in my bag. I spritz some on, hoping Daniel notices and that he likes it, and then I move from the porch toward the cottage to leave, like I've done every night for the last couple nights.

It doesn't get easier. I'm never not scared of getting caught.

It's black in the cottage when I go in. I feel my way with my hands.

I haven't gotten more than a couple steps when a lamp in the living room flicks on. Dull, yellow light enters the room, not reaching the corners so that they stay dark.

I flinch, taking a step back, my hand going to my heart.

Emily is on the sofa.

"What are you doing?" she asks, pulling her hand away from the lamp, her voice doomy.

Slowly, she pushes herself into a sitting position as I ask, without answering her, "What are *you* doing? Why aren't you in bed?" But then I see. The pillow. The blanket. She *is* in bed. She and Nolan must have gotten in another fight and she's sleeping on the sofa. I wonder what this one was about. His job or lack thereof. Her being overly controlling or him questioning her parenting in front of us kids, or D: All of the Above. The possibilities are endless.

"I fell asleep on the sofa," she says, as if it happened by accident, as if she didn't intentionally lift a pillow from the bed and bring it downstairs with her, as if Nolan didn't intentionally close the bedroom door after she left.

"Well?" she asks before I can really feel sorry for her.

"Well what?"

"You didn't answer my question. What are you doing awake? It has to be almost midnight." It's not just that I'm awake. It's that I'm fully dressed, though, if she notices, she doesn't say.

"I was thirsty, okay? I wanted water," I say, moving around the edge of the sofa for the kitchen, her eyes following me as I go.

"Did you sleep at all, or have you been awake all this time?"

"I was asleep. I woke up and I was thirsty," I say again. "Is that not okay? To drink water?"

"No, it's fine. I was just curious." She pauses, then asks, "Is that what you wore today?"

I look down, like I don't even know what I have on. It isn't what I wore today. But I say, "Yeah. Don't you remember? I guess I must've fallen asleep in it."

She stares too long. Nods. Says, "I guess so." There's another pause, and then she says, tilting her head, "You smell good. Is that perfume?"

My stomach tightens. Dramatically, I inhale. "I don't smell anything."

I reach into the cabinet for a glass, filling it with water that I don't even want, that I won't drink. "You should go upstairs and sleep," I say. I tell her good-night. I go back onto the porch with the glass. I sink down into bed, lying on my side. I pull the covers up to my neck, feeling this nagging pain in the pit of my stomach that I won't be able to see Daniel tonight after all.

It's not only that I want to go, that I want more than anything to be with him.

It's that I wonder what happens when I don't show up. I wonder what he'll do.

COURTNEY

I sit in the front seat of my car, still parked outside of the Matthewses' house, thinking about something Joanna just said, how Sam wouldn't give up on finding Kylie. I need to be doing more to find Reese. I can't only rely on the police to do it.

I search online on my phone for Daniel Clarke, and though Clarke is a common enough name, I find only one living on Moon Road, which is a mile and a half from where Joanna and Sam live.

I start the engine. My GPS takes me to Moon Road along the backroads, which are a far cry from the nearby vacation resorts where suburbanites with nice and sometimes luxury cars spend their time roughing it in the woods. The disparity is evident. Though the scenery around here is breathtaking, it doesn't nullify the poverty we've seen, people living in small, dilapidated houses and run-down trailer parks.

Tourism is big, a boon to the economy, and yet I wonder if the locals don't resent people like us for coming into their town, for using their lakes and woods as our summer playground. Nearly all of the houses around here are unmaintained, situated on large, heavily wooded lots with rusted, if not wrecked, cars on the lawn beside things like hot water heaters and washing machines that decorate the property like yard art. At some of the homes, people sit outside, on sunken front porches (a man on one, smoking what I think, at first, to be a cigarette, until I see the bulbous end of a crack pipe) while other homes look like they've been abandoned or are uninhabitable. It's unsettling and strikes me how very different rural poverty is from urban poverty. It's out of view, tucked away on backwoods streets as opposed to homeless people living on city street corners and in slummy housing projects with boarded-up windows that are infiltrated by gangs. But that doesn't mean it's any less prevalent.

I reach Moon Road, which is narrow and potholed. Above me, trees overhang the street, blotting out the sun. I drive slowly, leaned forward in my seat, searching for Daniel's house. Eventually I find the address on a rusted mailbox that sits at the end of a driveway, its post becoming uprooted and pitching forward toward the street: 126 Moon Road.

My stomach tightens. By instinct, I lift my foot up off the gas. I press lightly on the brake and the car slows to a stop at the end of the driveway. I feel my breath change as I take in his house, which is some type of depressed manufactured home with a detached garage that's just barely bigger than a shed.

I lift my foot from the brake. I press lightly on the accelerator and ease the car over the curb and into the driveway where I stop again, sliding the gearshift into Park. I sit, leaned forward in my seat, eyeing the single-story house through the windshield, with its low-slung roof and the tiny, jalousie windows that must allow almost no amount of light or air to get into the home.

I imagine the darkness inside the house. I imagine the stale, unventilated air.

He's like a cat you let outside to roam. It's gone so long, you think it's dead—that a car or a coyote got it—but then one day, he just reappears as if no one was ever looking for him.

I tell myself to leave, to go back to the cottage, to Elliott and the kids.

But instead, I let go of the gearshift. I turn the engine off. I bring my hands to the seat belt, which I unbuckle, slowly feeding it into place.

I set my hand on the door handle and pull on the lever, opening the door to get out.

The house sits on dirt and is surrounded, like everything else around here, by trees. Outside, I get assailed by mosquitoes, thousands of them that must breed in the dense woodland and leafy debris that surrounds the small home. I close the car door quickly, but still, some get in. A chill runs through me, the outside temperature colder in the shade. My senses are heightened; I'm overcome with a profound sense that something isn't right, though I tell myself it's nothing. The police were already here. They came to look for Daniel and he wasn't home.

It's not intuition. It's just fear speaking.

Daniel Clarke, I remind myself for a third time, isn't here.

I move away from the safety of my car. The world around me smells damp, earthy, dirt-like. Outside the house, a firepit filled with ash sits cold beside cigarette butts, beside empty cans of Pabst Blue Ribbon beer and cheap plastic lawn chairs that are knocked over and lying on their sides on the dirt. There is no grass to speak of, which makes the land feel depressed and neglected. The ground is soft, the sun unable to penetrate the trees to ever dry the earth fully. With every step, I leave footprints.

I circle the exterior of the house. There is litter strewn on the ground from garbage cans that have been knocked on their side, their contents scavenged by wildlife. There are tire tracks in the dirt, like from a bike or an ATV.

My chest feels heavy, a weighted blanket lying on it.

I imagine Reese here, her desperate screams going unanswered.

I make my way to the back of the house, which butts up against the woods. There is no porch or deck to speak of; on the back of the house, the sliding glass door drops down to the earth, where more trash—more cigarette butts, more beer cans—has been left on the ground.

I go toward the door, to see what I can see through the glass. I close in on it, cupping my hands around my eyes for a better look.

But then I stop. Because the door, I realize, is open, an eighth-inch gap running between the frame and the glass panel.

My jaw goes slack in disbelief. I lower my hands to my sides and stare at that gap. *Don't*, I tell myself—willing myself to turn around, to go back to the car, to drive back to the cottage and forget all about the open door.

But instead, I reach out. I set my hand on the handle, feeling the splintered wood against my skin. I pull without thinking, and it's reckless and impetuous. The door slides easily open along the track, the cool summer breeze whooshing in and moving the broken vertical blinds just inside the open door so that the vanes clang into one another, making noise like a dull wind chime.

It's not too late, I tell myself. I can still close the door, turn around, go home.

I do none of those things.

Instead, I climb the stoop and enter Daniel Clarke's home, sweeping the blinds away with a hand, moving past them. I leave the sliding glass door open behind me.

I don't think about the fact that I'm trespassing or about getting caught.

I only think about finding Reese.

The smell that greets me is rancid, like rotting meat in a trash can. It stuns me at first, stinging my eyes. Standing there in the kitchen, trying to ascertain the source of the smell, I wonder if the police entered the house when they came to look for Daniel, or if they just knocked on the door and then left when no one answered it.

What if Reese is here?

I want to call out for her. But instead I keep quiet. I hold my breath, practically gagging on the smell, dragging myself across the room, my heartbeat drumming in my ears.

The ceilings of the house are low. The walls are a wood paneling from some other generation. Stained high-pile brown carpeting lines the floor except for in the kitchen, which is a faux brick linoleum. Everything is brown and dreary. As expected, there is almost no natural lighting coming in through the small windows. There is no air.

Dirty dishes sit in the kitchen sink and on the table. On them, a half-eaten bagel, cereal floating in spoiled milk and a crust of bread, which the ants have found.

I press a hand to my nose to hold back the smell. I make my way further inside the home, into an adjoining family room, which is unexceptional except that the TV is on though it's on mute. On the screen, Steve Harvey hosts an episode of *Family Feud*, his mouth moving though no sound comes out.

I've lost track of what day it is. What time. I wonder how long that TV has been on and if it's been on for days. I spin in a slow, lazy half circle. Behind me sits a narrow hallway, which is dim, windowless, the already-inadequate light that comes in from the small, slatted, louvered windows barely able to reach that far.

I make my way toward the hall. I reach for a light switch at the entryway, but either the ceiling lightbulbs have burnt out or the fuse is blown because, when I flip the switch, the hall stays dark.

I stand there, wondering what's down the hall, wondering what happens beyond the ninety-degree turn where I can't see. I try to summon the courage to move forward, to look. My breathing is shallow, my mouth dry, my body heavy. I fall back a step first, thinking about leaving, but then I start to move forward rather than away by instinct, treading across the thick carpeting, my body moving as if separate from my brain.

Elliott doesn't even know where I am. He thinks I'm at the
store, picking up groceries.

If something were to happen to me, he wouldn't know.

If I never came back to the cottage, he wouldn't know where
to look.

He's like a cat you let outside to roam.

You think it's dead—that a car or a coyote got it.

Then one day, he just reappears as if no one was ever looking for him.

I come to a bathroom first. Small, boxy, the smell of urine
strong. I leave the light off; I don't bother with the switch. Standing in the open door, there is just enough light for me to see that
the toilet has been left open and unflushed. There's a rumpled
towel on the floor and the shower curtain is flung open, bottles of
shampoo and body wash lying on their sides, open, spilling out.

I round the corner. Just beyond the bathroom is a bedroom.
The bed is unmade, a stained white sheet untucked and falling
off. There is a blanket on the floor and a flat, rumpled pillow
at the head of the bed. Dresser drawers are open, clothes wilting from the drawers. On top of the dresser is a small amass-
ment of expensive-looking jewelry completely unbefitting for
this house and this room. A pendant necklace, drop earrings, a
woman's wedding band, loot he has yet to pawn, I can only assume. A side table light has been left on, the glow of it faint but
visible. I try to imagine the last time Daniel was here, thinking that it was dark from the light left on, and wondering if it
was nighttime, sometime after dark, or early morning before
the sun came up. I imagine him waking up, snatching clothes
from the dresser drawers, leaving in a hurry with the light and
the TV still on, the back door open.

Why was he in such a rush?

I turn around. Fleecy pink fabric catches my eye, peeking
out from beneath a wrinkled, pleated bed skirt, the color out
of place in the insipid room. I bend down and grab for it, pull-

ing it out from under the bed, knowing right away what it is, the recognition coming as a punch to the gut. My diaphragm spasms. The pink is Reese's fleece sweatshirt. It's a cropped thing with a wide neck that she cut herself to show more skin, much to Emily's dismay; it's meant to be off-the-shoulder, and I can picture Reese wearing it, her sunburned shoulder and bare midriff exposed, the pink of her skin rivaling the pink of the shirt.

I take it by the shoulders, my hands starting to shake as I unfurl the shirt for a better look. There is blood on the sleeve. Reese's sweatshirt, Reese's blood.

Just then, something outside startles me. A sound, though I don't so much hear it as I feel it—a low-frequency vibration in my chest—and I bolt suddenly upright. The sound is something subtle. It's insidious, a predator lying in wait to ambush its prey. It makes me wonder—as I turn without hesitation, taking the sweatshirt with me and scurrying down the hall to get back in my car and leave—if I heard it or not.

But as I rush down the hall, the sound comes again, far more evident this time. Far closer.

I only make it as far as the family room.

In my peripheral vision, I see the shadow of a man's head pass by the windows, and I know that I won't have time to get to the sliding glass door, to run outside and back to my car. My legs founder, feeling tingly, gelatinous, the blood rushing to them. I let go of the sweatshirt by mistake, watching it plunge to the floor as I crouch down by instinct, searching the house instead for a place to hide.

But I'm too slow. It's too late.

There is nowhere to go before the front door swings violently open and I find myself staring down the dark barrel of a gun.

REESE

Sometime later, I try again to leave the cottage, hoping it's not too late, that Daniel is still waiting for me by the lake and that he's not mad.

I get back out of bed. I stand on the porch, trying to see through the glass and into the darkness of the living room. I give my eyes time to adjust and when they do, I see that Emily hasn't left the sofa.

Still, I reach for the door handle. I curl my hand around the knob again, opening it more slowly this time. I hold my breath as I do. I hold every part of me completely still. Only my arm moves, pushing on the door, my eyes on Emily, watching for signs of life. I hear her breathe. A vibration like a gentle snore comes from the back of her throat, and I think that she's asleep.

I lift my foot. I take one hesitant step forward and then another. And then the next. All the while I don't breathe. I move across the room. Ten feet from the door, Emily inhales all of a sudden and I freeze, becoming paralyzed. My lungs are on fire. She rolls over on the sofa, mumbles something in her sleep. It's incoherent, which is how I know, or how I think I know, that she's asleep. I take another step toward the door. Once there, I have to turn the dead bolt. I don't flick it. I fold my fingers around it and move the dead bolt, as slow as fuck. I lift my fingers. I reach for the door handle, wrap my hand around it. I

open the door, step out. I pull the door closed, leaving it unlocked, and then I wait on the deck, not moving but breathing
slow, controlled breaths, counting to one hundred in my head.
Only then do I drag myself across the deck and down the stairs,
into the dirt. I stand just beyond the deck railing, watching the
cottage, wondering what would happen if I never came back.

I head into the woods. It takes a while to get to the lake, but
when I do, I don't see Daniel where he usually is, on the pier.
I feel a heaviness in my whole body because I'm too late and
he left.

I stand there, staring out over the lake, wondering if he
was angry when he left, if he went home or if he went looking for me.

I turn to go back to the cottage alone. Only then do I hear
the sound of rocks skipping on the water further down the
beach. I spin around again, my eyes following the sound, and
I just barely make Daniel out as he stands facing the water. As
I watch, his dark silhouette grips a rock, swinging back before
releasing it. The rock disappears over the blackness of the lake.

He never turns around. With his back to me, he says, "I
thought you weren't going to come. I thought you were blowing me off," his voice different than before, deeper.

"I know. I'm so sorry. I tried to get out like an hour ago,
but my mom—"

He doesn't let me get the rest out. "Your fucking mom,"
he sneers, sending another rock soaring out over the lake, and
though it vanishes in the darkness, I hear the sound as it bounces
on the surface. Once, twice, three times. He turns slowly to
me. I can't see his expression as he says, "I'll kill her if she ever
tries keeping you from me," though I don't think twice about
it because it's just something people say.

I'll kill you if you tell anyone what happened . . .

I'll kill you if you lose my favorite shirt . . .

It's not meant to be taken seriously. It doesn't mean anything.

"I'm so sorry, Daniel," I say to him, my words coming fast, worrying that he isn't into me anymore, that he doesn't like me because of this. "I wanted to come sooner. I tried. I promise it won't happen again. Are you mad?" I ask, my teeth biting down on my lower lip, tears building in my eyes.

Daniel's voice loses its edge. "I could never be mad at you. I told you before, Reese. I'd stay out here all night if I had to. Anything to see you. Come here," he says, and I don't even hesitate. I cross the grass, going to him.

His eyes, when I reach him, are intense. He looks at me and I feel weak in the knees. He's never looked at me this way before. I hold in a breath as he takes me by the hand. He leads me into the woods and there, in the trees, he turns me around to face him. He says nothing at first as he slides a hand under my shirt with an ease and efficiency to it that tells me he's done this before, that he's felt up other girls before. The look in his eye changes, no longer cold, but something else, something that makes me both lightheaded and hyperaware of my own skin.

His thumb moves across my chest like a match, lighting me on fire.

"Is that what you want?" he asks, my breath hitching as he slowly slips his hand out from under my shirt, pressing it between my legs, making me gasp. "To be with me?" I nod, short of breath, imagining it as heat fills my face.

Him and me together. No one telling me what I can and cannot do.

"Is that okay?" he asks, watching me from above, his eyes dreamy in the sky's faint glow. I bob my head, my words and breath lacking. "I can stop if you want," he says, but I shake my head and breathe out no because I don't want him to stop.

His hand moves inside my shorts and then he leans in, says into my ear, "Take your shorts off." His breath is warm against my skin. I don't hesitate or even think about what I'm doing or what's going to happen when my shorts are off, but instead I undo the button and slide the zipper, I latch my thumbs into the waistband of my jean shorts and shimmy them down over my hips and thighs, stepping out of one leg so the other lies wrapped around an ankle, exhaling, my eyes sinking closed as he touches me in a way no guy has ever done before.

Heat floods me. It fills my legs, my chest, my face as I stand, wanting more than anything to be transported, to be carried away, to not overthink, and yet I'm in my head too much, wondering if I'm doing this right, if I look stupid.

"You're so hot," he says then, as if hearing my thoughts, and I open my eyes, see him watching me in the moonlight, a rapt smile on his perfect lips, making me believe it, making my self-consciousness disappear in a puff of smoke. Poof! I am hot. I stare back, becoming less inhibited now, wanting this, wanting him like I've never wanted anything in my whole life. I reach for him, touch him outside his clothes, our eyes locked, a silent conversation happening between them, his breath quickening, becoming harmonious with mine.

"Do you wanna?" he asks, breathy, excited, and I nod without reserve, my heart feeling like it's going to explode out of my chest as he steps out of his jeans like they're on fire and we lower ourselves to the cold, hard dirt, and I tell myself to remember everything about this moment. The way he lifts my shirt over my head, watching, enrapt, as my hair falls around my shoulders. The way he sweeps my hair gently back, taking me in, his eyes feasting on me, saying it again, how I'm so hot, how I'm so fucking sexy, making me believe it. The way he presses into me, laying me gently down on my back, asking if I'm okay and if I'm comfortable. The way he parts my legs with his knee, lowering himself between my thighs, spreading them wide. The way he kisses me first, slowing the pace, touching his lips tenderly, unhurriedly to mine until I lose myself in his kiss, in him, thinking how perfect this night is, all alone in the woods, watching the moonlight as it comes and goes from behind the clouds, flickering through the trees, dousing us in a soft warm white light, and thinking how I couldn't have dreamed up a better scenario for my first time if I tried, because this is magic, the stuff of fairy tales.

He pulls his lips from mine, propping himself above me so he can see my face. He asks again, "Are you sure? You can say no if you want."

But I say yes, arching my back, lifting my hips to him because I've waited my whole life for this, and I'm sure.

"I'm sure," I breathe, letting my head sink back against the earth, pressing my eyes closed, holding my breath and bracing myself, overcome with a mix of nervous anticipation and desire, waiting for it to happen, wanting it to happen despite knowing it's going to hurt, because Skylar told me it would, though she also said, *Promise it will be worth it.* "I'm sure," I say again when nothing happens, and then, when still nothing happens, I open my eyes and gaze up, seeing him suspended above me like a statue.

"Did you hear something?" he whispers, every part of him completely still, staring deep out into the woods, searching the darkness.

"Hear what?" I ask.

"I don't know. Just something."

I hold my breath. We listen. And then I hear it too. And my heart stops. All the sensations I was feeling just a moment ago are gone, dried up, evaporated, replaced by a fear that spreads to every cell in my body.

There's movement in the trees, something substantial, more than a bird or a breeze.

He springs from me, reaching for his jeans, stepping into them while I grope blindly on the dirt, the scant moonlight slipping behind a cloud, not enough for me to find my missing clothes.

The sound gets closer, more definitive. Something's there.

Or someone is there.

COURTNEY

My vision is blurred. Spots dance before my eyes, which have become accustomed to the dimness of the house, making them more sensitive to the light that pours in the open door all of a sudden.

My heart is in my throat. It beats so hard my blood pressure drops. My ears feel clogged, which makes it hard to hear anything but the beating of my own heart.

I throw my hands up in the air, flinching in anticipation of the gun going off. I put them in front of my face and brace myself for the searing pain of being shot.

I imagine that.

I imagine what it would feel like to be shot, to have bullets enter me.

"Please," I beg, my voice desperate. "Please don't shoot. Please don't hurt me."

I press my eyes shut tight. On the other side of the room, I picture Daniel Clarke's face behind the gun, which I remember as sharp and angular from that day I saw him at the pool with Reese, with knitted, bushy eyebrows and long, unkempt hair. I imagine the intensity of his eyes, a vein on his forehead engorged.

When he speaks, the voice is unexpected and familiar.

"Mrs. Gray," he says, and at first I'm so taken aback by the sound of my name that my reaction is delayed. My brain stops working, processing.

How does he know my name?

Slowly, I open my eyes. I realize that the man in the room with me is not Daniel Clarke.

It's Detective Evans, who stands just inside the open door, pointing his gun at me.

"Detective Evans? Wh-what are you doing here?"

"A neighbor called," he says, his voice controlled, sedate, unlike mine. He doesn't lower his weapon. "They said they saw someone trespassing on Mr. Clarke's property, entering his home." He pauses, throwing the question back at me. "What are *you* doing here, Mrs. Gray?"

His expression is stony and cold in a way I've never seen. It takes a minute for him to lower his gun, and even when he does, it's still slow, deliberate.

My knees buckle. I stumble backward in relief. I sag against a wall, letting it support me. My muscles feel heavy and weak. Tears well in my eyes and I fight them, not wanting to cry in front of Detective Evans or the other officers who come into the house behind him with their guns also drawn, lowering them at Detective Evans's request.

"I asked: What are you doing here, Mrs. Gray?"

"I'm looking for Reese."

"This is private property. You're trespassing."

It takes effort, but I push myself up off the wall. "I'm looking for my niece," I say again, more sure this time, as if looking for Reese gives me the authority to break into someone's home.

"And so are we," he says. "You have to trust us, Mrs. Gray. You have to let us do our jobs. You can't just be breaking into people's homes on a hunch." He pauses, finally returning his gun into its holster, holding my eyes the entire time. "I could arrest you for trespassing, you know."

"Then do it," I say, daring him, watching for a reaction. But Detective Evans does nothing, holding my gaze. "Her sweatshirt is here," I tell him. "He has her."

"A sweatshirt alone is not incriminating. It doesn't mean anything. We don't know how it got here. Maybe she gave it to him. Maybe she left it in his car and he brought it inside for safekeeping. You said they were hanging out. So maybe she was here. It doesn't mean he did something to hurt her. It doesn't mean he knows where she is."

My voice tightens as I say, "There's blood on it," and for the first time, I get a reaction from him, something subtle but noticeable. A shifting of his body weight.

"Where is the sweatshirt?"

"Here," I say, motioning to it, leaving the sweatshirt where it is. "I found it in the bedroom. The blood," I tell him, "is on the sleeve. It's right there," I say, because the blood is visible without even having to touch the sweatshirt. "Reese is hurt. He did something to her," I say, watching as one of the other officers slips his hands into gloves and moves past me for the shirt, lifting it and showing the blood to Detective Evans, who nods, telling him to bag it.

He says to me, "We don't know for sure that the blood is hers, Mrs. Gray. We can't just assume."

"Of course it's hers. Who else's could it be?" I ask, but even as I do, I know the answer. Bile rises up inside of me and I press a hand to my mouth. I see that baseball bat in my mind's eye. I see it covered with blood. I see it in Reese's hands, the bat bloodied before she administered another blow to Emily, lying unconscious on the floor, drops of blood jettisoning through the air and onto the sleeve of her shirt.

"Here's the problem with breaking in to find evidence," he says, and I flush with shame, feeling embarrassed by the incongruity of it, because of his youth, because he could be twenty years younger than me, and yet in a position of such authority that I feel inferior, like a child. "If Mr. Clarke did something to hurt your family and this sweatshirt is proof, a judge could say that it's inadmissible because of the way it was obtained. The defense could claim you planted that sweatshirt here to set Mr. Clarke up. That you put the blood on it."

"I didn't," I assert.

"I didn't say that you did. I'm just trying to tell you why breaking in to obtain evidence might be problematic, in addition to the fact that it's illegal. You have to trust me, Mrs. Gray. I am trying to find your niece. I am trying to figure out who killed your family. You have to let me do my job and not do anything that's going to impede in this investigation."

I nod, feeling suddenly so tired and defeated that I start to break down. The rancid smell of rotting meat in the house makes me think of bloat and of maggots as I picture Emily's and Nolan's hollowed-out bodies getting ravaged by maggots. The temperature in the house seems to rise all of a sudden too, so that I'm overwhelmingly hot.

Detective Evans notices. "Is everything alright?" he asks, and this time, his tone has changed.

I pluck at my shirt. I lift it from the skin so that it billows, though there is no air in the house to get in. "It's so hot in here. And that smell . . ."

"Why don't we go outside and get some fresh air," he suggests, and I nod, grateful. I follow him through the open front door and outside, where he says, his voice far more lenient now, "We'll run some tests on the shirt and see if we can determine who the blood belongs to. Maybe it's hers and maybe—"

He turns to face me. At the same time, the wind rushes me, blowing my hair back. The lighting is better outside too so that, for the first time, he sees the bruising on my cheek.

He becomes still.

"You want to tell me what happened?" he asks.

The answer is a resounding no, I don't want to tell him what happened. But I can see on his face that it isn't so much a question as it is a command.

Tell me what happened.

I stay quiet, keeping it to myself.

"Mrs. Gray?"

"It's nothing. It's not what you think."

Detective Evans watches me for a minute. He throws a glance to the other officers, saying, "I think we're done here. You two can go. Take that back to the station and log it," about Reese's sweatshirt. He watches as they head to their squad car, parked at the end of the drive behind mine, and pull away.

Only when they're gone does Detective Evans turn to me. He lowers his guard. His features soften, the taut lines on his forehead relaxing. "I grew up," he says slowly, "with a father who had a temper. He hit things, walls and doors mostly, but every now and then my mom would be on the receiving end of his rage."

My words are a whisper. "It's not like that. It's not what you think."

"Isn't it?"

"No. My husband didn't do this to me."

"Then who did?" When I say nothing, he says gently, "There are fingerprints on your face. Someone did this to you, Mrs. Gray. If not your husband, then who?" He watches me closely, his eyes reading mine. He cocks his head, the wind moving his hair. Mosquitoes circle our heads. One lands on his arm and he kills it with his hand. "Was it Wyatt?"

My face gives me away.

"It was Wyatt, wasn't it?"

"You can't get him in trouble. Please. He didn't mean to do it. It was an accident."

"Tell me what happened."

"He was sleepwalking. He woke up in the middle of the night, looking for his lunch. He was so worried about being late to school because he couldn't find his lunch. I tried to wake him, to get him back in bed. He lashed out, because he was having a dream someone was trying to kidnap him and he fought back. He was asleep. He didn't mean to hit me."

"He thought you were this kidnapper?"

"Yes."

"Are you afraid, Mrs. Gray?"

I hesitate because the question takes me by surprise. "Of course I am," I say. "Someone killed my brother and sister-in-law. Someone has my niece. Of course I'm afraid. I'm fucking terrified. Shouldn't I be?"

"But are you afraid of Wyatt?" he asks. "Do you feel unsafe living with him?"

Do I feel unsafe living with Wyatt?

"You can tell me, Mrs. Gray," he says when I hesitate, reaching out to touch my shoulder. He lowers his gaze. "It's my job to protect you, to keep you safe." I look up. I meet his eye, feeling all of a sudden like I could cry.

It's my job to protect you.

Elliott hasn't said as much to me, though that doesn't mean he wouldn't, or that he's not trying to protect me. But when Detective Evans says it, I believe it.

After what Wyatt did last night, we slept with the bedroom door closed and locked. And then this morning, I tiptoed around, afraid to wake him before anyone else was up to protect me from him. Because I'm afraid. Because yes, I feel unsafe living with him.

But I say, "No," because I don't know what would happen to Wyatt if I confessed to Detective Evans that I was afraid of him. "I told you that it was an accident. He didn't mean to do it."

Detective Evans nods, thoughtful at first, letting go of my shoulder and bringing his arm back to his side. "You said that when he was sleepwalking, he was worried about his missing lunch and about being late to school?"

I nod, remembering the way Wyatt spoke to me last night, the words he used. *Are you fucking deaf? I'm going to kill you if I'm late for school.*

I say, "He was looking for his lunch in the refrigerator, but it wasn't there."

Seconds pass. Detective Evans is quiet, contemplative, as if processing what I've said, trying to imagine Wyatt searching the refrigerator shelves in the middle of the night, thrusting other items aside to search for a lunch that isn't there.

He asks, "Doesn't it stand to reason then that if he was dreaming about being late to school, he was not dreaming about an intruder in your cottage?"

His questions knock the wind from my lungs.

Was Wyatt dreaming about a missing lunch? Or was he dreaming about an intruder?

Or was he dreaming about nothing at all?

Was he awake? Was he only pretending to be asleep?

Before I can find the words to respond, Detective Evans says, "There's something I've been meaning to tell you."

"What's that?" I ask, breathless.

"While we were searching the cottage the other day, there's something we didn't find."

"What?"

"Benadryl."

My first instinct is to protect Wyatt, to come to his defense. "Maybe it wasn't in a bottle," I suggest. "Maybe it was a tablet, in a blister pack."

"We looked, Mrs. Gray, but we didn't find a blister pack either. Neither a bottle nor a blister pack."

"Wyatt wouldn't lie, if that's what you're suggesting. Maybe he was mistaken. Maybe Emily gave him something else for his allergies," I say, but even as I do, I know as good as anyone that few things would have had the same sedative effect as Benadryl, making it possible for him to sleep through what happened without waking up.

Maybe Wyatt is lying after all.

There are mosquitoes beside my car. Dark clouds of them float on and around the doors and windows so that I don't know how I'll get inside the car without letting them in.

As I reach for the door handle, another car passes by on the street, catching my attention, and I turn to look as the car drives past. As I gaze toward the street, a familiar green catches my eye, visible through a small break in the trees.

My hand falls away from the car's door handle and I find myself drifting to the end of the driveway, where visibility is better, where I can see all the way across the street to the house on the other side.

The green is sage-like compared to the green of the trees. Still, in real life, the color is more vivid than in Sam Matthew's Polaroids, though the house and the shed look more aged at the same time. The *Welcome* wreath is gone, removed from the door, and I imagine a rusty nail left in its place. The window boxes sit empty except for weeds.

A heavy feeling fills my whole body. There is a tightness in my chest. I tune out everything else around me—the bite of mosquitoes, the hushed, hard-to-hear sound of Detective Evans's voice speaking to me from behind, the cool breeze blowing through the trees and upsetting the leaves—focusing only on the shed.

The green shed.

I gravitate toward it. Without meaning to, I leave the drive-way and stray into the street, where another passing car nearly hits me, and I feel Detective Evans's hand on my elbow, pull-ing me back.

"Mrs. Gray? Is something wrong, Mrs. Gray?"

I can't respond. I'm lost in thought, wondering if Kylie's friend still lives there, wondering if it's only a coincidence that Daniel Clarke lives in the house across the street from the place where Kylie was last seen.

REESE

"Reese? Is that you?"

He shines his flashlight on me, an actual flashlight, its beam shockingly bright.

"What are you—" he starts to ask, but then he looks down, sees my clothes on the ground and realizes I'm not wearing any. He shines his flashlight off in the distance, where Daniel goes running through the woods.

Heat creeps up my neck for my face. Uncle Elliott doesn't finish his question. He doesn't have to. He knows what was happening, or what *almost* happened if he hadn't messed things up for me.

"Who is that?"

I shrug. "Just a friend."

He grunts. "Just a friend, huh?"

He bends down. Scoops my shorts and shirt up from the ground, tossing them to me. He turns his back to me, like he didn't already see everything, and says, "Put your clothes on."

"Don't look at me," I say, though he's not. I say it anyway. I step out into the open to get dressed, knowing I'll never be able to look Uncle Elliott in the eye again and *not* think how he saw me naked, though I try to rationalize it in my head, to tell myself that he didn't see anything in the dark.

Except for the flashlight's bright beam.

He saw everything.

"I'm done. You can turn around."

He does. And from the sad, stuffy look on his face, I expect him to say something all preachy about safe sex and stranger danger and shit.

What I don't expect is, "You know I'm going to have to talk to your mom and dad about this."

But that's what he says.

You know I'm going to have to talk to your mom and dad about this.

I feel the tension in my muscles first. My whole body tightens. My eyes narrow, my breath suddenly shallow. It doesn't cross my mind to beg and plead for him not to.

Instead, I say the first thing that comes to mind.

"If you say a word about this, I'll tell them that you were being inappropriate. That you said things. That you touched me. That you made me do things to you."

He goes white. He jerks back before putting on a brave face, faking bravado.

"You wouldn't."

"You wanna bet?"

"That's a very serious accusation, Reese. Do you have any idea the implications of telling lies like that?"

"Do you think I care?" I ask. Because I don't.

I'll say whatever I need to say to make sure he doesn't snitch or that, if he does, no one believes him.

COURTNEY

I go through it in my mind as I drive back to the cottage. Kylie Matthews went missing five years ago, when she was eleven, on the cusp of twelve. Five years ago, Daniel Clarke would have been nineteen. According to Joanna, the summer that Kylie disappeared was the summer she first discovered boys and bras and that she had her first crush.

What if Daniel Clarke was her first crush?

I wouldn't put it past him at age nineteen to have a thing for an almost-twelve-year-old, though it fills me with feelings of rage and disgust. It's not that different than seventeen and twenty-four. It's the exact same age difference, in fact. Seven years.

I come home empty-handed.

Elliott flings open the front door, and before I can put the car in Park, he's outside, bounding down the steps to the drive. "You've been gone for almost two hours. Is everything okay? What took you so long?" he asks, pulling my car door open for me.

"I'm sorry," I say, getting out.

Elliott doesn't give me a chance to say more before he goes around to the back of the car to open the liftgate and help with the groceries, but there are none.

"Where's the milk?" he asks, confused. "Where are the

bags?" I stand there beside the car, struggling to come up with the words to explain to him how I lied, how I never had any intention of going to the grocery store. "Courtney?" he asks.

Behind us, the cottage door is open, flies and mosquitoes getting in. Mae stands just inside the open door, staring out at us, looking so sad my heart aches. Her hair is tangled and there are dark circles under her eyes. I wonder if, every time I leave, she secretly hopes that I'll come back with Reese.

"I didn't go to the store," I say, bringing my gaze back to Elliott.

He stands incredulous before me, crossing his arms. "What do you mean you didn't go to the store? You were gone for hours, Court. Where did you go?"

I step closer, keeping my voice low. "Please don't be mad."

"Mad about what? What did you do?"

"I met a couple yesterday while we were searching for Reese. Sam and Joanna Matthews. I went to see them."

"You what?" he asks, upset and confused. "Why wouldn't you have told me? Who are they?"

"Their daughter went missing five years ago when she was eleven years old. They never found her, Elliott," I say, thinking again of Sam searching for five years, collecting his own evidence in a shoebox, doing anything he could to find Kylie and bring her home. I flash forward to five years from now, to a world in which we've never found Reese, thinking of the sad look on Mae's face and it never going away.

"And what do you think, that the same person who has her daughter also took Reese?"

There is cynicism in his voice. Skepticism. He's mad that I lied. He thinks it's improbable that the same person who took Kylie also has Reese.

I shrug. "I don't know. Yes. Maybe."

"Five years is a long time, Courtney," he says, stopping short of telling me that it's impossible these two things could be related, though I know that's exactly what he's thinking.

"Thousands of people go missing every single day, and that was years ago. This girl, Kylie, is probably dead, and whoever took her is most likely long gone. That same person didn't take Reese."

"How do you know? How can you be so certain?"

"It just seems unlikely. If you're talking about some serial kidnapper, wouldn't there be more than two missing girls over the course of five years?"

"I don't know. Maybe. I went to Daniel Clarke's house too," I say, getting the words out before I can change my mind. "The boy, the *man* that Reese was hanging out with here at the resort. I found his address online and I went to his house."

Elliott is floored. His eyebrows lift, his jaw drops.

"You did what?" he asks in disbelief. "Fuck, Courtney." He drags his hands through his hair.

"He wasn't there," I say quickly.

"That doesn't matter. Dammit. What the fuck were you thinking? Do you have any idea how stupid that was? What if he'd been home? What were you going to say to him?" Elliott isn't upset with me, I don't think. He's scared that something bad could have happened if Daniel came home when I was there. I got lucky.

Elliott's attitude changes. He uncrosses his arms, reaching for and reeling me in. "Why didn't you at least tell me where you were going? I would have gone with you," he says, holding me so close that I can feel his heart beat through his shirt. "You and I are on the same side," he says. "We want the same thing."

"I know. But what would we have done with the kids? We can't leave them alone, and if I had told you where I was going, you wouldn't have wanted me to go."

"From now on," he says, "we tell each other everything.

Promise?" he asks, and I wonder what Elliott means by *we*. Does he mean *me* specifically, because I've been keeping secrets from him? Or does he mean *we*, because he's been keeping secrets from me too?

It comes rushing back in that moment and I find myself thinking again about the blood on his shoes, about how Emily wanted to talk to him that night, how she had something to discuss with him in private, but how Elliott doesn't remember. I shouldn't doubt him. He had been drinking that night—we both had. It *is* possible that he forgot about Emily leaning in, saying, *Do you think I could talk to you tomorrow in private? I have something to ask you*, except that, at the time, he said yes. And not only did he say yes, but he hesitated first, a flush of red on his neck that I told myself was from the alcohol.

I pull free, looking Elliott in the eye. He steps back, increasing the space between us. "What?" he asks. "What is it?"

"It's nothing," I say. "Forget about it."

"Tell me."

"It's just . . ."

"What?"

"What do you mean by *we*, Elliott? What have you been keeping from me?"

Elliott's gaze darts to the police officer. He squints in the sunlight before lowering his eyes back to mine. He says, his voice colder than before, "Is this about the blood on my shoes again?" I don't say, watching as he inhales, as he blows out a noisy breath. "I told you. It was probably mine. I probably cut myself with the fishing line."

I shift in place, trying to slow my breath.

Because he didn't. He didn't tell me that. The first time I asked him about the blood on his shoes, he said it was from bleeding the fish.

His story's changing.

Elliott steps closer, closing the gap between us. He wags his finger at me and says, "To be clear, I didn't actually mean *we*, Court. I meant *you*. I was trying not to make you feel bad for lying to me. You told me you were going to get milk, and then you go and almost get yourself killed. *You* need to start being honest with *me*."

Maybe he means that.

Or maybe he's deflecting blame.

He says, "All you had to say was yes, that you promise not to keep things from me anymore. You didn't have to turn it into a whole thing."

I wonder if I did that, if I turned nothing into something.

Elliott starts to walk away, to close the liftgate. "Listen, before we go in," I say.

"What?" he asks, his movements jerky as he jabs at the button on the back of the car. "What now?"

I hesitate at first, but then say, "There's something else I have to tell you, something Detective Evans told me. It's about Wyatt. The Benadryl."

Elliott pulls his eyes together, trenches forming between them.

"What about it?" he asks.

"He didn't take it like he said he did."

"How do you know that?"

"Because they searched the cottage. There was no Benadryl there. Not a bottle of it and not pills. I think . . ." I say, my mouth dry. "I think that Wyatt was lying about taking Benadryl."

"Why would he lie about that?" Elliott asks, but the answer comes to him just as soon as he does, and his posture stiffens, straightening. Without the Benadryl, Wyatt would have heard people screaming. He would have heard Emily and Nolan begging and fighting for their lives. He would have heard Nolan being beaten to death just outside his bedroom door, the heavy, deadened sound of the bat striking human flesh and bone. He would have woken up at the sound of it, maybe risen from bed and gone to the door, laid his hand on the handle, opened it.

"What do you think Wyatt is keeping from us?" I ask. "What did he see?"

"I don't know, I—" Elliott starts to say, but he stops all of a sudden, his words evaporating into air. His eyes lift, looking past me.

I spin around. I follow Elliott's gaze to see Wyatt, standing in the open door beside Mae.

"Are you talking about me?"

REESE

The new girl and her family check in to the resort the next afternoon. I'm at the lodge with Cass and Mae when it happens,
when I see her walk in with her dark brown hair, her flawless
skin and the kind of smile that actually turns heads. There is
grace in the way she walks, and I'd bet my life that back home—
wherever home is for her—she's popular, has a lot of friends, is
captain of the volleyball team and is the kind of girl that every
guy wants and that every girl wants to be.

I stand there while Mae and Cass take an eternity to pick out
a movie to rent, giggling, putzing around, staring at the poster
of that missing little kid again. As I do, I watch the new girl
float around the lodge, examining things—the moose heads
and taxidermy fish, like I did my first time here—put off by her
confidence but also completely mesmerized by it.

I hate her. I want to be her.

Later that afternoon, I take Mae and Cass to the pool alone.

On the way there, I see Daniel from a distance. I haven't seen
him all day, not since Uncle Elliott found us in the woods together. He's standing by the pool again, skimming leaves off the
water with the net. When I see him, I stop without meaning
to, my mind wandering, going back to last night in the woods,
imagining him leaning in, breathing into my ear to take my
shorts off, so that Mae runs into me from behind.

"Why'd you stop?" she asks.

I don't say. Instead, I say, "You guys go. I'll be right there," not taking my eyes off him.

Mae and Cass jog ahead. I hold in a breath, feeling my smile slowly build. I watch him drag the net over the water's surface. I take in his hair, his eyes, and go mentally back to last night again, to him asking, *Do you wanna?* before laying me down on the ground. Lowering himself between my legs. My heart beats hard again, remembering how everything happened.

Or almost happened.

Daniel looks up. I wave, hoping to catch his attention, but he doesn't see me. I start walking again, faster this time to catch him before he goes. I close in on the pool. It's busy now, all the chairs spoken for, so that Mae and Cass fling their shoes and towels on the ground and go running into the pool, jumping in without testing the water first.

I reach the gate.

It's as I open the gate that I see her. The pretty new girl from the lodge.

She sits on one of the chairs across the pool from Daniel. She's leaned back, her already-tanned legs spread out in front of her. Her eyes, as far as I can tell, are closed, and her face is turned up to the sun, her long hair falling over her shoulders.

I look at Daniel.

He sees her too.

And it's the look on his face and how completely dialed in he is that makes it hard to swallow, hard to breathe. There's a pain in my throat. My lungs tighten.

Time slows down.

I look at her again. I look at him.

The girl must have ESP because she opens her eyes just then, like she knows someone's watching her even with her eyes closed. She looks around the pool, wondering who. She finds him, and when she does, she pulls her knees into her chest. She sits up straighter in the chair and shields her eyes from the sun.

They stare at one another for so long that I start to feel physically sick. I lose my balance, stumbling back a step from the gate. I stand there, frozen, as some little kid comes running past, almost pushing me out of the way to get in, his dad, behind him, muttering something like *slow down* and *not a race*.

"You coming?" the dad asks, holding the gate open for me. I shake my head and mumble no. "Suit yourself," he says. Instead, I watch Daniel wave at the girl. His smile is cool and effortless, the kind of smile I feel in the pit of my stomach because it's not for me and it's not intended for me to see.

The girl smiles back, a smile that slowly widens, changing the look of her whole face, making her even prettier if possible. She lifts her hand. She waves, and then Daniel waves again, like he didn't already wave first. She throws her head back and laughs.

My heart hurts.

I wonder if this is what a heart attack feels like, or if this is worse.

COURTNEY

Detective Evans asks for my permission to speak to Wyatt alone. We're at the police station, getting our fingerprints taken. The station is compact and uninspired, windowless, the ceilings low, the lighting artificial and harsh.

"He doesn't need a guardian present?" I ask.

"No. Not if you say that it's okay for me to speak with him."

I say that it is, before Detective Evans leads Wyatt to a nearby room, and I watch from a distance, through the glass, put off but also mesmerized by Wyatt's indifference and self-control. He sits low in the chair, hunched over the table that his elbows rest on. I watch his mouth move, trying to read his lips, but I can't. When he speaks, it's brief, but when Detective Evans speaks, it goes on much longer, and then they sit in silence, neither of them moving until Wyatt sits back in his chair, sinking even lower, his eyes looking down at his hands while Detective Evans watches him, and though Detective Evans looks young to me—he's probably fifteen or twenty years younger than I am—he's a full-grown man in comparison to Wyatt, both physically and mentally, sitting there at the table in pants and a button-down, cuffed once at the wrist, the long sleeves covering his arms despite the fact that it's warm in the police station.

This goes on for almost twenty minutes.

Detective Evans is serious when he comes out of the room.

"What did he say?" I ask, going to him.

"The same things he's said before. When we pointed out the discrepancies we've found, he couldn't explain them. He said he didn't know where the Benadryl came from and he doesn't remember dreaming about a lost lunch. He only remembers having a dream that he was being taken."

"What does that mean? Are you going to keep him here?" I ask, still wondering what Wyatt saw that night and why he's keeping the truth from us.

"No," he says. "He's not under arrest. You can take him home with you. Listen," he says, sensing my hesitation. "If anything happens, if you ever feel scared, there is an officer just outside the cottage."

I avoid his eye. I don't know what I was expecting, but it's not what I wanted to hear.

"Are you okay?"

"Yes."

"What aren't you telling me?" he asks. I want to be honest with him. I want to be able to tell him that I think Elliott is keeping something from me and that I do feel afraid living with Wyatt. But I think of how that would go, the consequences of telling the truth.

"Nothing," I tell him. "I've told you everything I know."

"You have my number," he says, touching my shoulder with his hand. "You can call me anytime, day or night. I don't mind. This is a small town, Mrs. Gray. I can be anywhere in just a few minutes."

I nod, touched by his kindness.

That evening, I find myself sitting at the Matthewses' kitchen table. Joanna invited Sam to sit with us, but he said, "I'm good here," opting to stand instead, leaned against the countertop in his work clothes. His shoulders round forward, and there are dark circles under his eyes that have probably been there for as long as Kylie has been gone. He holds a beer by his side by the neck. He offered me one too, which I took, sitting across from Joanna, telling them what I discovered about Daniel Clarke.

"You said he lives on Moon Road?" Joanna asks, her voice quiet over the sound of a ceiling fan whirring above us like white noise, which Sam turned on as we came into the kitchen.

I nod and her eyes become wet. She reaches for a purse lying beside her on the table, digging inside of it for a tissue that she presses to her eyes. "That's where Kylie's friend Abby lived too. On Moon Road. They don't live there anymore, I don't think."

"The house looked pretty abandoned."

"It might be," Sam says. He's soft-spoken, sedate. He looks different from the man in the photograph in the living room, the one making silly faces for the photographer. This man has lost weight. His face has thinned down and there is a sadness in his eyes. "From what I heard," he says, "they were behind on paying their property taxes. I think they foreclosed on their home a couple years back. Abby's parents may have gotten a divorce. They moved away. I think her brother is the only one who stuck around. I used to work with her father," he says by means of explanation. "I didn't know him well, but word spreads."

Joanna says, "The police found Kylie's bike not far from their house. It was about a quarter mile away, off some wooded road, lying maybe ten feet into the trees. The police thought someone tried to cover it up." She pauses, thoughtful, and then says, "Kylie was at Abby's house all summer," staring down at the tissue in her hands. "She practically lived there. I knew that the two of them were close, inseparable even, but I never thought—" She stops all of a sudden and I feel weighed down by her guilt, by her grief. She closes her eyes, blaming a lack of mother's intuition for not knowing that Kylie was most likely spending so much time at her friend Abby's house that summer not because of Abby herself, but because of the boy who lived across the street.

"Of course you didn't," I say, reaching across the table for her hand. "How would you have known?"

Joanna lifts her head. She says to me, "I should have asked her about it. I should have asked her why they spent so much time at Abby's house and never came to ours. I should have invited Abby over more. There was a change in Kylie that year, one I knew instinctually had to do with boys. A change in the way she dressed and behaved. She had more confidence, but also more sass. At the time, I told myself it was the coming teen years, and I'm sure that was part of it." She pauses, thinking back. "I remember that I found her looking up things on her phone."

"What kind of things?"

"Like how to tell if a boy likes you and how to kiss a boy. I didn't read too much into it because I kissed my first boy when I was ten on the school playground, because my friends dared me to." She smiles, all of a sudden wistful, looking over a shoulder at Sam. She asks, "Do you remember?"

He takes a sip of his beer, and then he smiles back, nostalgic. "How could I forget?"

"It was Sam," she tells me, though she doesn't need to. She brings her eyes back to mine. "My first kiss. Love at first sight, or something like that. Though I don't know that *I* was *his* first kiss, because all the fourth-grade girls liked Sam."

"You were the only one I had eyes for," he says, coming up from behind to set a hand on her shoulder, and she chuckles, reaching her own hand back to hold his. I look away. They've known each other their whole lives. I think of all that they've been through with losing a child, finding it remarkable that it hasn't torn them apart but has maybe brought them closer together.

Joanna says to me, "I didn't think it was unusual that Kylie would be curious about any of these things at her age. That's normal, right?" she asks, as if for validation, and I tell her it is. It is normal for an eleven- or twelve-year-old to show an interest in boys. Joanna nods, as if relieved by my answer, but then, a breath later, a visible wave of panic and regret washes over her. She says, her voice changing, becoming higher in pitch, "I didn't ask her about it though, about those searches on her phone. Maybe I should have asked her about them. Because if I knew they were in reference to someone much older than her, I would have—"

She stops all of a sudden, dropping her head into her hands to cry. Sam turns to set his beer on the countertop. He comes to her, squatting down beside her chair. He pulls her in, and as I watch, her head falls to his shoulder and he wraps his arm around her back.

"What would you have done?" he asks, stroking her hair, his voice tender and affectionate. "You would have stopped her, told her no, refused to let Kylie go to Abby's house anymore?" He pauses for breath and then says, "Kids do what they want to do, Joanna. She would have found another way, and she would have resented you for it in the process."

He pulls slightly back, lifting her chin so that she's forced to look at him. He says, "You're a good mom. You did everything you were supposed to do. There's nothing you could have done to change what happened."

I feel guilty making them relive this. But at the same time, they might be the only ones who can help me figure out what happened to Reese. And if I can do that, then maybe I can find out what happened to their daughter too.

I look away, giving them space to grieve. My eyes move around the room, finding three photographs of Kylie that hang by magnets on the refrigerator door. I push my chair back, standing from the table to go to them. In one, she's dressed as a pirate for Halloween. In another, she's on the beach, laughing as a wave crashes into her from behind. In the last one, she stands before the front door with a backpack slung over her shoulder like it's the first day of school. I reach for that one, lifting it from under the magnet, bringing it closer for a better look.

In it, I see something I hadn't noticed before.

Reese bears a slight resemblance to Kylie. It's nothing glaring, but it's in the long, wavy hair and green eyes—though Reese is older, of course, her features more mature, the cheekbones more prominent, with less baby fat, and her lips more full.

"She looks like Reese," I say, wondering if this is the same niggling thought I had about the family portrait in the living room, that vaguely familiar, elusive thing my mind couldn't quite reach. I swing back around, turning to face Sam and Joanna. "She's lovely," I say quickly. "But in this picture, something about her looks like Reese to me. The hair, maybe, or her eyes."

Joanna glances at Sam, saying something under her breath that I don't catch.

"Excuse me?"

Joanna looks at me. "I said that must be his type."

My stomach tightens. There is a bad taste in my mouth.

Maybe Kylie and Reese weren't chosen at random.

Maybe Daniel has a weakness for girls like them.

Joanna's voice is desperate, her eyes wide as she says, "The police need to find him, Courtney. He needs to pay for what he did to our girls."

REESE

That night, Emily organizes a family baseball game.

"Everyone plays. No one is exempt," she says, before I can even protest.

I go through the motions. I put on my shoes. I follow everyone else—Emily, Nolan, Wyatt and Mae—blindly out of the cottage, though I fall immediately behind, not keeping pace. Mae looks back, teases, "Hurry up, slowpoke," before turning and running down the hill to Cass, who waits up ahead, beside her own cottage with Aunt Courtney and Uncle Elliott.

Uncle Elliott.

He's looking off into the distance at first. When he knows we're coming, he turns to look at us. He gazes sideways at me out of the corner of his eye like he doesn't know where to look, like he's trying hard to act normal. I don't buy it. I see the tension in his jaw, the way his chin is lifted and his posture stiff. I somehow managed to avoid him all day because he never came to the pool, because Aunt Courtney said he had a migraine, which came as a surprise to everyone. No one knew he ever got migraines.

"How are you feeling?" Emily asks, reaching them first.

"Better," he says.

Mae takes Cass by the hand. They run off ahead. Everyone

else follows, trying to keep up, except for Uncle Elliott, who lingers behind.

"You coming?" Aunt Courtney asks, reaching out to him, her smile warm and her eyes kind.

"You go ahead. I thought I'd wait for Reese to catch up."

"You didn't have to do that," I say as I reach him.

He says nothing to that. Instead, he asks, "Can we talk?" as we start to walk. He's anxious. Up close, there is tension on his face, his skin red, one of his eyes bloodshot. He rubs at the back of his neck. He doesn't wait for me to say if we can talk. Instead, he says, "I want to talk to you about last night."

There is an air of desperation in his voice, which is strained.

"Well, I don't want to talk to you," I say, not looking at him but keeping my eyes ahead where the gap widens, everyone else walking fast to catch up with Mae and Cass, who run.

In nothing flat, he reaches out to grab my arm when no one's looking, his hand a death grip. He stops me. He forces me to turn and look at him, the pressure in my arm throbbing.

"Stop playing games with me, Reese. We need to talk."

I pull my arm away. "Get your fucking hands off me, you creep."

I don't raise my voice. No one hears because they're too far up ahead to hear, but still, I see the fear crop up on his face.

I'll tell them that you were being inappropriate. That you touched me.

He pulls back. He drags his hand through his hair. I see the movement in his throat when he swallows. He shakes his head and says, "You don't know what you're doing."

I hold his eye. I say, "I think I do."

He goes completely still.

"You think this is funny," he says. "You think this is a damn game."

I don't know why I do it. It's not him I'm mad at. It's Daniel.

Daniel's the one who hurt me. But for whatever reason, I take my rage out on him and say, "I don't think there's anything funny about child predators," before turning and trotting off ahead without him, leaving him standing open-mouthed behind me. I meet up with everyone else. My heart is beating harder now, and I can't focus because I can still feel his hand on my arm, and every time I blink, I see Daniel staring at that girl. I see him wave, I see her wave back, and then he waves again. It plays back over and over again in my mind. Daniel stares. She opens her eyes, catches him staring. He waves. She waves. He waves again and she laughs. Over and over again until I want to scream.

It takes a minute for Uncle Elliott to come.

"What's wrong?" Aunt Courtney asks when he does, going to him. "Is it your migraine again?"

He presses the space between his eyes, says, "Yeah. I think so."

There isn't an actual baseball field for us to play on. It's just grass. We don't have any bases, and so I stand, watching as Emily lays down random things like a frisbee and paper plates, weighing them down with rocks, but even as I do, I'm still thinking about Daniel and something Skylar told me once about how, when you give guys what they want, they don't want you anymore.

"Earth to Reese . . ." someone says, and I come to. Everyone is watching me now, waiting on me to begin.

"This is so stupid," I mutter under my breath. "Why do I have to play?"

"Because we're all playing," Emily says, as if that's an actual answer.

There are eight of us here, which means four on each team. Emily assigns teams lest anyone's feelings get hurt—which means Mae, because Mae would have no doubt been last to get picked and she would have cried. I wind up on a team with Nolan, Uncle Elliott and Mae, and though Emily claims she tried to be fair, she takes Wyatt—high school all-star—for herself. He has a batting average of something like .500, which means that when Wyatt swings, he doesn't miss.

Wyatt is up to bat first. Within a few seconds, we're losing. The next three batters strike out and then our team is up. Nolan gets on base first. When it's my turn, I can't hold or swing a bat to save my life, though I don't even try, not really, because I don't care about something as stupid as baseball. I can't stop thinking about Daniel. About that girl and about Skylar's words. *When you give guys what they want, they don't want you anymore.* I should have listened to her. I should have known better.

Wyatt stands on the mound, sneering at me, saying, "Imagine not even being able to swing a bat," and Emily tells him to be nice, that we can't all be as good at baseball as him.

I feel Uncle Elliott's eyes on me the whole time. When I look over, his jaw is clenched, his feet are spread wide apart and his arms are crossed, like he's silently raging.

There is a part of me that almost feels guilty for threatening him. Though, if I'm being objective, he's the one who started it, I think, looking down at the red mark from his hand still on my wrist.

He's the one who threatened to tell.

It's after eight now and people are hungry. The game went longer than expected and we haven't had any dinner yet. Mae is whiny. She says that her stomach hurts, and Emily coddles her, saying she'll cut her an apple while Dad puts something on the grill, as if she can't just cut her own stupid apple. But I'm not complaining. Because when Emily is hyperfocused on Mae, then she can't pay any attention to me, which means that I drop back. I lose them. I take my time getting back to the cottage, going my own way.

I take the path through the woods. It's the golden hour now, which used to be Skylar's and my favorite time of day, when we'd go out into the field by her house and take turns posing for pictures. The world is gold. The sunlight is soft and dreamy. It creates long shadows in the woods while the temperatures drop and bugs come out, fireflies creating light. I think of all the pictures I have of Skylar and me posing in the golden hour. Once they covered her Instagram page. Now she's taken them all down. The only pictures she has on there anymore are of her and Gracie.

As I walk through the woods alone, I hear voices carrying from the other side of the trees.

I draw in a breath.

Daniel.

My breath is shaky. I creep out from the trees, staying far enough back that they can't see me. I find Daniel and the new girl standing face-to-face beside a cottage. As I watch—not breathing and anchored in place like a ship—she asks, "When did you get this?" running her hand up his arm, over his tattoo. She traces it, a king cobra, which is long and coiled around his forearm and up his bicep, its mouth open, fangs and forked tongue jutting out. He tells her how he and a couple buddies got them, and she asks, "Did it hurt?"

"If it did, I don't remember," he says. "I have something for you," he tells her, reaching into his pocket. "Close your eyes and hold out your hand." She does. He lays something in the palm of her hand, and I don't have to see it to know. "Open your eyes," he says. When she does, she lifts a bracelet from her hand, and I watch him clasp it onto her thin little wrist, asking, "Do you like it?" She nods.

"How long are you here for?" he asks, leaning in.

She sinks back against the cottage, letting it bear her weight, and says, "A week."

"That's all?" he asks, coming closer, closing the gap, thinking they're alone, that no one can see them.

"Yeah," she says, her face turning pouty. "That's all."

He strokes her cheek with the back of a finger, says, "Then we have to make the most of it," and it feels like time slows down. Like it stops. My vision blurs, a feeling of vertigo rushing me. The world spins. I set my hand on a tree for balance, feeling the rough bark beneath my palm, telling myself he didn't say what I think I heard, but he did. It's exactly what he said. I bite my lower lip hard so I don't cry, tasting blood.

Then we have to make the most of it.

The same thing he said to me.

I run as fast as I can back to the cottage. When I get there, Emily is in the kitchen making dinner. She turns, sees me when I come in. My hand is on my stomach. She asks what's wrong, and I tell her I have a stomachache, that I think I might be sick.

"Maybe you're just hungry," she suggests, as if it could be that easy, as if heartbreak could be likened to hunger and cured with food.

"I don't think so. I don't think I can eat."

"Well, you have to eat something."

"I can't," I say again. "I'll puke if I do."

She watches me for a long time. Then she says, "Okay," letting me off the hook because of the look on my face and because she thinks I might actually be sick. I fight tears, desperate to get out onto the porch, to be alone before I start to cry.

Outside, everyone eats but me. I hear them through the screens of the porch, where I lie in bed with my back to them, listening to them laugh and to their conversations. The adults are drinking. Everything gets funnier the more they have to drink, though every now and then their voices go quiet, whisper-like, and I wonder what they're talking about and if they're talking about me.

And then I hear my name and I know. They are talking about me.

"What was wrong with Reese? Why didn't she eat with us?"

"She said her stomach hurt," Emily says.

"That's too bad. She seemed fine when we were playing baseball," Aunt Courtney says.

"I don't know about *fine*. She was pretty moody."

Nolan scoffs. "What else is new? She's always moody."

My throat tightens.

Aunt Courtney says, "I didn't mean that. I just meant that I didn't hear her say anything about her stomach bothering her during the game." She pauses, says then, "Can you imagine how hard it is to be a teenager these days, with social media and all that? It's not like when we were kids. We had it easy in comparison."

"Do you think she's on drugs?" Uncle Elliott asks from out of nowhere, and I know that's what he wants them to think. That I'm on drugs. "I just mean the moodiness. I'm not saying she is, but it's a sign. Being sullen, depressed, hostile, withdrawn."

People are quiet, imagining me as all these things, deciding in their minds that Uncle Elliott is right, that I probably am on drugs.

Emily asks, "Like what? Like weed? Where would she even get that?"

Nolan's voice is loud, patronizing. "Anywhere, Emily. Don't be so naive. Half her school probably smokes weed."

"Shhh," Aunt Courtney says. "You don't want her to know

we're talking about her." She asks then, "Have you checked on her since we've been home? Have you made sure she's okay?"

"No," Emily says. She goes quiet and I think that's all, just *no*. But then she says, "Maybe I will. Maybe I will go see how she is," and for a minute, I flash back to when I was young, when Emily would come into my room at night and lie down beside me when I had a bad dream or didn't feel well or couldn't sleep. She would burrow beside me under the covers, nuzzle in close and run her fingers up and down my back until I fell asleep.

But then Mae came and everything changed. Because Mae almost died. Because, when she was born, there was a lack of oxygen and blood flow to the brain due to something with her umbilical cord, because the cord came out before Mae did. Her skin was blue when she was born and her breathing was weak, which I only knew because I stood there that night, hidden behind an open door, when Nolan came home from the hospital, telling my grandparents about the color of her skin and how they weren't sure she was going to survive the night. The doctors had all sorts of scary prognoses should she actually survive, like cerebral palsy, epilepsy, more. She stayed in the NICU for weeks, on a breathing machine. Emily stayed too (feeling guilty somehow, as if it was all her fault) and when they came home, Mae almost never left Emily's arms. Something had changed. I was seven at the time, and though I knew Emily still loved me, I could tell she loved Mae more.

"I'll be right back," Emily says now, and I imagine her setting down her drink, pushing her chair back, standing up, and I decide that when she gets here, I'll tell her everything. About Daniel. About what happened. About how much my heart hurts.

But then, before she can leave to come to me, Uncle Elliott's voice cuts in, and he says, "Are you sure you want to do that?"

Emily asks, "You don't think I should?"

"Well," he says, "I'm just thinking she's probably asleep, right? If she was telling the truth and really doesn't feel well. You should let her sleep."

My anger grows. Uncle Elliott is only saying it to protect himself, to keep Emily from me so that I can't say anything to her about him.

"No," she says, "I guess you're right. I don't want to wake her. She should sleep if she's sick."

And just like that, someone gets more for them to drink. The laughter starts up again. They move from the deck to the firepit, where I can still hear them, though their voices are softer, dulled down by the distance.

I put a pillow over my head so I can't hear them at all. I don't actually know that I'm crying, but all of a sudden my face is drenched with tears that seep into the pillowcase, making it wet.

Sometime later, I come to. I must have rolled over in my sleep, because my body faces the other way, across the porch, out the window and toward the firepit, which has gone cold, taking any traces of light with it so that I can't see the empty camping chairs or the empty bottles of booze.

It's not quiet outside. Bugs like crickets and cicadas make noise. Thunder rolls across the sky in the far-off distance, while, closer by, embers sputter in some dying fire that's been left to burn out all on its own.

I don't know what time it is. I don't know how long I've been asleep, or how much time has passed since everyone went in. I slip my hand out from under the covers, reaching for my phone on the nightstand, seeing that it's two thirty in the morning.

It's black outside, though it's not black inside the cottage be-cause someone left the kitchen light on before they went to sleep, which they never do, which tells me they were too drunk when they went to bed to remember to turn off the light.

Images of Daniel and that girl come rushing back to me.

I roll over in bed. I turn the other way, toward the screen closest to the bed. I close my eyes again, wanting to fall back to sleep and forget, to lose myself to unconsciousness, to never wake up.

A noise comes to me from outside. It's close by, a heavy, deadened sound like when walnuts fall from trees.

I throw my eyes open and search.

It's too dark outside to see anything. The kitchen light is a disadvantage. Because of it, I can't see out, but if anyone is standing outside, they can see right in.

I hold my breath, fixating on the world outside, trying to get my eyes to adjust, staring but not really seeing anything.

Lightning flashes in the sky, and in the blaze of light it gives off, I see him, a dark silhouette standing at the tree line, facing our cottage.

I gasp, telling myself to be quiet, to hold still.

He comes forward. As he gets closer, the moon just barely illuminates his edges from behind, so that they're woolly and unfocused. I inhale, staring at him standing far enough away that I can't make him fully out, but close enough to know he's there. To hear him breathe.

I lie perfectly still and he comes closer, stepping up to the window, his face coming into view. I watch his eyes, which reflect the kitchen light, glowing outside.

"Where were you?" he asks, leaning out to touch the screen.

Slowly, I push myself up to a sitting position. I drag my body to the far side of the bed, furthest away from the screens. I pull my knees into me, wrapping the covers over them. "What . . . what are you doing here, Daniel? It's the middle of the—"

"I said, where were you?" he asks again, cutting me off this time, and I go silent because there's a bite to his words, an edge to them I've never heard before, at least not directed at me. He says, as if upset, "I waited for you for hours. You didn't come. If you weren't going to come, you should have told me."

"I . . . I don't feel good," I say, hearing and feeling a vibration to my words that I know is fear, though I tell myself not to be scared, that I don't need to be scared because it's just Daniel, and Daniel wouldn't hurt me, except that he already has. I think of him leaning into that girl tonight, stroking her face with the back of his finger, saying, *Then we have to make the most of it.*

"You sure about that?" he asks.

"Yes. I feel sick."

"You're not lying to me?"

"Why would I lie about being sick?" I ask.

"I don't know. You tell me."

I hesitate and then I say, "I saw you with that girl."

"What girl?" he asks, like I'm dumb. Like I didn't actually see them together. When I say nothing, he sighs and says, "That was a mistake. A lapse in judgment. She has a boyfriend, for one, and is stuck up as hell. I don't like her." He pauses, takes a breath, says in some sickening, sycophantic way, "I like you, Reese like the candy," as if trying to butter me up, to get back on my good side, except that this time when he says it, it isn't cute. This time, it gets under my skin. He asks, "Is that why you're mad? Is that why you didn't meet me at the lake?" softer, crooning. He sets his hand on the screen again, pressing so that the edges of it start to peel away from the frame. If he pressed any harder the screen would break and then he'd be on the porch with me. "Come outside," he says. "Let me make it up to you."

I say, "No." Because he doesn't actually like me. I'm an idiot for thinking a guy like him ever would.

He pulls a face. "No?"

"No."

It takes almost no time at all for him to ask, "Why, Reese, because you have so many guys waiting for you back home?" He laughs, but it's not a funny laugh. It's cruel. Tears sting my eyes, and I think of all the things I said to him that I never said to anyone else. "You said so yourself. They don't like you. No one thinks of you like that. No one thinks you're pretty."

No one thinks you're pretty.

My heart hurts. There's a squeezing feeling in my chest, my ribs. My chin trembles.

"You're not crying, Reese, are you?" he asks. When I say nothing, he says, "So you're not sick then," running his hands through his hair, his cruelty turning to anger. "So you were lying."

"Just leave me alone, Daniel. Go away."

"You're making a mistake, Reese. You'll be sorry," he says.

"I don't care. Just go away."

He stands there a long time. Saying nothing. Breathing hard while I don't breathe. While I hold my breath, my heart pounding inside of me until it hurts.

"You'll regret this," he says. "Do you hear me? You'll fucking regret this."

I won't. The only thing I regret is ever liking him.

He backs slowly away. When I can't see him anymore, I slide down in bed, lying on my side with the covers pulled up to my neck.

I think he's gone, that he's left.

But then, from outside, I hear the flick of a lighter and see the glowing cherry at the end of a joint. I smell weed.

He's not gone.

He's still out there, watching me from the trees because I'm backlit by the kitchen light, on full display.

Lightning flashes in the sky again. Thunder rolls. It never rains.

I stare at the glowing red embers, at the movement of them as he inhales and then lowers his arm to his side, over and over again.

In time, he puts out the joint so I can't see where he is anymore.

It doesn't matter because even if I can't see him, I know he hasn't left. He's still there.

He's still watching me.

COURTNEY

In the morning, I find Mae crying for Emily when I get up. She's disconsolate, curled into a ball on the sofa, folded over and weeping into the arm of it. I sit down beside her and rub her back, and then later, once I've managed to calm her down, I show Elliott the key to the cottage next door. "Ms. Dahl said the police have finished their investigation and that we can go in and take what we need. The kids might like some of their and Emily's and Nolan's things," I say, thinking it might help Mae if she had something of Emily's to hold.

Elliott agrees, though we haven't been on the best terms since our argument yesterday afternoon. Instead, we've avoided one another, giving each other a wide berth, which is hard to do in a cottage this size.

Still, he comes with me. We don't tell the kids where we're going, only that they should stay inside, lock the door, and that we'll be back in a couple minutes. Elliott and I are quiet as we climb the hill to the cottage, the tension in the air palpable. I didn't sleep again last night, lying awake beside him all night. He never reached for me. He didn't whisper an apology in the darkness. He didn't tell me good-night or say that he loved me. I didn't say anything either. Instead, I lay there, thinking through things, trying to remember every moment of the last few days, the details I might have forgotten.

There was one.

It came to me in the middle of the night. I remembered that the night before Reese disappeared, she and Elliott were in the small kitchen together in Emily and Nolan's cottage. They were talking, which I remember only because Nolan, Emily and I were waiting for Elliott for so long that eventually I took his turn at rummy so the rest of us could play.

"Are you sure you want to do this?" Elliott asks now as we arrive at the cottage. He turns to me, standing before the front door with the key in his hand.

I don't answer. Instead, I search his face, his eyes. Elliott's chin juts out, his jawline hard. As I watch, he reaches up to rub his temples as if feeling a headache coming on.

I say, "I thought about something last night."

"What?" he asks, frowning, and already, I can hear the impatience in his tone.

I take a breath, steeling myself. "That last night that we were here, in this cottage, we were playing cards." Elliott nods. "You and Reese were in the kitchen together for a while. I only remember because it took so long for you to come back that I took your turn for you."

"So?" he asks. "Is there a question there, Court, or is it just an observation?"

I swallow with effort, my throat so tight it hurts. "I guess I was just wondering what you two were talking about in the kitchen for so long."

Elliott harrumphs. "Fuck, Courtney. This again?" Though he doesn't exactly mean *this* because I haven't asked about this before; he means, in general, more questions. "I don't know," he says, flinging his hands up in the air, exasperated. "Who's better, Taylor Swift or Billie Eilish? If cats are better than dogs, global fucking warming . . . That was days ago. How would I remember what we were talking about? Did Reese ever have any conversations of substance anyway? She had no respect for anyone and didn't care about anything but herself."

I flinch, feeling the color drain from my face. It's not just the fact that he's speaking of her in the past tense like she's dead. It's the cruelty in his words. Is he only misplacing his anger at me, or did something happen between them that night that I don't know?

I take a step back, my eyes wide.

Elliott asks roughly, "Are we going in or not?"

I nod, unable to find the words to speak. I watch as he forces the flat metal key into the groove, turns the knob and throws open the door to the cottage.

I'm not prepared for what we find. I don't know what I was expecting, but this isn't it.

Nolan and Emily's cottage hasn't been cleaned. It's exactly as it was the last time I was here, except for the bodies, which are gone.

The blood is not gone. It's still there. Standing just inside the open door, I see all the way onto the screened-in porch where the bloodstain remains on the walls, dried-up beads of it like teardrops. The bed on the porch has been moved. Even from the front door, I can see that it's been pushed roughly out of the way, I imagine to make room for the coroner's gurney to fit, so that Emily's body could be lifted from the floor. There's blood on the stairs too, dripping down the wall.

The smell is not gone. It's something pungent and metallic, like rust. The windows are closed, trapping it in the cottage with Elliott and me.

Elliott gags on the smell, pressing a hand to his mouth and nose to keep it at bay.

I don't ask him if he's okay. I take one look at the inside of the place, and I leave.

REESE

The next night, I wake up. I open my eyes to find Daniel standing outside again, a murky figure watching me sleep. I don't move. I hold perfectly still. My breaths are shallow, not enough oxygen filling my lungs, so they're on fire. I try not to blink, wondering if he can see that my eyes are open, if they glow.

But then I realize something is wrong.

He knows I'm awake. He comes closer, and as he does, the floorboards creak, the soles of his shoes putting weight on the wood.

Because he's inside.

He's on the screened-in porch with me.

I scream, pulling back to the far side of the bed as Daniel sprints across the room, putting a knee on the edge of the bed so that it sinks with his weight. In a breath, he leans over me, clamping down on my mouth with one hand.

In the other hand, a knife.

The blade, in the moonlight, is long and sharp. I become motionless.

I can't think.

I can't breathe.

I squeeze my eyes shut tight, as Daniel leans over me and says, "I don't want to have to hurt you." I struggle to breathe under the weight of his hand. "Look at me, Reese," he says. "Look

IT'S NOT HER   263

at me." I open my eyes, see him suspended above me, his face close, his eyes hollow and black. "Are you going to be quiet now?" he asks, and I nod, gasping as he moves his hand. In the darkness, he sits down on the edge of the bed, his breaths quick and shallow like mine, visible through his shirt.

He touches my hair. He runs his tacky fingers the length of it so that it tugs at the scalp. I sob and he asks, "What's wrong, Reese? Why are you crying?"

"You're hurting me," I moan.

He lets go of my hair. He lies down, stretching out beside me in bed, pressing in so close I feel his heartbeat on my arm.

"I'm sorry," he says. "I don't want to hurt you."

He searches for the edge of the sheet with one hand. He finds it and slips his warm, sweaty hand under the covers, the knife in the other hand, above his head, in my peripheral vision. "Is that better?" he asks.

I hold still. I don't move. His hand finds the hem of my shirt, slipping under, touching me like he has before, but this time it's unwanted. This time is makes me want to scream.

Tears burn my eyes. I breathe out, "I want you to go."

"No, you don't, Reese," he says, running his fingers up the side of my ribs. "You like me, remember? A lot. You told me so."

"I don't like you. I want you to go."

"No, you don't."

"Yes. I do."

He takes his hand out from under my shirt. He props himself on the other arm, moving the knife to his right hand. "It doesn't have to be this way," he says, pressing the flat part of the blade to my neck, and I lift my chin, arching my back. I cry out from the cold, softly moaning as he drags the knife across my throat, wondering what would happen if it wasn't the flat part of the blade but the edge. How deep it would cut, how much it would bleed, if I would die.

"Take your pants off, Reese."

"No. I don't want to."

"I don't want to have to ask you again. Just do it, Reese. This doesn't have to be so hard."

"You're scaring me," I whimper, my hands shaking as I push my pajama pants beneath my hips, and he moves himself on top of me.

"You know I don't want to do that," he says again, pressing himself between my legs, trying to convince me, to win me over, as if I have some say. His voice is soft, smarmy. He says, "You told me you want to be with me. I know you still want that, Reese. I want that too."

I brace myself for it to hurt. But before anything can happen, from somewhere deep inside the cottage, a noise comes through the open door. Daniel looks up. His eyes go to the knife, and then something flashes on his face. Something dark. He slides off, puts his finger to his lips. *Shhhh.*

He starts to stand up, his eyes on the open door. As he does, I don't hesitate. I react, catching him off guard. I smack his hand, and as I do, he loses his grip on the knife. It falls onto the bed. Surprise crosses his face. We both reach for the knife at the same time, scrambling, though somehow, I'm the one who manages to come up with it.

I brandish it in front of me, my hands shaking. "Get back. Get away from me."

He rises from the bed, standing at the edge of it.

He laughs, mocking me. He swings his own imaginary knife out in front of him. "*Get back. Get away from me.*" And then, all of a sudden, he stops laughing. His face gets serious. His tone is patronizing as he asks, "What are you doing, Reese? You know you wouldn't use that. You wouldn't hurt me."

He comes closer. "Why don't you just give it to me so no one gets hurt." He raises an open hand for the knife as if to take it.

Instinctively I thrust it forward, a short, straight jab that connects.

Daniel flinches as the blade razes his skin. He looks down at his hand. When he looks up again, his eyes are cold. "You bitch," he says, and though it's dark in the room, I can see the blood on his hand. "You stupid bitch."

He comes at me again, but this time, when I raise the knife, he stops. Because he knows I would use it. I would hurt him.

For a long time, he stares at the knife, and then my face, and then the knife again.

"You're nothing," he says, reaching down to the floor for my pink sweatshirt, which he wraps around his bloody hand. "You're not even worth it."

I watch him cross the cottage. He walks out the front door, leaving it open.

My heart pounds. My legs give. I sink to the edge of the bed, sliding to the floor, crying.

I hope it's the last time I ever see him.

COURTNEY

We grab our things and leave the resort.

The motel, when we get to it, is even worse than I imagined.

"Where will everyone sleep?" Cass asks, taking in the two sagging double-size beds in the small room.

"You can sleep with Dad and me, and Mae and Wyatt can have the other bed."

Wyatt takes issue with that. "I'm not sleeping with her. I'll sleep on the floor."

"Let's see about a cot then," I say because I can only imagine how filthy the carpeting is.

Cobwebs hang from the corners of the room. When I pull back the quilt, the linens are stained, a pale red the color of terracotta or salmon flesh, which makes me think of blood.

Incidentally, the police don't clean up from a crime scene when they're through with it. That's up to the homeowners to do, which Ms. Dahl neglected to tell me when she gave me the key. Maybe she didn't know. Or maybe she just didn't say.

I look around the room. I'm not even sure why the motel is still in business, why the health department or some other entity hasn't shut them down. My stomach sinks.

Even here, Emily and Nolan are still dead. Reese is still missing.

I don't know why I thought this would be any better.

—

"I'm going to shower," I say, needing a minute to myself more than anything.

I set my bag on the dresser, gathering clean clothes from inside of it before going to the bathroom, where I try closing the door, but the latch is misaligned. It doesn't stay shut. Instead, it floats immediately open, and I have to push it closed for a second time, pressing more firmly this time, wishing for a lock, which the door doesn't have.

Hesitantly, I strip my clothes off, keeping my eyes on the door. I drop them into a pile by the toilet, running the water so hot that at first it scalds me and I have to turn the knob and scale back on the heat. The water smells like sulfur. Some of the shower tiles are missing while mold grows in the grout. I let the water run over me, using a small, generic travel-size bar of soap to scour myself clean, though no matter how hard I scrub, I can't erase the image of the blood in Emily and Nolan's cottage from my mind. It's still there.

It will always be there.

The bathroom is full of steam when I turn the water off. I peel the curtain back to see that the mirror is completely fogged up.

I don't see at first that the door has popped open all on its own.

I don't see anything through the thick water vapor, not until I reach for a towel on the toilet seat with nothing on to find Wyatt standing on the other side of the door, looking in at me through the crack.

I get dressed. I don't tell Elliott about Wyatt, because Elliott and I are barely on speaking terms, but I keep my distance from him.

A little while later, Detective Evans texts to say the fingerprint results have come back. He stops by the motel to speak to me, and when he arrives, I meet him outside, leaving Elliott in the motel room with the kids.

We stand in the parking lot, the sound of passing traffic on the street ambient noise. There, Detective Evans tells me that all of our prints were found in the cottage. The ones left with blood, however, belong to none of us. They belong to someone else, someone whose prints are not in their database.

It's cold outside, the warm day disappearing with the sun. Night has fallen.

I shiver, though it's not only from the cold.

The motel sits on a rural highway, where the occasional car or truck passes by. The motel's parking lot is small. There are only a couple cars besides ours. I could be wrong, but I don't think they're vacationers like us. I think they're unhoused people living temporarily in the motel, which is only one floor with rooms entered from the outside.

"Forensics analyzed the blood on Reese's sweatshirt. It wasn't hers," he says. "It didn't belong to either Reese or her parents."

"Then who?"

"Daniel Clarke. He says it's his."

My jaw goes slack in disbelief. "What . . . what do you mean he says it's his? When did you speak to him?"

"He's back home, Mrs. Gray."

"Why didn't you tell me? Where has he been?"

"That's why I'm here. I came to tell you. According to him, he drove west, sleeping in his truck at rest stops. He made it as far as the South Dakota border before turning around and coming home. Thought he'd go see Mount Rushmore but then changed his mind."

"He's lying," I say with unwavering belief.

"I don't think he is. We checked his bank statement. There are receipts for gas and food all along Interstate 90. And traffic cams show that your niece wasn't with him." He pauses, angles his head the other way and says, "He isn't like you and me. He's a loner. A drifter, a stoner. He's gotten in trouble for things before—like trespassing and robbery—but never anything violent. He was a couple years younger than me in school. As far as I know, he's always been like this." He shrugs, though this is the first time Detective Evans has mentioned having firsthand knowledge of Daniel Clarke. It takes me aback, and I have to regroup and remember that both men are about the same age. I've never asked Detective Evans about his personal life, if he grew up here and why he became a detective. It never crossed my mind, but now it does, though there are some things I can answer for myself now, like that he did grow up here, and he knew Daniel when they were boys. "He said he just needed to be alone."

"What did he say about Reese?"

"That he was into her. But she didn't reciprocate."

Except I saw her by that little pool house, and it seemed like she did reciprocate. That she *was* very much into him.

Detective Evans says, "He said something else."

"What?"

"He said that Reese came after him with a knife. That she stabbed him with it, which is how his blood wound up on her sweatshirt."

"He's a liar. He's making that up."

"I don't know. It's a case of he said, she said, but I can tell you this—there were knife wounds on his hand."

"Why would Reese do that if not in self-defense?" I ask, remembering what Mae said, how she overheard Reese that night, saying that Daniel was hurting her and how he was scaring her.

"We asked him what happened. He didn't have much to say,

nothing kind, nothing that bears repeating," he says, and I feel myself get upset, thinking of him trash-talking Reese.

"Are you sure he didn't hurt her?" I ask, imagining if Reese did eventually turn down Daniel Clarke's advances and he got mad. If he lost his temper.

But Detective Evans says with confidence, "I'm certain."

"How can you be so certain?"

"Because by the night she disappeared, he was already gone."

REESE

There is blood on the floor. I don't see it until morning, when the sun comes up and I go back onto the porch for the first time since Daniel left. I didn't sleep on the porch. I didn't sleep at all. Once Daniel was gone, I closed and locked the front door, and then I lay on the sofa with my eyes wide, staring at the front door, knowing that just because it was locked didn't mean Daniel didn't have a key. He does. He has a master key to all the cottages. He can come and go whenever he wants.

There are only a couple drops of blood. They're on the wood floor. I grab the edge of the rug and pull it over to hide them. The knife was in my hand when Daniel left. There's blood on it too. After he was gone, I opened the nightstand drawer, slipped it in, knowing I have to get rid of it.

When the sun comes up, Emily finds me lying on the living room sofa with my pillows and a blanket.

"Reese?" she asks, standing above me. "What's wrong? Why didn't you sleep on the porch?"

I get to my feet. "I'm not sleeping out there anymore," I say. "Someone else can sleep there, but not me."

Emily, for once, doesn't object. Instead, she watches as I grab my bags from the porch and march upstairs with them and into Mae's room, where Mae is still sleeping.

"What are you doing?" Mae asks, coming to when I come in, rubbing her eyes, still groggy from sleep.

"What does it look like I'm doing? I'm sleeping with you, you idiot," I say as I pull the covers back and lie down beside her in the flat, cramped bed.

Out of the corner of my eye, I think I see Mae smile.

That night, Aunt Courtney, Uncle Elliott and Cass come over for dinner. After what happened last night, I'm anxious. I can't relax. It's loud and hot in the cottage, the windows open but no air moving around the room. My clothes are uncomfortable. The sleeves of my shirt chafe.

"What's wrong?" Emily asks.

"Nothing."

"Why aren't you eating?"

"I am," I say, stabbing at a potato and putting it in my mouth, but it's hard to move the food around and chew.

After we're done, I can't find my phone. I look everywhere. "What are you looking for?" someone asks as I pull pillows from the sofa and search behind them for it.

"My phone. Has anyone seen it?"

No one has. Everyone helps look until, from across the room, Mae asks, "Is this it?" and when I turn, she's holding my phone in her hand, grinning like a little brat. Cass stands next to her, her face red, trying not to laugh, though eventually, they can't hold it in anymore. They die laughing, falling into each other, and my stomach drops because they didn't just happen to find my phone. They had it all along. They did something to it. Mae knows the password to my phone because of all the times I let her go on TikTok and YouTube when Emily says no, saying the videos are inappropriate and addictive, which they probably are, but Mae's not as naive as everyone thinks.

My password is Mae's birthdate, because mine seemed obvious. I regret that now.

"Give me that," I say, snatching my phone back from them, my hands shaking. I look down to see a bunch of Instagram notifications pop up on the screen, though I haven't posted anything to Instagram in months and shouldn't be getting so many, if any.

"I hate you," I say. "I actually hate both of you."

They laugh again. I swipe up to unlock, and then I find the app and open it. All of a sudden, it's hard to breathe.

They've posted a picture of Skylar and me. From my own phone. And not just any picture, but one of us from back in eighth grade that I should have deleted long ago, that I never should have even kept. In it, we're smiling and happy, though my face is covered in acne, which it was before Emily took me to see her dermatologist, worried that if we didn't get it under control it would scar. I also have braces, big silver brackets with teal rubber bands that the orthodontist let me pick out, which I thought was cool at the time, but is now humiliating. Everything about this is humiliating.

Their dumb caption: *My bestie.*

They don't know that Skylar isn't my bestie anymore. That Skylar actually hates me.

Mae and Cass don't know what they've done. They think it's funny, a stupid joke.

They don't know that my life is over.

There are three likes and over thirty comments already, in the last two minutes alone, which are beyond cruel.

You wish.
Nice face.
Who actually liked this?
This is so cringe.

My face gets hot and red, and I fill with rage, humiliation, shame.

I look up over my phone to see Mae and Cass still giggling their dumb heads off—gasping for air, holding their sides while I want to die—about what they did, how they pranked me.

Aunt Courtney asks, "What's so funny over there?" saying something to Emily about how nice it is to see the three of us having fun together.

No one tells her. Instead, I lean into Mae and Cass and slur under my breath, "You're so stupid. You're both such fucking idiots. If you ever touch my phone again, I'll kill you."

"No, you won't," Mae says, sticking her tongue out.

"Watch me."

"Then we'll kill you back."

"You couldn't. Because you'd be dead."

They turn and go running upstairs, laughing so hard they run into a wall. A door slams. Emily turns around, asking, "Where did Mae and Cass go?"

I'm so stupid. I'm so fucking stupid. How could I ever leave my phone alone?

It's not just the picture of me. It's because Skylar's in it too, like I'm needy and obsessed, like I haven't gotten the memo that she doesn't like me anymore, that she's not my friend.

You're so desperate for attention.
Skylar doesn't even like you. No one does.

Emily says something. "Reese? Did you hear me?" she asks when I don't respond.

I look up. The four of them sit stooped over the little living room coffee table, playing cards and drinking.

"No. What?"

"Why don't you come play with us?"

"I don't know how to play," I say, because the last place on earth I want to be is with them. I take my phone and go into the kitchen, because it's the only place in the cottage where no one is. I hunch over the ugly green countertops with my back to them, rocking in place, being a sadomasochist, not deleting the picture Mae and Cass posted, but reading the comments as they come in, believing them.

> **You should do everyone a favor and KYS.**
> **Loser.**
> **Lame.**
> **No one likes you.**

My mind is all over the place, though the last thing I'm thinking about is Uncle Elliott.

The problem is that he's still thinking about me.

He comes up from behind. "Listen," he says, the word a sharp, hissing sound like from a snake. I turn to find him standing in the kitchen with me, in the open doorway, so that there's only one way out and it's past him.

"What do you want?" I snap, wanting more than anything to be alone.

He throws a look back over his shoulder. When he brings his eyes back to mine, he's on edge, talking under his breath, his words coming out fast. "Can we just call a truce?"

"Hey, Elliott. Can you grab me another beer while you're in there?" Nolan shouts out from the living room.

Uncle Elliott calls back, "Sure. Corona or Spotted Cow?" his voice all of a sudden relaxed, like he's unagitated, except for the fact that his eyes never let go of mine.

"What do you say, Reese?" Uncle Elliott goes on, coming closer to me, lowering his voice again. "Can we pretend like it never happened?"

And I would just say yes. Because it's not like it matters. What happened between Daniel and me is done. I don't ever want to see him again, for as long as I live. I don't actually care what Uncle Elliott tells Emily and Nolan. So what if I get grounded. Nothing matters anymore.

"Sure."

"Say it," he says.

"Say what?" I ask.

There's a tightness on his face and around his eyes. He blinks a lot, dragging his hand through his hair before looking back over his shoulder and then again at me as he says, leaning in, "Say you won't tell those lies about me. Promise me, Reese. On your life."

"*On your life,*" I mock, not laughing. I shrug him off. "I said yeah. Besides, it's not that big of a deal."

"It is that big of a deal. Do you have any idea what they do to sex offenders?"

I ask, "If you didn't do anything, then what do you have to be so worried about?"

"Just promise me, Reese. Say you won't say anything."

"I—" I start to say, but then Nolan appears all of a sudden and slaps Uncle Elliott hard on the back. Elliott spins around.

"Never mind," Nolan says, "I'll get it myself." Elliott's face is blank. "The beer. Don't tell me you forgot already." Nolan rolls his eyes, goes to the fridge for his own beer, turns back. "What's this very clandestine conversation about?" he asks, teasing, his eyes going between Uncle Elliott's and mine.

"Why don't you tell him," I say.

I take the opportunity to make my escape. I cross the room, go to sit in the blue velvet recliner alone, pulling my legs into me, finally deleting the picture Mae and Cass posted from my Instagram. It's gone, but it's not so easy to forget.

You should do everyone a favor and KYS. Loser.

I don't stop there. I go into my settings and, in an instant, delete every single one of my pictures and videos like they never even existed. I consider deleting the whole damn page, like I never even existed.

Uncle Elliott turns from the kitchen. His eyes move in my direction and I hear Nolan ask, "Tell me what?"

Uncle Elliott shrugs him off. He takes a sip of his drink, watching me over the bottle. I look away, but when I look back, his eyes are on me, his face different than before. He releases my eye. He looks to Aunt Courtney sitting on the sofa alone (the spot beside her his) and says at random, "Hey, Court," his words loud and abrupt, calling attention to himself.

She looks up (everyone does). She meets his eye and smiles. Her voice is tender, teasing as she says, "Hey, Elliott."

"I was just thinking that I might get up early and go fishing tomorrow morning."

He lifts his beer again and drinks, then lowers his beer to his side.

"Okay," she says, pulling playing cards from her hand and laying them down on the coffee table, and then she asks what time he thinks he'll go, and he looks at his phone to see when the sun will rise. At the same time, we hear the bedroom door fly open. Mae and Cass come running down the stairs into the living room again, Mae announcing to everyone, "We want to have a sleepover tonight. Can Cass sleep here?" looking directly at Emily, hands in the prayer position, practically begging. "Pleeeease?"

It's not that I care if Cass sleeps here, because I don't. It's that I'm still mad at them—so mad that I could rage—and I'm not giving up the bed because I am never sleeping on the porch ever again. That bed is mine.

"They are not sleeping here," I say in front of everyone. "No fucking way. I am not listening to them all night."

On the sofa, Aunt Courtney stiffens. I can see on her face that she wants to grab Cass's precious little ears (though it's not like she doesn't hear kids swearing at school) and cover them, and I hate myself for acting like that. Emily tries apologizing for me, for my language, for my behavior, but Aunt Courtney just shakes her head and says, "It's fine. Elliott will probably just go to bed early, so he can get up early and fish. We can keep them. And then another night they can sleep at your cottage."

Emily says okay. Mae and Cass run upstairs to pack Mae's things. I envy them because they have each other, and I have no one.

Uncle Elliott gives them the key to their cottage and they go running back alone for the night, no doubt planning their next dumb prank, a way to get back at me for being mad at them.

I'm sitting on the bed alone, on a patterned quilt with bears and trees on it. Mae and Cass are gone now; they're at Aunt Courtney and Uncle Elliott's cottage for the night. I have the room all to myself and I should be happy about it—it's what I wanted, right?—but instead, I wish someone was here with me. I stare at the wall. There's an empty space in my chest. It hurts, like someone took my heart out, and now there's a hole left behind. I think over and over again how I will never have friends, how I will never fall in love, how no one will ever like me.

The room is small. The double bed practically fills it. I go on my phone (though I know I shouldn't, but I can't help myself) to see that Skylar has been with Gracie again. I wonder if she saw what Mae and Cass posted before I finally deleted it, if she read the comments, if she agreed with them. She hasn't texted me in days, not since I sent her the picture of the taxidermy fish and she told me it was cool. She doesn't know anything about Daniel.

I wish I could tell her.

I wish I could tell someone.

I wish I could tell someone that I'm lonely and scared. That I feel like no one likes me. That I worry no one ever will. That I'll be alone forever.

Voices carry upstairs and through the open door. It makes it ten times worse. It makes me feel even more lonely than if I was in the cottage alone. There is a thickness in my throat. The need to be friends with Skylar again is so intense it feels like physical pain.

I have my back to the door. I don't hear him come in at first. I don't know how long he stands there in the hall, watching me from behind, until I hear the sound of his annoying little laugh.

He says, "Imagine having no friends."

I whip around. Wyatt stands behind me, leaned into the doorframe, looking smug as fuck. His arms are crossed. He turns and looks at himself in the bedroom mirror and fixes his stupid hair. When his eyes come back, he looks down on me literally and figuratively.

He sneers.

I say, "Imagine being an asshole."

"Where's your boyfriend?" he asks, looking almost proud of the fact that he is an asshole, not denying it.

"I don't know," I say. "You tell me."

Wyatt's laugh is arrogant. He stands up straighter and comes further into the room. "I guess he doesn't like you anymore."

I try to pretend his words don't hurt. "I guess not," I say, though I don't tell him that he never did actually like me. Of course he didn't. Because what would a guy like Daniel ever want with a girl like me?

"What do you want, Wyatt?" I ask. "Why are you even here?"

"Why not? It's not your room. It's not your house. I can go anywhere I want."

I push myself up from the bed. I breeze past him for the door, our elbows bumping. "Watch it," I say, even though I'm the one who ran into him. He laughs. I go downstairs, trying to get as far away from him as I can. But Wyatt walks behind me, down the stairs and into the living room, where people still sit, playing their dumb cards.

I say back, over my shoulder, "You're such a little shithead. Go away. Stop following me."

"Reese, please."

No one cares that Wyatt is provoking me. They only care about what I said.

I go out onto the porch because, even though it's the last place in the world I want to be, it's the only place where no one is.

I stand at the screen, looking out, wondering if Daniel is out there somewhere, watching me.

It's not dark yet, though the darkness is coming. It will be here soon.

Emily comes to stand on the porch with me. "We have people over, you know? You can't just behave like that. Do you want everyone to think you're—"

"What?" I ask, spinning around to look at her, cutting her off but then wondering what she was going to say. That I'm out of control? That I'm a freak? "Am I embarrassing you?" I ask.

She pulls the door shut because I am. I am embarrassing her. She cares more about what other people think than that I'm upset. She doesn't even ask what's wrong, why I'm mad, what Wyatt did.

Instead: "You can't speak to your bother like that, Reese. Just because you're upset doesn't mean that it's okay to call him names."

"Do you even care why I'm upset? You don't," I say, answering for her. "All you care about is that I called him a shithead and that I embarrassed you in front of Uncle Elliott and Aunt Courtney. You care about everyone else but me."

She crosses her arms and says, "I don't know what happened upstairs, but I'm sure whatever it was, that your brother doesn't deserve to be called names like that."

My hands curl into fists. Sad, angry tears fill my eyes.

"You really are so gullible. You think Wyatt is the perfect child. You have no idea that he's been selling Grandma's antique silverware right under your nose for money to gamble with."

She pulls back, upset not that Wyatt would do something like that but that I'd tell more lies about him. "Wyatt wouldn't do that," she says. "He knows how much Grandma's things mean to me."

The door opens and Wyatt comes out. The look on his face tells me he heard what I said. He knows I was talking about him, that I told on him.

Emily's eyes flick to him. "She's lying," he says, all innocent-like, and I can already tell she believes him over me, that she genuinely thinks he would never do any of those things.

He can do no wrong in her eyes.

I go on. I tell her, "Not only that, but he's been selling drugs right here while we're on vacation. He meets random people in the woods and sells them actual drugs."

She laughs. "You don't expect me to believe that Wyatt is a *drug dealer*. He's fourteen. Where would he even get drugs?" Before I can tell her, she says, "It's not nice to tell lies, Reese."

Wyatt sneers like it's funny.

I throw my hands up in the air. "This is unbelievable. This is genuinely unbelievable. Why don't you just take his phone? Just *look at* his phone. You'll find everything there. Betting apps. Probably texts and Venmo payments from his *customers*."

On the other side of her, Wyatt's gaze is intense. His arms

hang long. As I watch, he flexes his fingers and then curls them into a ball. Flex and then curl. "It's not true," he says, his voice toady, sucking up to her, and I wonder what he'll do to get back at me for telling. "You know I would never do something like that, Mom. I don't know why, but she's making it all up. I don't know what I did to upset her."

I push past both of them for the door. I walk out of the room. I go into the living room, moving with such momentum that everyone in the room stops dead and watches. Emily follows me in, muttering something under her breath about how this isn't done and how we'll talk about this later, as if I'm the guilty one, as if I deserve to be punished for telling the truth.

I spin around. I look her right in the eye and say, "I hate you. I wish you'd die."

Emily grimaces. She draws physically back from my words. She takes a deep breath to try to get a hold of her emotions, because people are here, people are watching. I turn away. I go running up the stairs, my feet pounding. I go into the bedroom and slam the door. It doesn't stay shut. It bounces back open and so I slam it again.

I stand in the room at the foot of the bed, shaking, taking slow, uneven breaths.

I meant what I said. I *do* hate her. I hate all of them. I wish they all would die.

I sit down on the edge of the bed, heart pounding, and imagine it.

COURTNEY

I lie awake all night staring up at the cracked plaster ceiling. A long rift, like a winding river, snakes across it and I lie there all night, waiting for chunks of plaster to come raining down on us while we're in bed.

There is a streetlight outside in the parking lot that shines in through the window. It makes a loud humming noise that makes it impossible for me to fall asleep.

Daniel Clarke is no longer a suspect. Because by 6:00 p.m. on the night that Emily and Reese had that fight, the night that Emily and Nolan were killed—as the four of us, Emily, Nolan, Elliott and me, sat around playing cards and drinking—he was already in Stewartville, Minnesota, getting gas from a Kwik Trip before heading further west, which leaves only a handful of suspects.

Daniel Clarke didn't kill them. He didn't take Reese.

Wyatt sleeps on the floor. I see him out of the corner of my eye, his lanky body spread out face down on the quilt we dragged from Elliott and my bed so that Elliott and I sleep under only a thin sheet. We found an extra blanket in a drawer for Wyatt, which is pulled to his waist. He lies shirtless and facing away from me so that I wonder if he's asleep or if he's lying on the floor with his eyes open, staring at the blank wall. I listen to the sounds of his breath, trying to decide.

I'm going to kill you if I'm late for school.

Kill you.

It wasn't so much what he said but the way he said it, the merciless look in his eye and his strength when he hit me.

Beside me, Elliott lies with his heavy arm around my waist, binding me to the bed. Earlier, he tried talking to me when I came back in from speaking to Detective Evans. He pulled me aside and said, *We need to talk about this.*

I asked, *Talk about what?*

He said, *About why you don't trust me.*

I do trust you, I said, but it's not true. He's keeping something from me. I think about the blood on his shoes, about the picture of Reese on his iPad, and how Emily said she wanted to talk to him that night before we left. I find it too convenient that he doesn't remember her saying that, just as I find it too convenient that he doesn't remember what he and Reese were talking about that night in the kitchen.

I spend my night in a constant rotation of thinking about Wyatt's cold eyes and the drops of blood on Elliott's shoes, trying to explain them to myself, to justify them. There have been cases of people driving in their sleep, of them strangling and stabbing loved ones for no reason at all and not even knowing what they'd done. Stress (like the loss of loved ones, for example) causes people to have more vivid dreams—an excess of vivid dreams. So maybe Wyatt went from dreaming about a lost lunch to an intruder in a flash (though he only remembered one of these dreams), and maybe the blood did belong to the fish, and Emily didn't want to talk to Elliott about anything more than his alma mater because Reese will be applying to colleges this year.

Maybe neither of them did it.

Or maybe one of them did.

I tell myself not to sleep, not to blink. To stay vigilant.

Only one thing keeps me from losing my mind: the girls.

Their safety. They're the only ones I know for certain are innocent in all this.

The buzz of the streetlight hums all night. Trucks pass by on the street, the rumble of their engines loud. At some point, Wyatt kicks the blanket off him all of a sudden. As I watch, frozen, not turning my head but looking out of the corner of my eye, he pushes himself up from the floor. At first, he stands in the center of it, and then he takes a few steps before reaching out to turn an imaginary knob, to open an imaginary door.

Wyatt is asleep.

He's sleepwalking again.

He walks out of his nonexistent door. He goes to stand at the edge of Cass and Mae's bed, on Cass's side, and I start to grab for Elliott, to shake him awake, wondering what Wyatt is going to do and if he's going to hurt her.

But then, before I can react, Wyatt turns around, swiveling his head as if lost and looking for something. He crosses the room, going to the far corner of it. I can't see what he's doing, but with his back to me, I hear the sudden, urgent spray of urine against the wall. He's mistaken it for the bathroom. It goes on a long time and under different circumstances I might say something, I might try to stop him, to wake him up, to lead him to the bathroom instead. But I don't dare because I'm afraid.

When he's finished, Wyatt takes himself back to the floor, lying the opposite way as before with his head toward the door. A second later the smell of urine reaches me, and I know that I should get up and clean it, but I'm too scared to move.

In time, the sun rises. It slips through the flimsy, semi-sheer curtain panels and into the room with us, waking Elliott. I'm already awake and so I see him come to, the slow process of regaining consciousness, of opening his eyes, observing his surroundings, remembering where he is and that he's in this shitty motel.

His words, when he speaks, are a whisper. "How'd you sleep?" he asks, his face so close I smell his dried-out morning breath.

"I didn't," I say softly.

"Not at all?"

"No." I shake my head. "Not at all."

"You must have slept at least a little bit."

"I don't think so."

He reaches out, runs a hand the length of my hair, and I feel my whole body stiffen. "I don't want to fight with you," he says. "We're both under a lot of stress. Can we call a truce?" he asks, and I wish it was that simple, that easy. Still, I nod, telling him what he wants to hear. In the other bed, one of the girls makes a sound and we hold still, holding one another's eye, waiting for her to go back to sleep again because it's too early for anyone but us to be awake, to come face-to-face with reality.

"You must be exhausted if you didn't sleep," Elliott says. He breathes in, noticing the scent of something pungent in the air. "Do you smell that?" he asks, pulling a face because of it.

I nod, whispering, "It's urine."

"Urine?"

"Wyatt was sleepwalking again. He mistook the corner of the room for the bathroom."

His forehead furrows, his eyebrows coming together. "What do you mean? That he peed in the room?"

I nod again, imagine the dry urine on the wall, seeping into the carpeting. Elliott sighs, dragging his hands through his hair. "It's too early for this. I'm going to take a quick shower and see if I can't find us some coffee."

I nod. The mattress sinks when he moves into a sitting position, gravity pulling me to its center. He gets out of bed. He stretches and then moves quietly across the room, stepping over Wyatt. I hear the bathroom door partially close, not latching because of the way the door doesn't properly latch. For a moment, it's quiet as I imagine Elliott stepping out of his clothes before the water turns on, the sound of it changing as Elliott pulls that little pin that diverts the water from the bath to the showerhead.

I reach over to the nightstand for my phone, which is dead. I went to bed without charging it. I feel Elliott's side of the bed for his phone, though it isn't here. He must have taken it into the bathroom with him. I run my eyes across the room, seeing Elliott's iPad poking out from a large pocket on the side of his bag, which lies just beside Wyatt's feet.

It takes effort to push the sheet off myself, to stand. To get to the iPad, I'll have to step over Wyatt, because the bag lies just on the other side of him and there's not enough space in the small motel room for me to go around.

I creep slowly forward, praying the floor doesn't squeak and that he can't feel my presence.

Standing beside his makeshift bed, I watch Wyatt. He lies on his back now with his eyes closed, and I wonder if he's asleep or if he's just pretending to be. As I lift a foot up from the floor and go to step over him, all I can think about are Wyatt's eyes flying open, him reaching out and grabbing me by the ankle, pulling me onto the ground with him.

But Wyatt doesn't move. He continues to sleep as I step over him, setting my foot down on the other side, and reaching for the iPad, pulling it into my grasp.

I get back in bed, under the thin sheet. I start to search for *people who kill*, needing—desperate—to see some sort of studies or theories on why people kill and the types of people who do to reassure myself that no one in this room would do such a thing, but as I start to type, *p-e*, a list of previous search results come up, including *Pearl Lake depth*, which gives me pause.

My shoulders tighten, my hands all of a sudden clammy.

Pearl Lake is the name of the lake that the resort sits on.

Why would Elliott ever need to know its depth?

I go to the page Elliott searched. I skim. Pearl Lake is over 1,500 square acres in size with a maximum depth of forty-three feet, though the average is only nineteen. It goes on to say that there are steep drop-offs along the shore, making parts of it unsafe to swim. The clarity of the water, according to this article, is low, which means you wouldn't easily be able to see things floating beneath the surface.

I throw a glance toward the bathroom door, which I can't quite see from where I am.

I listen for the sound of the shower to go off.

I pull up the entirety of Elliott's browsing history. It's sorted by date and, at first glance, is not unusual, things like his email inbox, YouTube videos, Facebook and frequent checks of the weather. I look closer, examining them one at a time, seeing that just a couple days ago Elliott accessed a *Help Find Kylie Matthews* page on Facebook. He must have been curious. He must have wanted to know more about her and her case, other than what I told him the other day. I become curious too, scrolling through the most recent posts.

Four posts from the top is a post from none other than Elliott Gray. My heart stops. Because not only has Elliott been going onto the *Help Find Kylie Matthews* page, but he's been posting on it. And not just any post, but a picture of Reese's face.

My throat tightens. Time slows down. I feel dizzy, refusing to believe what I'm seeing.

His post reads: *Is this her? It looks like the age progresed picture.*

He's spelled progressed wrong. But that's not all. He's suggesting that Reese is the missing Kylie Matthews. He's also given the address of where to find her, of where she is—of where she *was*—at the resort, in cottage number eight.

There are some similarities in their appearance, sure, but Reese is *not* Kylie Matthews, which Elliott knows. It's ridiculous to think. Until recently, Reese had never stepped foot in this part of Wisconsin. Five years ago, when Kylie went missing, Reese was going into eighth grade. Cass and Mae were five at the time—about to start kindergarten—and, because of Emily's frequent work travel, the four of us spent a lot of time together while Wyatt was off at various baseball camps. I remember it well. I teach preschool; I had the summer off. I took the three girls to the zoo, to the aquarium, shopping. Reese was sweeter then than she is now. She had a soft side, a way with Cass and Mae. They looked up to her. I remember Mae riding on Reese's back for what felt like hours at the zoo that summer until my own back hurt from watching. She never complained. I have pictures of it.

Reese is not Kylie Matthews. It's not even a question.

Why would Elliott suggest that she is?

The comments are practically decisive.

I definitely see the resemblance.
OMG.
That has to be her.

Elliott's Facebook post is dated the night before Reese went missing. That was days before I met Sam and Joanna Matthews. It was days before I told Elliott about their little girl, Kylie, who was missing, which means that he knew about her before I did.

Yet he acted so surprised when I told him.

How did Elliott know about Kylie Matthews?

I think back. I rack my brain, trying to make sense of it, going back to the beginning, to why we're even here. Elliott was the one who suggested we come to this resort. He's been here before. He came years ago with a bunch of college friends; it was a couple weeks before a buddy of his was to be married, his last hurrah as a bachelor. They were going to drink entirely too much and do guy things like fish, hunt and cook things they killed over a fire. They stayed at the same resort when they came, which is why we chose that one, at Elliott's suggestion, because he said it was nice enough, rustic, clean, and that it had some charm.

Is it possible Elliott was here that same summer Kylie disappeared?

Is it possible he did something to hurt her, if not on purpose then by accident?

I'm so lost in thought that I never hear the shower water turn off.

REESE

After everyone leaves, I open the bedroom door. I come out of the room and stand at the top of the stairs, looking down on Emily in the kitchen. She stands with her back to me, hunched over and crying, her hands clinging to the edge of the sink before she lets go, putting her face in her hands.

Slowly, I come down the stairs. I step on a loose floorboard, which squeaks. Emily spins around, startled by the sound. One hand goes to her heart and the other to her eyes, wiping them to try to hide the fact that she's crying. There's an ache in my throat all of a sudden, because she's so upset, because I don't know that I've ever seen her cry like this before.

"Reese," she says, short of breath, her face puffy and red. "You scared me. I didn't hear you come downstairs. I didn't know you were still awake."

I swallow. "What's wrong?" I ask, my voice weak.

"Nothing," she says, turning away from me again, starting to scrub at the dirty dishes in the sink. "I think I just had a little too much to drink."

She's lying. She just doesn't want to tell me what's wrong, but I know that it's because of me, because of what I said.

"I'm sorry."

"No, it's fine. I just . . . I didn't hear you is all. I thought you'd gone to bed," she says, thinking the reason I'm apologizing is because I scared her.

"No," I tell her, reaching the bottom of the stairs, coming closer. "I mean, I'm sorry about what I said before."

She looks back, waves her hand like I didn't say that I hated her and wanted her to die, like I said something else, something less savage. "It's fine."

"What did Wyatt want?" I ask, because he was just here, talking to her. I heard his voice. I couldn't hear what he said, but it was probably about me, about how I'm a liar.

She turns back around toward the sink, reaching for a towel for her hands. "Medicine. For his allergies."

"Oh."

"You were right, by the way," she tells me.

"About what?"

"About Wyatt. About what he's been doing." Her eyes fill with tears again. "I'm sorry I doubted you, Reese. I'm sorry I didn't believe you."

"How do you know?"

"I looked at his phone like you said. He really is a shithead," she says, and I laugh, because in my whole life I never would have expected Emily to say something like that. She laughs too, a half laugh, half cry, and then we're both laughing, and it feels like the first time in a long time that it's happened.

I say, "Shhh. We should be quiet. He'll hear us if we're not."

"Don't worry," she says, waving me off again, dropping the towel to the counter. "Your brother should be dead asleep by now. I didn't have any Benadryl so I slipped him an Ambien instead to help him sleep. I had one left in my pill organizer. I figured he wouldn't notice the difference. They're both pink," she says, shrugging, and I smile because it feels like a secret between us, something only she and I know.

"I didn't mean it," I say again. "That I hate you. Or that I want you to die. I was just mad. I say things I don't mean when I'm mad."

"We all do, honey. It's human nature." She reaches out a hand to me and says, "Come here. Let's sit on the sofa," and I take her hand, which feels foreign in mine. It's been so long since we held hands that I forgot what hers feel like, though they're soft, the nails long and clean when I look at them, though as I do, I realize she's not wearing her wedding ring. "Do you know why I'm hard on you sometimes?" she asks, sitting beside me so close that we touch.

"Because you love Wyatt and Mae more than me?"

"No," she says, her face pained. "That's not true, Reese. I don't love them more than I love you. I love all three of you the same," she says. She holds my eye and says, "It's because I worry the most about you. You just seem so angry and unhappy all the time. I hate seeing you like that. I only ever want you to be happy." She pauses, looking at me, searching my eyes, and then says, "You remind me of myself when I was your age. You're in such a rush to grow up, to push the limits, to be twenty-five and not seventeen. You want time to go faster," she says, and I look away because it's true, because she knows me better than I thought she did. She reaches for my face, turns it so that I'm looking at her, and says, "I was that way too. I couldn't wait to be an adult. I rushed things. Your father was the only man I ever dated. I didn't know anything else. People told me that I should experience things, like dating other men and living on my own before I got married, but I never did because I was so afraid of being alone."

"I didn't know that," I tell her.

"I never told you. To be honest, I don't know that I ever really loved him. I thought I did, but you can't really know things like that when you're nineteen. I loved the idea of him. I loved that when I was with him, I wasn't alone. Not physically anyway."

"You shouldn't stay with him if you don't love him," I tell her, thinking how she can still be happy. How it's not too late for that.

She nods and tells me how she plans to talk to Uncle Elliott in the morning and see if he'll help her file for divorce. I should be sad, knowing my parents are getting a divorce. But for whatever reason, it makes me happy, because I want her to be happy. I want both of them to be happy.

"Are you okay?" she asks, and I say yeah.

"I know being a teenager is hard," she says. "There are so many emotions, so much angst. Just slow down, Reese. Be happy with who you are now. Don't rush things. Be a kid while you can. I promise it will be worth it."

She asks me about Skylar. I tell her we're not friends anymore. "I figured as much."

"How?"

"I saw the necklace of hers, the one you borrowed, in the trash."

I let her think the necklace really was Skylar's. Because telling her about Daniel, too, would be too much for one day. Another day I'll tell her about him.

She says she's sorry about what happened with Skylar. "Losing a friend is never easy. Maybe you two will work it out eventually, but either way, I promise you it will be okay, Reese. It doesn't feel like it now, but there is a whole life after high school. One day none of this will matter anymore."

I believe her. It makes me feel better.

"The best is yet to come," she promises me as she reaches for me, as she wraps an arm around my shoulder and I lean into her, resting my head on her shoulder, thinking how I haven't been this close to her in years. Physically. Emotionally.

It's dark outside now.

The darkness creeps into the cottage through the open windows.

I try not to let the fear in too, knowing most bad things happen after dark.

COURTNEY

"What are you looking at?" Elliott asks.

I look up. He stands in the hotel room, wet, a towel wrapped around his waist. He's shirtless, his hair standing on end like he towel dried it, but didn't touch it with a comb. Steam enters the room from the bathroom, suspended behind him like a cloud. There is artwork on the wall, which feels so out of place in this squalid room. It's something mass-produced and in a dime-store frame that hangs at an angle, the plaster behind it cracked. The image looks cheap and unexceptional, a painting of a lake that could be any lake in the world.

But a lake.

I think of the search I found on Elliott's iPad just now.

Pearl Lake depth.

The thought comes to me like a knockout punch: blinding, unexpected and from out of nowhere.

I realize the one place no one has yet thought to look for Reese is in the lake.

"Sorry," I say, feeling pain, a tightness in my chest all of a sudden, whispering, not for the kids' sake but because I don't trust my own voice. I don't trust it not to tremble if I speak at full volume. "I forgot to charge my phone last night. It's dead. I hope you don't mind that I borrowed your iPad."

"Of course not," he says, running his hands through his hair, flattening it and pushing it back from his eyes. "But you didn't answer my question."

"What question?"

"What are you looking at?"

My throat tightens. On the screen before me, which, thank God, he can't see from where he is, Reese's teasing, sun-kissed face stares back at me.

"Nothing," I say, turning the iPad off before I have a chance to close out of Facebook or to clear my own search history. "I was just mindlessly scrolling."

"It didn't look mindless. It looked pretty intent."

He holds my eye for longer than is normal.

"No, not intent. Just out of it. I didn't sleep at all last night," I tell him again. "Did you say something about coffee?"

"Yeah. Just let me get dressed first, and then I'll go see what I can find."

After he's gone, I get out of bed and pull the curtains back to let the early morning light into the room. I plug my phone in to get at least a few minutes of charge, and then I shake Cass and Mae gently awake, leaned over them, whispering at them to get up and get dressed, that we're going to go for a ride.

I stare at Wyatt on the floor for a long time, trying to decide whether to take him or to leave him. And then another memory slams into me of Emily and me one night, years ago, sitting too close together on the sofa, an empty bottle of wine on the coffee table before us, having one of those no-holds-barred conversations where we held nothing back. "If anything happens to Nolan and me, you'll take care of our kids, won't you?" she'd asked, sloping toward me, her face too close, her eyes wide and watery, and I said yes, of course, asking that she do the same for Cass.

"Of course," she said. "I'd take care of her like she was my own."

I shake Wyatt awake. When he comes to, blinking the world into focus, he's lost. He looks around, remembers where he is, what's happening, that he's on the motel room floor.

"What's wrong?" he asks.

"Can you get up?" I ask, urgency in my voice, though I try not to let the panic in too, and scare the kids. Elliott searched online for the depth of Pearl Lake because he needed to find the deepest part to sink Reese's body in so she wouldn't rise back up and be found.

What I don't understand is why. Why would Elliott do this?

"Why?" Wyatt asks.

"We need to leave."

"Where are we going?" he asks, his voice tired and testy but, at the same time, compliant. He pushes the blanket back and gets up off the quilt, reaching for his clothes in his bag.

"To talk to the police."

Quickly, I throw my hair into a bun, slip into a bra, grab my purse, and we go outside.

The parking lot is nearly empty.

Elliott has taken the car.

REESE

There's a knock at the door. It's a gentle thumping sound, so that at first I'm not sure if I heard it or not. If it was real or just the wind moving the door.

Still, I flinch, the soft, rhythmic sound moving up my spine. *Knock, knock, knock.*

My throat goes tight. My breath is shallow.

Beside me on the sofa, Emily looks up, which means she heard it too. Someone *is* really there. I didn't imagine it and it isn't the wind. Emily starts to get up, to make her way toward the door, but I blurt out, "No, don't," while grabbing for her hand. "Please don't open it," I say, pleading, my eyes wide and locked on hers as she turns back to face me. I take her in in that moment. Her golden blond hair and her soft blue eyes. She squeezes my hand, which is all of a sudden cold, clammy, shaking. Hers, on the other hand, is warm. Her posture is relaxed. She gazes down at me and smiles, pulling her eyebrows together in genuine surprise. "Why not?" she asks, as I feel her pull away again, her hand slipping from mine.

"Just don't," I say. "Please don't open it."

"Don't be silly," she says lightly, taking her first step toward the door. "It's fine. It's probably just Mae. She probably forgot something and came back for it or changed her mind and wants to sleep here," she says, which wouldn't be unlike Mae—Mae always, *always*, forgets things, and she always gets homesick at sleepovers and wants to come home—but that's not what this is.

It's not just a hunch. I know. I feel it in my gut.

It's not Mae on the other side of the door.

COURTNEY

I pull the motel door closed behind us, gesturing for the kids to hurry as we make our way across the parking lot. The police car, the one that's supposed to be there watching us, sits empty, and I imagine the officer inside the motel office looking for coffee or a place to relieve himself.

Outside, it's calm and still, the sun still rising. The angle of it is low, so that the light comes sideways and through the trees. The street, a state highway, is only two lanes. Phone lines run the length of it with birds perched on the wire. There is a gravel shoulder on one side, which is where we walk in a single file line, me in the back so that I tell the kids to "Scooch over. Not so close to the street," as the occasional car whizzes past. Each time, I wonder if the car is Elliott's. He'll go back to the motel room when he finds coffee, and when he sees we're not there, he'll come looking for us.

"Where are we going?" Cass asks.

"To the police station."

"Why didn't you just talk to the policeman at the motel?"

"I need to speak to Detective Evans."

"Why didn't we drive? Where's Daddy?"

The questions are endless. I manage to placate Cass and Mae with excuses, but Wyatt doesn't believe them so easily. He glances back, knows I'm not telling them something.

"Car," he says, seeing it over my shoulder, and I feel my whole body stiffen, wondering again if it's Elliott, imagining him leaving our cottage that night after I'd fallen asleep, going to Emily and Nolan's cottage. Killing them, taking Reese. Rowing out into the center of the lake, where the depth is greatest, and then easing her over the edge of the canoe, weighing her down, sinking her in.

Was she alive when he drowned her? Or was she already dead?

Was the blood on his shoes hers? Or was it Emily's or Nolan's?

"Let's move into the grass, closer to the trees," I say, trying to control the tremor in my voice, pressing my hand against Mae's back, who walks just ahead of me, though the trees are missing their lower branches and provide minimal protection. It doesn't help that Wyatt has on a red sweatshirt and that he's tall, standing out like a sore thumb. I want to tell him to take it off, to leave the sweatshirt behind, but I also don't want to worry the kids.

Mae whines, "I'm tired. I can't walk so fast."

The car drives past, a dusty little blue sedan. It edges too near the shoulder, kicking up gravel as it goes, and I think how not twenty seconds before, we were standing on that gravel.

In the distance, from the opposite direction, another car comes, drawing nearer, its headlights bobbing with the bumps in the road. I imagine Elliott again, in the car, in the canoe early that morning, blood on his shoes, maneuvering Reese over the edge and into the water without so much as a splash.

"Can we go a little faster?" I ask, pressing harder on Mae's back as the car approaches, wondering if I should instead tell the kids to run.

REESE

Things move quickly now.

They happen fast, before I can speak, before I can process what's happening. Before I can reason with her, before I can beg, before I can say to Emily what I'm thinking, that I'm scared and that I know it's not Mae on the other side of the door.

I try grabbing for her hand again, but it gets around mine this time. It drifts further out of reach. I watch as she moves toward the door. As she reaches for the handle, I feel a scream well up in me that won't come out, that can't come out because it's trapped. I squeeze my eyes shut tight and bury my face in my hands.

I can't see anything with my eyes closed.

The turning of the dead bolt startles me. I moan, but if Emily pauses, if she looks back, if she hesitates at all, I don't know.

The door rasps as it opens. The cool nighttime air rushes in.

Outside, the sound of bugs gets louder.

Emily's voice is bewildered when she speaks.

"Can I help you?" she asks, her voice formal and cold in a way that confirms all of my beliefs.

It's not Mae at the door. It's someone she doesn't know.

"Kylie," I hear and, all of a sudden, incomprehension edges out fear. The voice is not Daniel's, though it belongs to a man, someone whose voice I don't recognize. Slowly, I lower my hands from my face. I open my eyes to find him standing just on the other side of the door looking in, straight past Emily and to me, his attention rapt.

It's in the way he looks at me that makes the fear come instantly back.

His eyes are damp. His chin trembles, his mouth falling open.

His voice is full of emotion, shaking and in disbelief as he says, "It's you. It really is you."

He steps in, over the door's threshold, so that he's in the cottage with us.

Emily's laugh is strangled. "I'm sorry, sir," she says, trying to be polite, stepping in front of him to stop him from coming all the way in. But Emily is something like five foot two and this man is tall, his chin at the top of her head.

He comes in anyway. He steps easily past her so that when she speaks again, her voice has changed, becoming firm. "I think you're mistaken, sir. This is my daughter, Reese. You must have her confused with someone else."

She reaches for his arm, which he shrugs off.

The look of recognition on his face and in his eyes is beyond doubt.

He puts a hand to his mouth. He lets out a sob, something involuntary that sends me to my feet, that makes me go around the back side of the sofa so that there's something between him and me.

It doesn't stop him. He comes across the room, his head cocked, staring at me, not blinking.

He says, "Do you know how long I've been looking for you?" his eyes wide and bright. "Do you know how long *we've* been looking for you? Your mother and I. We've looked everywhere for you, Kylie. We never stopped searching."

My voice trembles when I speak, my whole body shaking. "Mom."

He crosses the room, scrambling around the arm of the sofa, moaning as he comes right up to me before I can run, touching my hair, Emily's frantic voice in the background telling him no, to stop, that he has the wrong person, that he needs to leave, her hand grabbing for his, though he brushes her off harder this time so that she falls back, bumping into the edge of the coffee table and losing balance.

"Mom," I say again, fear in my voice. He sweeps me into his arms and then he pulls back, cradling my face in his hands.

"We've searched everywhere. For years. I never gave up. Look at you," he says, running his hands over my hair again, the clamminess of his hands pulling at my hair. I sob and he says, "I'm sorry. I'm so sorry, baby," his voice wild as he lets go of my hair, setting his hands on my shoulders. "You're all grown-up."

My eyes bulge. I can't blink, I can barely breathe.

"Mom."

Emily comes forward again. She lays her hand down on his arm, pulling as hard as she can. "Get away from my daughter. Get your hands off her. She's not who you think she is." In an instant, the man throws his elbow back. It hits her square in the face, her head snapping back with such momentum that I don't know how her neck doesn't break. I gasp, watching in horror as she rights herself, her eyes dazed, blood leaking from her nose.

But the man is unaffected. He never once looks at her to see if she's hurt. He doesn't ask. He never takes his eyes off me as Emily stumbles backward, her hand pressed to her face.

"Do you know who I am?" he asks, as I try backing away. "Do you remember me, Kylie?"

"Leave me alone. Don't touch me. You're scaring me."

Emily stumbles. She finds Wyatt's baseball bat leaned by the front door, where someone left it. She jacks it up over her shoulder with both hands. She comes after the man, grunting from the effort. At the same time, he looks back. He hears her or sees it out of the corner of his eye, sensing the blow. At just the right time, he turns; he catches the barrel of the bat in his hand as it comes raining down. He tugs once. That's all it takes. Because Emily's hands are wet with blood, they're slippery and weaker than his. They can't grip the bat.

He takes it with ease. He drives it instantly backward, plunging the knob at the end of the bat into her stomach. She cries out, clutching her stomach, crumbling to her knees, gasping like she can't breathe. I start to cry, "Get up, Mom. Get up," wanting to help her, but instead backing further away, putting distance between myself and him, because the man is reaching for me again. He's telling me we have to go, that this woman isn't my mom, that my mom is waiting for me at home, that this woman stole me, that she took me from him. He starts to cry then, actual tears. "God," he says, "Joanna is never going to believe it's you. She's never going to believe you're home."

I can feel my heartbeat thrash in my ears.

Emily's voice is rasping as she tries to get up. "Run, Reese," she puffs out, using what little strength she has to reach out, to curl her hands around his ankle, holding on to him so I can go.

She says it again. "Reese. Run," and I do. I turn, running onto the porch, where I try to break out through the screens, tearing one from the frame, thinking that if I can get out, I can get help. But in the few seconds I have before the man kicks Emily's hands off of him, before he grapples with her for the baseball bat and I hear the dull, horrifying sound of the bat against bone, the rip doesn't become big enough for me to get out.

As footsteps approach, I turn, looking for a place to hide. I throw myself under the bed, lying flat on my stomach beneath it, my whole body trembling.

It's darker on the porch, though it's not black because the light from inside the cottage reaches it. He carries the bat when he comes, setting it gently on the floor. He doesn't see me at first. He only sees the tear in the screen, which he goes quickly to, fingering it, examining the size of the hole, peeling it back to look out into the dark night on the other side.

My heart thumps against the wooden floor. I hold my breath. I see Emily through the open door as she struggles to get up, pushing against her body weight, but then losing her grip so that her hands slide out from under her and she falls back down.

I eye the bat on the floor, calculating the time it would take for me to get out from under the bed, to run to it, and if there would be enough time.

There isn't.

He turns away from the window.

"I know you're in here," he says, his tone soft, warm. "Don't be scared, Kylie. Please. It's just me, your dad. I'm not going to hurt you. It's time to go home, baby girl."

This man is not my dad. My dad is sound asleep upstairs, sleeping like the dead. I wish that he would wake up. I pray to God for him to wake up, thinking of all the times he slept through his alarm clock going off so that Emily would have to splash cold water on his face, or the one time the fire alarm got coated with dust from the new floors going in, and it went off in the middle of the night. Nolan slept through that too.

I scream silently in my head. *Please wake up. Help us.*

He doesn't.

The man comes to stand at the edge of the bed. He knows where I am. He knows that I'm here, that I'm lying under the bed. My breath shudders and I try to hold it, to control it, to not let him hear me breathe.

All of a sudden, he bows down. He crouches close to the ground, his eyes locking with mine. "Get away from me," I scream. "Leave me alone."

"This doesn't have to be so hard," he says, just like Daniel said, reaching under, wrapping his hands around my ankle, pulling as I kick.

Emily's face is wild, harried when she finally comes in. There is blood in her hair, a small pit along the hairline. It drips down the side of her face, into her eyes. She sways. Still, she bends down; she tugs on the man's arm as he tries dragging me out from under the bed by my feet. At first, when she pulls, he loses his grip. She manages to get his hands off me, long enough that I squirm further away, almost to the other side of the bed, where I will be free and where I can make a run to the front door for help.

Before I can, he flings her off him hard. She falls all the way to the ground. In an instant, he gets up. He searches for the bat, picking it up where he left it. He hoists it over his shoulder, bending his knees, leaning over, putting his whole body into the swing, and I'm so fucking scared all I can do is cover my ears so I don't hear the sound as her body lurches before becoming still.

"It's time to go, Kylie," the man says, reaching under and pulling me easily out from under the bed, the wood floors making it impossible to resist, to find a toehold, to anchor myself under the bed.

In the distance, a door opens. The man looks up. He lets go of my arm. He tightens his grip on the bat as Nolan calls down over the stairs. "Emily?"

I whimper, "No, please, stop," reaching for his leg as the man turns, as he makes his way from the porch toward the cottage. "Please don't hurt him."

Through the glass, I see Nolan standing in the upstairs hall, looking around. He's leaned over the stair railing, covered in shadows, an almost negligible glow from a night-light lighting up his face. He's squinting, trying to bring the cottage into focus, though he doesn't wear his contacts when he sleeps and without them, he's blind.

The man steps into the cottage. "Emily?" Nolan asks, his voice dulled down by sleep and the distance. He brings his gaze toward the man, though because he can't make out the man's face without his contacts in, he only sees that a figure has appeared and is crossing the room quickly, going toward the bottom of the stairs.

I scream, but there's no time for him to react.

I watch as Nolan's face changes as the man comes into focus and he realizes it's not Emily. It's someone else. Someone he doesn't know. A stranger.

He stumbles back a step, shielding his body. He only ever gets one word out. *Who.*

I don't watch it happen. Instead, I press my hands to my ears, my body curled around Emily's, to block out the sound. "Wake up," I beg into her ear. "Please wake up. I need you."

COURTNEY

When we arrive at the police station, Detective Evans doesn't take us into an interrogation room as I imagined he would. Instead, he gets me coffee with sugar and cream, and we speak at his desk. Cass and Mae take the two small chairs for themselves. Detective Evans offers to pull up another chair for me, but I say that it's fine, that Wyatt and I can stand, though Wyatt wanders away and finds somewhere else to sit.

I look back at Detective Evans, who's watching me.

"I was looking on my husband's iPad this morning. I found something."

"What did you find?" he asks.

I clear my throat. "Some recent searches about Pearl Lake," I say, "and a Facebook post he made to that *Help Find Kylie Matthews* page a few days ago." I pull up the post on my own phone. I set it on the desktop for him to see, watching as he brings the phone closer to his eyes.

I'm standing behind Cass's and Mae's chairs. I have a bird's-eye view of them so it's hard to miss Cass nudge Mae under the table. As she does, I start to pay closer attention.

Mae looks at Cass. From her profile, her little chin starts to quiver. Cass looks carefully, almost negligibly back. Their eyes meet. Cass shakes her head so subtly I almost don't notice, before she lowers her own eyes to the desk and Mae follows her lead.

Mae brings her hands under the table. From behind, I see her breath start to hitch, her shoulders undulating like a wave as she fights tears.

Beside her, Cass is stoic. She sits tall and quiet with her hands in her lap, unnaturally still as if—if she doesn't move—we'll forget she's even there. Until she notices Mae starting to cry and she lightly kicks her under the chair, her foot sliding gradually over, weaving around the legs of the chair, pressing into her.

The more Mae tries not to cry, the more she does.

Detective Evans notices and looks up from the phone. "You okay there?" he asks Mae, unsurprised that Mae is upset because her parents are dead; why wouldn't she be? She nods, wiping her nose on the sleeve of a shirt.

Except that something is starting to register. I've picked up on an idea, my mind latching on and trying to disentangle it.

These aren't tears of sorrow. They're tears of guilt.

Cass isn't supposed to use Elliott's iPad without asking. But sometimes she does. Sometimes she sneaks it when he's not paying attention and goes on it anyway.

The night that Reese disappeared, they were on Elliott's iPad. They had gone back to the cottage from Nolan and Emily's place, and were alone with it for hours. I remember how I went up to the loft to turn the TV off in the middle of the night and slipped the iPad out from under Cass's arm. I left it on the counter to talk to her about in the morning. But by morning, Emily and Nolan were dead and I wasn't thinking about the iPad anymore.

It's not just that.

I think of the way *age progressed* was misspelled on the Facebook post, with only one *s*. Anyone could have done it. Anyone can misspell or mistype a word. But it's something two ten-year-olds are more likely to do.

My mouth falls open.

"Why would you do this?" I ask, my voice hollow and numb.

Detective Evans looks up. I feel his eyes on my face, though I'm looking down at Cass and Mae.

Cass doesn't even try to deny it. Instead, she says, her eyes jerking up all of a sudden to mine, throwing her gaze back over her shoulder to where I stand, "We didn't know. It was a joke. We thought it would be funny."

Funny.

They don't understand the gravity of it. They don't understand the million reasons why what they've done is wrong. Not only were they toying with two grieving parents, dangling a carrot in front of their eyes, but they used Elliott's iPad without asking, they used his Facebook account to post something under his name. Nolan and Emily are dead because of them. Reese is missing because of them.

"Can someone catch me up? What am I missing?" Detective Evans asks.

"Tell him," I say to Cass. "Tell him what you did."

Cass shakes her head, her hair falling in her eyes.

"No. You," she says.

I'm short of breath as I tell him, "They made the Facebook post. They used my husband's iPad to go on Facebook, to share that picture of Reese, to pretend she's that missing girl and to tell everyone where she is. Did you take that picture of her?" I ask, thinking how I was so certain that Elliott had done it, that Elliott had sat there on his pool chair taking surreptitious pictures of our teenage niece and that Reese had caught him and flicked him off.

Cass nods. It wasn't Elliott taking the pictures. It was Cass and Mae.

"How? How did you even know how to do all that?"

Cass shrugs. *It was easy*, her body language says. They're ten, but so much more internet savvy than me. Years ago, I let Cass set up her own Instagram page on my phone just for fun, telling her she had to ask permission before following anyone or accepting friend requests, and that it was for family only, to follow her cousins, aunts and uncles, things like that. You're supposed to be much older than she was at the time to have your own Instagram account, but how hard is it to lie about a birthdate?

It didn't go as planned. I blamed myself for not paying better attention to what she was doing online, for not realizing that Cass had, at some point, made her page public. She said it was an accident, but I wasn't so sure. Either way, by the time I figured it out, Cass had over five hundred followers, was following close to a thousand accounts and was DMing strangers. So much for asking permission to follow people. I made her close the account down. I thought our troubles with the internet were done then. I thought she'd learned something from that experience, but it turns out that I was wrong.

"What did you think was going to happen?" I ask.

Cass says it again, how they thought it would be funny.

"You didn't think someone would go looking for her and believe that Reese really was this missing girl?"

She shakes her head. "No. She doesn't even look like her."

Maybe she does and maybe she doesn't.

But who's to say what a grieving parent sees when they want so badly to believe?

Detective Evans digs into it for all of five minutes. The Facebook page, he tells me, is owned by Sam and Joanna Matthews. They started it shortly after Kylie went missing, because word spreads quickly on the internet. Their reach was so much greater than simply hanging posters around town. There are billions of active users on Facebook and over a thousand following their page, though it's had less and less activity over the past year, other than the celebration of sad milestones like Kylie's birthdays and anniversaries of the day she disappeared.

Until one night less than a week ago when someone claimed to have found Kylie alive.

Detective Evans pushes his chair abruptly back, the legs scraping across the linoleum floors, and stands up from the desk.

"Where are you going?" I ask, watching as he runs his hand over the gun in his hip holster as if to make sure it's there. He reaches onto the desktop for his keys.

"To speak with the Matthewses," he says.

"Then I'm coming with you." I look back over my shoulder, meet Wyatt's eye. "Wyatt can stay here with the girls."

Detective Evans shakes his head. "I can't have that, Mrs. Gray. You need to stay here, to sit tight," he tells me firmly, leaving no room for debate. "If she's there, I'll bring her back to you."

REESE

He pulls me through some field by the hand. I'm crying. Tears flood my eyes, spill over and down my face. My nose runs, snot mixing with tears with saliva that trickles from the edges of my mouth so that my whole face is wet. I try to pull my hand away, to let go of his, to turn off and run some other way, but he tightens up on his grip, saying stuff like, "I know. I know you must be so confused. You must not remember. It's been so long. I'm sorry I had to do that. I'm sorry you had to *see* that. I didn't want you to have to see that. But those people, Kylie. They took you from your mother and me. They're not good people. They're bad people. Very bad people. Keep running, Kylie. We're almost there. It's not much further now. God," he says, "your mother is going to be so happy. So surprised."

He's kind to me. Gentle, other than the death grip on my hand. When I fall, my hand pulling out from his, I try crawling away. But he takes me by the upper arms and helps me to my feet, asking, "Are you okay? Are you hurt?" running his hands over my hair, and I shake my head, feeling myself shut down before he reaches for my hand again and we begin to run, my feet and legs moving so fast I can't feel them anymore.

I can't stop thinking things like if only she hadn't opened the door.

If only I had stopped her.

If only I had remembered Daniel's knife in the nightstand drawer.

I think of all the things I could've, should've, would've done differently.

I have only one free hand. At one point, I manage to get my phone out of my pocket with that one hand, but when I turn it on, the screen light is blazing in the darkness. I move fast, opening Snapchat, going to the chat screen. That's as far as I get. He stops all of a sudden. I don't anticipate it. I keep running forward, his hand on mine stopping forward motion so that I jerk back, feeling something in my shoulder pop. He says, "What's that?" turning to look at the screen, his face haunted in the phone's light.

When I look up, there is blood on his face.

"Nothing . . . I . . ."

There's sudden movement. He comes at me fast. It happens before I know what's happening. My hands go to my head by instinct, to protect it. I wince, cowering, and then my legs actually give out. I fall, curling into a ball on my knees, shaking, blubbering.

His voice is so nice.

He lowers himself beside me. Runs his sticky, bloodied hands over my hair.

"I'm not going to hurt you. I'm not mad, Kylie. I'm not mad at you," he says, folding his hand around the phone and easing it from me. I don't try to resist, I let him have it. "It's not your fault. It's theirs. They did this to you. They made you forget who we are."

He helps me to my feet, which I don't feel move though I know they are, because we're gaining ground, we're getting somewhere, but I don't know where.

All the while I wonder if Emily is alive. If Nolan is alive. Or if they're dead. If he killed them.

There is a parked car up ahead. He opens the back door and

the light turns on. He pushes me in and then closes the door. He gets in the driver's seat. The light goes off.

He drives away down the deserted street, leaving the headlights off at first. As he does, I tug desperately on the door handle, trying to get out, but the door doesn't budge. He set the child locks in advance.

He knew I might try to run.

I press myself into the door as he drives. He says stuff like, "You don't need to be so scared," and, "No one is going to hurt you," and, "I know you must be confused. It's a lot to process. But you have to believe me, Kylie. You have to trust me. Those were bad people. They took you from your mother and me. They're not who they say they are."

I say nothing. We come to a house. The porch light is on. He pulls the car into the driveway and puts the car in Park. We sit there with the engine off as he turns around in his seat, beaming in the glow from the front porch light. "Your mother is going to be so surprised. I always told her I'd find you. I always said I'd bring you home one day. And now I have, just like I promised her I would."

He gets out of the car. He comes around to open my door, reeling me in by the arm, though I try grabbing at things to stop myself from being dragged out of the car.

"Don't be scared. You're safe now. I promise. It's all over. You're home."

My legs are stiff as we walk. They don't work right. My knees lock and I trip, but he holds on to my arm. He leads me to the house where he unlocks the door, and we go in, into a dark living room. He reaches down and turns on a lamp, filling the room with light. "Do you remember our house?" he asks, talking fast, excited, his eyes bright.

I've never been here before.

"Sam?" a woman's weary voice calls out. "Is that you? Where have you—"

She comes into view, standing there in her pajamas, the hall behind her dark. Her eyes bulge, her mouth drops open and she gasps.

"What's going on?" she asks, her voice now strained. She doesn't know where to look first, at him or me. "What is that on your clothes? Is that—"

It's blood.

His voice is loud. "Look who's here," he says, laughing like he didn't hear her, like he doesn't care that he's covered in someone else's blood. He grins like a madman. "Look who I found."

She gives a slight headshake, pulls her eyebrows together and asks, "Who did you find?" her face blank.

He gives a strangled laugh. "Kylie. It's *Kylie*, honey."

She looks again, running her eyes over and examining me. "That's not her," she says.

He drags a hand through his hair, his smile fading. He looks at her in disbelief. "What do you mean it's not her? Of course it's her."

He turns to me, his voice desperate, insistent. "Show her. Show her your necklace."

I don't know what he's talking about. I shake my head. He says, "The one that was in the picture of you. The one we gave you, honey." He gets flustered when I don't know. He motions to a picture above the fireplace of this man, this lady and a little girl, of them making silly faces. In it, the girl wears my gold necklace, the one Daniel gave me, the one I threw away. "That necklace. Show her, Kylie. Show her you still have it."

But the woman doesn't care about the necklace. She says, "I'd know my daughter anywhere, and that's not her."

He looks harder, and this time, he starts to second-guess

himself. He finally sees it. I'm not who he thinks I am. I'm not the person he wants me to be.

He gets choked up, he cries big, fat tears.

"Oh my God. It's not her. It's not her," he sobs over and over again to the woman, and then, to me, "You look so much like her," he says, reaching a hand out to touch my hair, though I recoil. I pull back so hard my head slams into the wall, seeing Emily's body heave on the porch floor as he hit her again and again with that bat. "You look so much like my baby girl. Oh God." He sobs, dropping his head into his bloodied hands. "What have I done? *What have I done?*"

"What are we going to do with her?" he asks after a minute.

He won't look at either of us. He can't.

They talk about me like I'm not in the room with them.

"I don't know," she says, shaking her head.

"Well, we can't just bring her back. She's seen my face. She saw what I did to them."

"To who? What did you do, Sam?" she asks, though she sees the blood all over him and knows.

He shakes his head. Even he can't say.

She says, "Just give me a minute to think."

"We need to get rid of her before someone comes looking for her. If they find her here . . ."

"I know."

They lead me down some dark, unfinished stairs. They open a panel in the wall and leave me in the basement crawl space.

Because now that I'm here and after what he's done, they can't just let me go.

COURTNEY

After Detective Evans leaves, I manage to get a hold of Elliott, who's been driving around town, searching for us, certain that after he left for coffee, someone broke into the motel room and took us.

"Jesus, Courtney," he says. "There you are. I've been calling you. Where are you? Why didn't you answer your phone?"

I tell him to come to the police station. I tell him I'll fill him in on everything when he gets here, feeling guilty for thinking he could have done this. He left the cottage at five o'clock to go fishing, like he said. He didn't kill Emily and Nolan. He didn't take Reese.

Cass and Mae still sit on chairs beside Detective Evans's desk. They're playing tic-tac-toe on scraps of paper they find, because they're bored and have nothing else to do, and I wonder how long it will take for them to come to terms with what they've done. There will be no punishment for them, nothing in the legal sense. Impersonating someone on Facebook can be a crime, but at their age I can't imagine they'll get anything more than a slap on the wrist (if anyone will take the blame, it will be Elliott and me, for not keeping a better eye on them). I wonder how long it will take for the weight of what they've done to sink in, if it will happen days from now or if it will be years before it happens, when they're older and their prefrontal cortexes are finally fully developed. Maybe then they'll realize they're culpable in two murders, if not three.

Reese.

I can't stop thinking about her. I can't stop wondering if she was in Sam and Joanna's house when I was there.

I think of what Joanna said to me that night as she, Sam and I sat around their kitchen table talking, about how Kylie and Reese, with their similar hair and eyes, must be Daniel's type. She looked me right in the eye that night and pleaded, her voice desperate, *The police need to find him, Courtney. He needs to pay for what he did to our girls.*

Our girls.

Except Daniel didn't do anything to Reese, which she knew. She intentionally misled me.

I can't stop wondering if, when I was there, Reese was in a closet or the basement somewhere. If she heard my voice and my footsteps, but if she was gagged and unable to scream.

Or maybe she was already dead.

Because it would have been a liability for Sam and Joanna to keep her alive, if and when they realized she wasn't Kylie.

REESE

It's uncomfortable in the crawl space. It's maybe two feet tall, which is not enough room to ever sit up. I lie on my back or sometimes on my side when my back gets numb. The ground is hard. There is a single exposed lightbulb that they leave on, the pull string within reach if I wanted to turn it off or on. I have options. A blessing. Something to do to pass the time, pulling the string, turning the light off and then on, off and then on, or wrapping the end of it around my little finger and watching the tip of my finger turn purple, wondering if the same would happen if I could tie it around my neck.

They bring food and water down for me to eat and drink, though all I can do is prop myself on an elbow to eat. They let me out sometimes to stretch my legs, to use the bathroom, one keeping an eye on me, the other on the front door. They put me back when I'm through, opening the door and watching me crawl back into my cave, and I don't ever resist, because the memory of what the man did to Emily and Nolan is always there. Ever present.

And then one day when the little wall hatch opens, the face on the other side is not theirs. It's someone else, a man with red hair.

"Reese?" he asks. "Are you Reese Crane?" I nod, my hair in my eyes. "We've been looking for you."

Aunt Courtney is the one who tells me they're dead, sort of.

She sits on the edge of the hospital bed, her face splotchy like she's trying not to cry. She pats my leg over the blankets and sighs, having trouble finding the words.

I say, "They're dead right?"

She nods, confirming it. And then we sit in silence, because neither of us knows what to say, until she says, "It will be okay. I know it doesn't feel like it now, but we'll get through this to-gether."

She didn't have to tell me. I already knew, because if Emily and Nolan were alive, it wouldn't have been Aunt Courtney to come into the hospital room to see me first. It would have been them, my mom and dad. But they couldn't because they're dead. Because that man killed them, because he thought I was his missing daughter, Kylie. Why he thought that, I don't know, except I think it had something to do with the necklace Daniel gave me; I think that maybe it was hers. Still, I don't know how or where Daniel got the necklace, and I don't know how that man knew where to find me. I ask Aunt Courtney if she knows. Her eyes get all wet again, and then she takes my hand into hers and says, "We'll talk through everything later. For now, rest. Let's take care of you and get you all better so we can go home."

Home. It's a word that doesn't make sense to me anymore, like when you say something so many times it loses meaning in your head. Home. I don't even know what that is anymore.

I nod anyway. "I . . . I didn't tell them."

"Tell who what?"

"Those people," I say. When I was locked in their basement, I had time to kill and nothing to do but think. I thought about dying. A lot. I thought about what it would be like to be dead and buried. I thought about the cemetery that Daniel took me to.

"The Matthewses?" I nod. "What did you want to tell them?"

"I think I know where their daughter is."

The police officer is in the room with us now. He stands at the foot of the bed. He turns his head too fast when I say that. I have a startle reflex that I didn't have before. When someone moves, I jump. When someone coughs, I jump. When someone breathes, I jump.

"I'm sorry," he says, seeing me gasp, jerk, pull away from him in bed though he's ten feet away, not even close to entering my personal space. "I didn't mean to scare you."

"It's okay," I say, telling myself I am okay. I'm in the hospital room with Aunt Courtney and the police. I'm okay. Still, there are burning hot tears in my eyes. Aunt Courtney scooches closer to me on the bed. She squeezes my hand, holds my eye, gives a sad smile.

"Can you tell me where?" the cop asks.

I nod. "There is a cemetery by the resort. In the woods. I was there one day. I saw that lady from the resort there too."

"What lady?"

"The one who owns it. Ms. Dahl or whatever. She was laying flowers on an unmarked grave. Maybe that's where their daughter is. Maybe she's who's buried there."

COURTNEY

I'm allowed to watch. I'm not in an observation room staring through one-way glass, like you see on TV. Instead, the interview room is monitored by cameras and microphones, and I sit in someone's empty office and watch the interview on a monitor, alone.

Ms. Dahl sits in a chair in the interview room. The room itself is small and bare, with what looks like a card table and four chairs, only two of which get used.

Detective Evans sits across from her. "Tell me what you know about Daniel Clarke."

Her jaw is set. There's an edge to her voice as she says, "I thought I already did."

"Tell me again," Detective Evans says.

"I knew his mother," she says. "She was my best friend ever since we were little kids. I helped him out after she died, because I felt sorry for him, because he was one of those kids who got the short end of the stick, and because I didn't do something more to intervene when she was still alive. I always felt guilty about that. Helping Daniel out was my penance. His dad was a deadbeat and his mom drank herself to death. She choked to death on her own vomit. But you probably already knew that, didn't you?"

He says nothing to that. He stares back, pensive, and then he asks, "What do you mean when you say you helped him out?"

"I gave him a job. I let him work at my resort, though he wasn't ever gonna be employee of the month, but it was something, a paycheck at least. I should have fired him more than once."

"For what?"

"Not doing his job. Stealing things from the guests."

"What do you know about the night Kylie Matthews disappeared?"

"I remember that night. At the time," she says, "I didn't even know the girl was missing. It wasn't until the next day that I found out who she was."

"Who *who* was?"

"The girl that Daniel was burying."

In the other room, I blanch.

Detective Evans says nothing.

"The night it happened, I was out walking in the woods after dark," she says, going on to explain as she sags back in her chair. "I walk before bed sometimes because I don't sleep well, and I found that a little activity before bed helps me sleep. When I came to the cemetery, I saw him. Daniel. He had his back to me. I couldn't make out his face because he was looking the other way and because he had some sweatshirt on, the hood pulled clear up over his head. But the sleeves were pushed up, like this," she says, pulling up on the sleeves of her own shirt, "and when the moonlight hit it just right, I could make out his tattoo."

"And that's how you knew it was him?"

"Yes. I didn't tell anyone what I saw that night."

"What exactly did you see?"

"The girl. Her body. She was lying on the ground behind him. I couldn't see her face either, but I could tell it was a body.

She wasn't moving. I assumed she was dead. Daniel had a shovel and he was digging. I watched him dig. It went on for hours until he was short of breath and spent, but he went on digging with an energy and a determination I've never seen before or since from Daniel. And then, when he was done, he threw his shovel down and he went to the girl. He hoisted her limp body up onto his shoulder, and then he laid her down in the grave."

There is a sour tang in my mouth, a burning in my throat. I eye the garbage can in the corner of the room, wondering if I might be sick, thinking of that poor girl and of Joanna Matthews sitting at home, feeling aggrieved that Kylie wasn't back from her friend's house yet, and of Sam, waiting in his car for the train to pass. They had no idea what was happening to their daughter in that moment.

Ms. Dahl's gaze wanders around the room, locking eyes with the camera so that it feels like we make eye contact. "The next morning I went back, hoping I'd imagined it. The place where he buried her was as plain as the nose on your face, the only saving grace that no one but me ever visited that cemetery. No one ever said Daniel was smart. He didn't leave the place very tidy."

"Did you think about going to the police and turning him in?"

"No," she says. "Never. Daniel had it rough. Whatever happened between him and the girl, he didn't mean for it to happen."

"What did you do when you saw the way he'd left things, *not very tidy*, as you say?"

"I helped smooth out the dirt and I came back the next day and threw some grass seed down."

Detective Evans says, "You understand, Ms. Dahl, that you're also culpable for her death?"

"Failure to report is not a crime."

"But you're an accessory after the fact. Like you've just said, you helped hide the body. You helped cover up the gravesite."

She turns away from the camera, looks back at him, says, "So arrest me then."

Detective Evans offers to drive us back to the resort to pack up the rest of our things so we can go home. The investigation is through. Sam Matthews confessed. He killed Emily and Nolan and he took Reese. He and Joanna then kept her in a basement crawl space, which makes me wonder if the first time I stopped by their home unannounced, they weren't doing laundry, but keeping a close watch on Reese, who says she couldn't hear anything from down there, not when the hatch was closed. My guess is he never expected me to take him up on his offer of stopping by their house; he only said it to draw my attention away from him as a suspect.

They'll both go to jail, Sam for longer because not only is he charged with kidnapping, but with murder.

The necklace that Reese was wearing, the one I recognized in the Matthewses' family portrait on their fireplace mantel, the same one she had on in the photo Cass and Mae took of her that day by the pool on Elliott's iPad, was made of beads to create the dots and dashes of Morse code. It spelled out *daughter*. Sam and Joanna had given it to Kylie for her eleventh birthday. How it came to be in Daniel's possession, no one knows, but we can assume that at some point, he stole it. What we do know for certain is that that, coupled with Cass and Mae's Facebook post, is the reason Sam believed Reese was Kylie. It makes me feel sad for him, sad for all of us.

"I would appreciate that," I say to Detective Evans, about the ride, "if it's not an inconvenience." The kids and I don't have a car here. Elliott has it. He's at the hospital with Reese because I didn't want to leave her alone. When I asked Elliott if he minded keeping her company, he said he didn't, but that he wasn't sure Reese would want him there. I asked why. He was quiet at first; he didn't want to tell me. I kept pushing and eventually he told me how a couple nights ago, he took a walk when he couldn't sleep and came across Reese and Daniel in the woods, which set off a chain reaction of events that caused hard feelings between them, but nothing that had to do with what happened to Nolan and Emily.

I'm not sure if we've made amends yet, he said, and I told him it might be a good opportunity for him and Reese to work through things, because right now, what she needed more than anything was a friend.

While we were talking, I asked why he searched for the depth of Pearl Lake, and he told me it was for when he went fishing, because he thought he'd have better luck where the water was deeper. Then he pulled his eyebrows together and asked back, *Why did you think I wanted to know the depth of the lake?*

I couldn't bring myself to say that it was because I thought he killed Reese. Because I thought he killed all of them.

Now Detective Evans shakes his head, looking as tired and defeated as I feel. "It's not an inconvenience."

He's been solemn since he came out of the interrogation room, since he listened to Ms. Dahl confess to watching Daniel dig a grave that night to bury eleven-year-old Kylie inside.

"Are you okay?"

"Yeah," he says, but it's so sparing, I don't believe it.

"Kylie was a little girl. She didn't deserve what happened to her. It's understandable to be upset."

He nods, his eyes not meeting mine.

"You ready?" he asks, reaching for his keys.

"Yes," I say, and then to the kids, "Let's go. Detective Evans is going to drive us back to the resort so we can get our things and go home."

"Home?" Cass squeals, suddenly looking up from her chair, her eyes wide. "Like *home* home?"

"Yes," I say, though it lacks Cass's same enthusiasm. "Like home home."

We can go home now, back to our lives in Chicago, though I don't know what that looks like anymore. It's not the same. It's changed. Reese, Wyatt and Mae won't be going to their own home. They'll be coming to live with Elliott, Cass and me, the six of us under one roof, all of us different than we were before we stepped foot inside these cottages. Not only will they have to leave their home, but they'll have to leave their friends and school too. Mae will have Cass, but Reese and Wyatt will go to a school where no one knows them and where they know no one. Wyatt will be fine—he'll make friends through baseball—but I worry about Reese starting her senior year somewhere new, though maybe she will be happy for a fresh start.

Detective Evans leaves the police station first. He holds the door open for us, and we follow him out of the building and onto the street, where the wind has picked up, blowing trash and trapping it against the curb. In the distance, the sky darkens; a summer storm slowly moves in.

We stop by the motel first. The kids and I run inside to grab what's there, which isn't much, just a couple bags that we never fully unpacked. We drive to the resort next to get Emily's, Nolan's and the kids' things from inside their cottage.

"Stay here," I say to the kids, as Detective Evans and I step out, leaving them in the car with the windows cracked for air. "We'll only be gone for a couple minutes."

We make our way to the cottage. After we get what we need, Detective Evans will drive us to the hospital, and there, we'll wait for Reese to be discharged. Then we'll go home.

"What happens now?" I ask on the way. "Will you arrest Daniel Clarke for Kylie's murder?"

"We'll speak to him," he says. "I don't know that Ms. Dahl's testimony is enough to convict him, but it should be enough to reopen the investigation."

"What would you need to convict him?"

"Forensic evidence or a confession."

"Do you think he'd ever confess?" I don't know anything about Daniel Clarke. I don't know what really happened between him and Reese. I don't know how close Reese came to being another one of his victims. But I'll never forget what Mae said. How Reese was crying. How she was scared. How he was hurting her. He deserves to pay for whatever he did to her.

He says, "No."

"The other day you said you knew him."

He turns to me and says, "I said he was a couple years younger than me in school. I knew *of* him."

"What was he like?"

"Not the kind of guy you'd ever want your niece to date."

We reach the cottage. I follow Detective Evans up the deck stairs and to the front door, steeling myself for what awaits us on the other side. He presses the key into the lock. He turns the handle, swinging the door open, but this time, as we go in, I try to see it the way Sam Matthews did. I imagine walking in and finding the girl who I believed was my missing child. I imagine Cass here, with people who stole her, who kept her from me for five long years. I would have been out of my mind and I would have done anything to have her back.

"What did Sam Matthews tell you about that night?" I ask as we stand there in the great room, my mind flashing back to Emily and me, all those months ago, planning this trip, wanting to go together so that our families could bond and for the shared memories. It was Emily's idea, but I was completely on board. Reese, in particular, was getting older, and Emily worried that any moments of togetherness were fleeting; she would go to college soon, and if we didn't take this trip now, the opportunity might be lost. Emily imagined Reese going somewhere far away and never coming back. She planned everything, down to our meals and how we would spend our free time, because she wanted everything to be just right.

"Why do you want to know?"

"So I can picture it."

"No," he says firmly with a curt headshake. "Don't do this to yourself, Mrs. Gray."

Tears well in my eyes. "Don't you think that what I imagine in my mind is so much worse?" I ask, biting down on my lower lip.

He's quiet, thinking deliberately through his words.

"No. I don't," he says, and I feel the tears fall from my eyes, though I don't bother to wipe them away. Detective Evans is quiet. His face changes; he watches me, holding my eyes, the look in his empathetic. "I'll just say this," he says after a minute, his voice soft and warm. "The medical examiner said that while Mr. Crane might have been taken by surprise, Mrs. Crane had defensive wounds all over her hands and arms. She fought. She fought like hell for her family."

I nod, my throat tight and my heart heavy. "That sounds like something Emily would do."

We get to work, packing Emily's, Nolan's and the kids' things so we can leave, and then, when we're done, I follow Detective Evans out of the cottage for the very last time.

Before we go, I turn back for one last look.

Standing in the open door, I close my eyes. I see Nolan and Emily in the kitchen, Emily with her Old Fashioned, laughing like she was our first night here. I smile, hearing her voice and remembering.

I don't know how long I stand there until I feel Detective Evans's hand on my elbow, and I turn to him. "Are you ready?" he asks, and I nod, fighting tears as we leave and make our way toward the car to go home.

DETECTIVE EVANS

"Do you mind if I text you sometime, to see how you're doing?" she asks. We're at the hospital, standing just outside the main entrance doors, the four of them with their bags. Beside us, my car still runs, rain coming down hard though, under the covered entryway, we don't get wet. "You can say no," she says, rambling now, her smile nervous. "I don't want to cross a line or make you feel like you need to stay in touch with me. I'm sure you have boundaries when it comes to your work."

I say, "Of course you can text me. I'd like that."

Mrs. Gray grows quiet, her light brown hair moving in the wind, though she holds it back from her face. "I guess this is it then," she says when she speaks, setting her bag down on the sidewalk and coming in for a hug that surprises us both.

She lets out a sigh as she pulls back. "Sorry," she says with a sad little smile, struggling to find the right words. "I just can't thank you enough for everything you've done for us, Detective. If it wasn't for you, I don't know how we would have gotten through the last few days."

"Call me Josh, please. And I should be thanking you, Mrs. Gray. You're the one who figured it out. You found Reese."

She nods, knowing she did. I, myself, was on the wrong track. I don't know how long it would have taken me to figure out

that the Matthewses did it, though I'd like to believe I would
have eventually gotten there.

"Courtney," she says.

"Pardon?"

"If I'm going to call you Josh, you're going to have to call
me Courtney."

I nod, thinking we're having a moment. She glances back
to make sure the kids aren't listening, and then she looks at me
again, leans in, confessing, "I'm not sure I'm ready to go back
home and deal with everything that comes next," and I honestly wish I could say something to make it better, something
more genuine than what I say.

"You can do this. I know you can."

She's quiet. Then she nods, reaching for her bag. "Say goodbye to Detective Evans," she tells the kids, and they mumble
their goodbyes.

"Bye, guys," I say. "Be good."

I give them a little wave as I get back in my car. I pull away,
watching them get smaller in my rearview mirror until they
disappear. I breathe out a sigh of relief when they're gone. Because their perception of me won't be altered. Because after they
leave, Mrs. Gray will still think of me as one of the good guys.
She won't know what I did.

It's a twenty-minute drive back home. The rain is coming
down even harder now, hammering the windshield, the wipers
whipping back and forth but hardly able to keep up.

I spend most of the drive mulling over something Ms. Dahl
said this afternoon in the interrogation room, when she was
describing what she saw that night. How she said she watched
Daniel dig that hole in the cemetery with an energy and determination she's never seen before or since from him.

I looked up at the time, reading the expression on her face

and trying to decide if there was some hidden meaning in there, but there wasn't, which made it all the more ironic.

Because it wasn't Daniel she saw.

It was me.

When I get to my house, I pull into the driveway. I park the car and then make a run for it, getting wet from the rain, thinking of that night, of the cemetery, which I only knew the way to because of the times Daniel and I met there to get high, sitting on his mother's grave, smoking a joint. Daniel wasn't just someone I knew of. He wasn't some random kid a couple years younger than me in school. We might not be friends anymore, because people change (although Daniel never changed, he's still that sad sack I knew in high school), but I knew him my whole life, because he grew up across the street from me.

I flip on the living room light. I make my way to the bathroom, unbuttoning my shirt as I go. I peel it off and then set it on the counter by the sink, staring at my face in the mirror, which has changed, become more defined these last few years. I'm not that same round, baby-faced kid that Daniel knew, who could barely grow chin scruff.

It all changed the night that Kylie Matthews died. I changed that night.

I reach down, set my hand on the short sleeve of my t-shirt, still wet from the rain. I hike it slowly up, exposing my bicep, which I manage to keep covered in public. To this day, I have a hard time looking at it, though I force my eyes to lower, to make contact with the snake's fierce white eyes, which stare back into mine.

There were four of us who grew up on the same street and went together to get them, Daniel, Jeremy, his kid brother Adam and me. We used fake IDs and blew money we stole, because we thought we were cool at the time and we wanted the world to know it. We made up some fake gang—the King Cobras—and told everyone we knew we were in it, spending our free time when we were kids smashing mailboxes and robbing gas stations, stupid shit like that. We never got caught; we always got away with it, which gave us a high like we never had at any other time in our lives. We were invincible, untouchable. We had power. People listened to us. They were scared of us. We meant something.

The rest of the time, we were nobodies. We meant nothing to anyone, not even our own folks.

I didn't mean to hurt Kylie Matthews. It was an accident.

My kid sister had her over all the time. They were practically joined at the hip. She'd come over and the two of them would make fun of me. It was relentless. They'd sit in the same room with me and laugh about everything I said and everything I did. The way I walked, the fact that I was tall or that I had some patchy facial hair coming in. It made me angry.

One night, not long after it happened, my sister, Abby, knocked on my bedroom door. "Josh?" she asked, poking her head in.

"What do you want?"

She came into my room without saying, sat down on the edge of the bed, picking imaginary fuzzes from the quilt. By then, it had been a couple weeks since it happened. For the first few days, I was convinced I was going to get caught. It wasn't so much an *if* but a *when*. The police questioned me that first night, same as they did Mom, Dad and Abby, and I kept imagining them coming back, taking me away in handcuffs, locking me up.

But at the one-month mark, when the police seemed to have no leads and I started to think I might actually get away with it, the fear morphed into guilt, into nightmares, into me not being able to think about anything else but running Kylie Matthews over with my car. I hated myself for what I did.

I hated the person I was. I made the decision to change, cutting myself off from Daniel, Jeremy and Adam because I didn't want to be like them anymore. After high school, I joined the academy because I thought that if I could help other people, it might make up for what I did to Kylie, and in some effed-up way, it did. Those times I broke up domestic disputes or talked a man down from a bridge, the guilt would let up, if only for a time. I wasn't a murderer. In those moments, I was a hero. I was the good guy.

Still, when I'd see her folks around town, I'd think about confessing, because if I did, I wouldn't have to keep my secret anymore. It weighed on me, it preoccupied me to the point that there were physical effects. I couldn't sleep, I could barely eat.

But then I thought of everything I'd lose if I told them the truth. My family, my freedom, my future. In other words, everything I took from Kylie.

I kept my mouth shut. I told no one.

"She liked you," Abby looked up from the bed that night and said.

"What do you mean?"

"Don't be dumb," she said, rolling her eyes. "You know what that means."

"You're lying."

"Am not."

"Then why was she always ragging on me if she liked me?"

She gave a little snort. "Are you really that dense?"

Over and over again, I relived that day in my mind. I still do, trying to change the outcome every time. I remember watching from my bedroom window as Abby and her friend left our house, riding away on their bikes. I got in my car, thinking I'd follow them, maybe try to scare them or something, to teach them a lesson. I didn't get far when I saw Abby pedaling back, alone. I could've turned around. I should've turned around and gone back home. But for whatever reason, I didn't; I kept going. I found Kylie not much further up ahead. I remember that I honked and she looked back over her shoulder and smiled. I kept swerving the car, pretending I was going to hit her, and then swerving back. She was laughing at first. She thought it was funny, until I cut too close once and she got scared, calling me an idiot through my open window, shouting about how I was so dumb and how I was so stupid.

I did it again, to scare her, cutting even closer this time.

I didn't mean to hit her. It just happened. I clipped the back bike tire with my car. She fell off and into the street just ahead of me. I couldn't hit the brakes in time. To this day, I still feel what it felt like to run her over with my car. It nags at me. It haunts my dreams.

It was all adrenaline then. I didn't think. I reacted, lifting her from the street and setting her in my trunk. I hid the bike and then I drove back home and crept into my family's shed for a shovel when no one was looking, and then I drove out to the cemetery.

I just didn't know that someone else was there, that someone was watching. Ms. Dahl.

Tomorrow morning, I'll pick Daniel up. Daniel and I haven't been friends in years, not since I cut things off. He thought I believed I was better than him. It wasn't that. It's that I wanted to be different, I wanted to change. I wanted to make up for what I did, to atone. Daniel broke into my house and stole my things. I caught him in the act. I was a cop by then. I could have shot him or, at the very least, brought him in, but I didn't because we were friends once and I owed him that. Instead, I told him to get his shit together and do something productive with his life, but he chose to do neither.

He had his chance. I don't owe him anything anymore.

Justice will be getting Daniel off the streets. He's done enough bad things already—stealing from people, chasing after young, pretty girls and then hurting them—even if he didn't lay a hand on Kylie Matthews.

Tomorrow I'll take him in and ask him what happened that night. I'll tell him what Ms. Dahl saw, how she identified him digging that hole in the cemetery. There will be no way to prove it was me because, even if they exhume Kylie's body, any forensic evidence will be gone by now. If Daniel tries to make the argument that there are four of us walking around town with the same tattoo, no one will believe him because he's done nothing with his life, while I'm a detective. I protect people.

I'm one of the good guys.

It's a mantra I repeat to myself before I fall asleep at night, as I lie there in bed seeing Kylie's face in my head, in the trunk of my car, her pale, unmoving body beside jumper cables and a lug wrench, her knees bent, her eyes glassy. I say it over and over again until one day, I might actually believe it.

I'm one of the good guys.

★ ★ ★ ★ ★

ACKNOWLEDGMENTS

One thing I've learned is that, no matter how many books I write, it never gets any easier. Without my incredible network of brainstormers, early readers and emotional support people, I couldn't do what I do. Thank you first and foremost to my editor, Erika Imranyi, and literary agent, Michelle Brower, for the amazing feedback that helped make this book what it is. Thank you to the entire Park Row Books and Trellis Literary Management teams, including Emer Flounders, Justine Sha, Brianna Wodabek, Rachel Haller, SarahElizabeth Lee, Allison Malecha, Tori Clayton, Elizabeth Pratt and everyone else who played a part in getting this book into the world—from copy editors to proofreaders, to the Art department for another stunning cover, to Sales, Marketing, Publicity and Foreign Rights. Thank you to Brittani Hilles at Lavender Public Relations, and to Hilary Zaitz Michael and Carolina Beltran at WME for continuing to champion my books in Hollywood.

Thank you to the many booksellers, librarians and influencers (too many to name, though I'm eternally grateful to you all!) who have been so instrumental in getting my words into readers' hands. My books wouldn't be what they are without you advocating for and constantly supporting them. Thank you, thank you, thank you.

Thank you to my dear friends Erica Gnadt, Janelle Kolosh, Marissa Lukas and Vicky Nelson for being my earliest readers and for the honest and insightful feedback. Thank you to my family, especially Pete, Addison and Aidan, for always being the best cheerleaders.

It truly takes a village to bring a book into the world, and I'm so fortunate for mine.